THE BOOK OF LIGHT

THE DARK LIBRARY SERIES
BOOK THREE

MORGAN REILLY

LIBRA'S INK
PUBLISHING HOUSE

*To Dr. Paula Buck & Dr. Mary Pharr
for nurturing my love of story craft with the beauty of mythology and epic
storytelling.*

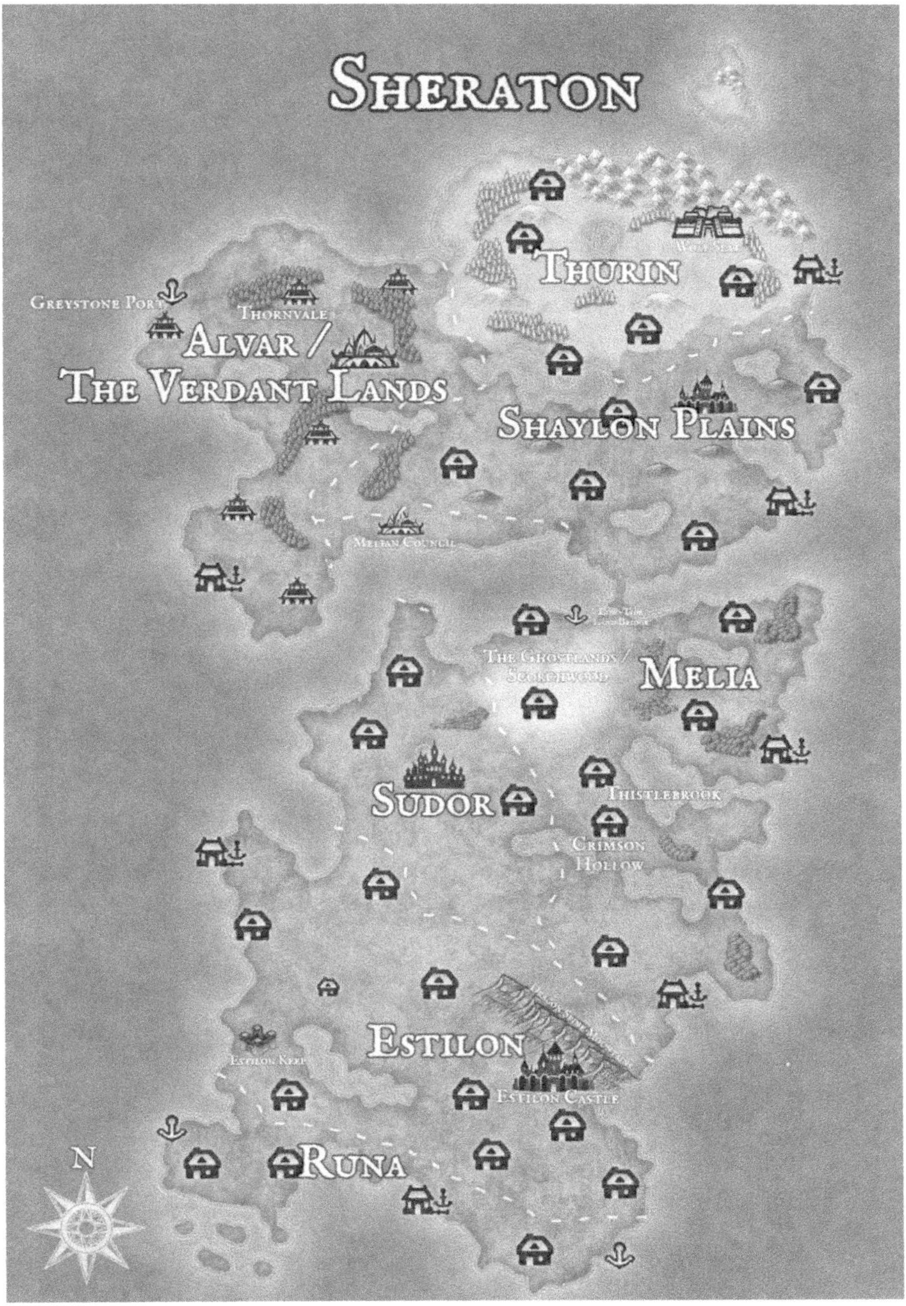

SHERATON
THURIN
ALVAR /
THE VERDANT LANDS
THORNVALE
GREYSTONE PORT
SHAYLON PLAINS
MELIAN COUNCIL
THE GHOSTLANDS /
SCORCHEWOOD
MELIA
SUDOR
THISTLEBROOK
CRIMSON HOLLOW
ESTILON
ESTILON KEEP
ESTILON CASTLE
RUNA
N

N
FROST
WEST HILLS
BROCK
FIEL
VALEBROOK
ILEDEN

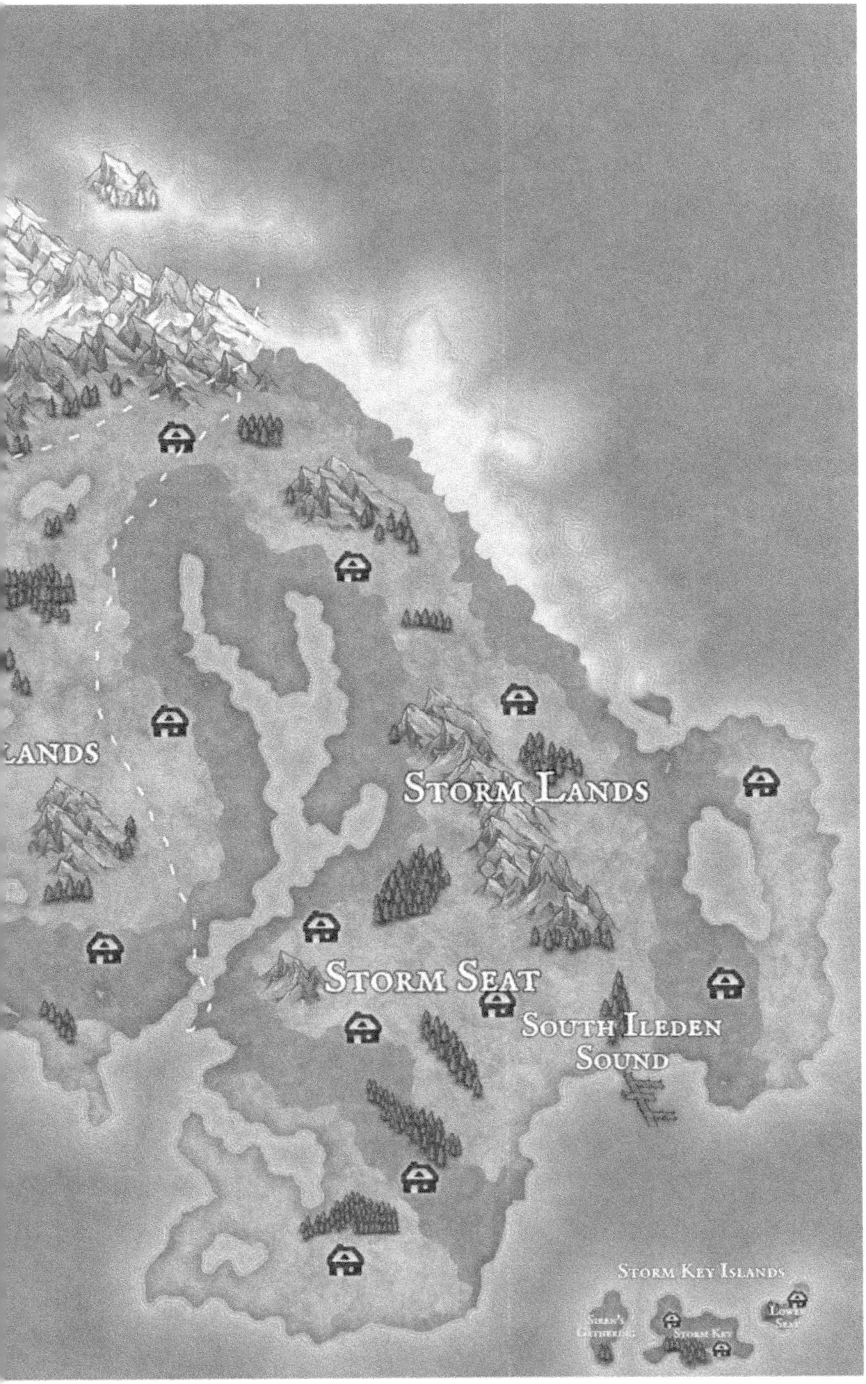

LANDS
STORM LANDS
STORM SEAT
SOUTH ILEDEN
SOUND
STORM KEY ISLANDS
SIREN'S
GATHERING
STORM KEY
LOWER
SEAT

To Shanna, goddess of water, patron of sea and magic,
To Brena, goddess of fire, patron of artistry and creation,
To Erys, goddess of air, patron of storms and rain,
To Rhiann, goddess of earth, patron of land and fertility,
To Anya, goddess of order, patron of life and justice,
To Aishlin, goddess of chaos, patron of death and crossroads,
We swear our undying fealty.

CHAPTER I

Chaos tingled beneath Neeve's skin, her palms itching to cast.

"We can do this," Eira said, taking Neeve's hands. Her grip was firm, her icy blue eyes shimmering beneath the full moon. "We were so close before."

They sat at the center of the crossroads, their prayers to Aishlin complete. The night breeze played with their hair, sweeping strands around their faces, Eira's straight, chestnut locks the opposite of Neeve's moon-white curls. The cold ground beneath them siphoned their warmth, and Neeve shivered, anticipation feeding the chill that coursed through her blood.

Neeve closed her eyes, picturing her parents' faces. "If they would tell us where they go, we wouldn't have to spy."

"Not just where, but *why*. It can't be simply because they enjoy the landscapes."

On the few trips where Neeve and her sister had joined them, the work was simple: search the land for its history while preserving it. Her father updated his map while her mother searched the earth for whatever relics she could unearth—stone icons for the goddesses, ore and gems, broken clay bowls and pots, all of them important.

"Proof that we have lived and learned and loved," her mother would say. "And time layers upon itself, giving us all it can so that we keep going."

Neeve regarded her best friend with gratitude. "Thank you, Eira. Truly."

"It's nothing. The more we practice, the more control you'll gain."

Control with chaos. Control with magic that was difficult to reach. But with Eira's magic connected with hers, Neeve could scry, stretching her sight beyond herself.

Neeve cleared her throat, sitting taller, the boughs of trees blocking the star-studded sky from view. White light shimmered through the dark branches and leaves.

"Kaeli and Robert, givers of life and blood." She breathed through the tingle of Eira's magic joining hers, the spell gaining strength. "Where have you gone?"

Her parents had waved from the wagon, their destination somewhere in Sudor. With the kingdom now ruled by Estilon, research would be freer, *safer*, or so they said.

They'd waved with bright smiles, her mother's mining tools reflecting the sunlight, the leather and cloth covers of her father's books warm from the afternoon.

"Show me."

The wind whispered through the leaves overhead as though answering her call. It carried the crisp scent of autumn, of damp earth and fallen leaves.

Neeve pulled at the shadows of night, giving them shape. A raven regarded her from midair, its wings flapping slowly as it hovered, the ethereal gleam in his black eyes regarding her, awaiting instruction.

"*Show me.*"

The raven flew, and Neeve closed her eyes, connecting her mind to his sight, just as Eira had shown her.

"Excellent," Eira whispered. "Very good, Neeve."

Their minds soared to the sky, flying beyond Brightmere. Their village was so small compared to the land around it, compared to the places her parents had described to her.

"It's working," Eira said. "Just like before. But go farther, Neeve. You can do it."

Channeling her blood bond to her parents, Neeve let the magic guide her, shadows and chaos coursing through her skin like static lightning. Her sight reached west, flying over trees and lakes, following a stream. The thread pulled tighter, tethered to Neeve, before it stopped.

"Go." Neeve's grip tightened on Eira's hands. "*Go.*"

The thread snapped, the magic ending.

"No!" Neeve's eyes shot open, meeting Eira's own disbelief with her own. "It was working!"

"I don't understand."

Neeve pressed her palms to her eyes, pulling the vision from memory. "Gods damn it all, it was *working*." She searched through the boughs overhead for glimpses of starlight. "When will I be strong enough?"

"Have you tried naming the raven?" Eira asked.

"What? Like a pet?"

"Calling him a name would give him an identity," she said. "It may strengthen the bond between you."

Neeve wasn't sure how strong a bond could be between a girl and the shadows, but she considered it. "Titus?"

Eira nodded. "A good name. But what if—" Eira winced, stopping herself. "What if your parents don't want to be found?"

"What do you mean?"

Eira blinked, hesitating before she answered. "Why do they leave? They're barely home before they're off again."

"Archeology." The word was almost a reflex. "Researching history."

"For months at a time?"

"Their plans are Sudor and Melia this time," Neeve defended. "It's not like they went to Runa. Or Ileden."

"Then why can't we find them? Even with my magic—"

"It's me." Neeve curled her lips against her teeth, biting to keep them from quivering. "It has to be."

"No." Eira took Neeve's shoulders, moving closer so that their knees touched. "You're more than strong enough. Whatever is holding you back, we'll get through it. You've already made a lot of progress."

Without another word, Eira took Neeve's hands in hers, holding them at their chins, and pulled her closer so that their foreheads touched.

"My mind to your mind," she whispered. "My sight to yours."

"What are you doing?" Neeve asked.

"Showing you what I see."

The trust between them ran deep, Eira as beloved as a sister. Though they'd linked their thoughts only once before, the experience had shaped their approach to what their chaos magic could do. But Neeve's aspirations outweighed ability. She wanted more.

"My mind to your mind," Neeve recited. "My sight to yours."

Then, together, their voices synchronized, "My mind to your mind. My sight to yours."

There was music when Neeve entered Eira's mind. Violin, played softly by expert fingers, the strings singing with every loving note. It drew her in, as though the bars of each measure lined the road for her to follow. She moved on tiptoe, seeing light bloom in front of her as a field of wildflowers surrounded her.

"We should return here." Eira's smile came through her voice. "We swore we would never get old, Neeve. Let's hold on to what keeps us young."

Eighteen was hardly old, though Neeve and her sister, Gretchen, had to live more independently than they'd like.

Neeve spun among the flowers and tall grass, the afternoon of Eira's mind bright and welcoming. She would dwell there forever if she could.

"A field, with a river, and a waterwheel." Neeve pictured a cottage, the image almost appearing in the distance. Eira had conjured it almost perfectly before the shimmer of it faded.

"We'll build a house," Neeve said. "Raise chickens."

The sound of a gentle brook soothed her as she heard clucking. Neeve's heart warmed, watching her friend granting each of Neeve's wishes.

"We'll both live here," Neeve said. "What would you have? A field full of horses?"

Eira was silent, the hold on Neeve's hands loosening. The vision flickered, the sunlight dimming, the breeze turning far too cold.

"Eira?" Neeve pulled her magic back, slipping free of Eira's mind before she opened her eyes. "Are you—"

Blood oozed from Eira's nose and ears, the red rivulets tinged black beneath the shadows of the trees. She stared at Neeve, tears mingling with the blood.

"Eira!"

She collapsed, eyelids fluttering before they closed.

"Eira!"

CHAPTER 2

A week of confusion, of accusation and anger.

A week of Neeve, powerless to save her friend, to reverse whatever it was she'd done.

"You were in her mind?" Eira's mother raised her hand, palm and fingers poised to slap Neeve before she balled a fist, trembling. "What have you done?"

"How dare you toy with such magic?" Eira's father loomed over her, his dark eyes accusing. "How dare you—"

"Back up." Gretchen moved between Neeve and Eira's father, hazel eyes alight with defensive rage. "Eira let her in."

Neeve's voice quivered. "It was her idea. We were creating—"

But Eira's mother overshadowed Neeve's words, aiming her rage with sound. "You liar! Spread your deception elsewhere and stay the hells away from my little girl!"

There was nothing the village healer could do. A human with shelves full of herbs possessed little against a wound caused by magic.

"We need a lightborn," her mother said, stroking Eira's hair. "Divine healing is the only thing that will fix her now."

"Alvar," her father said. "The healing houses. Earthborn and lightborn train there."

Neeve's throat tightened as she tried to swallow, and in the days leading up to their departure, they had refused Neeve any chance to say goodbye.

Eira was motionless, eyes open without seeing. The only proof of life was the color on her cheeks.

What have I done?

"When will you be back?"

They didn't answer, the wagon disappearing out of sight as Neeve wept in their wake.

THAT NIGHT, Neeve stared at the ceiling of the room she and Gretchen shared, her sister shifting in the bed beside her.

"It's all my fault."

"No." Gretchen pulled Neeve into a tight embrace, her arms locked around her as though ready for Neeve to resist. But Neeve melted, the warmth and strength of her sister's arms anchoring her. "No, Neeve. Don't you dare believe it."

"We've mindwalked before," Neeve said, her voice muffled between Gretchen's shoulder and her pillow. "The magic worked perfectly."

But if it was so perfect, she thought, her own voice accusing her, judging her, *why is Eira going to die?*

If Neeve had known, none of it would have happened. If she'd have known, Eira would never have left.

Go wish for the power of the gods. Her own voice mocked her. *Go to the crossroads and strike a deal. Ask to see the future and avoid all other failure.*

The frigid touch of guilt burned, killing all that it touched as the frost spread a hole within her.

Failure would only come if I did anything with magic.

At this, the voice was silent.

Strike a deal to take my magic. She choked back a sob, burying her face. *Whatever pathetic magic there is, wipe it away. Wipe it all away.*

A chasm split in her core as though her magic had already gone, an unseen force consuming it, leaving her hollow. For a power so thin, the hole within her spread wide, its edges dissolving to nothing.

But what would I give in return? She nearly asked herself aloud, stopping only as Gretchen exhaled, her consciousness close to the fringes of sleep. *What do I have to offer?*

Neeve turned, Gretchen humming as she shifted. Where exhaustion claimed one sister, the other remained in the agony of wakefulness, thoughts careening to a waterfall that led to a fathomless void.

Neeve could fix this, for herself and for Gretchen.

Leave the offering up to the chaosborn to decide. A lifetime of service? Unyielding devotion to Aishlin?

Neeve swallowed, her throat raw. Her chest was far too tight to breathe. But the idea took shape, the seed finding root in her mind's fertile soil.

Banish this magic for good. Live a normal life. See Eira again and beg her forgiveness.

Eagerness surged in her heart, the decision made. The problem had a clear solution.

And she would find it at the crossroads.

NEEVE GREW up with stories of the magic of crossroads, as though Rhiann had carved them with the specific purpose to amplify magic and divinity.

And for this, she would need the touch of a god.

Go at midnight.

Face the north.

One wish may be granted.

The full moon had reached its peak when Neeve slipped out of her cottage, Gretchen asleep and unaware, Samson remaining at her side.

"Stay here, good boy," Neeve had said, stroking her dog's head. "I'll be right back."

The nearest crossroads was half hour's walk from her village, where Neeve and Eira had practiced their chaos magic together. The night was cool and sky clear, starlight and moonlight guiding her every step as though earth and sky conspired with her midnight plan to see it done. She allowed herself a few reverent glances skyward, despite her hurried footsteps. Hope waited on the horizon, with Neeve's promise to herself almost fulfilled.

I will never make another mistake like that again.

Her skin puckered as magic tingled beneath it. A gentle breeze danced through the grass and leaves, whispering answers to the questions that raced through her mind. If only she knew the language of wind and trees.

The fear of outcomes had held Neeve in place these last seven days. She pressed against the bars of a cage she'd made, but opening the door for freedom was impossible, the task insurmountable. Not without help.

This was the first step.

"Wherever you are..." Neeve closed her eyes, breathing in the cool touch of night. Her lips quivered as she pictured Eira's smile. "Please be well. Please be *safe*."

Touchmagic and blindly exploring chaos had nearly cost Eira her life. Neeve clung to the threads of friendship that remained, desperate to atone for what she'd done.

"I'll do better," Neeve said to the night. "I'll *be* better."

Her boots were quiet on the worn path toward the crossroads, her steps measured and rhythmic against the ambient sounds of night. An owl hooted overhead seconds before a fox cried out. Crickets chirped. Branches swayed. The calm beauty of another world comforted her as she tiptoed through the dark.

When she reached the intersection of paths, the worn clay still held the grooves of the last batch of travelers reaching their destinations. She stood at its center and faced north.

"What will it hurt?" She looked down at her feet, clothes too thin for the chill that swept over her. She curled her toes and fingers against the cold, skin puckering to gooseflesh.

"I promise." A man's voice behind her. She spun, eyes wide, her white-blonde curls thrown over her shoulder. "It won't hurt."

He was tall, his broad shoulders carrying the white beams of moonlight as a nightly mantel. She stepped back, catching a flash of red in his irises as he moved closer.

A chaosborn. Granter of wishes. Dealmaker.

"What's your name?"

She hadn't expected his beautiful voice, smooth even as it rumbled. She imagined her hand against his chest, feeling the vibration of his voice with the rhythm of his heartbeat. "Neeve."

"*Neeve.*" He said it with a smile, his voice low just for her. "Bright. Radiant."

Blood rushed through her. *This was a mistake.*

"Neeve of Brightmere?" When she nodded, he stepped closer, eyes sweeping over her face and hair. "Your hair is the color of moonlight. And your eyes..." He studied them, the corners of his mouth angled up. "The same green as devil's ivy? Or the leaves of seraphim rose?"

She was stock still, her breath catching in her throat, unable to tear her eyes away.

"My name is Mal'Erick." He offered a slight bow. "It's a pleasure to meet you, Neeve."

She struggled to form the words as he held her without touching her. "Mal'Erick Chaosborn."

He smiled, the laugh lines around his mouth flattering. "If I asked you to say it again, would you indulge me?"

She hesitated, but something within her wished to, feeling power in the act. "Mal'Erick."

He'd closed his eyes, his expression serene. Her heart fluttered, watching him linger in this moment with her.

"You've come seeking my help." His voice was soft, confidential. He opened his eyes, the moonlight glimmering in his burgundy irises. "You only need ask, dear one."

"I—"

Her desire was so stupid. So ridiculous. *Take away my magic?* Why, when she should learn to control it? Or, better still, why seek his touch when she could abandon it herself?

She glanced over her shoulder, eyes scanning the path she'd taken, her heartbeat thundering in her ears.

"Wait." He opened his hand to her, his palm inviting. "Tell me."

She stared, fascinated with the thin streak of light across his cheekbone. Her palm itched, eager to take his hand.

"Tell me, dear one."

She slipped her fingers over his palm, surprised by its warmth, by the tender way he wrapped his fingers around hers. "I want you to take my magic."

"Take your magic?" He studied her eyes as though he could read every thought. His thumb rubbed her knuckles. "May I know why?"

"I didn't mean to hurt someone I care about," she said, though the firm tone in her voice wavered as her breathing came fast. "I'm not strong enough."

"Do I have your permission to see?" She held her breath as he stepped closer, as he touched one of her curls. "Bright, radiant Neeve."

"See what?"

"How the magic was used. How you reached it. Then I can trace its thread."

"And remove it."

"If that is your wish," he said. "And if it will not harm you, I will."

"I don't want to hurt anyone else." She turned her face, ashamed by the emotion that affected her voice. "I don't want to be afraid."

"Look at me, dear one." He raised his hand, poised to cup her cheek. "Let me see your magic."

She forced herself to focus, though her eyes were desperate to study the shadows that buried themselves in the hollow of his throat, to trace the fringes of light that highlighted the cupid's bow that crowned his lips. Heat bloomed over her face, her blood rushing fast through her veins.

A lock of hair fell around his eyes, touching the arch of his cheekbone.

"Ah." He hadn't touched her face, but Neeve's check felt his warmth. "There's something..."

He narrowed his eyes as his gaze bore into her, somehow with neither pain nor pressure. Neeve held his arms with both hands, bracing herself for what might come as he explored her mind.

He blinked, eyes searching hers, lips parted to speak. But the words were slow to come.

"What is it?" She tightened her hold on his arms. "What did you see?"

"Your magic." He shook his head. "It's shielded by a ward."

She stared, disbelief sinking like a boulder in her core. She released him, hands dropping.

"You fear your magic for its ineptitude," he said, "but it isn't a lack of skill. There is a barrier, one created to block your power."

"But—" She shook her head. "That's impossible."

"I'm afraid I must go back on my promise."

She didn't realize what he'd meant at first. Then, "It's going to hurt?"

His smile was sympathetic as he held out his hands, and when she took them, his long fingers rested open, giving her room to refuse. But she didn't.

"Take this barrier," she said, "and take my magic."

Kindness mingled with sadness as he nodded. "If that is what you wish, dear one."

Dear one, as though he knew her, as though she was already his.

I am no one's, she reassured herself. *I am my own.*

But his eyes, his voice. She couldn't deny how she enjoyed hearing him say her name. He'd captivated her within the very first second of meeting. It was the first step into an unknown world she wanted to explore fully.

"Breathe. I'm with you."

She obeyed as his presence entered her mind, his magic easing through with care. Closing her eyes, areas of her consciousness suffered fleeting congestion, the pressure building and releasing.

"There," he whispered. "Don't let go."

She tightened her grip, bracing herself, but nothing could have prepared her for the stab of pain at her temples, the pressure mounting behind her eyes. She cried out, bringing their hands to her mouth to muffle the sound.

The magic had no room in her skull, in her skin. She would burst into a million pieces.

Until, as quickly as it had come, the pain was gone.

Her breathing was deep and labored, exhaustion sinking into her muscles and bones. She tottered on her feet until Mal'Erick caught her, bracing her against his chest.

"Breathe," he said, smoothing her hair from her face. "I've got you. Breathe."

Her eyelids fluttered, her body almost weightless. Her mind was freer, her eyes sharper.

He helped her to stand, hands on her shoulders. "The barrier is gone, but your magic remains."

She blinked up at him. "What?"

"I'm afraid I can't remove it, dear one. It's a part of you."

Her anger flared like a spark igniting a fuse. "You said you would. We had a deal."

"It's impossible. Not without killing you." He paused, his burgundy eyes captivating. "Your blood is godborn."

Godborn. "That—that's not possible."

"I couldn't remove it in a thousand lifetimes, at a thousand crossroads."

An emotional whirlwind raged within her. "I'm godborn?"

He released her shoulders. "A child of light. But I conjure shadows."

"Anya and Aishlin share blood, dear one. Our magic forms a balance that each may tap into, with practice and focus."

Light. She staggered back, eyes unfocused. "How…"

"The block in your mind was placed there with magic," he said, "and it has shielded you from the memory of it. This magic feels old. It's settled within you."

"Taking root in my mind…" Neeve stared at her hands, curling and uncurling her fingers. Magic tingled in her palms. Eagerness. *Power.* She summoned tendrils of light around her fingers, feeling their warm touch over her skin. But she shivered, accustomed to the cool touch of shadow and dark. "How did this happen?"

"I'm sorry, Neeve." He moved closer, cupping his hands beneath hers as her light remained. But he didn't touch her. His proximity was a reminder that she wasn't alone. "I wish I had the answer."

"Me too." She pressed her lips together, frustration slipping into her tone. "Who would do this to me?"

"I didn't see," he admitted. "The memory was buried when the ward was created."

She looked up at him, dispelling the magic. *Courage, Neeve. Courage.* "What do I do now?"

"What do you want to do?"

His simple question didn't have a simple answer.

"This is a part of me," she said, her gaze moving to the lock of hair that dangled near his eyes. The wind touched it, the gentle sway pleasantly distracting. "If I have to live with it, then I will have to learn how to use it."

A hint of a smile toyed with his lips. "A wise answer. From what I saw, you've used your magic through touch."

"I didn't have a teacher," she said. "My friend and I taught one another. But we had no idea. Light magic, when I've cast shadows in chaos."

"The twins can offer their children that kind of connection," he said. "If I wished to, I could summon light, though it wouldn't be as powerful as yours."

"And your shadows would be stronger than mine."

His calm regard was her answer.

"If you wish it," he said, "you will have a teacher."

The thrill of his offer met her relief. "You will?"

"Absolutely." The moonlight sharpened the angles of his face, added clarity to the depth of his burgundy eyes. "If you'll have me. We will figure this out together."

"Yes. I accept."

I accept.

I accept.

I accept.

CHAPTER 3

I accept.

Neeve's feet carried her home, but her mind was elsewhere. Mal'Erick's voice filled her, the lingering fringes of his consciousness whispering back the moments they'd shared.

If you wish it, you will have a teacher.

I accept.

His voice. His hair. The gentle way he held her with his hands and eyes.

Dear one.

She pressed her fingernails into her palms, the chaos beneath her skin eager for use.

No, not chaos. *Light.* But the urge to cast was no less urgent. Twins of light and shadow, both calling in equal measure.

With the cage door opened, what could her power accomplish?

A prisoner of her own mind, locked in a tower. A songbird in a cage. No longer.

This magic feels old. It's settled within you.

Her heart thundered in her ribcage, fury coursing through her blood as she walked home. The cool night was a sweet contrast to the heat in her skin.

If I asked you to say it again, would you indulge me?
Mal'Erick.

She'd enjoyed saying it as much as he'd enjoyed hearing it.
Mal'Erick.

The village was quiet with sleep, midnight having passed and dawn still hours away. She walked the thoroughfare, passing the blacksmith and potter, the tanner and the tavern. Brightmere was small, particularly in its prejudices and tendencies to mind other people's business. But it was quiet, and the neighbors mostly left Neeve and Gretchen alone. After what happened with Eira, the village's glances from a distance were more tolerable than the alternative, with busybodies bringing Eira's family covered dishes as their cover to fish for gossip.

A man emerged from the tavern, its amber light flooding the street. Voices carried as he slurred through a common drinking song off-key, swaying where he walked. Neeve stepped to avoid him, but he reached for her, bleary gray eyes bloodshot.

"You can never trust the sea at dawn!"

She attempted to yank her arm free, his grip strong as she worked to peel his fingers back, light flaring in her hands.

His life unfolded behind her eyes, flashes of his past and present progressing down his life thread, leading to a grisly ending. Neeve blinked against the horse's hooves and wagon wheels crushing her.

She pulled free, staring at him in horror. From his perspective, the terror of the moment was brief, but for her, the horse's screams and rattling wagon lingered in her ears. She cupped her hands over her ears, but the same came from within, inescapable, looping as the images of his death repeated over and over.

She witnessed the moment he would die.

Oblivious, he fumbled onward, legs unsteady, singing voice absorbed by the night sky.

"When?" she whispered, forcing her mind to recall the images slowly, to study whatever distorted details she could manage through the blurred vision.

She had no recollection of reaching home, awareness only reaching her after Samson nuzzled her hand, his tongue startling her to waking.

She scratched behind his ear, panic chilling her core, spreading through her veins with every heartbeat.

More flashes came of Samson as a pup when he found Gretchen in the field outside of Brightmere. And then—

Neeve gasped, recoiling, staring into his loving brown eyes in horror. "Not you. No. *No.*"

She pulled free before the vision of his death came. What she glimpsed was Samson in old age, white fur replacing the golden yellow, his eyes tired but no less full of love. He would live a wonderful, comfortable life, but the thought of his passing made Neeve's bones weak, as though they'd crumble.

"Samson." Emotion welled. "What have I done?"

<hr>

NEEVE DIDN'T SLEEP. Dawn found her huddled by the hearth, teeth gnawing at the calloused skin around her thumb, barely blinking as the fire devoured what remained of the wood.

Gretchen emerged from the small hallway of rooms, her waves mussed from sleep. Her tired face scrunched as she studied Neeve. "You look like hell."

I made a deal at the crossroads.

Would Gretchen demand that Neeve take it back?

I'm Lightborn.

There was no taking it back now.

"Neeve. You're not blinking." She snapped her fingers twice in front of Neeve's face. "What's wrong?"

The words spilled out of her, the pressure of them too much to carry. They filled her stomach, her chest, her throat. Her body was far too small for the volume of space everything demanded.

"I went to the crossroads last night." She swallowed, her throat raw. "I asked him to take my magic."

Gretchen stood straight, drowsiness fading as her eyes widened. "Him? Him who?"

"The chaosborn as the crossroads."

"What are you saying?" Gretchen stared as though to read the meaning on Neeve's face. "You met a strange man last night?"

"A chaosborn," Neeve repeated. "I asked him to take my magic."

Gretchen's mouth opened and closed, strained sounds coming through until they eventually became words. "Why would you ask for something like that?"

"What happened to Eira," she said. "If I'd have known—"

Gretchen kneeled in front of her, the firelight behind her limning her warm blonde hair in an orange glow. "Your magic—"

"There's more."

Neeve closed her eyes, clasping her hands against her chest to avoid touching her sister, to avoid seeing how she would die.

"There was something in my mind, Gretchen." Neeve nearly choked, her breath catching, the words jamming the passage of airflow. "Something blocked my magic before. Something strong. And he—"

She shuddered to breathe, her chest aching as her breath struggled to fill it.

"Did he hurt you?"

"No." Neeve's curls swayed as she shook her head. "He removed the barrier. The wall. Whatever it was. And my magic—"

Gretchen's hazel eyes stared in terror. "What is it, Neeve?"

"I'm godborn."

Her sister blinked, the words slow to sink in. "What?"

"You must be too." Neeve wiped her face, feeling the trickle of tears falling. "Lightborn. That's what—"

"There's no way." Gretchen shook Neeve gently. "There's no—"

"I saw a man die."

The room stilled.

"I touched him. He staggered out of the tavern and touched me, and I pulled his hand off my arm—" Her breath caught. "I saw how he's going to die."

Gretchen's hands lifted, but she stayed close. "Because you touched him?"

Neeve almost showed her hands but kept them tightly closed and pressed against her pounding heart. "He'll be run over, but I don't know when."

"That chaosborn did this." Gretchen stood, her hands balled into fists. "What's his aim, here? What does he want?"

"That's not what happened, Gretchen. Please—"

"How could you go to the crossroads? How—" She stopped herself. "You were alone and let someone alter your mind. Your *mind*." Gretchen was awestruck. "What if something happened to you? Just like Eira?"

Neeve's lips trembled, the pit in her core growing wider, swallowing her whole. "What blocked my magic, Gretchen? Why can't I remember? Did I—Was there—"

Gretchen was quiet, the moment passing between them as guilt settled in her core. Hurting Eira. Making a deal. Seeing death.

"The godborn who gave you this power," Gretchen said. "He can take it back, right?"

"He didn't give me power," Neeve said, her voice quiet. "He unlocked it."

"Can you—" She hesitated, a hand going to her forehead as she exhaled. "Can he put it back?"

Neeve pressed her hands harder against her chest, willing her heart to stay inside.

Gretchen's tone was firm. "Will you see death every time you touch someone?"

She was afraid to say yes. "He's going to teach me. Gods, I—I thought *I* was weak. All this time."

Gretchen reached to embrace her, only to recoil. Tears welled in her eyes.

"I'm going to figure this out," Neeve said. "I swear it."

"We're figuring it out *now*." Gretchen picked up a blue shawl draped over the back of the nearest chair. "We're going to the crossroads together."

Gretchen threw the shawl around Neeve's shoulders, shoved her feet into her boots, and pulled Neeve out the front door with Samson at their heels. But the village greeted them with noise and movement as the sisters walked toward town.

"Gods above," Gretchen said, surveying the village. "Is it market day or something?"

Traffic was heavy down the thoroughfare, with horses and wagons passing from the south, crates and barrels among their loads.

Horses and wagons.

Neeve touched her face with trembling fingers, the phantom sensation of the horse's hooves on her nose and cheeks.

"Wait." She slipped free of Gretchen's arm and walked toward town. "Is it—"

"No." She reached for her arm, but Neeve pulled free. "Let's go to the godborn first."

"It might be too late."

"What? I didn't hear you."

Neeve's steps quickened, Samson barking as he remained by Gretchen's side. Neeve's eyes passed over every face, looking for the man and the horse that would trample him. But everything had happened so fast…

"Oy!"

A man cried out. A horse whinnied.

Neeve ran.

She saw him now, either still drunk or horribly hung over, lumbering through the street.

"Watch it!"

But the man didn't stop, his steps taking him straight to the horse.

Neeve's hand gripped his arm and pulled hard. He lost his balance and fell, taking her with him, the road dust stinging their eyes and filling their lungs. Neeve coughed as the man wheezed and sputtered as a crowd gathered, voices calling in urgency.

"She just saved his life!"

"Gods above, that idiot nearly died."

"Are they alright?"

The drunk regarded Neeve with sobering eyes, blinking in confusion. "Where the hells am I?"

Gretchen rushed to her, her blonde waves a mass around her shoulders as she kneeled beside her. "Are you crazy? You could have died!"

"I had to," Neeve said. "I had to try to stop it."

"Try to stop it?" A bystander stared at her. "His death?"

"He was going to die?"

"Gods above, can she see death?"

"A deathseer?"

"This isn't mist arcana, is it?"

The crowd collectively recoiled, wide, suspicious eyes staring. *Deathseer.*

"Dark chaos magic," one said, his voice low with superstition. "Toying with the threads of someone's life."

"It's not—"

But one spoke over her. "How much of your soul did you give for it, girl?"

"I didn't!" Neeve searched every face, begging for understanding. "That's not what this is!"

But that's exactly what it was: Deathsight. And it had always been a part of her.

Deathsight with light magic. Anya, just like Aishlin, remained connected to the life threads of all things.

Gretchen helped Neeve to her feet, careful not to touch her hands.

"You're a deathseer?"

Neeve whirled on the man who asked, venom ready to strike, but was taken aback by the state of him—pale, thin, eyes bloodshot.

"I want to know—" A cough interrupted him. He held a handkerchief up to his mouth, red lining his lips. "—how much longer I have. My family—"

He wheezed, unsteady on his feet. Neeve helped him before she thought better of it, hands meeting the skin of his frail arm. The flashes came slowly at first, showing a carefree youth that bloomed into an adulthood full of promise. He married the love of his life, and they shared three beautiful children. But something took hold of his body, leaving him on the threshold of death when he should have had decades of his life left.

"I don't care if you're using mist arcana to see," he said, meaning the words as a kindness. But bitterness soured in her stomach.

"I'm not using mist arcana," she said. "That poison can rot."

"I'm no one to judge." He coughed into his handkerchief, now more red than white. "My father died of this, and it took him quickly. I can only hope my children don't—" He wheezed a deep breath, the sound damp and hollow. "A cruel fate."

The man's death was near. In the vision, Neeve counted four more sunsets before his final breath would leave him.

"Four days," she said. "Gods, I'm so sorry."

He nodded, pulling a purse from his belt and handing it to her. "Four days. It's not nearly enough time. I'll prepare what I can for them."

Neeve moved to hand him back his money. "Sir, I—"

He shook his head. "Aishlin graced you with deathsight, and you have given me a chance to make sure my family is cared for."

"Anya," Neeve said, grateful for an ear that listened. "I'm lightborn."

"Anya. May her grace guide your days." He wheezed, his lungs rattling with breath. "Four days. I will make them count."

He turned and walked away, his movements slow. It wouldn't be long before his strength left him.

"Seven hells." Gretchen touched Neeve's shoulder. "Are you alright?"

"I hardly know." Neeve held the purse of coins to Gretchen, an idea sinking its hooks into her mind. Death reading done, coin in hand... "We can afford to eat for a week off this."

Their cabinets would be empty no longer. Neeve would help her sister to thrive despite their parents' absence.

"I know that look," Gretchen said, patting Samson's head as the dog whined beside her. "What is it?"

"Everyone wants to know how they're going to die." Neeve tapped the fabric pouch, making the coins clink and jingle. "Some will pay well to know."

"We're going to the crossroads." Gretchen's voice was firm.

"I'll go," Neeve said.

"Neeve—"

"I'll take care of it, Gretchen. He'll teach me."

Gretchen pressed her lips together, nostrils flaring. But she conceded as they separated, Gretchen heading home as Neeve walked toward the crossroads.

CHAPTER 4

The crosswords were different in daylight.

Neeve stood at the center, the cross of paths meeting beneath her feet, and held Mal'Erick's name on her tongue. When she summoned him, would it please him to see her? Or would he be cross at her recent return?

She closed her eyes, remembering him in shadow and moonlight, remembering him in voice and touch. Seeing this ethereal being in daylight would make him real.

Do I want him to be real?

She looked around, wondering if she would glimpse his thick dark hair, his piercing eyes. How did the magic of crossroads work, if anyone could summon a child of gods?

Say his name, Neeve.

Her fists were tight at her sides.

Call him.

She slowly opened her eyes, lips parting, the sunlight warm as it shimmered through the trees.

"Mal'Erick."

She waited, the world remaining the same as the seconds passed.

"Hello, dear one."

She whirled, the chaosborn appearing behind her.

"You've returned, Radiant Neeve."

"I—"

It was a foolish thing to meet his gaze. The deep wine-red would drown her the longer she stared.

Mal'Erick swept a curl over her shoulder. He hadn't touched her, but her shoulder flared with heat as though his fingertips had grazed her. "You look troubled."

Courage, Neeve. Tell him.

She straightened, taking a breath before the words came. "I have deathsight."

Had softness dulled the edges around his eyes? "Deathsight?"

Her fingernails would break the skin of her palms if she didn't loosen her hands. "I saw someone's death."

He studied her face, eyes flickering over every inch. "Gods, I hadn't anticipated this."

"Neither did I. It was—" Words failed as a chilling surge of stress flooded her core.

The horror and fear were unexpected effects of the gift, as had been the peace of letting go. The sick man, knowing his family was cared for, added a layer of comfort to an otherwise disturbing power. That reassurance had balanced everything.

And the coin he'd paid her ensured she and Gretchen would eat.

"Did you learn how the barrier came?" he asked.

Neeve shook her head, hands gripping her skirt, the fabric wicking moisture from her palms. "How do I control it? How can I hug my sister without seeing her die?"

Gods, what about her parents? To have them return home, only to see when...

Neeve closed her eyes, pressing her lips together to keep them from trembling. If they hadn't left...

Her breath caught as Mal'Erick touched her face, his palm forming to her cheek. She looked up at him even as tears welled in her eyes.

"Your mind is strong," he said. "I saw that when we broke the barrier and your magic was set free. But the heart is a different thing."

"I don't want the power to control me." *Nothing will control me. No cage will contain me. Never again.* "It is mine to wield, is it not?"

"It is." His thumb stroked her cheekbone. Neeve found it difficult to concentrate. "I will help you."

"Chaos helping with light? Will it—" She hesitated, the rudeness of the question tightening the muscles in her throat and chest. "Will it work?"

"Anya and Aishlin are bookends. Order and chaos created the world. They created us."

Relief helped her to breathe, though distant whispers in her mind warned her of the aftermath with Gretchen. She would *not* be pleased.

"Your first lesson." Mal'Erick dropped his hand to offer it to her. "If you're ready."

When her fingers slipped across his palm, he didn't close his grip, as though to give her a way out. She could let go anytime she wanted, and he wouldn't stop her.

"Create a guard that you control," he said. "Only incredibly powerful magic should have the strength to breach it, especially against the ward of a godborn."

"Godborn," she repeated. "I still can't believe it."

"Your experience with magic is impressive despite the block. And without a teacher, no less."

All experience had come with Eira, the pair learning without fear of consequence.

"And the cost was significant," Neeve whispered, reliving the moment Eira's parents took her.

The sunlight danced over them as the boughs swayed overhead. Tilting her head skyward, Neeve squinted at one ray of sun. "Light magic feels foreign to me. Chaos still tingles beneath my skin."

"Light creates shadows, dear one. You are both cause *and* effect."

They were quiet for several seconds, the whispering trees the only ambient sound above and around them.

"If you allow it," he said, "I'll show you where your ward is weakest. It will be uncomfortable, but I promise you, dear one, I won't hurt you."

His words were steady, his eyes sympathetic. The softness of his voice caressed her like the morning breeze.

She nodded. "I'm ready."

"At your word, this ends." He squeezed her hand for courage. "You are in control, Neeve."

You are in control.

She said the words again, more to herself. "I'm in control."

After a breath, Mal'Erick began. His presence created congestion, a second consciousness existing alongside her own. Pressure mounted slightly, and Neeve winced.

"Are you in pain?" he whispered.

"No, I'm alright."

He pressed her hand to his chest, the steady rise and fall coinciding with his heartbeat, offering a grounding rhythm. "Tell me the moment you want me to stop. Promise me."

"I promise."

He searched, the seconds ticking by, Neeve focusing on her breathing to match his.

"There," he whispered. The sensation of congestion deepened. "Tell me what you feel."

"Like there isn't enough room in my head."

"Your ward is strong against basic magic," he said, "but anyone practiced, or someone like me, could push through and meet only a little resistance."

The pressure in her mind released slowly, and his consciousness left her. He waited silently, eyes searching.

"How do I make it stronger?" she asked.

"What makes you feel safe?"

Her brow furrowed, the question almost intimate, the answer elusive. Until, "My sister."

"I sensed a strong bond. Familial."

"How do I—" She hesitated, not wanting to sound ignorant or petulant. "How will that protect my mind?"

"The wards are as strong as your will," he said. "Or they're as strong as your connection to what you see. Your sister would make a great champion for your mind, since you feel safe with her."

Neeve nearly laughed, imagining Gretchen poised to fight any intruder stupid enough to cross her path. Hazel eyes alight, fists ready, teeth bared. Gretchen's innate warrior's spirit had trained Neeve in the art of self-defense and self-preservation from an early age. "Pity to the poor soul who tries to cross her."

But for herself, for the power opened to her and the light she wielded...

Her mind—her body—had been a prison, but now, her hands had become symbols of incredible power. She regarded them with a perspective nearing objectivity before reality touched her once more, reminding her of what she'd lost and what there was to gain.

"What do you do?" When he didn't answer right away, she boldly met his eyes, determined to know his answer. "How do you block your mind?"

"Diamond glass," he said. "I imagine that I'm surrounded by glass made of diamonds."

"Diamond?"

"Created under extreme pressure," he said. "And only something powerful can crack or break it."

Something impenetrable to help control her power while keeping her out of a cage.

"Maintain the protection of your mind," he said. "Mastery comes with practice and time, but don't be surprised if you feel fatigued."

"Practice," she said, sensing something in his voice.

Scenarios raced behind her eyes. This mysterious, handsome chaos-born teaching her how to hone her magic.

Light and shadow. Order and chaos. She was grateful he didn't make her choose.

"You're kind to want to help me," she said. "But I am curious why."

"I want to see your magic grow," he said, "You've already accomplished remarkable things."

But Neeve's insides tightened. *Remarkable things* almost took Eira's life. *Remarkable things* left her nearly alone again. She praised the goddesses that Gretchen and Samson were with her.

"Don't get lost in the sea of your mind," he whispered, as though he could read her thoughts. "You're learning how to harness incredible power. And you've courage enough to practice wielding it. There are few who could manage it, dear one."

Though his confidence was bolstering, she wasn't sure she belonged among the powerful wielders of incredible magic.

Believe you do, she told herself, *and your place is there, right beside them.*

"Alright," she said. "But I have one question."

He raised an eyebrow, his smile devilish. "Only one?"

"You said diamonds are created under extreme pressure."

"I did."

She hesitated, the question sounding ridiculous now that it was seconds from her lips.

"Ask me, dear one."

He offered his hand to take, which she did mindlessly. The sensation of his touch grounded her, even while her mind was calm and her body relaxed.

"You're diamond glass, aren't you?" She nearly gulped, the question no longer amorphous but given voice. It was too forward, too personal. "You were created under extreme pressure."

His amusement didn't lighten or flicker. If anything, his closed-mouth smile widened. "In a way, aren't we all?"

CHAPTER 5

In a week, Neeve had followed the life threads of nearly a dozen people, all of them paying to know when they would die.

In a week, every villager subjected Neeve to suspicion and side-eye glances.

Deathseer.

Chaoswitch.

Soul-giver.

Few listened to the truth, and even fewer believed it. But her purse and pantry were full.

"An interesting outcome." Neeve walked beside Gretchen through the village, eager to buy ingredients for the evening meal. "This should take care of us for a little while."

"I don't care about the money." Gretchen kept her voice level, even as the tone betrayed her frustration. "I care about *you*. Are you sure about this?"

"No." Neeve wouldn't lie to her sister. "I have a lot of questions, and I—" She pressed her lips together, tempering the frustration simmering within her. "I feel betrayed, Gretchen."

"Gods, Neeve, I wish I could hug you."

"You can." Neeve took Gretchen's hand as proof. "I've been practicing."

"You swear?"

Neeve answered by embracing her, and Gretchen's arms tightened, Neeve melted, an emotional surge causing her throat to tighten.

"My training with Erick is going well," she said.

Gretchen quietly chuckled, her hold steadily tightening as she came to trust the outcome. "He's *Erick* now?"

Neeve inhaled slowly, hoping the delicate warmth on her cheeks didn't show. "A natural nickname to give, I think."

Neeve had come close to seeing Gretchen's death once since her trainings with Erick began. He visited nightly, helping her to learn what her *godborn power* could do. But the path ahead was long, even with all the progress behind.

"How did this happen?" Gretchen asked.

"Would it sound foolish if I admitted that I've tried not thinking about it?"

"No. But I can't help it." Gretchen pulled back, smoothing Neeve's hair from her face. "You're godborn. Am I? Do I have a barrier blocking my magic?"

"Have Erick—"

"No." Gretchen's smile was strained. "I think I'd rather not know."

"Mom and Dad would, wouldn't they?" Stress tightened Neeve's stomach. "They would know."

Gretchen's brow furrowed, hesitating to admit it. "We can't know that for sure."

"What else would make sense? A stranger blocking my magic?"

Gretchen didn't answer.

"If we ever see them again," Neeve said bitterly, "I have a lot of questions to ask them."

"There was something when I was young," Gretchen said. "A trip you took to Alvar."

Neeve stared, no memory surfacing. "We went to Alvar?"

"Not *we*," she said. "Mom and Dad took you when you were small. You cried a lot, like you were hurting or sick, so they took you to a healer."

"All the way in Alvar? Without you? How could they leave you here alone?"

"I remember staying with a neighbor. Everyone called her Grandma."

Neeve's memory strained for any connection, but she could find none. Worry needled her insides, her stomach unsettled.

"Mom and Dad." The sting of betrayal sank deeper. "How—"

How could they? The question breached a chasm in her chest, her heart throbbing as it continued to beat through an internal catastrophe.

Dusk was imminent, the colors of the sky vibrantly warm as they steadily shifted to the cool tones of night. Neeve and Gretchen had settled on stew and, with her recent reading, they could afford meat.

"Samson will be happy," Gretchen said, her tone lighter. But both sisters shook in terror as glass shattered and voices rose from the tavern.

"You useless bastard!"

Two bodies flew from the front door in a tangle of arms and legs, rolling down the wooden steps and onto the dusty road. Neeve and Gretchen stared in horror as two men fought, their fists and feet hitting wherever they could land, until one of them wasn't moving. His opponent landed punch after punch against a motionless face, blood splattering his arms and face.

"Stop!" Someone reached for the assailant's arms. "Stop! He's out!"

The attacker, panting, leaned back, the man beneath him still.

"Serves you right," he growled. "Never look at my wife again."

"I don't think he will." A villager approached slowly, reaching a tentative hand toward the man on the ground. After a moment's contact, they recoiled. "Gods above, he's dead!"

Guilt flashed on the man's face, his jowls shaking as he refused to believe. "I didn't kill him! I swear, I didn't!"

"Neeve," Gretchen whispered. "Isn't that—"

But Neeve recognized him as the sisters moved to get a better look.

The dead man on the ground had been the one she saved.

Visions of his death beneath the hooves of a horse, beneath the wheels of a wagon. Neeve saw them all again, quick flashes of fear and trauma flooding her mind, anxiety writhing in her stomach.

"He wasn't supposed to die," Neeve whispered.

"Let's go." Gretchen tugged at Neeve's arm. "Let's make supper."

Neeve allowed herself to be led away from the scene, horror meeting anger in a strange partnership within her.

"That was his life, Neeve," Gretchen said. "*His*, not yours."

His life. *His life.* Neeve had seen its end and stopped it. What if...

"What if I didn't stop it?" she asked. "What if he was always going to die? No matter what I did?"

"You mean like fate?"

Neeve didn't answer. Fate sounded like an excuse, a way out when nothing else made sense.

"Actions have consequences," she muttered, more to herself than to Gretchen. "Our actions. Our *choices.*"

"His choices landed him in trouble both times," Gretchen agreed. "You didn't do this. And I don't think *death* did, either." She looked ahead, holding tighter to Neeve's arm. "I don't think of death as an entity. It's more of a concept of what happens to our physical bodies."

Neeve normally loved when Gretchen philosophized, but her words didn't land as she'd hoped.

"Death is always for the living," Gretchen said. "The souls of the deceased go on to whatever's next. And there *is* something next. Magic is proof enough of that."

Neeve half-listened, but Gretchen's voice echoed in her mind.

Death is always for the living.

Was his end in a tavern brawl meant for Neeve to see?

Are you angry that I adjusted your timeline? She aimed her thoughts at the amorphous concept of Death, as though he walked with her unseen. *Are you displeased that a mortal could thwart your plan?*

Magic tingled in Neeve's palms, itching to be used. She glanced down to see threads of line illuminating the creases in her palms.

But how much thwarting had she done, really? The man was dead, after all. And the village knew what she was.

Deathseer.

CHAPTER 6

Three Months Later

"You had a reading today."

In her backyard, the sun near to setting, Neeve stood with Erick, his fingertips on her temples.

"A young woman," Neeve said. Her fingers still knew the memory of the cloak she held to see its maker on her deathbed. Loving hands had crafted every stitch, the deep crimson lined with a soft black. "Asking about her grandmother. She was afraid she made her sick."

"But that wasn't the case?"

Neeve shook her head. "The natural order of things. Age and a tired body."

"Was she relieved to know?"

"I think so, but her grief is still heavy."

"Grief always is."

Grief in loss. In *choice*. For Neeve, one led to the other.

Erick swept a lock of moon-white hair from her face. "Let's see how much you remember."

She rose to his challenge, mischief conjuring a smirk. "I remember it all. Barricade myself in diamond glass. Nothing can come through this shell. Only I'm allowed in."

"Good. Remember: the magic obeys *you*. It's strong because of *you*." An eyebrow rose. "Though I'm curious."

"Curious about what?"

"I thought your protection manifested as Gretchen."

"It did." She paused before going on. "You use a powerful object, something that you can create and keep. But Gretchen—"

She'll die someday. Neeve blinked, focusing on the locks of dark hair that fluttered around Erick's eyes, afraid of what her mind would see.

"I think I understand," he said. "It's better if you use something that belongs to you, something you made, rather than what depends upon another."

"Yes." Relief soothed the tightness in her chest. She didn't have to say it, to put words to it.

"Leaning on others can be hard," he said, "but that's a part of loving them."

In the waning daylight, his irises were black glass. Their up-turned almond shape enhanced the mischief and bravado that flashed within them, but she knew their softness and their intensity. If he let her, she could stare into them for hours and still not discover their full depth. She would willingly lose herself in them without a shred of remorse.

"I have to trust myself," she whispered. "My magic is strong, but that's what makes me afraid. I don't want to hurt anyone else."

"I wish you could see what I see," he whispered. "A powerful young woman. Capable. Remarkable. *Radiant.*"

Heat painted a flush across her cheeks.

"How can I make it easier?" he asked. "How can I help you?"

"I don't know. I can't—"

Her chest tightened as it had done so many times before, when she thought too hard and too clearly about Eira, about what happened and what should have been.

"The past was never meant to haunt you, no matter how recent its reach remains." He held her shoulders, leaning slightly to level his gaze with hers. "Let it go, dear one."

Her lips trembled, so she took a sharp breath of cool air and let it out before it could settle in her lungs. "I almost killed her, Erick. I was so *stupid*. So careless."

"It wasn't stupidity or carelessness." His voice was firm, though his touch remained gentle as he lifted her chin. "I saw it all when I read you. Your excitement. Your joy. It was *pure*."

Neeve almost closed her eyes, taken by the warmth of his hand, the gentle whisper of the trees.

"You have so much light in you now, even with the shadows that linger."

She collected herself, the emotional swell ebbing. His hair hung low, the breeze toying with strands that dangled over his brow. His lips parted to speak, the cupid's bow drawing her attention before returning to his eyes.

"Block me."

She had no other warning as he filled her mind with magic. There was never pain, but the pressure built before she could will it out. Her unbreakable shell shimmered blue-white in her mind's eye, like cut glass reflecting moonlight.

Your mind makes it real, Erick had said. *Believing it makes it real.*

Trust. Acceptance. Forgiveness.

I wish you could see what I see.

"Good," he said, his thumbs trailing along her jaw as he pulled his magic back. "Very good."

He let her go, though he didn't move. His proximity was as much an anchor as his hands had been. "I have an idea."

She tilted her head. "I'm listening."

"Our magic. Light and shadow."

"*Our* magic." But it made her smile. "Flatterer."

He chuckled, shifting his weight on his feet. "Sometimes you catch me off guard."

Neeve stared in awe. Mal'Erick, charismatic and confident, *flustered*. "What do you mean?"

"A look, a word. The way the light fills your eyes."

Neeve took his shoulders and give him a gentle shake. "You said something about our magic."

"I did. What have you learned of light and chaos and the magic they bring?"

Neeve considered as she sifted through superstition and prejudice that circulated among those who didn't know or understand Aishlin and her kin. "Chaos is shadows and moonlight. Illusion."

He smirked. "You just described the night we might. Though the *illusion* part came later."

He touched near his eyes, which he'd never hidden from her. For others, Erick set his mask firmly in place, shifting his eye color to a rich brown.

"One interesting thing about chaos magic is its limitless potential," he said. "The same could be said for earth magic, which can connect to the weather and tap into the power of the storm goddess, or for light magic that can burn as hot as Brena's forge."

Neeve understood the intention behind Erick's quiet coaching, but the *limitless potential* set her heart racing. She almost pulled her hands free from his, sensing the tingle of perspiration in her palms.

"Just like light magic, chaos can tap into the life threads of all living things, as you know, Mindwalker."

"*Mindwalker.*" Neeve almost laughed. "How do you make it sound so remarkable when it scares me to think about?"

"Because it *is* remarkable. What happened before won't happen again."

Her breath caught, the fringes of confrontation teasing her. She would have to face it, no matter how she tried to avert her gaze. "You don't know that."

"I do, because I'm coming to know you, Neeve of Brightmere. It won't happen again because you won't let it."

She said nothing at first, wishing that his confidence was her own. "How does this relate to what you were saying before? About our magic?"

"Right. Threads of life, mindwalking, illusion. And light magic is sunlight, healing, and warmth that can be weaponized in a fight. But how do you find the relationship between your light magic alongside the chaos magic you're used to casting?"

"How do I find it?" She considered her answer. "It's easy to cast. The shadows still come when I call."

"Curious, though I shouldn't be surprised." A pleased smile graced his mouth. "A lightborn mastering the dark."

"Hardly mastering." But she couldn't deny how her heart hammered against her ribcage at his impression of her. "But I wonder how one can call upon both. Shouldn't the shadows be repelled by the light?"

"Not if the magic comes from the same place, which, as children of Anya and Aishlin, our god-touched bloodline *is* that place."

She turned her hands over as his hands still cradled them, curling and uncurling her fingers as she imagined light-laced threads of shadow curling around them.

"Light and chaos," she muttered, thinking about Eira. "Is that why—"

Eira had agreed so readily to the magic that left her broken at Neeve's feet. Was Neeve's use of shadow magic somehow out of place or corrupted because of her lightborn blood?

"Neeve?"

Her eyes flitted to Erick's, reading the worry in his look. Her hands slipped free of his.

"Talk to me," he urged, his voice gentle. "What is it?"

"You know about her," Neeve said, the specific words and details still too hard to say. "About what happened."

"Since the day we met," he said. "I saw exactly why you were there at the crossroads."

It came as a relief that she didn't have to tell him. There were so many words she didn't have to say, and that knowledge loosened something invisible that had tightened across her chest. She would have sunk to her knees in gratitude if they hadn't locked up beneath her, if Erick hadn't steadied her with his hands on her shoulders.

"Did I—" She swallowed air, her lungs simultaneously full and not full enough. "Before, with Eira, my magic—"

"No, Neeve." His hold was firm and his eyes piercing. "Your power didn't do that. Your magic didn't."

Neeve forced herself to remember, discerning through the memory if she'd unwittingly subjected her friend to an outcome that left her broken.

"She was as eager to try as you were."

As eager as you were. The truth both helped and hurt, but the sting faded as her body pushed through the flood of panic.

"Breathe slowly. I'm here." He tightened his grip just enough. "I won't let go."

Her back and shoulders ached for the pressure of his arms, something to hold her tight enough that she would feel rooted where she stood.

Don't let fear win. She recited the words over and over, her voice echoing in the chambers of her mind. *Don't let fear win.*

"It's still with me," Neeve said, her voice quivering. "As though it was yesterday."

"Your kindness carries it," he said. "Most wouldn't let it burden them."

"It feels wrong to let it go."

"Why?"

She bit back against the answer.

"You don't deserve to be punished, Neeve."

He saw too much. He *knew* too much.

She inhaled deeply through her nose before easing it out through pursed lips, forcing patience into her lungs. Her vulnerability made her shiver, but there was relief in Erick knowing her. Forming the words around her fears was exhausting.

"You're going through a lot to protect Gretchen *and* yourself, pushing yourself to learn that which should have been yours all along. You're doing well, Neeve."

"I don't want to see her die. I don't want to see *anyone* die. Seeing the end of her life thread, I—"

A sob escaped. She pressed a fist to her mouth.

"You don't have to say it," he whispered. "I know. I know about the people you've tried to save."

Three, not counting the man who died in the tavern fight. And two of them survived past the assigned time when they would die. One died sooner, and Neeve couldn't rectify if her touch to alter his direction had hurried the timeline.

Assigned time. But that was fate's touch, giving them a deadline.

Deadline. Neeve shook her head, wishing to be anywhere other than in her own head.

Some had their destinies altered, but others had theirs diverted, the end still meeting them as though every life thread fell prey to the shears in the hands of fate.

"They say you shouldn't tamper with what will be," he said, "but I find it difficult to sit back and watch when my actions may yield a different outcome."

"What if it doesn't change?" She braved a glance at him then, already vulnerable, already exposed. He could see right through to her throbbing heart. "What if you try, and they still die?"

"You're thinking about the drunk in the tavern brawl."

It was cruel to reduce him that way. "Yes. And others."

"What you did saved his life. What *he* did paid a hefty cost."

He was right, but Neeve suffered her anger at such powerlessness, even still. Would her actions yield nothing, after all? Could she defy death if she saw its path and interrupted its course?

"The same could be said for the others, but it's more than their life threads that play a role. Everyone makes choices that have consequences. Sometimes, they overlap."

"Tangled threads," she muttered, imagining unseen lines glowing outward from their chests, intersecting with other lines like a growing web of lives.

"Why can't I read you?" Her question was sudden and unprompted. "We've touched without my ward in place."

"Your ward may have been down," he said. He followed her arms down to her wrists, his fingers gentle as he took her hands. "Mine was not."

A tinge of hurt stung at the thought of him guarding his mind against her. But reality set in, and with it, comfort. "You're protecting me."

"My godborn life hasn't been the most pleasant. And I'd rather not show you the manner of my death."

Protection for both of them. She would have done the same if their roles were reversed.

The panic eased its hold, relief flowing through her blood. His presence unwavering, Erick had seen her through the grip of her fear. She wouldn't forget that.

His brow furrowed as her eyes misted. She blinked away the sting.

"Sometimes, I hate my magic," she said. "It's a burden to learn it. To *control* it. Giving in would be easier." She scoffed a laugh, turning her eyes up to keep the tears from falling. "Gods, I sound so childish."

He cupped her face, his palm warm against her cheek. "It requires more strength to fight back, to keep it from taking you."

"Thank you," she said, blinking through the sting as she tried to smile up at him. "I don't know what I would have done without your guidance."

"You would have found a solution." Then, quietly, he chuckled. "Or Gretchen would have. But Neeve—" He paused, the words almost there. "Would you believe me if I said I cared for you?"

She raised an eyebrow, heart quickening, even as her own mischief surfaced. "That's not your charisma talking, is it?"

Erick, caring for her, feeling for her the way she felt for him—the thought sent her spirit skyward.

"My—" Surprised, the weight of his mood lifted, his expression smoothing. "You think I'm charismatic?"

Charismatic and a flirt. Though she was proud to have surprised him. "I believe you. Though, I feel I should ask..."

She let her thought dangle on purpose, pleased when he leaned closer.

"Ask what, dear one?"

She met his eyes with mischief flashing in hers. "Isn't it exhausting, flirting all the time?"

The rumble of a chuckle sent her heart soaring as it fluttered against her ribs.

He tucked her hair behind one ear. "Not when it's you."

"You make it seam as natural as breathing."

"Again, only when it's you."

She stood with him, glad for his anchoring touch, for the softness of his voice.

"I should go," she said, the last glimmer of daylight leaving the horizon. "Are you staying for supper?"

"Not this time, which will make Samson happy."

"He just needs to get used to you."

"A season is plenty of time to learn that I am a trustworthy guest in your home."

"Goodnight, Erick."

"Goodnight, Neeve."

She turned for the back door, stopping as Erick took her arm, his hold gentle.

"I meant what I said. You have great potential."

She looked at him over her shoulder. "Thank you for helping me unlock it."

"If you'll let me. If you'll let yourself turn the key."

But what if the lock is broken?

CHAPTER 7

Neeve breathed in the steam from the boiling pot, the potatoes and onions merging beautifully in the homemade stock. After a fitful night's sleep and a slow morning, Neeve took the domestic reins to prepare lunch while Gretchen practiced throwing knives outside. Neeve counted the rhythmic *thud, thud, thud* of the blades hitting their wooden targets as she stirred.

Ever since Gretchen was ten, she'd honed her skill with knives and small daggers. "*The carnival's in town!*" And she'd been so excited. But Neeve and their parents hadn't expected her desire to *join* them.

She may have lost the dream of running away with the carnival, but she never lost the joy of throwing knives.

Neeve opened the kitchen window and moved the shutter aside. Gretchen's back and shoulder were barely visible. "Do you think Erick will surprise us with a visit? I swear, he can smell our food for miles."

"He's not here for the food," Gretchen answered, punctuating her statement with a *thud* as another knife landed. "He's found something *sweeter*."

"*Gretchen.*"

A knock at the door made both sisters freeze before Neeve heard Gretchen yank her knives free from their wooden target. She peered through the window with eager eyes, her brown waves framing her face. "What are the odds?"

"I'd say pretty high, knowing his daily visitation record."

But it wasn't Erick. A tall man with broad shoulders offered a slight bow, his clothes framing his lithe body with soft earth tones and durable fabric. His brown leather boots had seen a lot of miles, by the look of them.

"Are you Neeve?" His long hair was bound at his neck, making his soft gray eyes appear sharper, keener. The dark golden brown locks shimmered in the sunlight.

Magic tingled in her palms, channeling shadows and light. How would this encounter go? "I am. What brings you by?"

"I heard from the villagers that you give death readings." Sadness laced his smile, lips closed, laugh-lines deep.

Neeve stepped aside, letting him in. Samson rose from his place by the hearth, studying the newcomer.

"Are you sure you want to know?" Neeve always asked, even as the man placed a small purse of coins in her hand. "You can't take back the knowledge once it's learned."

"In my line of work," he said with a quiet chuckle, "it would be a good idea to have an advantage."

The skin on the back of her neck prickled. "Your line of work?"

"I'm with Moonblade." He tugged at the silver chain beneath his collar to show the silver charm of a crescent moon diagonally crossed with a dagger. "We've had our hands full lately. The Wandering Order is getting bolder. One of their Preceptors was sighted in Shaylon Plains a day or two ago."

Preceptor. Neeve's knowledge of the cult didn't extend to titles or rankings. It was the same with Moonblade, if they had such things as officers and leaders. Her parents had spoken of Moonblade before their last departure months ago, but the addition of an ally against the cult only worsened Neeve's anxiety. Too much conflict, too many threats, and Neeve's parents were out among them all.

Neeve showed her guest to the table and invited him to sit. "What's your name?"

"Darrow."

Neeve held out her hands for him to take. "I have to walk through moments in your life in order to reach its end." She offered a kind look, suspecting his end may come in violence. "It will take time, and I will learn things about you that you may not wish others to know."

"I understand." His hold on her hands didn't waver.

Passing along Darrow's life thread was smooth. *Easy.* There were turns and paths and layers, just like in any life, but Darrow's was straightforward. Even as a member of Moonblade, whose survival centered on secrecy and discretion, his heart laid bare for Neeve to see.

Tears welled in Neeve's eyes, watching scenes from his life, seeing his father when Darrow was young. They'd stood at his mother's grave, his father openly weeping, Darrow touching his bowed shoulders while his own tears fell.

Time progressed to Darrow's initiation into Moonblade, his necklace earned once he'd completed his first mission. Darrow's bloodstained hands had accepted the token, the silver glistening in the firelight.

Recent days showed Darrow kneeling at a freshly dug grave beside his mother's. He'd wept alone, no one beside him with a touch of comfort, his fists trembling at his sides.

Neeve's breath caught in her chest as she inhaled, trying to steady the welling emotion with little success.

His hold on her hands tightened.

Then the moment came. Gray accented the hair above his ears with signs of age lining his face. But there was no violence around him, no battle being fought, no cultist aiming death at him. Beauty surrounded him—a clear blue sky, an overgrown field swaying in a gentle breeze, the world brilliant in bright, pure color.

He clutched his chest, struggling to find his breath, and fell to his knees. The world turned black before Neeve could fully see his end.

"Your heart," she whispered, her throat tight. "It's years away. Gray hair and crow's feet. Walking—a dirt path along a hillside. A field of wildflowers."

Neeve released his hands, wiping her eyes with her fingers. "Gods, I'm sorry. It's just—it reached me."

"This can't be easy for you," he said, his voice low and quiet. "Thank you for doing this."

She nodded, taking a slow, steady breath through her nose.

"My father," he said, but hesitated.

"He passed," she said. "You were at his grave." She sniffled, wiping her face again. "The reading showed me."

"I've only just been able to return. I was in Sudor when I heard the news. The mission—I couldn't leave."

He struggled, looking down at his hands, his index fingers worrying the skin around his thumbnails.

"My parents had a trip out of town, too," Neeve said. "Leaving is never easy."

"Neither is staying." He met her gaze then. "It was hard on him. It must be hard on you."

Neeve's brow furrowed, his knowing reminding her of Erick, how he could read her and see her and know without Neeve having to say a word.

"You saved his life," Darrow said. "My father."

"I did?" The wrinkles between her brows deepened.

"The wagon. He was nearly trampled and run over."

Her eyes tingled anew with fresh tears forming, guilt swirling midst the fountain of emotions brought by the reading. "I'm so sorry. The tavern fight. I didn't see—"

Darrow held up his hand, his expression kind. "My father was a reckless drunk. I am responsible for it, not you."

"No—"

"I shouldn't have left. But the money from Moonblade was more than I could ever make with a trade. I did what I thought was best."

The coin from Darrow's reading bore the same guilt-laced meaning. Neeve, doing what she thought was best by finding an optimistic outcome to a grim, dark power.

Ironic, that her light-given power came with shadows of its own.

"Thank you, Neeve," he said again, standing. "For saving my father when you did, and for reading my future."

But it wasn't enough.

Neeve couldn't speak as he bowed and stepped out, latching the door quietly behind him. She sat in stunned silence for several seconds before Gretchen stepped in, resting a hand on her shoulder.

"Are you alright?" Gretchen asked.

Neeve nodded, wiping beneath her eyes again.

"I was worried something would happen," Gretchen said. "When he said life was hard for you, too. Then bringing up his father."

Neeve noticed Gretchen toying with one of her throwing knives. "The reading would have shown me if he meant harm."

Gretchen's hazel eyes pierced into Neeve's. "And you would have set him on fire, right?"

"Maybe not arson, but there definitely would have been burning."

A series of frantic knocks shook the door.

"Gods, another one?" Gretchen moved to answer, but Neeve stopped her.

"I'll get it."

She wanted to be there to see Erick, to have his eyes read her and know.

But, once again, a stranger waited on the other side. A middle-aged woman glanced over her shoulder, trembling hands worrying the hem of her shirt. Her clothes were dirty, boots mud-caked. She'd seen better days, and when she looked at Neeve, she dropped her eyes, watching her fingers work the fabric.

"Eye contact won't hurt you," Neeve said without thought, stung by this stranger's behavior in the wake of Darrow's kindness. She called over her shoulder to Gretchen, "Looks like a reading."

"I heard you're a deathseer," the woman muttered.

"I am."

She untied a bulging pouch from her belt for Neeve to take. "I can pay. A lot. I need a reading right away. Please."

Neeve ushered the woman inside. She placed the pouch of coins on the table with shaking hands.

By the hearth, Gretchen rested her hand on Samson's head as both watched their guest. "That bracelet is beautiful."

An ornate knot pattern decorated the metal cuff, the engraving resembling a bird. But the woman drew her sleeve over it quickly, still not lifting her eyes.

"I'll prepare some tea," Gretchen said, reaching for the kettle.

But the woman refused. "There's no time."

The sisters shared a knowing glance before Gretchen said, "I'll wait outside."

She slipped out, leaving Samson with Neeve.

"Please, have a seat." Neeve kept her voice level, as though soothing a frightened animal. "What brings you in?"

She pulled and twisted her fingers as she sat. "I'm going to die soon. I need to know when."

Alarm furrowed Neeve's brow as she reached for her guest's hands. "Are you sure you want to know?"

"I wouldn't have come here if I didn't." She clipped her tone as though to verbally slap sense into Neeve. She took Neeve's hands, her grip aggressive.

Neeve recoiled but hesitated to yank her hand free. "There's no going back, once it's done. There's danger in knowing."

"There's danger in *not* knowing. Just do it." The woman closed her eyes. "Please, by the gods, just do it."

Neeve would have refused her, if not for the weight of the coin purse on her table. The woman's rudeness didn't detract from Neeve's empty cabinets. The reading would be over soon enough, and Neeve could afford to buy Gretchen and Samson quality meals for the next several days.

"Say nothing," Neeve instructed. "Keep your eyes closed."

After waiting for a breath in silence, Neeve pushed through, her approach careful as always. She wove through the length of the woman's remaining days as the images flashed like sunlight through the wind-shaken boughs of forest trees.

But the tone and progression changed, moving faster, the sense of urgency far too strong.

"Something's changed in your life." Neeve didn't open her eyes, following the thread. "Things haven't always been this way."

"Please, get on with it," the woman begged, her voice and hands trembling. "How and when do I die?"

"Silence." Neeve's abrasive tone matched the woman's. "I have to walk the path before I can see its end."

For some, the journey was direct. But this woman's thread had tangled. Neeve struggled to maintain pace.

Brilliant green lands with a backdrop of blue and white mountains filled Neeve's sight. Here, there was more land than people, with few faces passing by until one—a female face made of stone, framed by trees and sky. Warmth and love swelled within Neeve, reflecting the woman's feelings as Neeve passed through her memories. Even in her loneliness, the woman had something she held dear.

"Your relationships are short-lived," Neeve said. "No attachments to speak of."

"I can't. This is a waste of time."

The woman moved to break the bond, but Neeve was the first to break contact, throwing the woman's hands aside. Frustration simmered hot beneath her skin as she regarded the woman's disrespect in kind.

"You're right. This is a waste of time." Neeve pointed to the front door. "Get out."

"You dare—"

"You're the one who dares." Neeve's palms itched to conjure, the light burning to be of use. She only needed to whisper, and they would do her bidding. "Either let my magic work, or stop wasting my time. I will not say it again."

"You stupid—"

"*Get out,*" Neeve said, her voice both lower and louder. Light bloomed with her anger, enhancing the firelight from the hearth and sunlight from the windows. Her skin prickled as the tiny hairs stood on end. "*GET OUT.*"

The woman rounded on her, motion and sound happening too quickly to process until Neeve suffered the sensation of falling. The woman whispered quickly, slamming her hand onto the table with a scrap of parchment that caught fire. A symbol Neeve didn't recognize burned into the paper before a flash fire reduced it to ash.

At Neeve's descent, she reached for the woman's leg, fingers gripping her ankle and pulsing chaosmagic through her touch. The woman cried out before kicking back against Neeve's face. Neeve saw blinding stars limned in darkness, blinking and staring as they whirled.

Samson barked, lunging for the woman, but she bolted, the door crashing against the house at her thunderous exit. Sunlight poured into the room through the open door.

Neeve gasped for breath like a fish out of water.

Then her vision went dark.

CHAPTER 8

A hand on her shoulder, the grip heavy and tight, shaking her.

"Ma'am? Are you all right?"

Something cold and wet touched her nose. She recoiled, wincing as Samson grumbled close by.

"By the gods. What happened?"

"Hm?" Neeve groaned, opening her eyes. She was level with the floor and Samson, whose brown eyes met hers.

Gretchen looked her over. "Are you hurt? Is there any pain?"

"Some." Neeve's voice was raspy as though from disuse. She let Gretchen help her up, her hip and back aching from the fall. "Oh, gods, I feel awful." She pressed her hands to her head, palms against her temples. The pressure within thumped like a heartbeat. "What *was* that?"

"Do you remember anything that happened?" Gretchen asked. "Where's my sister?"

Neeve blinked at Gretchen. "What?"

"She was here with another woman, performing a reading."

"Gretchen." Neeve gripped her sister's arms. "What do you mean, *where is my sister?*"

Gretchen didn't blink for several silent seconds, confusion graduating to realization. "Neeve?"

"What's wrong with you?"

Gretchen touched Neeve's face, shoulders, and arms, her motions erratic. "Something's happened." She smoothed Neeve's hair, her touch different. "You need to stay calm."

"Spit it out. What's wrong?"

Gretchen steadied Neeve on her feet as she helped her to the washbasin. She took up their mother's antique hand mirror, the patina on the bronze light and dark from the touch of many hands.

The reflection was a woman near to eighty years old. Her hair was a powdery white, thin around her shoulders, the voluminous curls withered and limp. What remained untouched by age were her eyes, somehow keeping their vibrant green brightness as if they were still young.

Neeve touched her hair, seeing her aged hands in the reflection. Wrinkles, liver spots, arthritic joints.

She shoved the mirror away, rage burning through her blood. "She cursed me!"

The rhythm of her headache was no longer a heartbeat. It was a war drum.

She spun on her heel, practically running out of the house, eager for a sign of where the woman went. But Neeve's body was not strong enough to keep up with the rage that burned. She cried out when her back and hips seized, using the doorway for support.

"Gods above," Gretchen said, doing a terrible job of hiding her amusement. "You look like Gram."

"This isn't funny." Neeve swatted at her, Gretchen succumbing to a fit of giggles. "This isn't funny, Gretchen!"

"It can be undone, though, right?" she asked, pinching Neeve's wrinkled skin. "Break the curse, go back to normal?"

"If I don't die of old age first!"

Reality broke through as Gretchen's expression sobered. "Gods, Neeve. I didn't think."

Neeve's eyes narrowed, forcing herself to see through blurred vision. Her spine popped in realignment when she straightened her aching body. She growled through the fleeting pain that fanned the fire burning in her core.

"She'll wish she'd never been born." The flash of rage in Neeve's eyes was dangerous. Her fingernails almost cut into her palms. "Maybe that's why I couldn't get a clear reading. Because I'm the one who kills her."

"Neeve—"

"She crossed the wrong deathwitch."

"*Neeve.*" Hurt reached Gretchen's voice. Her grip on Neeve's shoulder tightened. "You hate that word. You're not a deathwitch."

Guilt stabbed her pounding heart, some of her anger receding. "I do. I'm sorry."

Gretchen took her arm, helping her to hobble toward the dining room chair. As soon as she sat down, her bones and muscles relaxed, the pain easing.

"What do you know about her?" Gretchen asked. "Is there anything from the vision that can help?"

"There wasn't much. Her life is pretty empty."

Neeve closed her eyes, trying to remember the images of the woman's life.

"Neeve?"

"Hm?"

"Don't fall asleep."

She opened her eyes, her glare lethal. "I'm not falling asleep."

"Sometimes the elderly just *nod off.*" Gretchen pressed her lips together, the corners turning up. "How do we fix this?"

"She's made my body age so fast." Neeve pressed a hand to her forehead, the light flutter of anxiety making her heart race. "What if something happens?"

"What do you mean?"

"I'm so old, Gretchen." Neeve looked down at her body, her torso and limbs almost unrecognizable. "Did she curse me to die?"

Gretchen, shocked, stared at her sister with mouth agape. "I thought—" She gestured vaguely. "I thought this is just superficial, that you're the same on the inside."

"It doesn't feel like I'm the same. Gods, I feel like Gran."

They sat in heavy silence as Neeve massaged her hands.

"I need to find her." Neeve stood, hips and knees creaking. "She has to make this right, or so help me..."

Neeve hobbled to the shelves where they kept books and herbs. She pulled one volume down and flipped through the pages with one hand while the other was supporting her, palm planted against the edge.

"The bracelet she wore." Gretchen wrapped her fingers around her left wrist. "The engraving style doesn't look like it's from Sheraton. Ileden, maybe?"

"The bird design? You sure?"

"I'm sure. But I can't remember where I've seen it before."

Their parents had a few volumes on the pantheon of goddesses, on the symbols of the varying styles of magic connected to each goddess.

If the symbol was a bird, Neeve suspected its meaning.

"I think it's here." Neeve hobbled to the bookshelf by the door and took the book, trying not to look at the age spots on her gnarled hand. There was a chapter devoted to each goddess, and Aishlin, after Anya, was near the beginning. "Yes. It's here."

She touched the symbol of a crow, the style of weaving similar to the bracelet. "It's common among chaoswitches."

After a beat, Gretchen asked, "How did you know to look there?" She touched the edge of the open page. "I wouldn't have thought of it."

"This is one of dad's favorite books," Neeve said. "Whatever they did, I did." Hollowness ached in Neeve's heart. "I would have followed them to the edge of the earth."

Gretchen embraced her, arms tight, head leaning on her shoulder. "I would have followed them, too."

But the sisters were alone, bearing the catastrophe of a curse without them. Neeve could die, and their parents wouldn't know until their return.

Neeve's eyes itched, her chest tightening, as anxiety's icy touch spread through her blood. She blinked, focusing her attention on the scripted words on the pages.

"Ileden," Neeve muttered as she read, remembering what Gretchen had said. "The cuff could be from Ileden. Maybe Hymoor?"

"Hymoor?" Gretchen leaned back, studying Neeve's face. "What do you mean?"

"Where this woman is from. Followers of Aishlin are more common in Hymoor, but it's near Ileden, where the bracelet could have been made..."

"Neeve, you're not thinking—"

"I don't know what I'm thinking."

"She's still here somewhere." Gretchen's voice was full of caution. "In Shaylon Plains."

"Right. *Right*." Neeve closed her eyes, rubbing them softly. "We need to find her. That bracelet could be her magic focus. If I destroy it, would that end the curse?"

"We'll figure this out," Gretchen said. "Do you need to lie down?" There was no trace of teasing in Gretchen's voice.

"I can't," Neeve said, taking the book to the dining table. "We need to learn everything we can."

But even as she spoke, fatigue steadily spread like ink soaking through parchment.

"Let's get you to bed," Gretchen said. "You're body's just been through something quite traumatic. Your mind has, too."

"I don't—" But Neeve could neither fight nor deny the toll the spell had already taken. "Admitting it feels like giving up."

"It's not." Gretchen squeezed Neeve's shoulder. "Rest."

"Just a few minutes. Until I get my bearings."

"I'll wake you up after a little while." Then, mischief returning, Gretchen added, "Don't worry, Gran."

"*Damn it, Gretchen.*"

CHAPTER 9

The streets bustled with merchant carts and pedestrians as Neeve hobbled along the dirt path to the center of town.

"Did you see a woman with brown hair?" she asked the nearest villager. "About this high?"

They looked at her aged hand as she estimated the woman's height, but they shook their head.

"Have you seen a woman—"

"Did you see—"

But her questions yielded nothing on the street.

Gods, where is Darrow? A desperate hope. A Moonblade assassin could track her easily. But his tall form was nowhere in sight.

"Woman lose her daughter?" someone asked.

"Not sure. She looks upset."

No one recognized her. No one whispered *deathwitch* as she walked among them.

Determined, but with a quivering fear of disappointment, Neeve entered the tavern, brimming with patronage.

"Excuse me," she said to the nearest man, "I'm looking for someone."

She recognized him from the tanner, the shop just outside of the village. His calloused hands held the handle of his tankard, and he smelled strongly of conditioning oil and leather. "Lose someone, old woman?"

She bit back her scathing reply, opting for more sweetness. She needed him compliant. "A woman, brown hair, a little taller than me. She'll look frightened or scared."

"Of you?" The man chuckled, lifting his tankard to his mouth. "She owe you money?"

"A woman like that tried to sell me a bracelet." The local blacksmith, seated near the tanner, held up his thick wrist and wrapped his thumb and index finger around it. The tips didn't meet. "A nice silver cuff. But she wanted too much for it."

"Did it have a design?" Neeve asked. "Did you see a crow?"

"Aye," he said. "That's the one. Great craftsmanship."

"A silver cuff?" A new voice, a baritone with a hint of raspiness. The man who spoke stepped forward. "She might be the woman I'm here to see."

"Popular lady," the tanner said, looking from the man to Neeve. "She owe *both of you* money?"

"She ran away from home," the man said, his piercing blue eyes arresting in their pointed stare. "Her family asked me to find her."

Neeve couldn't read any emotion on his face, the crow's feet around his eyes emphasizing his keen sight. His hair, dark brown with a few strands of gray above his ears, combed back away from his face, bringing out the hang of his brow and the sharp edges of his cheekbones.

"That's exactly where she's lookin' to go," the blacksmith said. "Tried some sob story about booking passage to Ileden to get me to agree to her price." He scoffed, shaking his head. "Silver ain't worth *that* much."

Booking passage to Ileden.

Gretchen wouldn't like this.

"How long ago did she leave?" Neeve asked.

"Just before I got here." He considered, rocking his hand in a seesaw motion. "Maybe twenty minutes?"

"And the nearest port?" the blue-eyed man asked. "Her family is desperate to get her back."

"South, not far," said the tanner. "Passage ain't cheap."

"Thank you." The blue-eyed man bowed his head before leaving the tavern.

"You good, old woman?" the blacksmith asked Neeve. "You look pale."

Neeve nodded, pressing a hand to her clammy forehead. "I just need some air."

She stepped out, the breeze cooling and fresh. *Ileden*. And passage was expensive. Would the woman try her luck and get on a ship? Or would she be bound to Shaylon Plains a little longer?

"He comes to Brightmere often enough," someone said with disgust. Neeve's eyes found the speaker, a man whose gossiping tongue bore Neeve's name often. "Follows her around like a lovesick puppy."

"She shouldn't be here," their companion said, shaking their head. "That kind of darkness belongs in Willow Hill, far away from us."

"Saying nothing of the brunette." The man chuckled crudely. "That gorgeous lass needs a strong man to protect her from her dark witch sister."

"She probably uses dark magic too, you idiot. Those two nutcases are inseparable."

Neeve whispered, calling to the shadows to curl around the ankles of the two men. Even as a lightborn, practicing more light magic in the days in the crossroads, reaching for the shadows was as easy as breathing.

The pair screamed as they hopped, trying to avoid the swirling darkness, and Neeve hobbled on, hiding in plain sight. She worked to hide her smirk of triumph.

"How the hells did they find us?"

"You idiot, she has eyes everywhere!"

"Run!"

Their thunderous footsteps retreated in diminuendo as Neeve continued on, nearly cackling in their wake.

"Oy!"

Older children, not quite in their teenage years, shoved another boy. The victim, Neeve recognized, was the baker's son, Zayn. He often ran deliveries around the village.

"I said give it back!" Zayn demanded, scrambling up from the dusty ground.

Mouthy boys. Ornery bullies. And there was Neeve, in the right mood and temper to engage them.

One boy held something in his fist, stretching his arm high while the Zayn jumped, pushing him, trying to reach it. But the heckler tossed it to a comrade who followed the same juvenile tactics, only this one shoved the baker's son down again.

"Hey!" Neeve hobbled, her body limiting the power of her confrontation. "What in the seven hells are you doing to that boy?"

"Tend to your own business, Granny," one said with a laugh.

Granny. The heat of her anger rivaled the volcanoes in the Ashlands.

She helped Zayn stand up. Other than his pride, he was unhurt. "Did you two wake up with the sole intention of being idiots to ruin someone's day?"

"I said tend your own business." The largest of the two straightened, extending his shoulders back.

"They don't stop," Zayn said. "If they want what you have, they take it."

"Shut it, troll," the other said, standing behind the biggest.

"You're the only trolls I see," Neeve said. "Return to the bridge you came from."

Zayn stifled a laugh.

The biggest one crossed his arms. "Where'd this old hag come from, anyway?" He narrowed his eyes at her. "I don't recognize you."

Oddly, *old hag* didn't offend her as much as *Granny*. "Know everyone here, do you? Your brain can handle that much information?"

He snarled, growling at his friend, who chuckled.

"But I know *you*." Neeve pointed at the tallest boy. "Your mother harvests herbs and flowers for the apothecary to trade for medicines for your father's illness." She tsked her tongue. "Your parents are going through enough, boy, without you adding to their troubles."

"Don't you talk about my parents like that!"

"Like what? Like the hard-working people they are, having a boy who likes to take things that don't belong to him?" Her gaze moved to the second of the bullies. "And *you*." He recoiled from her pointed finger as though she'd slung a curse. "Your mother is a washer woman for the tailer and works long, hard hours to meet ends after your father left."

"You dusty old—"

"What's the trouble here?" came a man's voice, calling from several feet away as he approached.

"Hey!" Carissa, the baker, hurried toward them, her bright eyes aimed at the tallest boy with a lethal gaze. "I told you to leave my boy alone!"

The boys ran, even Zayn, but not before the largest boy rammed his shoulders into Neeve's. She crumpled to the ground like an empty linen bag, pain surging like lightning up her legs and sides. Nothing had broken, but plenty felt bruised.

The man hurried to her, his hands reaching to help her up. "Are you alright?"

"By the gods." Carissa hurried to her. "What did those little monsters do?"

"One boy shoved Zayn," Neeve said. "I stepped in."

"He pushed him?" Carissa's fierce expression held sadness. "Those boys only need a target, and they find an easy one in my son."

Neeve accepted their help. The man made sure Neeve was steady before letting her go.

"They have something I think belonged to him," Neeve said.

Carissa thought, shaking her head. "Not sure what it could be. There's not much we have at the moment."

Neeve used the man's arm for balance, her hip objecting to weight and movement. "Zayn's a good boy. We all think so."

Tears welled in Carissa's eyes before she blinked them away. "Are you alright?"

"I think so. Nothing that won't heal."

"May I walk you home?" Cassander asked.

"And I will look for my son," Carissa said, walking in Zayn's wake. "Good day to you both."

"Thank you," Neeve said, and turned for home with her escort, her body desperate for a soothing balm from the apothecary. One that smelled of camphor and worked instantly. "Are you new to our village?"

"I am," he said, the sunlight bringing out the warm tones of his brown skin. "I'm Cassander."

"Neeve." With her wards protecting her mind, she pressed her palm to his arm, gleaning surface thoughts as Erick had taught her. But Neeve didn't get far as magic tingled through his skin, the same as when she'd met Erick at the crossroads. Whether godborn or witch-made, Cassander had magic. "Nice to meet you, Cassander."

"Likewise."

"What brings you to the village?" she asked, letting go. "Visiting family?"

"No. I'm looking for someone. He may have passed by here a day or two ago." He gestured his thumb and index finger down his chin, drawing a point. "An older man with a thin face, bright blue eyes."

Bright blue eyes. Piercing. Neeve blinked at Cassander, her mind's eyes recalling the man from the tavern.

"You've seen him?" Cassander said, reading her expression.

"Not long ago." She pointed toward the tavern. "He left. I don't know which way he went."

"Gods." Cassander's dark brown eyes scanned the thoroughfare, golden light shimmering for a second before it disappeared.

"May I ask?" Neeve prefaced, echoing the man from in the tavern. "Does he owe you money?"

"No, nothing like that. He's a witch hunter."

Freezing water coursed through Neeve's veins, leaving her core chilled and hollow. *Witch hunter.* The Wandering Order was in Brightmere.

Cassander went on. "He's after a woman who cursed one of those cultists before leaving Ileden. She toys with dark magic but doesn't seem to have much skill in it. I've even seen trails from Moonblade in her wake." He scoffed. "She's made plenty of people angry, it seems."

Toying with dark magic, frantic with the imminence of her death. The panic in her eyes made sense. "I met a woman like that about an hour ago."

He regarded her then, nodding slowly. "Dark magic…"

"An aging curse," Neeve said quietly. "Any idea how to break it?"

He shook his head. "I'm sorry. That's likely to come from her."

"I was afraid of that."

"If I find either of them," Cassander said, taking her as far as the bend in the road toward her home, "I'll try to leave word."

His urgency was palpable, but a spark of hope kindled, having an extra pair of eyes searching for her. "Thank you."

But her heart didn't hold out hope as she watched him walk away.

"Excuse me?"

Neeve turned as a woman approached, her clothing simple but rugged. A traveler, if Neeve had to guess. Her blonde braid reached over her shoulder, the shade a warm golden hue that emphasized the striking color of her light blue-green eyes. Passers-by gave her second glances, especially the men, no doubt taken by her striking beauty. Neeve's own heart fluttered in her presence.

"I'm looking for a cobbler or a leatherworker." The woman lifted her boot, showing the separation of leather and sole. "Is there anyone in the village who could fix this?"

As Neeve pointed toward the tanner on the other side of the village, the woman's balance tottered. She collided with Neeve, nearly knocking her down.

"Oh, gods! I'm sorry! Are you alright, ma'am?"

Ma'am. A cruel reminder of Neeve's age in this foreign body.

"I'm fine," Neeve said, her tone light. "That has to count for something, after the day I've had."

"Thank you for your help," the woman said. "Sorry to bother you."

"It wasn't a bother." But Neeve was glad to be on her way home and away from those glancing her way as though they knew, as though they could see.

Solitude and tea were in order, and she couldn't get to them fast enough.

CHAPTER 10

The waning afternoon was warm, but the world was colder than before. Her body enjoyed the sun's heat, warming her on the surface, but it didn't reach beneath her skin. She hugged her blue shawl tighter around her hunched shoulders, better understanding how her grandmother had felt. The cold was deep set, as if it had burrowed its way permanently into her bones with no hope of thawing out.

Curse you. Neeve sneered, massaging her aching hands. *I never should have let you in.*

What if Neeve had finished the reading? Would the woman have left? Would she have killed Neeve for what she would have seen?

Whatever hunts you, Neeve thought, her mental voice full of bitterness. *I hope it finds you.*

There was still time before sunset when she considered whispering Erick's name. He'd told her to use it—*Mal'Erick*—if she ever needed him.

Would he come to her?

She bit her lips closed. *I can figure this out on my own.*

A chaoswitch, a curse, and a load of unanswered questions. The loudest of them was *why*.

"How do I break this?" She whispered the question into the dusk, the evening breeze taking them. "How do I get my body back?"

Her hands were gnarled and wrinkled, her shoulders bowed and back aching. She tried sitting up straighter, bones creaking, muscles pulling tight in resistance.

"Curse you to every layer of the hells," she said. "How could you do this to me?"

The question echoed in the halls of her mind, reaching an end devoid of a beginning. Her frustration, her anger—they had nowhere to go.

"Mal'Erick," she whispered. "If you can hear this, please."

She closed her eyes and waited, the silence painful in her ears. Until—

"Neeve?"

He appeared beside her, the waning light flattering the angles of his handsome face, brightening the richness of his burgundy eyes.

"You came."

Her voice wasn't hers anymore, and she'd almost forgotten. A cruel reminder as emotion appeared on his face—shock, questioning, worry. Tears stung her eyes before she blinked them away.

"Neeve." He whispered her name like a melancholy prayer. "What happened?"

"I seem to find myself under a curse. Gods, I—" She held her breath, emotions welling to the brink.

He knelt before her, taking her aged hands into his perfect ones. His touch remained gentle even as his tone sharpened, shadows dancing within his eyes. "Who did this?"

The intensity of his stare warmed her skin. She didn't dare look up, keeping her eyes on their hands, but he brought one to her cheek, lifting her face. His eyes were the most beautiful shade of wine with a trace of fire in them, allowing Neeve to see his anger while his hands showed his gentleness.

"Who did this to you?"

She shook her head, glad for the warm softness of his palm. "A woman. I don't know."

"Do you know her name?" A weighted question, carried by his dangerously low voice.

"No." But a small part of her had wished she did, the same that had wished for the woman's fears to find her. "She didn't like the reading. I moved too slow, and she—"

Neeve flinched at the hazy memory, body remembering the sensation of falling. Light flickered at the edges of her vision, her internal magic reacting to the memory.

Erick's thumb stroked her cheek as a tear fell. His eyes darkened as shadows deepened the cool red of his irises. "Every human leaves a trail."

"I asked around, and someone said she's trying to book passage back to Ileden."

"*Back* to Ileden," he repeated. "What brings her to Shaylon Plains?"

"It would seem she has caught the attention of the Wandering Order. One is close by, looking for her."

Red light flickered in his irises, traces of chaotic, infernal flame stoking within. "The Wandering Order is *here*?"

"Her fear is understandable. She doesn't deserve hellfire."

"Doesn't she?"

"I was condemning her before you arrived." Neeve took a deep breath, soothing the simmering boil in her core that wanted flames and fury. "But people do foolish things when they're scared."

"That doesn't mean she gets away with this." He stroked a thin lock of her white hair. "Her most foolish thing was harming you."

She turned her palm up in Erick's hand, the lines deeper as she opened and closed her fingers. "Can you break it?"

"No." He rubbed circles in the middle of her palm. "I would have to know the spell, its intent, what she used to make it, before I could even approach the idea of reversing it." He paused. "The witch that cast the curse is the one to break it."

Emotion tightened her throat as her despair grew. "I'd hoped because you're godborn..." She laughed without mirth. "But so am I."

Erick swept away another tear that escaped. "Tell me what you can remember."

She did, walking through every detail. "Gods, I've said this so many times—" She stopped herself, rubbing her forehead with her fingertips. "She's leagues away by now."

The sun disappeared, the orange and red diminishing to the deep blue of night that shimmered with infinite stars. Neeve read the anguish in Erick's eyes, even as his brow furrowed.

"We'll break the curse," she whispered to him, wanting herself to believe it, too. "This is far from over."

"Damn right, it's far from over." Red flashed in his eyes. "We'll find her, and we'll set this right."

She tightened her hold on his hand, seeking to soothe the anger that welled within him. But it welled within her, too, the smoldering light eager to do her bidding.

"Neeve." Wonder smoothed the lines on his face as he turned her hands over before taking a lock between his fingers. The powder-white, lusterless wave grew, shimmering, and curled with renewed youth. "*Neeve.*"

The skin on her hands and arms shifted, the liver spots fading, the arthritic joints shrinking. Her body sat straighter, relief spreading through her back and hips. The sun fully descended beneath the horizon as Neeve sat, renewed, cast on a moonlit glow.

"By the gods." She touched her face and arms. "Am I back?"

He tilted his head, studying her. "After sunset, it would seem so."

"Sunset." She blinked, thoughts moving far too fast. Light flared from her palms, her eyes adjusting to the dark with improved vision. "Can I heal the curse away?"

"I wouldn't think so." He rested a hand on her shoulder. "Don't push yourself too far."

Pushing a bit more yielded nothing but tiredness as light burned through her blood, searching for the *wrong* to turn *right*. She reined the magic back, something within her unsatisfied.

"The magic used against you," he said. "Strong transformation magic. The kind that doesn't require permission or any components from the target."

"Components?"

"Hair, blood, saliva. Any part of you that would be consumed by the spell."

"That kind of magic is rare."

"Very rare. And only done successfully by strong, practiced witch-es." He considered, deep in thought. "And it worked against a godborn."

"Will I age again?" she asked. "Is this curse short-lived, or will I age at dawn?"

"The spell doesn't feel quick." He rubbed the tip of his chin. "What I read is powerful."

But there was hope. Neeve would have her youth, even for half the day. She wouldn't waste away before her time.

"I heard the woman is trying to go back to Ileden," she said. "Run-ning away from the Wandering Order."

His expression darkened with worry. "Why come to Sheraton at all?"

"Did the Wandering Order follow her here? Has she already reached port? Can she afford to book passage?"

"Breathe," he said. "One thing at a time."

"The blacksmith said she tried to sell her bracelet." Neeve gripped her own wrist to illustrate. "She wore a cuff bracelet with a knot-work engraving that looked like a crow. Does that sound right?"

"Certain parts of Ileden, I'm sure. And Hymoor. It's possible she could be from Storm Key or South Ileden Sound." But he was thinking out loud by his tone and cadence. He spoke the words as though to cata-logue them. "But magic is everywhere, despite what some kingdoms would like."

"But why sell the bracelet for passage?" Neeve asked, thinking out loud. "She took the money with her."

"Money?"

"She flaunted a fat purse of coins, but never paid me."

His eyes narrowed. "I can't wait to meet her."

A whispering voice in her mind agreed, eager to see this woman meet her light and Erick's shadow.

"If we can't find her," Neeve asked, her vulnerability battling her courage, "what happens?"

"There's no way of knowing." He paused. "You really don't have a name?"

"I don't. She came in, demanded a reading, cursed me, and left. That *hellspawn*."

His sour expression lightened. "Oh, she's in for a rude awakening. I will have to get in line, it seems."

But Neeve didn't know how effective her efforts would be in a body like this one. Moving around the village had taken an unexpected toll, and magic required a lot of energy from her mind and body. What would traveling to Ileden be like?

"What are you thinking?" he asked, smoothing her hair behind her ear. "Tell me."

But she didn't know how. Uselessness and powerlessness were the coldest caverns of her heart that she barricaded herself from. Admitting to them would unseal all that should remain undisturbed.

"Mindwalking safely," she said. "Without hurting someone. Is that something you can teach?"

"I will teach you anything you wish," he said. "Mindwalking starts the connection between you and your target."

Neeve playfully winced. "*Target* sounds awful."

"Fine," he said with a smirk. "The *person*. Though, may I ask?" He paused. "Why would you like to know?"

She stalled, vulnerability compromising more than she cared to share. There were few words that would remain honest without omitting too much.

"Her thoughts will betray her," she said. "When we break this curse, I want to make sure she tells us the truth."

She felt the weight of his knowing stare. He could likely read the partial truth in her words.

"Too many would see that as an opportunity," she said. "If I want something or need something, I don't want someone to take advantage of me. Walking through their mind, gleaning surface thoughts—" She stopped, clearing her throat. "I don't want to be taken advantage of because of something I don't know."

He said nothing at first, regarding her with a look of knowing.

"Is that alright?" she asked.

"It's more than alright." He squeezed her hands. "Are you ready?"

She nodded.

"Look at me. *Really* look at me."

She obeyed, knowing the effect of his eyes. *A sea of wine*, and she would happily drown. But she kept her focus.

"Like I said, mindwalking comes from connection," he said. "And the quickest way to connect is to look someone in the eye. But it's more than simply *looking*. Reach for them. Your eyes, your hands, however you can tether your will to theirs."

Reach for him. She allowed her consciousness to melt with his, not expecting the warmth that spread through her. She exhaled, a completeness filling what she didn't know was empty.

"Erick—"

His mind was guarded. One barrier unlocked to make room for her entrance as she stepped inside. The atmosphere was calm, welcoming. She inhaled slowly, savoring the scents of wildberries and vanilla.

He released one of her hands so he could cup her cheek, his warm palm perfectly shaped, his fingers reaching into her hair as his thumb grazed the length of her cheekbone. With a simple lift of her chin, he would have her near his parted lips, and she could almost feel the sensation of his mouth against hers.

I will break worlds for you, Neeve. His voice whispered in her mind. *I only need your word, and I will see it done.*

I hear you. Can you— She blinked. *Can you hear me?*

Yes, dear one. But only through this magic.

Blushing, she managed a quiet laugh. *That's probably for the best.*

Laughter rumbled deep in his chest, his expression relaxing to levity that turned him years younger, the joy expressed smoothing lines of worry. She leaned into his touch, closing her eyes and easing out of the bond their minds had forged. He pulled her against his chest, arms tight as he held her with one hand gently combing through her curls.

"I don't think I'm the best candidate for your practice," Erick admitted with a quiet laugh. "There are parts of me I'm ashamed of, Neeve of Brightmere, but I wish for you to know all of me when I find the courage to bear them. Whatever you wish, I will see it done."

She returned his embrace, comforted by his companionship and his presence, by his selfless and earnest way of teaching, by his patience when she was still unsure.

But she could be sure of him. In that, there was no question.

"*Supper!*"

Even with Gretchen's summons, the two were slow to part.

———

ERICK DIDN'T JOIN them for the evening meal, which affected Neeve more than she cared to admit. His presence had become a part of her life, and her heart knew his absence. But she and Gretchen dined well and cleaned up together.

The only trouble came once Neeve spoke of the chaoswitch and her plan to return to Ileden. Gretchen's shift in mood was almost immediate, her mouth forming a line that progressively grew tighter and tighter.

"Why in the seven hells would she come to Sheraton?" Gretchen's tone was sharper than Neeve expected. She sensed Gretchen's mood stepping from a source of intuition. Did she already suspect Neeve's plan? "Why bring your danger to our door?"

Neeve stared out the kitchen window, the limited view of the landscape shrouded in night. "I wondered the same thing."

"Losing your temper and lashing out—" Gretchen stopped, whatever logic she'd formed fizzling to nothing. "But her reaction was extreme."

"She must have one hell of a temper."

Gretchen stopped, the edge of confrontation close. But she said nothing, her brow furrowing as she put the clean dishes on the shelf near the hearth.

Neeve didn't give a voice to the worries flowing through Gretchen's mind. Worries they shared. The night carried the tension as they eased into rest, lying together on their shared bed without speaking. Samson settled in his spot on the floor, sighing heavily before sleep came.

Shadows danced across the ceiling as Neeve shared, finding shapes in their formlessness. With a twirl of her finger, a tendril came to her, swirling around her hand and wrist with cold comfort. She hadn't channeled her chaos magic since her discovery at the crossroads, focusing on honing the light.

"What do I do?" she whispered to the amorphous conjuring.

If only the shadows could answer.

She sat up, careful of Gretchen, and padded to the front door. With quick hands, she slipped on her boots and her shawl before stepping out the door.

She moved in solitude through the dark, a thin mask of clouds veiling the stars and moon. The crickets and fireflies provided quiet ambience as she moved beyond Brightmere and settled on a mound of earth that barely qualified as a hill. But it was soft as she lay among the wildflowers, the cool grass soothing her as she stared at the misted sky.

What did the sky look like in Ileden? Would it be this clear? What Neeve knew of the continent was only what her parents had drawn on their map. "Beautiful country," their father had said, "prime for exploring."

What would a map of Hymoor look like once her father had drawn it? Would the landscape rival Sheraton in its size? Were there mountains? What sort of magic folk thrived there?

"Chaosborn," Neeve answered, remembering what she and Erick had said before. "Witches and the children of chaos."

How would a child of light fit in?

Aishlin and her twin were a pair made for study. Light and Dark, Order and Chaos.

What would Erick say if he were here? Something flirtatious?

She recalled the worry that lined his eyes, the anger that hardened his mouth. So much of him was out in the open for her to see.

Let it go, Neeve.

But the shadows that remained from her unguided study in chaos magic tingled beneath her skin alongside the warmth of Anya's light.

Opposites. *Equals.*

Is that why Eira's mind crashed after they connected? A lightborn had entered her consciousness with no idea about her size and power?

Neeve opened her eyes, forcing them to focus on what evening lights were visible. *Don't go down that road, Neeve. You won't like where it ends.*

But the tingle of anxiety had already slipped its cold grip into her core, her blood cooler in her veins than it ought to be.

Eira, she thought, almost like a prayer. *Are you alive? Are you coming back?*

Let it go, Neeve. Erick's words found no tether in her mind, and they floated freely without course or weight. *Let it go.*

"How?" she whispered. "Please, tell me how."

Erick, she thought, keeping his full name from her thoughts. But the desire to call for him gripped her heart in a vise.

She wanted his companionship.

She wanted *him*.

But she kept his name behind her lips unspoken.

CHAPTER 11

Neeve had returned in plenty of time before dawn, slipping back into bed without Gretchen's notice. Only Samson knew of his mistress's midnight absence.

The star-studded sky had been a comforting companion in the hours Neeve battled with her thoughts, but her rest and dreams remained troubled before waking even more tired than before.

Erick joined them for the evening meal after helping Neeve's magic and mindwalking. His hand found her shoulder as they collected the dishes for washing. "May I speak with you outside?"

He'd whispered his request, low enough for only Neeve to hear. She glanced at Gretchen, who was tending to the remaining food in the pot.

"Let's wash these at the stream," she said, gathering soiled bowls. Her hands shift from old to young. The sun had set on the second day of her curse.

Gretchen looked up, seeing Erick collecting plates. "It must be serious if Neeve's volunteering to clean up."

"*Ha, ha.*"

"Thank you, though," Gretchen said. "Clear the air *and* clean the dishes."

"Clear the air?" Erick asked, raising an eyebrow.

"Don't pretend you didn't notice," Gretchen said, a playful challenge gleaming in your eyes. "You changed enough subjects during supper to prove that."

"Alright, let's go," Neeve said quickly, leading Erick out through the back door.

When they walked far enough from the house, Neeve asked, "Is everything alright?"

Dusk had settled into night, and the deep blue night sky covered them with sparkling stars and thin overcast. The moon and stars highlighted the cool tones of Erick's dark hair.

"Shouldn't I be asking you that?"

She stayed silent, hugging the bowls to her chest, the savory smell of stew mingling with the cool nightly scent of the grasses, flowers, and pine. The steady flow of the stream added to the calming ambiance of the night bugs and birds seeking food and shelter.

"That cuff bracelet you mentioned."

"The one that might be from Ileden?"

"It would link her to chaoswitches," he said. "There are settlements in Ileden."

"In another continent." With a sigh, Neeve admitted, "It's all I've been thinking about."

They knelt by the stream and began their work, setting the dishes down on the bank and each dipping one at a time. Neeve's hand cupped icy water into one bowl, swirling it to dump what she could before her hands continued the work.

"Ileden is only a boat ride away," Erick said. "Curses were made to be broken." He ran his fingertips over the first plate as the flowing water swept over the dish and his hands. "We'll fix this."

"Thank you." A mass of curls fell over her shoulder, the ends nearly touching the stream. "You've been there for me ever since that day at the crossroads. I'm grateful, Erick."

She turned as he swept her hair back, hooking it with one damp finger to avoid it getting too wet. The depth of burgundy pulled her in, as though the world within him had a gravity all its own. She took his hand, her wet fingers curling into his palm, her heart fluttering as he returned the force of her grip.

"I can see this curse weighs on you," she whispered, careful of the moment that had somehow become so delicate. "I'm sorry."

"Don't apologize for her." He set the plate in the grass and covered her hand. "You asked me why I haven't let you read me."

She almost looked away, embarrassed. "That was such a forward question."

"I'm glad you asked it," he whispered, even though they were alone. "I don't want to burden you with something like that."

"What do you mean, *burden me*?" She studied his face, reading its earnestness. "Shouldn't I worry over burdening *you*? First, my selfish wish to get rid of my magic, learning how to be godborn, and now a curse that turns me into my grandmother."

He chuckled. "Your grandmother?"

"Gretchen won't stop reminding me about the resemblance." But she didn't let his amusement distract her. "If it's a burden, Erick, then burden me." She held his hands tighter. "We're friends, aren't we?"

His brows pulled together, the lines between them deep. "Friends are precious things, Neeve. And I—"

She waited a breath before asking, "What is it?"

His broad shoulders bore the hues of dusk as the sun painted reds and oranges across them. A strip of golden light painted across his face, highlighting the curves of his brow, cheekbone, and jaw. He didn't finish his thought, choosing instead to stare at her in the remnants of the sunset.

Bravely, she masked the fear that cooled her heart. "Show me what you want me to see."

"Are you sure? There's no going back once it's done."

"Do you want to go back?"

"No. But I know how you feel about your power."

"Seeing death is hard." She moved closer, still holding his hands as she adjusted her seat to be nearer to him. "Seeing *you* is easy."

The diminishing light made it challenging to see the depth of emotion welling in his eyes. "You'll feel differently after—"

"I won't," she interrupted. "But I don't want to force you. This happens only when you're ready."

He rubbed her hands with his thumbs, his palms and fingers damp from the stream. "I want you to know everything, Neeve. As selfish as that is."

"It's not selfish if I ask you to."

He studied her, eyes searching, before nodding. "Slowly. Deep breath."

As she inhaled, flashes of his young life entered her mind. His boyish burgundy eyes watching a woman with long raven hair walking away. A man's hand rested in the center of her back, leading her forward. Neeve felt the fringes of Erick's heartbreak, as though his grief lingered in the distance.

More moments came and went, human mouths shaping around the word *demonblood* as Neeve received the images without sound. Some raised their hand to the *cursed child* until he grew enough to fight back. His demeanor aged with him, sarcasm and apathy masking the heartbroken boy.

The cold steel of his heart had softened as romances developed. Youth held his lovely face as he admired a young man with deep red hair, the sadness that followed when their relationship ended. Next was the young woman whose blue eyes were striking as she held his rapt attention. Fleetingly, Neeve sensed how deeply Erick cared for them, the strength of his affection settling within herself.

She blinked, and there were people begging at a crossroads, deal after deal flashing behind her eyes before she saw her own. The sardonic view of humans seeking his aid faded as he regarded her with growing interest. Beneath the moonlight, Neeve had looked holy, as though her body glowed. He'd been so close to her. His eyes had captured her. Seeing it unfold from his perspective made her heart flutter.

One more image, one that took her back to his boyhood. The woman with the long raven hair had wrapped him in her arms. Too soon, she departed again, the man leading her away as Erick watched.

Erick retracted the magic, building his mental guards as Neeve gasped for breath.

"That woman." She searched his eyes, seeing the anguish he tried to mask.

"My mother." He smoothed her hair from her face, his fingers lingering in her curls. "I haven't seen her in a very long time."

"Do you—" She hesitated. "Do you want to talk about her?"

"Not yet." He wiped her cheeks with his thumbs. "The hurt is still near."

She threw her arms around his neck, running her fingers through his hair, breathing him in. His arms tightened around her as he buried his face in the curve of her neck, their embrace deep and desperate to keep one another from drowning.

"Thank you," she whispered, the words barely audible. "Thank you for trusting me."

Erick's heart pounded against her chest, having given her access to his inner sanctum where the most delicate parts of him existed behind fortifications long forged.

"You both alright?"

Neeve gasped and pulled back at the sound of Gretchen's voice. Samson's bark followed.

"We should go back," she said.

"We'll break this curse, Neeve," he said, slow to release her. "I won't rest until it's done."

"You will rest," Neeve quipped. "Your mind is sharpest after a full night's sleep."

He winked. "You've been paying attention."

She gathered the bowls after hurrying to finish the last one. He did the same with the plates before standing, offering her his hand. "What else have you noticed about me?"

"That you're adept at standing upright despite the largeness of your ego."

He chuckled. "Go on."

Neeve did, her heart warming as she continued to make him laugh. "You have a tone and cadence in your voice when you want something."

"I'm glad you can recognize it when you hear it."

"You smirk when you think you've won."

"And when have I ever lost, dear one?"

CHAPTER 12

Neeve greeted the morning with a grudge.

Her body ached as she sat up, bones creaking, muscles tight. Neeve touched her throbbing knees with gnarled hands. The curse of premature age hadn't left, after all.

There was little in the kitchen for breakfast. Barley, a few root vegetables, and apples weren't too inspiring for the morning meal, but it was better than nothing.

After breakfast, Neeve took to tending the beans while Gretchen walked Samson along the stream. She used a stool to sit beside the lush green plants, careful to pull away the suffocating weeds. The sensation was satisfying as each weed pulled free to its roots, and she tossed them aside one by one, the bed of beans looking better the world over.

"There's more room for you," she said to the plants, making sure the ground secured the poles holding them up. "Grow tall, my lovelies."

"That's her!" A youthful voice shouted, one she recognized. "She's at the deathseer's house!"

The two bullies from before had returned, with two more in their wake. Luckily, Zayn was not among them.

"Oh, by the gods," she said, sitting straighter, a few bones in her back creaking as she did. "Don't you lot have anything better to do? How old are you all? Ten? Eleven?"

One of the new boys spoke. "I'll be twelve in a week. How old will you be? Two hundred?"

Neeve couldn't help but chuckle. "What brings you by, then? You want your futures told?"

The son of the washerwoman stepped forward. "You don't get to talk about our mothers and get away with it."

"Talk about your mothers?" Neeve looked from one boy to the other, purposefully ignoring the other two. "What did I say?"

"You made fun of them."

"I did no such thing." Neeve adjusted her seat on her stool. "A gatherer and a washerwoman, doing the best for their sons who run amuck with stupidity. They have my sympathy."

One of the new boys moved forward, mischief glimmering in his eyes. "Sympathy from a *deathwitch* is as good as a curse." He said the word like a swear.

"Not a deathwitch," Neeve said, uncomfortable with the look in his eyes. "And not a curse." But she didn't back away as she met his gaze, settling in to the harshness she saw there. "There's a lot of anger here, Boy of Almost Twelve."

"Don't read me, witch."

"Then don't come here an open book." She narrowed her eyes. "Why are you so angry?"

He didn't answer, his lips tight across his teeth. Neeve looked at the other boys and asked them the same question.

"Tell me, where is all this anger from?" She looked at the primary antagonist from before. "You first. You took something from the baker's son. What was it?"

When he didn't answer, she asked, "How's your father? Is the medicine helping?"

"Why?" He sneered. "So you can curse him?"

"A witch doesn't curse unless she's a dark witch," Neeve said. "And even dark witches wouldn't use a curse on one already sick. Magic takes energy and resources, which are precious and few. Cursing the sick is a waste."

She pivoted on her stool and reached to pick berries from the nearby bush. Wildberries, a brilliant fuchsia color, holding remarkable sweetness, their fragrance reminding her of Erick. "Do you remember the baker boy's father? He died from a sickness."

"Yeah, I remember."

"He knows what you're going through." She offered him a wildberry, which he took but didn't eat until she popped one in her mouth. "His father died, bless his soul. That little boy lost his father, but you still have yours. Does his sickness scare you?"

The boy nodded.

Neeve offered him another berry. "That boy was scared, too. And now he helps his mother make deliveries from her bakery. You help your mom, too, don't you?"

His head bobbed again, emotion showing in his eyes.

"You're a good boy." She gave him another berry, then turned to the son of the washerwoman, handing him three berries. "And you're a good boy, too. I see you returning cleaned clothes to their owners."

"My father is an ass," he said, taking her offering. "Mama says that all the time. It helps her scrub out stubborn stains."

"You take good care and help your Mama," Neeve said, "and you'll grow up to be a good man."

"What's the point of all this?" said the fourth boy, one who hadn't spoken until now. Neeve had forgotten he was there. "What are we doing here? Making nice with a deathwitch?"

"Shut it," said the gatherer's son. Then, to his friend, he said, "Give Zayn back the—"

The second of the new boys had, at some point, procured a rock, smooth and perfect. He threw it with precision, breaking the side window of her house.

"Hey!" The two boys with berries rounded on him. "What'd you do that for?"

"You said she was a deathwitch! You said you wanted to show her who's boss!"

"We didn't want to break her house!"

"What have you boys done?"

They all turned to Cassander, walking up the path from town.

"They did it!" The boys with berries pointed fingers at the others, prompting them to run.

"This is a small village," Neeve said. "I don't know where they think they're going."

"We're sorry," one boy said. "And I took a hairpin from Zayn. He was going to give it to his mother."

"Ah, I see." Neeve passed the boys another berry. "Perhaps Zayn should get that hairpin back."

"Yes, ma'am."

The boys ran off, leaving Neeve and Cassander with the broken window. The warm sunlight of morning enhanced his remarkable looks, a golden sheen illuminating his rich sienna skin. But such regard only reminded her of her own looks. *Gram. Old Hag.*

"I was passing by," he said, sunlight shimmering in his dark eyes. "I overheard some of what you said. You handled them well."

"Thank you." She looked at the pieces of jagged glass set in the windowpane. "But my window is still broken."

He looked toward the marketplace. "Does your village have a glassmaker?"

"No," Neeve said. "One is in the next village, closer to the Melian border, which isn't far. A few hours on foot."

Cassander shrugged out of his vest, leather lined with simple cotton, and used it to grip and pull the broken pieces of glass from the pane. Neeve, inside, set a bowl on the table beneath the window for them. He dropped pieces in as she swept up the shards from the table and floor.

"Neeve!" It was Gretchen, coming back from Samson's walk. "That stupid witch was seen going south—*oh.* Hello."

"This is Cassander," Neeve introduced. "Cassander, this is Gretchen."

"Nice to meet you," Gretchen said, a strange smile tugging at her mouth before she took in the scene before her. "What on earth happened?"

"A few village children seem to have a lot of time on their hands." Cassander was careful as he removed a large piece from the pane.

Samson trotted to Cassander, tail wagging.

"There's a good boy." He looked from Samson to Gretchen. "This is your dog?"

"Yes," she said. "Samson."

He scratched Samson behind his ear. "Such a good boy."

"Thank you for helping." Gretchen gestured to the broken window. "What are we going to do?"

Neeve scoffed. "Hang a mirror?"

"Or Mom's painting." Gretchen grinned. "*The Forest at Dawn*."

Neeve groaned. "The color green waged war on the entire canvas."

Standing by Cassander, Gretchen traced the size and shape of the window with her index fingers. "It looks to be about the right size."

"Please pardon my rudeness," Cassander prefaced. "But I heard you say something about a witch heading south." He looked at Neeve. "The same woman who cursed you?"

"The very same."

Gretchen's eyebrows rose. "Have you two—" She snapped her fingers, remembering. "The news of the witch hunter. That came from you."

"It did."

Neeve continued to sweep, avoiding eye contact. "We'll fix it. We just have to find her."

He picked the last shard of glass out of the pane, thinking. "An aging curse is dark magic, toying with the threads of someone's life."

"Dark magic," Gretchen said. "As in Aishlin?"

Neeve winced, hating assumptions of *darkness* against the goddess of chaos. Shadows had been comforting to Neeve before Erick helped to unlock her connection to the light.

In an attempt at levity, Neeve asked, "If she were a follower of Anya, would I have been cursed to relive my youth?"

"Likely into your infancy," Cassander said, picking up her levity with a lightness of tone. "Not shorten your life, but prolong it, starting with us at our most helpless." He grimaced. "Gods, consciousness in infancy would be another form of hell, wouldn't it?"

Neeve returned to the bowl, full of broken pieces, and poured it in their rubbish bin. "How do we find one chaoswitch in all of Ileden?"

"*My, my.*" Erick approached, stepping around the modest wooden fence that guarded their plot of herbs. He held a pear in one hand and his knife in the other, the blade long and well kept. "Who do we have here?"

Cassander met Erick's gaze, recognition smoothing the expression he wore. "I'm only passing through. I don't want any trouble."

"What trouble?" Neeve looked up at Erick. "What's he talking about?"

"He's lightborn. I'm chaosborn." Erick's expression remained calm, even *disinterested*. "I don't want trouble, either, friend."

Neeve flexed her fingers, remembering his handshake and the power she'd felt then.

"I'm not that kind of lightborn," Cassander said. "There's a balance, and the sisters *are* that balance." A golden light shimmering across his russet skin and dark eyes for the briefest moment before fading. "Our *bloodlines* are that balance."

Erick scoffed. "Is that why the lightborn descended upon Willow Hill? Because of the balance?"

Neeve looked from one godborn to the other before resting her confused eyes on her sister. "What are they talking about?"

Gretchen's only answer was a shrug as she shook her head. "You're lightborn, too, right? But Erick didn't react this way."

"Because her power had been locked away from her for years," he said. "The chaoswitches of Willow Hill didn't suffer by her hand."

Cassander kept his focus on Erick. "And those lightborn were few and incredibly misguided. They're part of the reason I'm here." He regarded the others, golden light flickering in his deep brown eyes. "The man I'm looking for is a Wandering Order cultist. I've been tracking him, and he was last seen close by."

"I've heard," Erick said. "Something about a cultist following a witch who likes to sling curses."

"He's alone, so far as I can tell," Cassander said. "It's made it easier for him to travel quickly."

"What's his name?" Erick asked, a flash of red bright in the pool of wine. "His *full* name?"

Cassander's look darkened. "I don't know."

"Would you tell me if you did?"

For a moment, Cassander almost shook his head. Neeve could see temptation there, knowing the power a name would have for the godborn who possessed it. Erick had required hers when he enhanced her power.

"Fallon," he said. "I don't know if that's his given name or his family name. It's all I have."

"Fallon," Erick repeated. "*Fallon*."

Samson barked, staying by Gretchen's legs, looking up at Erick.

"The woman at the inn overheard her say she's returning to the Midlands." Gretchen shrugged. "It's as good a place to start as any."

Gretchen knew. She knew Neeve was going. Guilt tugged at Neeve's core, waiting for the inevitable, *And I'm going with you*. But Neeve couldn't explain the dread that filled her at the idea.

"Well, if this damned curse shortened my life expectancy by decades, then we need to move quickly." Which was the best way to get to the Midlands? Could Neeve catch up to her? "Do you think she's already caught passage there?"

"Depends on how quickly she can move," Cassander said, "and if anything stopped her."

But guilt tugged at Neeve's core. Both sisters traveling with Samson, alone on a ship among strangers, bound for a vast, strange continent with a dog to care for?

What was the alternative? Leave and trust the villagers to care for Samson? Trust that they would leave her home alone?

I can't let her come with me.

Gretchen couldn't leave, and Neeve couldn't stay.

Her clammy hands gripped the broom handle.

"You have a lot of vitality despite it all," Cassander said to Neeve. "That has to count for something."

"Oh, sure," Neeve said, the decision made. She would go to Ileden alone. "Vitality, fueled by bitterness and spite."

Gretchen snorted a laugh as Cassander pressed his lips together.

"That's my girl," Erick whispered, her face warming.

Cassander nodded to Neeve and Gretchen. "I'll take my leave. Again, if I hear anything, I'll try to leave word."

"Thank you," Neeve said.

Cassander returned to the path toward town, shaking out his vest and inspecting its seams before shrugging into it.

Gretchen patted Samson's head and turned for their backyard. "I'll see about making us something to eat. You two—" She gestured vaguely. "You two talk."

She disappeared around the corner before Neeve could say anything.

Erick cut a piece of pear and handed it to her. "Word reached me of a team of hooligans terrorizing an old woman near the deathseer's house. Your days have been rather active lately, dear one."

"Haven't I noticed." She shook her head. "Can't a body be left well enough alone?"

He chuckled, waving a hand toward the broken glass and the windowpane. Shadows emerged, nearly invisible in the blazing sunlight, and the shards of glass steadily returned to their original places. But the shadow magic left its mark, the clear glass darker than before.

Gratitude swelled within her...and something more.

"You've been so good to me, Erick. You're a wonderful teacher and friend."

"Thank you." After a moment, he asked, "Is that all I am?"

He'd shifted his eyes to brown and relaxed his mouth and jaw, but Neeve knew his desire for her answer despite the mask he wore.

Her answer was barely audible but for the breath that carried it. "No."

A moment passed between them before he offered her the last of his pear. "We'll break this curse. She can't hide from us."

"She *might* make it to the Midlands," Neeve said. "She wasn't successful in pawning her bracelet for money."

"*Yet*." He lifted his eyebrows. "Trust me. She won't get far."

Before Neeve could open her mouth to question him, he winked and turned to go.

"Keep yourself out of trouble," he called over his shoulder.

With an unexpected surge of playfulness, she answered, "No promises."

Pride lifted her chin and shoulders at the sound of his laugh.

CHAPTER 13

"Absolutely not. I'm going with you."

Well past sunset and supper, the sisters moved around their small room like a couple dancing. Neeve, enjoying the renewed energy after her returned youth, took full advantage while she and Gretchen worked.

While she and Gretchen *argued*.

"If you do, we'll have to take Samson."

"We can leave him with a neighbor."

"After what happened today? Those kids were ready to rip our house apart because of their serious lack of judgment."

Neeve folded a shirt to pair with her trousers and socks, still to be packed. "Damn it all, I'll need *dresses*. They're the only clothes that'll suit an *old woman*."

She traded the trousers for skirts and added two dresses before forcing the clothes into her open rucksack, covering wrapped jerky and dried fruit.

"Their parents wouldn't have lack in judgment," Gretchen said. "The baker is kind to animals. I wouldn't ask a kid to take care of him."

"I can do this, Gretchen." Neeve tucked two pairs of socks into a corner. "If I can't find her, I'll find someone there who can help. Magic leaves traces. If I have to, I'll get help to track the spell's trail."

"You're not thinking this through." Gretchen's voice rose with the argument. "You're just going to ask? 'Hi, I've been cursed to look like an old woman. What witch would do something like that?'" She scoffed. "Good luck with that."

"What else can I do?" Neeve matched her sister's energy, which wasn't the right choice. "We have to find her somehow."

"I agree, but you're not going to Ileden alone." Gretchen's tone was as resolute as Neeve's refusal. "You don't know where to start, and you'll be too far from home in a place you've never been." She shook her head. "Absolutely not."

"Someone has to take care of Samson and our home." Neeve looked down at their dog, happily panting from his spot on the floor. "I, personally, don't trust anyone else to do it. Except maybe Erick."

"Trust me to do what?" Erick appeared in the doorway, knocking twice on the jamb. "Whatever it is, I'm touched. Your front door was unlocked, by the way." He aimed a thumb over his shoulder. "You both should be more careful."

But his appearance did not deter Gretchen from her point. "And I don't trust strangers to tell you the truth when you ask about where a curse came from."

Erick regarded Neeve, knowing well enough to not interrupt Gretchen when she was making a point.

"We have the cuff," Neeve said, remembering, holding one wrist with the opposite hand. "We can ask around about blacksmiths and jewelers."

"The cuff came from Brockdon Fields," Erick said.

His assurance told Neeve everything she needed to know. Still, suspicion tickled the back of her neck.

Sending as much, he went on. "No harm came to a single living thing. She didn't even know I was there."

"Erick—"

"I won't apologize because I'm not sorry," he said, crossing his arms. The muscles and veins of his forearms flexed as he shrugged into his pose, burgundy eyes unwavering. Even smug, he was charming. "She's going back home. I heard her say as much, and the bracelet is her fare."

"Brockdon Fields." Gretchen pointed to the map. "That's in Midlands."

"We're already on our way to Ileden," Erick said, "and this helps us to narrow down that massive continent to a specific, single region."

"*We?*" Neeve looked from Erick to Gretchen. "He said *we*, right?"

"Oh, he definitely said *we*."

Was Gretchen *relieved*?

"You wouldn't be alone if he went with you," she said.

"Gretchen—"

"This is the only way I will get any sleep," she said. "And even that's a stretch. But the odds are higher."

"There's a delicious tea blend from Melia that can help with that," Erick said casually. "*Prince Charming* or something."

The sisters looked at one another, the only noise in the room coming from Samson, who grumbled at Erick before lying on his side.

"I don't like it," Gretchen said at last, "but I can agree to it if Erick goes with you."

Erick's eyes brightened, hands out at his sides like he was a showman on display, waiting for applause.

"I can't afford your fare," Neeve said bluntly. "Would you be able to book your own passage?"

"Don't worry about that, love. It's all taken care of." His confidence bloomed into a grin before he winked at her. "To Ileden, we go."

She pressed her lips together, folding her clothes, simultaneously frustrated and grateful. She wouldn't be alone, and she had a lead. That was something.

"Oh, before I go…" Erick revealed a small book from the back pocket of his trousers. "I found this little volume, which might be helpful."

Neeve took it, the leather binding modest but well made. The book was thin and fit in her open hand. Peeling back the cover revealed its inked title: *Spells and Curses of Order and Chaos.*

"Order *and* Chaos?" Neeve flipped through several pages.

"Curses aren't exclusive to the goddess of crossroads," Erick said. "Her twin has a few up her sleeve."

"I never would have imagined that," Gretchen said. "It makes me like her a little more."

"Thank you, Erick," Neeve said. "How did you find this?"

He winked. "I know where to look."

"So." Gretchen clapped her hands once, looking from her guest to her sister. "Now that you have a traveling companion, a lead, and a new book of spells—" Her eyes lit up, looking past Neeve. "Take the map."

"What?"

"You're going to Ileden." Gretchen pulled the frame from the wall and carefully separated the front from its backing. She lifted it free and passed it to Neeve. "Look at everything he's already marked."

Neeve was careful with the map, worn soft from many hands. The document wasn't very large, but the detail of Sheraton and Ileden was impressive, even up close. And there, where her father's handwriting had marked MIDLANDS, was BROCKDON FIELDS, the letters in the space between a series of hills and a thick arrangement of trees.

"They'd feel better knowing you had this," Gretchen said. "It'll help."

"What if I lose it?" Neeve's fingers traced the compass drawn on the bottom right. "What if I ruin it?"

"You know Dad can make another." Gretchen tapped her temple. "His memory is practically god-touched."

She was exaggerating, but their father's ability to recall detail remained impressive. Neeve obeyed, folding it carefully and tucking it into the cover of the book from Erick.

"Now, with all that settled," Erick said. "Let's get you packed."

Ileden.

The only place colder than Thurin with the added excitement of wilderness and animals and people devoted to the goddesses.

Would a son of Aishlin fare better there than here? Or would his odds be about the same?

Neeve watched the shadows and light flicker on the ceiling, sleep elusive. Samson snored softly from his bed.

It had been hours since Erick had left, but his presence remained.

Don't worry about that, love.

She brought a hand to her chest, rubbing the ache at her sternum.

Love.

Would you believe me if I said I cared for you?

Love.

"What time does your boat leave?" Gretchen whispered.

Neeve started with a gasp. "Gods above."

"Sorry." Gretchen stretched, draping an arm across Neeve's stomach. "Can't sleep?"

"The boat leaves at midday. And sleep is a ridiculous flirt, sometimes."

"That's too soon." Emotion was in Gretchen's tired voice, though she didn't cry. "We've never been apart like this before."

Silence passed between them, the anticipated weight of their separation upon them.

"Mom's knife is in their trunk," Gretchen said. "Make sure you take it."

"I hardly think—"

"Cassander said there's a witch hunter. You'll need it, Neeve. What if—"

Her voice quivered. Neeve reached for her arm, grounding her with a firm hold. "I'll pack it tomorrow."

"Wear it," she said. "Don't pack it."

"Alright. Please, try not to worry."

Gretchen sighed. "Too late."

Another pause settled between them, more tense than the first.

"Do you have plenty of money?" Gretchen asked. "Sell a few things before you go. And take Mom's poncho."

"I'll be fine."

But Neeve wasn't sure how true that was. She would have some money left after booking passage and could work odd jobs for food. Maybe sell a few readings, if it was safe. She couldn't assume Ileden would be more accepting of her magic or her deathsight. People allowed their superstitions and fears to think and speak for them.

"I was going to give you something for your birthday," Gretchen said. "But I think you need it now."

She rose slowly, padding to the small chest of drawers they shared. Digging into the top drawer, Gretchen pulled out a small box. "I had these made for us months ago, and it was hell keeping it from you."

Neeve sat up. "What is it?"

Gretchen placed the box in Neeve's palm. "Open it."

Slowly, Neeve opened the lid to reveal two silver rings, thin with delicate knot-work in the band.

"They're beautiful."

Gretchen took one and slipped it on her index finger. Then she slipped the other on Neeve's before clasping their hands, palm to palm.

"Together forever." Gretchen's grip was firm. "Never take it off."

"Never take it off."

They hugged awkwardly from their seats on the bed before the mattress sank and they toppled over, laughing. They lay on their backs, staring at the ceiling, the mood graciously lighter.

Gretchen exhaled a quiet laugh. "When you're old, even your voice sounds like Gram's."

Neeve sighed through her amusement. "I've been called an old hag by a bunch of hooligans, and now I'm Gram from my own sister."

"They called you a hag?"

"I almost mumbled gibberish to make them think I was cursing them. It's no less than they deserve."

"That's right." Gretchen giggled. "Disrespecting the elderly."

"Gods damn it all, Gretchen."

Gretchen snuggled closer, her serene expression relaxing as sleep took her.

Neeve closed her eyes, willing the darkness to wrap her in its embrace and lull her to sleep. But rest remained elusive.

CHAPTER 14

Clothes were different on her old body. The ring, too, was more snug around her aged finger. But Neeve let her form adjust, since it was so damned obstinate at succumbing to the curse.

She waited until sunrise to dress, doing her best with a skirt and foregoing any trousers. Gretchen rose with her, groggy but conscious, and insisted on breakfast after she forced Neeve to wear their father's belt with their mother's knife sheathed at her side.

"Eat as much as you can now." Gretchen joined her at the table, their bowls steaming between them. "You don't know when you'll have time to eat before you board the ship."

Neeve didn't argue, though her stomach was no place for food, as nervous as she was. Gretchen needed to do this for Neeve, and Neeve needed to let her.

Time was an active agent against her. It would be hours on foot before they reached the eastern port, and likely a week before the ship would reach South Ileden Sound.

"Maybe not a full week," Gretchen had said the night before.

It would be days, at any rate. How long before Neeve could truly begin her search for the woman who cursed her?

You've already started, she reminded herself. *You've started by deciding to go.*

What if I don't find her?

Gretchen's emotions were palpable as they ate in silence. Her sister was near to bursting into tears, the meal keeping her occupied enough to prevent a flood. Neeve tried not to grimace as she chewed and swallowed. The delicious food turned to sawdust on her tongue with the churning of her stomach.

Courage, Neeve. She swallowed her guilt with her food. *This may yield nothing, but you have to try.*

There was no promise that Neeve would find the woman who cursed her. There was no promise that she would reach a solution to this very serious problem. And she was stepping out into the unknown with a leap of faith that she wasn't ready to take.

Courage. And faith.

Both were in short supply.

Erick knocked on their door, prompting Neeve and Gretchen to share a surprised look.

"Before you think I'm strange or over-eager," he said from outside, "I saw the fire and candles from the window, and—wait. That *does* sound over-eager."

When Neeve opened the door, he flashed a grin. "Ready to go?" He gestured behind him. "Our chariot awaits, madam."

"You—" Neeve stared at the wagon drawn by a single horse. "You rented a wagon?"

"It'll be more than twice as long if we walk." He set his hands on his hips, puffing out his chest. "This will be faster and much less physically taxing."

Neeve didn't ask how much the ride cost, both flattered and embarrassed that he'd spent it.

"What if she's still in Sheraton?" Neeve asked, the familiar touch of fear chilling her core.

Erick grinned. "Dear one. I already checked." He tapped his temple. "When I saw her last, she was in the belly of a ship. And we will be hot on her trail."

Confidence filled the hollow in Neeve's stomach. "I suppose I am ready."

"Wait." Gretchen left and returned in a flash, holding a thick garment in her hands. "Mom's poncho. You'll need this."

She shoved it into Neeve's pack without ceremony and met her eyes, hers already welling up, lips down-turned and trembling. Gretchen looked years younger, like a child whose heart was breaking.

"Please be safe."

Neeve hugged her as she cried. "I'll be back soon. My normal, young self. No more old hag Neeve."

"And just so you know," Gretchen whispered, "Erick put some kind of spell on our purse. It's been months, but he asked me not to tell you."

Neeve froze, keeping Gretchen close as she shared this secret. "What do you mean?"

"The purse will never run out of money," she said. "Even if it's down to its last coin, there will always be another. A gold piece, too, the charmer."

Erick had done that, and Neeve had never known.

Gretchen would be alright. It was hell leaving her, but she would be alright.

"I'll return soon," Neeve said. "I promise."

"A promise that you'll keep." Gretchen kissed Neeve's temple as they parted. With tears misting her eyes, Gretchen looked up at Erick. "If anything happens to her, Mal'Erick, I'm holding you personally responsible."

His eyes widened for just a moment, the initial shock of her sternness hitting him. "I will keep her safe. I swear it, Gretchen of Brightmere."

Gretchen's lips quivered, but she waved, using both of her hands. "Come back soon." Her voice cracked. "I hope you find her."

"Me too." With her pack on one shoulder, Neeve stepped out, glancing back to Gretchen and Samson. Samson wagged his tail from beside Gretchen's legs. "Bye, Sam-Sam."

Gretchen rested a hand on the dog's head, wiping her face with the other.

"Let's hurry," Neeve whispered to Erick, eyes stinging. "I'm so close to changing my mind."

He put a hand on her shoulder, its warmth and weight giving her focus. "We'll be back soon. We have a significant lead, and we're moving toward it."

Neeve growled through her own welling tears. "I hate it when Gretchen cries. It makes me want to watch the world burn."

"I understand that feeling."

They boarded the wagon, and the driver clicked his horse on. Neeve waved at Gretchen, straining her arm and back as she turned to keep her sister in sight. Gretchen waved back with an enthusiasm that didn't match her tear-streaked face.

"You two aren't separated often, are you?" Erick asked, watching from his seat across from her. The wagon was open with enough room for Erick to stretch his long legs in front of him.

"Never." Neeve settled in, homesickness swirling in her core. She extended her legs parallel to his, leaning awkwardly against the short side of the wagon bed. "I don't know what I'm going to do."

He leaned forward, his expression soft with sympathy. "You'll win this. For her. For you."

"*Win*?" She almost chuckled, looking down at her hands as they toyed with a loose thread in her skirt. "You make it sound like a game or a fight."

"It *is* a fight." He didn't flinch. "You're fighting for your life, Neeve."

She took a sharp breath, pulled into his unrelenting gaze. He took her hand and squeezed it before letting her go.

"We're in this together," he said, squinting in the sunlight. "I gave your sister my word that I would keep you safe, and you have my word that we will see this curse broken."

"What if we can't find her?" She'd been afraid to ask this of Gretchen, to pose the potential of loss to her sister, as upset as she already was at Neeve's leaving. But she wasn't afraid to ask Erick. He was strong and constant, even in his mischief. "What if we can't break it?"

"We'll find her." His eyes darkened. "Even if I have to step into hell and rip her soul from death."

───

TWO HOURS PASSED on their journey to the coast, with conversation thin beneath the clear sunny sky. During the journey, Erick had moved beside Neeve as she dozed, putting an arm around her humped shoulders and guiding her to rest against him.

"Right about now, Gretchen would make some joke, calling me Gran." Neeve meant to laugh, but the sound came out as a punctuated exhale. "I can't seem to keep my eyes open."

"It's alright," he said, his voice gentle. "Rest while you can."

She did, easing travel time as she awoke to an unfamiliar landscape and the distance cry of seagulls.

Erick squinted against the light, using his hand to shield his eyes, while Neeve closed hers and aimed her face heavenward. How many more sunny days would she have?

"The sun feels good on my old skin." She laughed to herself. "My Gran used to say that. Now, I know what it means."

"Neeve, you're not old." His arm was still around her shoulders, and he pulled her closer.

She held out her hands, comparing her age spots and gnarled joints to his beautiful olive skin and long fingers. "My body would beg to differ."

He clasped one of her hands. "You are still Neeve, no matter what that witch has done." His thumb stroked the back of her hand, across the bones and veins. The skin didn't bounce back right away, its elasticity almost gone. "I don't see the curse when I look at you."

"You're sweet to say that." She appreciated the firmness of his grip, matching it with both of her hands surrounding his. "Thank you for helping me have courage. I—" She swallowed. "I wouldn't have gone this far without you."

"And we have farther still." He was closer to her ear, whispering to her, the softness of his voice spellbinding. "Courage, Neeve. The fight's about to begin."

She almost grimaced at the thought and how very real it was. Her days were numbered, and there was no way for her to know the count. Unless, of course, another deathseer crossed her path.

"Before, when I called your name," she said. "How does that magic work?"

"Similar to how the crossroads magic works," he said. "But there is a secret to it. One I'll share with only you."

He smirked as he leaned closer, his lips almost touching her ear. "I have given you the right to call for me, Neeve of Brightmere."

Shivers cascaded down her spine as warmth flushed her cheeks. "*Mal'Erick.*"

He chuckled to himself. "You don't say my name nearly enough to suit me. I love it when you do."

After a moment's pause, he went on.

"A godborn can give a mortal permission to call upon them. Few do, understandably. It's easy to be taken advantage of. And godborn don't have to answer, but the magic of the summons requires time and attention to dispel if it's unanswered."

The tingle in Neeve's palm reminded her of the power stored within her. She understood that magic required *time* and *attention*.

"I'm glad you came," she whispered. She opened her mouth to say more, but the words fell short.

"There is nothing on this earth that would keep me from you. Nothing short of death itself."

"Don't say that," she whispered, superstition making her shiver.

They soon rode through a bustling coastal town, its stone and wooden buildings tall and broad as people moved in and out of allies and streets. The driver navigated his horse deftly, following the main path through the center of town, heading straight for the docks.

"Do you know when the ship boards for Ileden?" Neeve asked, looking as far ahead as she could see.

"Midday," Erick said. "We have time."

"Aye, midday," the driver confirmed, overhearing them. "You have quite a journey ahead."

"Anything we should know?" Neeve asked.

"It's colder than you think," he advised. "And it's a wet-cold. Seeps into your bones." He glanced at her. "You'll really feel it, Gran. There's a tailor here that sells furs."

"Thanks." But she had no money for clothes. She hugged her pack closer, vastly under-prepared.

The driver stopped the wagon and said, "This is as far as I go. It was a pleasant drive."

"Thank you," Neeve said.

"Thank your friend." The driver offered Erick a nod. "He pays well."

Neeve internally winced, banishing the *how much* from her mind. "Thank you, Erick."

"I told you." He squeezed her shoulder. "We're in this together."

They found the dockmaster, who pointed to the ship headed to Ileden—the *Sea Sweeper*, captained by a man named Shea.

"That's him, with the red hair," the dockmaster said, pointing to the tall man on the deck. He looked as though he was born and raised on the sea, with the ship as his home. "He'll get you there fast and safe."

Erick escorted Neeve with her hand on his arm like a grandson walking with his grandmother. He did all the talking, booking their passage straight away and patting Neeve's hand as he played his part.

"You two can board." Shea looked at Neeve with a discerning eye. "Don't die on the ship, old woman. Your family won't have a body to bury."

She scowled at him, reserving every curse and swear word in her arsenal. "Watch your tongue, boy."

The captain chuckled. "As you say, old woman."

Erick chuckled. "Easy, Gran." When they were alone, Erick leaned close, a mischievous smirk flattering his features. "Pay him no mind. He won't get much sleep tonight, with the strange feeling that sugar ants are in his bed."

"Serves him right."

On deck, they sat where there was room, near others who were waiting for the ship to sail. To their right, nearly six feet away, was a familiar face that caught Neeve's eye.

"Cassander?" she asked, smiling. "What are you doing here?"

He smiled, too, waving and moving over as the sunlight glistened on his white teeth. "You made it. I wasn't sure if it would be this ship or the next one." He leaned close to her, whispering so that only she and Erick could hear. "Be on your guard. The witch hunter is on board."

Neeve straightened, though still hunched over, as every muscle in her old body was on alert. She'd all but forgotten about the witch hunter, with her own malady pressing on her mind.

Cassander darted his eyes to the right, and Neeve tried to sneak a glance.

"Tall, gaunt face," Cassander mumbled. "Silver thread in his bootlaces."

"Silver thread?" Neeve asked.

"The Wandering Order," Erick said. "It's a way to declare their membership without wearing full uniforms or badges."

"Most don't know it," Cassander said, "and few look at someone's boots. It's a good place to hide something like that in plain sight."

"Why silver?" Neeve asked.

"For purity," he said simply. "As though they're purifying the world from magic."

Her lip curled in disgust as her eyes wandered over the passengers' boots and shoes, looking for any trace of silver until her eyes finally caught the shimmer. The man turned, the light reflecting off of his lace. His body language was casual, his face frightfully thin. Shadows rested deep beneath his cheekbones and around his deep-set eyes, giving him a haunted look.

Neeve tore her eyes away, the hunger in the icy blue gleam of his eyes almost robbing the air of warmth. "Even with her curse, I pity her. He won't relent until he has her."

"I still haven't caught sight of her," Cassander said. "Nothing I hear is remarkable about her appearance or ability, but she's wanted by the Order for reasons unknown."

"The reasons don't matter when a witch hunter is involved," Erick said, bitterness in his voice.

"What are the odds he and I are after the same person?" Neeve asked. "What if this unnecessarily crosses our paths together?"

"It would explain her desperation for a death reading," Erick said.

"I'm not inclined to believe this is a coincidence," Cassander said. "Which means we'll need to be doubly on our guard."

To Erick, Neeve asked, "You've had experience with the Wandering Order?"

"A brief run-in," he said. "Nothing too daunting, but enough to make me aware."

"With Fallon?" Cassander asked, aiming his head carefully toward the witch hunter on the deck.

"No, another." Erick, still guarded, said little else, except, "I didn't exactly catch her name."

Neeve quickly imagined what Erick might have experienced or lived through in the hands of a witch hunter and shuddered, wrapping her knit shawl more tightly around her.

"The wind chill will only get worse," Erick said, his voice low as he smirked. "Stay close. I'll keep you warm."

"That's enough of that." With a smile, Neeve added, "*young man.*"

Erick burst out a laugh before he could stop himself, turning his face aside, his grin broad.

Captain Shea called for all hands to set sail. The crew worked quickly to get the ship out of port and into open water. The party of three watched and listened, the witch hunter remaining in their peripheral vision as they set their sights on the horizon.

CHAPTER 15

Passengers and crates crowded the ship's deck. Erick secured Neeve a seat while he and Cassander stood, blocking her from the wind. The overcast was a thick shield against the sun, and Neeve grit her teeth as a gust of wind swept through. Erick turned to give her a wider defense.

"I am at your service, Neeve," he whispered, enjoyment tugging at the corners of his mouth.

"Don't look so smug," she said, a slight shiver in her voice.

"I'm glad to be of use. And you're glad I've come along, aren't you?"

Neeve reached into her pack for the poncho, the tightly knitted wool felted and lined. Erick helped her pull it over her head. Cassander, from her other side, straightened the back.

"Better?" Erick asked.

"By the gods, yes. It'll please Gretchen when I tell her she was right." But even as the garment creating a sanctuary of warmth, Neeve swallowed against the guilt of leaving her sister behind. "And yes, I'm glad you're here." She lowered her voice, hating how vulnerable she sounded. "I'm glad I'm not alone."

A passenger nodded and mumbled a pardon as he side-stepped between Neeve and Cassander. She glanced up to watch him pass, eyes tracing the impressive width of his shoulders before noticing silver glistening beneath his collar. His boot laces were plain, but the silver around his neck—could that be—

But before Neeve could see or call his attention, another passenger passed by, a shorter, stockier man in fur-lined leathers and worn brown boots. The boat shifted, the turbulence of the water increasing with the change in weather. The passenger wobbled on his feet, reaching for a handhold and finding Cassander's outstretched arm.

"Thanks."

Another lurch, and they both fell on impact, the man's weight taking Cassander with him. Cassander pivoted to avoid landing on Neeve, but she reacted too quickly, bracing him with her hands as the ship's motion countered their best efforts. Neeve's power tapped into Cassander's life thread almost on reflex, the images filling her mind with sight and feeling of immense joy. And incredible heartache.

The flashes came slowly at first. A beautiful childhood in a place that seemed too ideal to be real, with lush green fields and dense forests full of enchantment. A life filled with joy, growing up lightborn, honing his powers, falling in love...

And wandering the lands in search of one witch hunter who'd entered his idyllic home and broke everything his withered hand had touched.

Fallon's blade glimmered in the sunlight as it sliced through each member of Cassander's family. Cassander barely survived, bearing the guilt of life in loneliness.

A life he would give to vengeance. One nearly at its end.

Blood everywhere. His body lying in an unfamiliar place. So much sunlight. So much grass. But what struck Neeve was his *acceptance* alongside his fear. How could someone have *both* as they were dying? Acceptance and fear were longtime strangers, but they harmonized in him in his final moments.

Hands cupped her face and turned her before Erick whispered, "Your eyes."

She closed them. "What is it?"

"They're white. Completely white."

No one had ever told her. As the magic faded, Neeve opened her eyes to see Erick's worry.

"Is it bad?" Erick asked.

"They're always bad."

"Thank you," the man said to Cassander. Then, to Neeve, "Apologies, ma'am. Are you alright?"

"I'm fine," she lied, not looking up.

The vision was clear: Cassander was going to die. The only thing she didn't know was *when*.

"Don't keep that darkness to yourself," Erick whispered.

She watched the man go to the other side of the ship to settle in.

Don't keep that darkness to yourself.

Don't let fear win.

I won't let go.

The crew worked to navigate around the storm and keep its rain and treachery in the distance. The passengers on deck shifted, making room for Neeve, Erick, and Cassander to sit together. Surreptitiously, they continued their watch on Fallon as he moved with everyone else, a predator hiding in plain sight as he pieced on food he'd brought. He didn't engage with anyone, bright eyes watching.

"While we're here in this little traveling party," Erick said, turning to Neeve. "Have you remembered anything since her reading?"

She exhaled through pursed lips. "I wish I could say yes."

"Any details could be useful," Cassander said. "What do you remember?"

Neeve stared ahead, letting her eyes get lost in the hazy storm-laced horizon as the ship navigated around a dark patch of gray clouds. Lightning struck in the distance, the flash of white surrounded by cloud and rain. Thunder soon followed.

"She doesn't have strong, lasting relationships," she said, recalling the conversation more than the vision itself. "I saw a statue of a woman surrounded by trees. Nothing familiar, but I remember the *immensity*." Neeve paused. "The statue could mean a lot to her."

"A statue with trees." Cassander ruminated. "It's assuming it's in Ileden, of course, but there are statues of Rhiann and Erys all over the continent. Especially Erys in Hymoor and Storm Seat."

"What about the Midlands?" Neeve asked. "Would she have a statue among trees?"

"The first thing that comes to mind is one in Brockdon Fields," he said. "Set in a pine forest."

"Oh, that's perfect," Erick said, bumping Neeve's shoulder with his. "That's on the trail of the cuff. The blacksmith is from Brockdon Fields." He grinned, winking at her. "Admit it. My sleuthing has paid off."

"I never doubted you for a moment."

Satisfied, Erick continued. "Why would they give Erys a statue in the woods? Shouldn't she be out in the open? High upon a rock or something, calling for the storm?"

"It's two-fold, as I understand it," Cassander said. "Trees attract lightning, and she's surrounded by wild nature to compliment Rhiann."

"*Rhiann and Erys, the sisters of earth and sky,*" Neeve recited. "*Shanna and Brena, lovers of sea and flame. Anya and Aishlin, twins of order and chaos.*"

"Shanna and Brena's story always touched me," Cassander said. "Lovers who struggle with distance but whose companionship never wavers."

"Shanna's water tempers the blacksmith's steel," Erick said. "One strengthens the other." His melancholy matched the bittersweetness in Cassander's eyes. "Still, to be apart from the one you love because of significant obstacles. Even the goddesses struggle."

"How very human of them," Neeve said with admiration. "I never thought of it that way."

After a moment's pause, Neeve went on. "Cassander."

His eyebrows rose. "Yes?"

"What happened just now, when that man nearly fell, I touched your arm." She waited a beat before she lowered her voice and continued. "I saw—"

She hesitated, the words somehow hard to bring to life.

"What did you see?" he asked, gently. "You can tell me."

But anxiety caged the words back, knowing the impact they would have.

So Cassander said them for her. "Did you see my death?"

She nodded.

He blinked once, his expression unchanging. "That is such a weight you carry, Neeve. I wish I could help you bear it."

Erick rested a hand on her arm as she continued. "It feels soon. I don't know when."

"Are we on this boat when it happens?" he asked.

She shook her head. "A green field. I couldn't tell if it was at the statue or somewhere else. There was daylight."

He was silent as he considered her words, looking down at his hands.

"Thank you for telling me," he said. "What do we do now?"

"Try to stop it. Though—" Neeve grimaced. "I don't know how."

"Yet," Erick said. "We don't know how *yet*."

"There was blood, and you were lying in the grass," she said. "That's all I could see."

A part of her wondered if the future for him had already changed. By telling him, had she saved his life?

A shiver ran through her.

Had she somehow made it worse?

She clasped her hands in her lap, keeping her touch and her thoughts to herself.

"How much of my life did you see?" Cassander asked, his dark eyes studying her face.

"Enough to know why you're following him." Neeve didn't have to say his name.

"I only survived by some cruel miracle."

"Don't say that," Neeve admonished quickly.

For Erick's sake, Cassander explained. "Fallon killed my family. I always suspected that I would meet my end as I pursued him." He offered Neeve a half-smile. "I made my peace with that a long time ago."

"You and I are similar there," Erick said. "I wouldn't rest of that bastard murdered everyone I loved."

"And now, we're all on the heels of a chaoswitch who appears inept at magic," Cassander said. "But is somehow remarkably successful at curses."

"It was a symbol on parchment," Neeve said. "She slammed it onto the table, and it burned away before I could see anything else."

"It takes a lot of skill to craft a spell that transforms a target without the proper reagents," Erick said. "Whoever made that sigil—if it was her or another—that maker is a powerful chaoswitch."

"And the three of us are on her trail," Neeve muttered, "right alongside a witch hunter."

"Let's not pull his attention from her," Erick said, "as much as we can. It seems she's the perfect thing to occupy his time."

Cassander raised an eyebrow, cautiously watching Fallon. "I couldn't agree more."

Dark magic, a desperate woman, and a bloodthirsty witch hunter.

Neeve hugged her poncho closer, the chill coming from within.

CHAPTER 16

Just before sundown, Neeve ducked beneath the hood of her poncho, waiting for her body to change. "We're going below deck soon, right?"

"Soon," Erick said, staying close to shield her from view. "Your marvelous hair will be the hardest to hide."

A touch of heat bloomed on Neeve's cheeks. "You'll look strange behaving this way with an old woman."

"It's none of their business," he said, "especially if it's someone I want to protect."

"Beds ready!" one of the crew called. "Below decks, if you please, ladies and gents."

The passengers filed down creaking wooden steps beneath the decks. Neeve tucked close to Erick as the passengers moved with them, a tall hooded man nearly bumping into her before excusing himself and giving her more room. She couldn't glimpse his face from beneath his hood, but thanked him quietly as Erick helped guide her in.

Hammocks and bedding waited for each of them in rows and columns, the hammocks rocking slightly back and forth like strange banners. The trio hurried to a corner where they could tuck themselves in, keeping all movement and sight in front of them with no chance of someone sneaking from behind.

"Keep watch?" Cassander asked. "Two asleep, one awake?"

Neeve grimaced. "Is that really necessary?"

Her voice had returned. She looked down at her youthful hands before meeting Erick and Cassander's gaze, their expressions explanation enough. She touched her hood, careful to hide every strand, but her curls had other ideas, strands peeking from the brim of her hood.

The last the join the passengers was Fallon, his sharp eye noting the faces in their shared sleeping quarters.

Neeve sipped from her waterskin, turning to hide her face. "Will they overreact if they suspect I'm cursed? Magic isn't outlawed here."

"Superstitions are rampant everywhere," Erick reminded her. "I'd rather not have someone accuse you of something ridiculous, like being a bad omen or a token of bad luck, and threaten to throw you overboard."

"They wouldn't do that." But she gulped, unsure.

"They've killed passengers for many reasons, be they legitimate or otherwise," Cassander said. "Fear is volatile."

"Point taken." But there was a bright side. "Does that mean I don't have to keep watch?"

Erick's amusement flattered his eyes and mouth. "Ever the optimist." To Cassander, he said, "We'll take turns shielding Neeve from view, in case anyone gets curious about the young woman they don't remember seeing before."

Cassander agreed. "Sleep completely covered, if you can," he said to Neeve. "Facing the wall would be better."

She adjusted herself to comply. "Why do I feel like a child being tucked into bed?"

Erick's devilish grin emerged, bringing Neeve to stare at his impeccable cupid's bow. "Would you like a bedtime story?"

Neeve laid down, hood up and blanket pulled high. She turned to face the wall, feeling the sensation of someone laying down beside her, his back against her back.

"Sweet dreams," Erick said.

Staring at the wall, heart fluttering like a bird within her ribcage,

Neeve allowed herself to relax against him. She closed her eyes, forcing her breathing to calm. Scents of wildberries and vanilla filled her, and she smiled to herself at Erick's use of magic, just for her.

————

SNOW-CAPPED MOUNTAINS. The peaks of tall pines. The statue of Erys, tall and impressive, serene and fierce.

Cassander, bloody in the grass.

The woman slammed her hand on the table, the parchment burning to nothing.

A broken circle and strange letters.

The woman's eyes piercing daggers through Neeve as she mouthed the curse.

Neeve clung to any dangling thread, but this one—knowing she would die—this thread didn't remain strong. It kept going, the fibers fraying as she pulled hand over hand. She threw the line away with a curse. There would be no salvaging it.

Neeve gasped, either in the dream or in sleep, as the images kept coming. Cassander lay on his side, dying, his mouth lined with blood. The wound oozed onto the grass and dirt, with streaks of golden white shimmering on the surface of liquid red. Neeve pushed him onto his back and pressed her hands to stop the flow, the light coming through her fingers. But his eyes were already lifeless. His light faded to nothing.

Horror and sadness strangled her as she fought the urge to scream. She blinked, staring at the dark wall of the ship, her breathing shallow. She pressed a hand to her chest, focusing on pressure and warmth, conscious of every measure of breath. The air smelled of salt and mildew as she filled her lungs to the brim, her chest aching to exhale until, at last, the pressure released.

Whose hand would stain red with Cassander's blood? Was he sentenced to die for crossing Neeve's path? What if she couldn't prevent this from coming to pass?

She forced herself back into the memory. Everything was cold in a way much deeper than ice and snow. It was a living cold, magically made, one that siphoned life from everything it touched.

The statue of Erys was an unexpected piece of the curse wielder's puzzle. Why, if the woman studied chaos? Or did she wish to return to the path of thunder after abandoning the storm goddess for Aishlin?

Unless Neeve had it all wrong from the start. Was the woman even a witch at all? Had she stolen her power?

The ship creaked and swayed with the undulating sea, and Neeve was grateful for the calm, as though Shanna herself wanted to soothe her to rest in her arms.

Why did you bring that curse? Neeve pulled the blanket closer, snuggling it around her shoulders and face. *You came prepared to strike against me. You had it ready.*

Fallon's hawk-like face frightened her in memory, his piercing blue eyes almost unnatural in their intensity and shade.

Was it meant for him? Did you waste your one defense on me? For a moment, Neeve nurtured the satisfaction of bitter justice. *How foolish you must feel.*

Neeve took a deep, cool breath, her body relaxing.

I'm strong, she thought, a part of her wishing to send these words directly to the woman's mind. *I'm strong, and I'm fighting back.*

Another breath, her heart and mind stronger.

Prepare yourself, witch, for the adversaries in your wake.

CHAPTER 17

When Neeve turned over and opened her eyes, she met Erick's watchful gaze, the dark brown barely discernible in the dark the moonlight gleaming through the portholes.

She sat up, seeing Cassander asleep beside Erick.

"Good morning," Erick whispered. "Did you sleep well?"

"Well enough." It felt like a partial lie as she remembered the dream. "You?"

"Like a rock." He passed Neeve her waterskin. "What did you dream about?"

She took a long draught of cool water, her consciousness clearing. But she didn't answer, pressing her lips together as she sealed her waterskin.

"It was during my watch," he said. "You gasped in your sleep."

She looked down at her hands. "Would it be ominous and creepy if I said I saw death?"

"Only to someone who isn't me." He leaned his head against the ship's wall. "Care to elaborate?"

She wanted him to know, to tell him everything, but the words wouldn't form, her body hesitating to give them breath and life.

He held his hand out for her, which she took. "What is it, Neeve?"

Wordlessly, he pointed to Cassander. Neeve nodded. He turned her hand palm-up and wrote a single word: *How?*

She wrote back, *Stab?*

"You don't know?" When she shook her head, he exhaled, his free hand combing his hair back. "Did you see anything new in the dream?"

"No."

He rubbed her fingers, keeping her hand in his. "I've been thinking about the Erys statue. Such an odd location for a chaoswitch. Unless that's where *she's* going to die?"

"I thought it was strange too, but—" She grimaced, words harder and harder to find. "I didn't feel death *there*."

"What did you feel?"

"Shame," she said, letting herself remember. "And sadness."

The passing silence was palpable, even with the ambience of the ship navigating the undulating sea.

"You don't have to be afraid, Neeve." He drew lines up and down the creases of her palm. "I will do everything in my power to keep you safe."

The urge to lean against him was strong, to close her eyes and imagine that they were on an adventure, not a journey fraught with danger, one that could end in death.

"It isn't only myself," she said. "You. Cassander. Gretchen." She opened her eyes and searched his, the dim light somehow both helping and hindering. "So many things are at stake."

He kissed her forehead, his lips lingering on her skin as butterflies swarmed in her core, their wings stirring up a hurricane within. Even with the curse and the stress and the suffocating powerlessness, he was there.

"What do you expect we'll face in the coming days?" she asked. "Is there anything you're worried about?"

"Oh, there's plenty to worry about," he said with a quiet chuckle. "Avalanches, bears, wild folk from the mountains."

She quirked a brow. "Aren't they a myth?"

"I assure you, Neeve, the bears are very real."

She shoved his shoulder, eyes lingering on the shadowed creases by his eyes as he smiled.

He glanced to the left, where Fallon rested with his back against the wall, arms crossed, the slightest bit of silver visible in his boot lace. He had fallen asleep far from them, not really in a clear position to see or hear anything. In his relaxed posture, he didn't seem bothered enough to keep watch.

"Superstition with anything related to Aishlin is everywhere," he said then. "My blood and chaos magic. Hells, even your deathsight, even though it's light-given. There's plenty to worry about."

At this, Neeve turned her hand in his to weave their fingers. "One man asked me if I'd taken mist arcana to see death."

Erick's scoff was almost silent. "They only need a reason to assume the worst."

"How did that happen?" she asked. "Mist arcana. How did it occur to someone to make a blend that affects those with magic?"

"Rumors say it was a magicborn." He paused, exhaling quietly through his nose. "Others, that it was a human desperate for power. Either scenario is probable, given the right circumstance."

"Have you—" But she stopped herself, the question far too personal.

"Once." He tightened his hold on her hand, their intertwined fingers comforting. His thumb stroked back and forth in a soothing motion. "I was young and suffering the pain of a broken heart."

Neeve looked up at him, the mischief in her eye gleaming. "The brunette or the redhead?"

He nearly laughed aloud, bringing his free hand to his mouth. "You wicked thing."

He pulled her closer, draping his arm over her shoulders, still holding her hand. "That poison was the scariest thing I've lived through, even compared to the day my mother left."

He paused, Neeve sensing there was more to tell.

"There is no control as power rushes through your blood. All you can think, all you can *feel,* is the need for more. Chaos coursed through me, demanding to be used, building within me with unimaginable pressure."

"What did you do?" She leaned her head on his shoulder. "How did you handle it?"

"Poorly," he said. "I hurt someone. The rush of power was replaced with ice-cold panic." He rested his cheek on her crown. "You told Cassander what you saw."

She nodded against his shoulder, her muscles relaxing, her body melting against him.

"Do you think you can save him?"

"I want to try."

"Me too." He rubbed her arm, his broad hand seeping more warmth through her poncho. "Are you cold?"

"The draft below deck has me concerned for this ship's integrity." After a moment, she looked up at him. "Are you alright?"

"Right as rain. Or should I say *right as chaos*?"

The shadowed shape of his lips was inches from hers. She cleared her throat, forcing her gaze to meet his. "Is it true that chaosborn are warmer than humans? That the cold doesn't bother them?"

The laugh lines around his mouth flattered him, even in the dark. "I didn't take you to believe in old wives' tales."

"You haven't put on a coat since we left Shaylon Plains," she said. "You don't feel the cold?"

"Notice that our friend hasn't, either?" He offered a nod toward Cassander. "Lightborn are the same. Perks of being the children in a bloodline connected with light and darkness."

"Then why am I so cold?" She hugged her poncho tighter. "If I'm godborn, the same as you?"

"I would think your human blood has something to do with it. Not to mention the curse." He paused, thinking. "It's likely affected your body's timeline, even with the godblood in your veins." He shrugged. "The further north we get, I'll feel it. But here, I'm fine."

There had been moments of vulnerability, flashes of his true self shown only when they were alone. His smile when she'd made him laugh. His unwavering stare as he trained her in magic. The flare of his anger as it burned on her behalf.

The longer she stared, the more she saw the veneer that protected him from the world. He'd curated and perfected each layer with flash and flair, all of it like a mask made of paper and ink.

Even with the weight of her deathsight, even with the toll such a gift had taken, Erick stayed with her, walking beside her along this path unknown to them both. Guilt soured on her stomach as she met his eyes. "I'm sorry."

"Why?" He tilted his head, confused. "Did you steal food out of my pack?"

"No—you have food?"

He raised an eyebrow. "Why are you sorry?"

"All this—" The words were the hardest part. The understanding of wrongdoing didn't always come with the tools to explain. "We're crossing into danger."

"That isn't your fault, Neeve."

"I couldn't have known that you'd get roped in like this. I know that. But we're on this ship with a witch hunter, trying to find some crazy woman who cursed me, and something terrible might happen."

"I didn't get roped into anything."

She managed a quiet chuckle. "The irony of me wanting to get rid of magic, only to unlock *more*."

"I chose to be at the crossroads, the same as you." He brought her hand to his chest, holding it to his breastbone. His steady, strong heartbeat thrummed beneath. "I could have walked away. I didn't have to appear at all."

"Why did you stay?" she asked, not unaware of the vulnerability in her voice.

It took him a moment to answer. "There was hope in your asking, hope and sadness. Your heart was broken, and I—" He exhaled, holding her tighter. "I was drawn to you."

A quiet laugh escaped on a breath. "And I thought it was because you like my hair."

"*Love*, dear one," he said. "But there is more to you than those glorious moon-white curls, and I am thoroughly enjoying myself as I learn it all."

It was easy to get swept up in his words. But fear held her, its icy touch making her shiver. "Are you disappointed?"

He leaned closer, resting his head on hers. "Not for an instant."

The shift was delicate as her body aged. Dawn had come, and with it, Godmother Neeve.

Godmother, she thought. *Much preferable to* grandmother, *I should think.*

Cassander groaned, stretching and waking. Neeve slipped her aged hand from Erick's and said, "Breakfast." She looked at their packs. "I'm assuming we're to fend for ourselves, like with supper last night."

"That, we do." Cassander sat up, reaching for his waterskin.

After a sip, he dug into his pack and produced a sandwich, breaking it up into pieces to share. Neeve did the same, sharing dried fruit and jerky, prompting Erick to sigh.

"All right, fine." He produced more jerky and pears from his pack. "Let's share because we care."

Neeve giggled, entertaining the idea that Erick had conjured his food in that moment, rather than packing for the journey. He didn't strike her as the *preparing* type. But he never failed to surprise her.

CHAPTER 18

Open water. Vast. Infinite.

Neeve's only experience had been lakes, easily traversed by fishing boats and skiffs. But on the sea, where the line of the horizon remained flat over endless water, Neeve stood at the boat's railing between Erick and Cassander, feeling small in a way that filled her with possibility.

When it was safe to appear as herself—Godmother Neeve—she let the sun warm her face as the sea breeze chilled her bones. She hugged her poncho tighter, eyes following the line where sea met sky and studied the faint blue outline of the distant mountains.

While Cassander leaned with his back against the railing, surreptitiously watching Fallon, Erick rested his arms on the wooden bar, his shoulder touching Neeve's.

"Is this the farthest you've been from home?" he asked.

"I think so, from what I can remember," she said, refusing to let the question of Alvar and healers take over her mind. There was no point dwelling on the question of what her parents had done and why, not when they were so far and out of reach. "It's humbling to think that this is my first real venture from home. No parents, no Gretchen."

"They're your home," he said. "Gretchen is, without a doubt."

She used her age and the sea as an excuse to lean against his arm. "I am far from home, aren't I?"

He bent his head to her, whispering into her ear to avoid the words being caught and swept away by the breeze. "When we're safe, we can try to speak with her."

Her green eyes were almost teal against the blue of sea and sky. "You can do that?"

"I can *try*," he admitted. "Do you have something that belongs to her?"

Neeve showed her ring. "She gave this to me before I left. She has its twin."

"Perfect." He stood upright, squinting beneath the sunlight. "We'll try as soon as we're able."

"Thank you, Erick."

He chuckled. "The spell hasn't worked yet."

"But you're willing to try."

Their eyes met, his masked brown to her vibrant green. His lips parted as though to say something, but perhaps thought better of it. Privacy would be in short supply for the rest of the week, barring any delays that the ship could face. They'd been lucky so far, avoiding storms and catching the wind beneath clear skies. But time remained sluggish, languid seconds passing at their leisure despite the desperation of the bodies moving within them.

"My parents went to someone in Alvar," Neeve said, unprompted. "Gretchen told me." She raised a shaking hand to her forehead, wiping away the dampness from the sea spray. "What did they do to me?"

He covered her other hand with his, squeezing her fingers. "We will learn together. You're not alone in this."

She closed her eyes, allowing his comfort to wash over her. "I am grateful for you. More than words can say."

His hold tightened, edging closer but keeping a modest distance as other passengers moved around the deck, enjoying the afternoon sun.

Two more sunsets passed before, at the following sunrise, Neeve heard the crew sharing stories of their favorite inns and shops to visit when they reached South Ileden Sound.

"Holly's has got the best meat pie in Ileden, mark my words." The crewman hummed as he remembered. "It's right near the port. Can't miss it."

"I hate docking ships in that damned place," one man said. "It's too bloody full."

"Careful of the *Queen's Pride*," the first said, a shadow in his words. "Heard what they did to the *Emerald Gem*?" He drew a line across his own throat, eyes wide and ominous.

"That was a storm, I heard."

But the first chuckled. "And that storm was named Sam Blackwood and Whitney Grainger."

"You alright, Neeve?" Cassander asked, nudging her arm. "You look lost in thought."

Pulled from her eavesdropping, she nodded. "Right as rain. Though this cold air is playing hell with my joints."

"A hearth fire awaits us," Erick said. "We should reach the Sound in a few hours."

"*Hours?*"

Hope kindled within, and sure enough, when the sun fell to afternoon, Neeve's heart skipped as she studied the skyline of South Ileden Sound, a bustling port city with several ships docked.

Look at how far you've come. She held the hem of her poncho in her hands, fingers worrying the edge. *Courage, Neeve, for you still have far to go.*

"Let's eat something before we go," Cassander said, reaching into his pack. Neeve's own stores were low, but she offered what she could.

Erick shared his final two pears. "We'll stock back up while we're here."

"South Ileden Sound, folks," the chief mate announced. "Tomorrow, we leave for the West Hills."

The passengers moved on the deck like a herd of livestock, waiting for the chance to move forward. Fallon was among them, preparing to disembark and shifting to be unobtrusive and very much out of the way of notice.

"Ileden is rich with religion and history," Cassander said, watching Falling without laying eyes on him. "The Wandering Order has had their hands full trying to fulfill their cultish demands. They have delusions of grandeur if they think they can squash magic in a land so wild as this."

Erick agreed. "The irony of a *cult* against magic, gods, and religion."

"Their dogma is their religion." Cassander's voice was rich with bitterness. "Their dogma and their misguided prejudice and anger. They would rather kill and die than learn and accept." His nose twitched in disgust. "I have no patience for that."

"Something we agree on," Erick said.

"From what I've heard, though," Cassander said, "they have yet to venture to the islands south of here." He chuckled to himself, as though privy to some secret or inside joke. "Storm Key is full of magic folk. Witches and worshippers. I defy any of the Wandering Order to make it out of there alive."

"Why the islands?" Neeve asked. "That can't be as hospitable as the mainland."

"They thrive there, from what I understand," Cassander said. "They go willingly to practice magic in peace. And some even manipulate the storms and waters to keep outsiders at bay."

"Sons and daughters of Erys and Shanna. Maybe some of Aishlin and Brena?" Then, with a flicker of shadows, he added, "Storm Key provides excellent ways to discard the bodies of the cultists stupid enough to step foot there."

"If the Order is more active in Ileden these days," Neeve said, thinking, "where could they convene without opposition? Surely, they face the wrath of witches and godborn?"

"A question I share," Cassander said.

"How long have you been on his heels?" Erick asked.

"Too long." Cassander glanced away before looking down at his hands, a few bites of breakfast remaining. "I should have ended this long before now."

"How?" Neeve asked. "How did they find you?"

She tried in vain to shove away the flashes of his death reading, remembering how his family had died.

"Cultists were in Melia, near the Ghostlands, looking for a healer. I didn't realize they were with the Order. I knew of one further east and helped them find her."

"Aren't you from Ileden?" Erick said.

"I grew up in Alvar," Cassander said. "My family has traveled back and forth. I've lived in Ileden for many years."

"What were doing in Melia?"

"Proposing."

Erick stilled, the sea breeze sweeping the levity from his face.

The crew worked mechanically, following orders and issuing call-outs as jobs were completed and the ship reached the dock without issue. Minutes later, the passengers disembarked. The trio rose, packs in hand, the mood heavy as Neeve understood why Cassander pursued as he did, across countries and continents. He would bring down the Wandering Order, or as many of them as he could, until his dying breath.

His dying breath. Neeve shuddered.

"I'm sorry," Erick said quietly, standing near Cassander and behind Neeve. Their fellow passengers passed them as the trio stood at the dock's entry into South Ileden Sound. "I wouldn't rest until every one of them fell to the bottom of the Seven Hells."

"That's nearly done," Cassander admitted. "Fallon has remained the most elusive of them all. He and a pair of Preceptors."

"Cunning bastard," Erick murmured.

"And cruel," he said. "He's a Warden with aspirations of becoming a Purifier."

"These names," Neeve said. "The Wandering Order has titles?"

"Ranks," Cassander said. "Seekers and Pursuers are the two lowest ranks. Glorified hunters. Inquisitors and Binders capture and question. Then, there are Wardens."

"Fallon," Neeve said.

"Wardens oversee imprisonment," Erick said, his tone dark.

"There are Preceptors," Cassander said. For Neeve, he added, "They train recruits and are second only to the High Arbiter."

"And one of these Preceptors," Erick said. "Is she a blonde woman?"

Cassander's eyes widened. "You've met her."

"Charis," Erick said. "Puts Fallon's dark desires to shame."

"The other is worse," Cassander said. "Elias. If he has a heart, it's made of nothing but darkness."

Neeve reached for Erick's arm, her fears shadowing her mind with imagined scenarios of Erick and Cassander at their mercy.

But those cultists know nothing of mercy.

Cassander and Erick, bloody and full of rage, slew every cultist who dared cross his path. The image didn't match the men beside her, not how she knew them.

Cassander's rich brown eyes squinted against the afternoon sun. A lightborn, touched by the dark. One who used his light as a weapon of cleansing fire against the bloodstained hands of the Wandering Order.

Anya, do not abandon your son. Give him your power and strength to fight the monsters of the world.

Monsters in human skin.

Neeve found Fallon's shape among the crowd. If she were to touch him, what would his death vision tell her? Did it align with Cassander's? Would they bring one another down together?

Or was Cassander's life the only one in Death's line of sight?

CHAPTER 19

Off the ramp, the port city of South Ileden Sound teemed with pedestrians navigating merchants, carts, and livestock, all of them treading on streets of dirt packed and worn with frequent travel.

Cassander watched a merchant offloading several wooden boxes to a man at the docks, who passed him a purse of coins in payment. "I wonder if he's going toward the Midlands."

Erick didn't look hopeful. Neeve busied her hands as Cassander approached the merchant, toying with the hem of her poncho.

"It's been a long time since I've been in a place like this," Erick said. "Years, I think."

"Where?" she asked, looking past the people up to the sky, as much of it as she could see over the tops of tall brick buildings. "Anywhere in Sheraton?"

"Alvar. I've often thought about going back."

Neeve almost asked him why he hadn't but feared the answer.

"Magic folk and humans alike," he went on. "Witches and godborn. It was filled with magic of all kinds."

"You make it sound ideal."

"It has its problems, just like anywhere. But its cities are beautiful.

Architecture, history, music." He looked around with a grimace. "Nothing like here."

Neeve watched Cassander shake the man's hand. His skin was a few shades lighter than Cassander's, a cool-toned compliment to Cassander's warmth. But Cassander's inherent glow shone with no need for comparison. Absently, Neeve imagined Cassander lighting up a room with magic shimmering through his skin, like a comforting, guiding beacon.

How long before his light would go out?

Cassander returned with a victorious grin. "We have passage!" He gestured back to the cart and its driver. "Meet Sven. He will take us as far as Storm Seat."

The driver's mismatched eyes crinkled at the corners. Neeve quietly admired their color difference—one dark honey brown eye, one the shade of mahogany wood—when she took his offered arm to step into the cart. Erick helped from her other side as she climbed, her joints aching.

The flashes were quick. Highwaymen down the path they were to take, waiting with swords and knives ready. Sven bled on the road as Erick commanded the horse to run like all seven hells were behind them, with Neeve and Cassander white-knuckling the cart to keep from falling out. Cassander was bleeding from his shoulder, Neeve from her arm, but Erick had a devastating wound at his back, the blood stain blooming on the fabric of his shirt.

"What path will you take?" she asked Sven, her words quick and tone urgent.

A storm loomed in the distance, the rumble of thunder a whispered promise.

He explained the road to her, where it veers left once they leave the city and then goes right, like a big S on the map, before going straight again.

"Why do you ask?" He looked from Neeve to the others. "It's the road I always take."

"Is it possible for you to go straight from here?" Neeve asked. "To skip the curve?"

Sven looked at her like she was a fool. "Hardly, ma'am. It's just weeds and wildflowers."

"Would you try?" Erick said, stepping in. Understanding offered confidence as he encouraged the driver to listen. "She has good instincts."

Their driver shrugged. "It's your money."

"Money?" Neeve asked, then looked at Cassander.

"That's already covered." Sven returned to the driver's seat and clicked his horse onward, the hooves clopping against the dirt path and the wheels squeaking into motion.

"What did you see?" Erick asked.

"Highwaymen. It doesn't end well." Sven, dead. Erick, dying. "Best to avoid it at any cost, even if he thinks I'm an old loon."

A few quiet moments passed, the sound of horse and cart rhythmic against the background of the singing birds and the whispering breeze. The fringes of a headache crept in, prompting Neeve to close her eyes. Seeing two deaths had taken its toll. Seeing Erick's death...

"You're going with us?" Erick asked Cassander. "Can't bear to be parted from us?"

"I think we're all on the same trail, from the way this looks. And perhaps Fallon may wish to stay close to us." Cassander cast a cursory look around. "No doubt he knows who I am, or at least suspects something. And he may be interested in who my friends are."

"Aw," Erick teased. "He said we're friends."

"You folks good with Storm Seat?" Sven asked, mounting the driver's seat. "Should be there before sundown."

Neeve looked at Cassander and Erick. "Let's hope it's well before then."

"All right," the driver said, shaking his head. "Going straight."

The terrain was uneven, Neeve using both Erick and the cart to keep her upright. Sven drove the horse slowly, steering the animal to take the grass instead of the clear path.

"There," Cassander said, pointing. "Is that—?"

There were men looking from the thin line of trees, a few of them stepping forward out of hiding, since the cart they'd seen in the distance was avoiding them completely.

"Highwaymen?" Erick asked loud enough for Sven to hear. "How many are there?"

"I can see four," Cassander said. "No telling how many are hiding in the trees."

"You knew?" Sven asked, turning his head to speak to Neeve, but he didn't take his eyes off the front of the cart. His horse stepped carefully, the wheels a little bouncy and uneven. "You knew we'd run into trouble, didn't you?"

"What will you do if I say yes?"

She felt Erick's hand on her arm, his hold firm.

"Your secret dies with me," he said. "Th—thank you."

She could hear the trepidation in his voice, but the gratitude was there all the same.

"That was a brave thing," Cassander said quietly. "You never know how people will react when they're exposed to that kind of power."

"I only hope he keeps his word," Erick mumbled.

"I still would have done it," Neeve whispered, "even if he reported us to the Order. He could have been killed for helping us."

"Not out of the kindness of his heart," Erick whispered. "He's been paid, Neeve. Besides, there's no causality between those two things. Circumstances happen. Our need for a driver and his want of Cassander's money wouldn't have caused his death. We're not responsible for what choices the highwaymen make."

Would Sven have taken the same path, with or without them? What if he'd delayed his departure by minutes or hours, or left sooner than planned because they bought passage?

Regardless of what could have been, all four of them still had their lives as they rode further into the morning.

The landscape was breathtaking, with rolling fields and tall trees as mountains lined the horizon. Neeve admired the peaks of the pines against the bright blue sky. And there, in the distance, was a statue of a woman, her face serene, her hands resting on the pommel of her sword, the point of the blade in the ground at her feet. Around her, worshipers and admirers had gathered stones and placed them by hand, the base taking the shape of a diamond.

"Another Erys statue?" Neeve pointed as Erick and Cassander looked. "That's not the same as the one I'd seen."

"You'll find them all over this part of Ileden," Cassander said.

"We're in Storm Country," Sven said. "Many here worship Erys and pray to her sister for a healthy harvest."

Storms brought rain, and rain bought life. The goddesses were each a point of balance, from sky and earth, from sea and fire, from order and chaos.

Shadows could not exist without light.

"What are you thinking about?" Erick whispered, bumping her shoulder with his.

"Order and chaos," Neeve answered simply. "Earth and sky."

He followed her eyes, nodding slowly as he watched the scenery passing by. "There is order and chaos in everything. The chaos of a storm, the wildness of briars. The order of rain nurturing plants and animals to grow. Each aspect of our lives carries balance, which we have the frustrating proclivity to tip or sway."

Cassander hummed in agreement. "Mountains erupting fire, oceans shifting and changing with the tide."

He let the image hang, Neeve filling in the gaps. Each goddess brought their own brand of chaos to the natural order. Brena with her fires, Shanna with her seas.

"Why is it that Aishlin is marked so heavily, when every goddess has chaos?" Neeve looked from Erick to Cassander and found that both were looking at each other, a hint of a challenge in Erick's gaze.

"Life grows within order," Cassander said. "Seeds planted and watered in fertile soil will grow. But the world is remade in chaos. Lightning strikes dried brush and causes a fire, turning it to ash. But the ash fertilizes the fallen seeds on the ground, and new brush grows."

"And humans," Erick said. "Humans are the very product of order and chaos working together."

"Our bodies represent order," Cassander said, agreeing. "Everything works in tandem and follows a set of rules and series of actions. But our consciousness, our independent spirits? Absolute chaos."

Erick winked at Neeve. "Give a sentient being free will and watch the world unfold."

Or give a silly young woman incredible power when she has no inkling how to use it. But Neeve kept that thought to herself, massaging the slight ache in her arthritic knuckles as Sven drove on.

CHAPTER 20

In the hours from the Sound to Storm Seat, Neeve and Cassander passed the time with Sven while Erick avoided small talk in favor of a book he pulled from his pack.

"Do you always travel so prepared?" Neeve tapped the cover of Erick's book. "Avoiding people at all costs?"

"Not all people," he mumbled, lifting an eyebrow at her. "Most. But not all."

"Would Sven raise an eyebrow if I read mine, too?"

"Only if he read the title."

The hills grew as Sven drove them north, the horse and wagon moving carefully toward the nearby township.

"Village is Sun Glade. Good people here," Sven said. "Honest folk. Hard-working. Some of them use magic." A note he added for Neeve's sake.

Children played behind a few buildings, laughing with one another. A dog barked as he fetched a stick they threw. Several men and women walked the worn dirt road, carrying baskets of either clothes or food or leading horses to the blacksmith at the other end of the street. This place felt a lot like home, bringing a tinge of sadness to Neeve's heart.

When we're safe, we can try to speak with her.

Neeve clutched her hands in her lap, eager for the chance to reach her sister, so far away.

"The inn here is good," the driver said. "I've spent many a night here between runs to the Sound."

"How's the food?" Cassander asked. "Anything we should try or avoid?"

The driver considered, impressed by the question. "You travel a lot, don't you?"

"A fair amount," he said.

How much of that travel came from his commitment to striking vengeance against Fallon for destroying his family?

Cassander was a son of light with chaos of his own.

"Definitely enjoy the apple cobbler," Sven said. "You'll not easily meet its equal. Avoid the leek soup." The driver grimaced, no doubt reliving the experience. "Anything but the leek soup."

The driver pulled up in front of a large wooden building, the thatch roof fresh, laughter and voices audible from outside.

"There's a ferry to the west," Sven said, as he climbed down from the driver's seat. "That'll take you faster to the Midlands than foot or cart. It's about an hour's walk, though."

"Does it go along the coast?" Cassander asked.

"It does." Then Sven added, "The fare's cheap, but he makes you work."

Erick didn't look eager. "What's the work?"

"Fishing."

"Oh." Erick shrugged a shoulder. "That's alright."

"It'll help the time go by faster," Neeve said. "I always enjoyed fishing with my parents when I was small."

Sven nodded kindly, likely equating the distance in age within a wider span of decades than was true. Neeve remembered fondly a past that was much more recent than what Sven likely assumed.

"Let's hope you enjoy it again." Sven nodded once, waving his farewell, and led his horse and cart further down the thoroughfare.

The three looked at the facade of the inn, the boisterous activity typically inviting to some. But Neeve noticed Erick shudder as he said, "Lovely. *People.*"

"Your favorite." She winked beneath his scowl, pleased to hear him chuckle behind her.

They stepped inside, Neeve's hips and back stiff as she wobbled forward. How she must have looked, bent and crooked, *so much like Gran.* Neeve hummed a laugh and missed her sister so much her chest ached.

Gretchen, she thought, saying her name like a prayer.

Gretchen, home alone, moving through the kitchen without stepping around Neeve. Sleeping in their bed alone. Existing in the days to come in solitude.

Leaving her, just as their parents had left them.

Gods, what have I done?

"There," Erick said, pointing at a table in the back, away from the door and windows. "Nice and tucked away."

"With eyes everywhere," Cassander said in approval.

Neeve sat, eyeing the room as Erick leaned against the wall for a better view of everyone in the room.

"I'll get our rooms and some food," Cassander said.

"Just one," Neeve said, passing him some coin. "Two beds, please." As he lifted an eyebrow, she clarified. "It's safer. We can still keep watch and take turns sleeping. And this time, I can keep watch, too."

"If you insist." And he left to speak to the innkeeper.

Erick grinned, leaning down to her. "And here I thought you couldn't bear a moment's separation from me."

"All this flirting will get you into trouble someday."

Mischief gleamed in his eyes. "Promise?"

"I am ninety years old, Mal'Erick." But she didn't push him away.

"Oh, using my full name." He winked, ready to say something else when Cassander returned with tankards of ale.

"Foods on the way. No leek soup." He looked from Neeve to Erick, reading the atmosphere between them. "Did I miss something?"

"They are taking them from their beds," someone said from a table near theirs. They raised their voice and punctuated those last three words with their tone, their index finger jabbing the table in an ominous rhythm. "*From their beds*, I tell you."

"Those are just rumors," said one with him. "Have you known someone taken? I haven't."

Neeve and the others stayed quiet, listening.

"They're movin' all through the Midlands, spreading their poison, scarin' folk. Even if it *is* a rumor, I still believe it because they'd do it. No question."

Those eavesdropping mumbled in agreement. Neeve shared a look with Erick and Cassander.

"Just our luck," Erick said. "If one cultist in our sights wasn't enough. The Wandering Order is actively leaving its mark, and we're walking right into their path."

"I didn't mean to bring this upon you," Cassander said. "I'd say we'll keep our head down, but I'm afraid that may be impossible."

"You didn't bring this upon us," Neeve said. "Our paths crossed because of what we're after."

"Because of what *he's* after," Erick said, looking around at the faces in the tavern. "That hawk-faced witch hunter."

"Why is he going to the trouble of pursuing her?" Cassander paused as the server brought three meals—hot stews with hunks of bread. He tasted the broth, nodded once in approval, and went on. "What's personal about one witch to drive you across continents?"

"If she's his real quarry," Erick said quietly. "We *assume* he's after her. I mean, it matches up. But it would be safer to think that he could be after anyone."

"You think it's me?" Cassander asked.

"It could be. Or it could be someone else." Erick scratched beneath his jaw, his lips pursed as he considered. "It's curious that we're all going to the same place, on the trail of the same woman who may or may not be bait."

"I'm glad we're not alone," Neeve said. "What we're doing, what we're *facing*." She tried in vain to push down the ill feeling in her stomach. "At least we have each other."

Cassander raised his tankard to her, and Neeve raised hers, and the pair of them eyeing Erick, resting his chin in his hand.

He sighed. "Oh, alright."

The meal began in silence, the trio listening for any other bits of information in the otherwise jovial atmosphere of the inn. But the conversation had shifted as the working crowd ventured in at day's end. At Erick's suggestion, they moved upstairs.

The room was accommodating for a mother and her two sons. No one blinked an eye as Erick helped Old Woman Neeve upstairs behind Cassander's lead, the brass room key in his hand.

"We take turns," Neeve said, impressed by the furnishings. There was a small table with a single chair, where a watchman could sit while the others slept. "We deserve as much rest as we can get."

She chose the bed farthest from the door and sat on the edge, her joints creaking and her back aching. She unfastened the belt with her knife and tossed it onto the table before sitting, relieved.

"Sunset is soon," Erick said, as though reading her discomfort all over her aged face.

Her gratitude for his attention and concern didn't outweigh her dislike at the worry lining his eyes. "I'll be right as rain after some rest."

Erick moved in front of her and held out his hands. "Would you be up for trying to reach Gretchen?"

Her aged hands slipped into his palms, his long fingers curling around them. The warm pressure was comforting.

"Deep breath," he said, sitting with her.

She closed her eyes, waiting for the magic, focusing on the pressure of his thumbs and the firmness of his grip. But no other sensation reached her.

She opened one eye. "Why are you smiling?"

"I'm holding your hands."

She jerked her hands free and swatted him, laughter brightening his handsome face. She eyed him when he held his hands out once more and took them slowly, chancing a glance at Cassander. He sat at the small table and sifted through his pack, but Neeve didn't miss the lift in the corner of his mouth.

"Be my anchor," Erick said, touching the ring on her finger. "You and your ring are my best chances of forging a connection."

Erick quietly incanted the spell, his magic tingling against Neeve's palms and fingers. Soon, something internal connected, a link forged, and he whispered, "Hello, Gretchen."

"Erick?" Gretchen's voice echoed in Neeve's mind, though she sounded far away. "Is that you?"

"Your favorite chaosborn comes with news."

"Gods above, Mal'Erick." But Neeve squeezed his hands, her heart racing with relief and excitement, her emotions at odds.

"Neeve?"

She gasped. "She can hear me?"

"She can," he said, "but I don't know for how long."

"Are you alright?" Gretchen asked. Neeve's heart ached hearing the emotion in her sister's voice.

"I'm fine," Neeve said. "We're in Ileden, resting in a tavern for the night."

"Gods, you're so far away."

Neeve's lips trembled. She tried to steel her voice against the emotion, to remain steady for her sister. "We won't be long. I promise I'll return soon."

"You both be safe," Gretchen said.

"Cassander, too," Neeve said. "He's with us."

At this, Gretchen laughed, though the sound still bore melancholy. "I've half a mind to be jealous, sister. Two handsome men escorting you to another continent?"

At this, Erick chuckled. "You flatter me, Gretchen."

"You'll flatter yourself if no one else does it."

"I miss you more than I can stand," Neeve said. "Are you alright?"

"Alright enough, being home alone. Samson is wonderful company."

Neeve's lips quivered as she struggled to make her voice level. "I'm sorry I left."

"I'm not," Gretchen said right away, as though she'd been ready. "Break this curse and come home."

"I will."

"I love you, Neeve."

Her voice trembled at last, the room too warm, her muscles too tight. "Love you too."

"I'll reach out again when we can," Erick said, squeezing Neeve's hands.

The spell's hold weakened, even as Gretchen said *I love you* once more before the line snapped.

Neeve met Erick's waiting gaze, tears already falling.

"You'll be home before you know it," he said.

She nodded, trying to steady herself, feeling the tightness of anticipation resisting the assurance he offered. He released her hands to cup her face, clearing the tears from her cheeks.

"You rest first," Erick said to her, rising from the bed. "You'll take last watch."

Neeve didn't argue, grateful for the bed and the rest, grateful to turn her face and close her eyes. She breathed through the surge within her chest, several more tears falling before her breathing regulated.

Break this curse and come home.

I will, Gretchen. I swear it.

She breathed slowly and deeply, listening to the quiet in the room as Cassander and Erick deliberated who should watch first as Erick took the second bed.

Cassander laughed. "Why ask if you already had a choice?"

"Because it's polite." Erick used the wash basin for his face before settling in to rest.

"You didn't mention the Wandering Order," Cassander whispered. Neeve heard Erick chastise him quietly, feeling their eyes fall on her. She remained still, feigning sleep. "Should Gretchen know?"

"She's not magical," Erick said. "She poses no threat to them."

Until they learn her sister's a deathseer.

Guilt churned within, but Neeve bit back against the swell. *She's alright.*

In the few moments of consciousness that remained, Neeve wondered if she could feel Erick looking at her from across the room, or if she'd imagined the sensation between her shoulder blades.

Rest well, Erick, she thought, pushing the wish toward him. *And thank you.*

Warmth filled her, spreading from the center of her chest all over her torso, through her limbs to the tips of her fingers and toes. She hugged the blanket tighter, grateful for its shape and weight, grateful for the soft pillow beneath her head.

She didn't feel the change as her body shifted to its younger shell. She only felt the slow and steady drift into the dark, quiet space reserved for sleep and dreams.

Rest well.

CHAPTER 21

Her shoulder shook with Erick whispering her name. His hand offered gentle pressure and warmth, lightly massaging her muscles as he stirred her awake. Her eyes opened, the world still dark, her body comfortable on the soft, warm bed.

"Last watch," he whispered. "Are you alright?"

Neeve shifted, blinking at him in the low light from the single burning candle. "Yes."

The room was warm, but her arms puckered with gooseflesh when she emerged from beneath the blanket and sat up. Erick swept a mass of curls over her shoulder, his fingers careful of tangles as he stared.

"Gods, above," he whispered. "You're lovely, even when you first wake up."

She closed her eyes, humming a laugh she didn't have the energy to project, and leaned against his shoulder. Words flowed through her mind as she moved to speak, but rest still gripped her even as Erick's arms enveloped her.

"I wish we could stay this way," he whispered.

Neeve inhaled, taking air deep into her lungs to force herself awake. "Watch will be over soon."

"You're right," he said, amused, "but I had something more *long term* in mind."

She took his hands and twisted out of his embrace, her body cold where his warmth had been. "Sleep here."

"You sure?"

Neeve looked at the other bed where Cassander lay on his side. "You want to share with him?"

Erick wrinkled his nose, crawling into Neeve's bed. "Not that he isn't an attractive man. He looks like a cuddler, which I can appreciate."

Neeve muffled a soft giggle as he laid back.

"I was going to stay awake with you so we could have some alone time." Erick wiggled his eyebrows until he yawned. "Gods, I can barely keep my eyes open."

He didn't bother with a blanket as he set his head on her pillow and exhaled in relief that Neeve, herself, could feel.

"You need to rest," she said, using her fingers to comb through and settle her hair, though the memory of Erick's touch lingered.

Deftly, she worked a braid over her shoulder, a quick solution to what was likely an unruly mess. The white-blonde curls wrapped around her fingers as she wove them together.

"I love your hair," he mumbled. He blinked so slowly that Neeve thought he'd closed his eyes. "Magnificent."

"Flatterer."

"Hm. This smells like you."

"Is that a good thing?"

A light smile curved his lips. "Heaven."

His breathing deepened, eyes closed, head slightly tilted to one side. Neeve indulged a long look, the shape and angle of his face pleasing to study. The reach of his cheekbones, the temping curves of his jawline. Neeve's fingertips could almost feel his skin beneath them.

She pulled the blanket over him, shielding him from the cold.

When the curse is over, she thought, promising herself. *Have courage, Neeve. When the curse is over.*

When the curse is over...

She watched her youthful hands toy with the end of her braid, imagining the woman reaching South Ileden Sound and securing passage to a place called Brockdon Fields. Neeve pulled out her father's map and traced a finger along the Midlands, stopping where the clear lettering labeled the region.

Where are you now?

She pulled for the one who cursed her, anchoring the tether on the bracelet the woman wore. *Show her to me. Connect us. Where is she?*

The shadows coalesced at her call, forming Titus, his silent regard watchful and knowing.

"I expected that to be more difficult," she muttered to the bird. "I suppose Anya and Aishlin are more connected than I ever realized."

Titus waited, and at her command, he slipped through the thin space in the uneven windowpane. Neeve closed her eyes, seeing through her conjured raven, as her magic reached beyond the tavern.

What if this magic could reach the woman's mind? For several racing heartbeats, the idea thrilled her. Walk through the chaoswitch's mind, learn her secrets. But the frost-touch of panic made her recoil, palms and fingertips itching with unspent chaos.

Darkness met her sight. Even as Neeve tried to reason why—not a strong enough connection to the subject, not knowing where first to look—she knew the truth.

Fear kept her magic tethered.

A cold pit of frustration bloomed in her core, even as determination warmed her blood. Half of her in fire, half in ice.

"You can't keep being afraid," she whispered, hoping the sound of her own voice would still the racing thoughts and hammering pulse. But her clammy palms caught a chill that she couldn't rub away. "You're in control. The magic obeys you."

But that's simply it. The magic obeys me.

And someone could get hurt.

"Don't let fear win." She rubbed her chest, applying pressure up and down her sternum, breathing with deep focus. "Don't let fear win."

Warmth spread from her palms, sinking into her chest until it touched her heart. Her light magic worked to heal and soothe. She sat this way for several minutes, forcing her mind to listen to and internalize the silence. Fringes of anxiety lingered, but she'd kept the worst of it at bay. This time.

Careful of the map, Neeve rummaged through her things and pulled the book of spells. She turned its pages slowly, reading titles in search of something, *anything*, that could help.

Anything to remind her that her magic was capable even while she feared its power.

For Inner Balance

In Times of Too Much Dark

In Times of Too Much Light

For Sleep

For Dreams

For Understanding

Absolutely nothing about *age* or *youth*. She turned to the first one.

For Inner Balance

Light a lavender candle and place it in a circle of Anya.

Arrange a circle of amethyst and quartz crystals around the candle.

Fill a small bowl with fresh rainwater. Add a pinch of salt and a sprig of rosemary.

Hold your hands over the bowl and recite:

Balance within, balance without,

Steady the soul, dispel all doubt.

Believe that you can. Believe that you will.

Knowledge of self. Trust, instilled.

Repeat until the words fill your heart.

Light a candle and say some pretty words.

That was it?

It would take more than a cleverly worded rhyme to rid her body of this curse.

Hope diminished to frustration as she closed her book and took Erick's from his pack. She sat close to the candlelight at the small table and skimmed through the opening pages. He'd brought some kind of adventure story, which intrigued her enough to return to the beginning.

But in the quiet space, reading the printed words by amber light page after page, Neeve's mind wandered over the path they'd taken, retracing their steps from the hills of Storm Seat to the bustling port of South Ileden Sound, over the Sea of Kings with the three of them simultaneously avoiding Fallon while keeping him in their sights. It reminded

Neeve of finding a spider, one she had to face and dispose of despite her body freezing in fear. She couldn't look away from it or it would dart away to hide. Not knowing would have been a worse fate than facing the beast head-on, rolled up parchment or house slipper in hand.

Though it was unlikely she could face the witch hunter with rolled parchment or a slipper, the imagined scenario amused her.

All this for a woman with a temper. Was she aware of the group who pursued her? Did she think Neeve would shrink into a corner and accept her fate? That Neeve would continue aging until her body turned to dust? She'd angered the wrong lightborn deathseer. And a small part of her hoped her fury-fueled tenacity would make Erick proud.

Bitterness and spite.

That's my girl.

A week had passed since the curse changed the direction of Neeve's life, rebounding between old and young as she pursued the unknown. What if this all came to nothing?

Bitterness and spite. And I am godborn. That has to count for something.

She considered Cassander, curious if he would use his magic in the same way that Erick would. Neeve stared at her open hands, eyes tracing the lines of her palms as the golden light filled them. The glow was faint as Neeve pushed the light to the surface. The room brightened. Her eyes had gone wholly white on the ship when she accidentally read Cassander's death. What did they look like when her vision adjusted to the dark? There was no mirror in the room, leaving Neeve to wonder.

Sun and moon. Light and shadow.

Hours passed as Neeve read, as she conjured light and shadow, mulling over the words of the spell.

Balance within, balance without,
Steady the soul, dispel all doubt.

She glanced at Erick's sleeping form. Warmth bloomed beneath her skin, picturing his cunning eyes, hearing his sharp words spoken through a slyly upturned mouth, his hands gentle as they touched her.

Mal'Erick. Dealmaker and unexpected companion, one who still hid so much from her and from the world.

He mumbled in his sleep, body shaking as his left leg jerked, the words indiscernible until she heard, "No."

His arms twitched, eyes darting behind closed lids, lips twitching into a sneer that formed a frown, his breathing coming faster. Neeve rose to him, reaching to pull him from the nightmare while there was still time to return to sleep, but he sat upright without warning, nearly colliding with her as she bent to touch his arm.

His eyes were wide and alert, searching between the dream space and reality. His pinprick irises found her, staring as though to discern that she was real. Recognition smoothed the lines of his face before he pulled her close, hugging her waist as he pressed his head to her stomach.

"Gods—" His voice betrayed him, breaking slightly beneath whatever nightmare had gripped him.

She rested a hand on his head, saying nothing as she combed through his hair. Her other hand rubbed circles against his back, the pressure firm and soothing.

His breathing steadied, but neither of them let go. She continued to touch him, her motions rhythmic and soothing, as his hold remained firm.

"You're alright," she whispered. "Just breathe."

He obeyed, every inhale and exhale measured and steady.

"Can you go back to sleep?"

He shook his head, still holding her. "Not for a while. Not after that."

She passed him his waterskin, and she took a sip from her own. But a sip was all that remained. "We should have filled these before going to sleep."

"I think I saw a well behind the tavern when we were coming in." He pressed his fingers against his eyes. "I'll get some. It'll probably help with this headache."

"Not alone, you're not."

His flirtatious smirk returned, though it wasn't strong enough to overshadow the terror that had been there moments before. "You're cute when you worry about me."

"*Erick.*"

"We can't leave Cassander alone, asleep and oblivious."

"Then we leave him a note." She crossed her arms. "You're not going out alone when Fallon could be right outside."

"That bastard probably doesn't sleep," Erick said. "It's only water. We'll survive a couple more hours."

"I could use a sip." Cassander propped himself up on his elbows, groggy but pleasant. "I'm awake."

Erick shrugged, standing up. "We'll be right back so you can go back to sleep."

"I feel alright."

But Cassander's words were slow, his breathing deep. Neeve and Erick shared a look before she reached for Cassander's waterskin to join theirs, and the pair stepped out in silence. They moved quietly downstairs before Erick led her to the back kitchen.

"There's a lot of iron here," he whispered, eyeing the pans hanging on the wall where the wood stove held an empty pot.

On the back wall beside the oven was a wooden door, locked.

"Hm." Erick pointed to the brass ring of keys hung beside it. "It can't be that easy, can it?"

"Let's hope it is." She reached for the keys and tried one that didn't work. But the second one did, twisting in the lock to free the latch.

They stepped out into a night that was pre-dawn, the remaining moonlight bright in a clear sky with fringes of yellow and orange peeking over the horizon. The well was in sight, though a good distance from the tavern. They walked slowly, Neeve staying close.

"I'm sorry about your nightmare," she said. "You're not getting any rest."

"I'll be fine. Maybe the ferry master will let me sleep instead of fish." Erick stepped ahead and turned to walk backwards, one eyebrow raised. "I can be very persuasive."

"Your confidence is inspiring," she said as they reached the well. She readied the waterskins as Erick lowered the bucket. "You're so—" She gestured vaguely, searching for the word. "You're so *sure.*"

"That part is thanks to you," he said. "You make it easy to be sure, Neeve."

Erick's flirtatious nature was one thing. Neeve's heart continued to flutter with every wink and comment. But this was different. This wasn't teasing. It was a *confession*. She had known his feelings, even as she worked to navigate her own, but this went beyond curiosity and the willingness to explore. He was *sure* about *her*.

Her palms itched to hold his, but she settled for their empty waterskins as Erick let the bucket fall and waited, listening for the gurgling water to fill the vessel. Neeve mimicked the sound, making him chuckle again, and he carefully brought it back up, mindful to keep it from hitting the sides and spilling.

"You don't have to tell me about your dream," Neeve said, taking Erick's waterskin first to fill it. "But I'm here to listen, if you need to say anything out loud. That always helps me."

He was quiet before thanking her. "Fallon had you, and something bound me. Chains of iron wound too tight. I couldn't move, and I watched as he—"

Red flashed in his eyes, his lips pulling from his teeth. Neeve slipped her hand into his, water dripping from her fingers.

"I'm here, Erick," she whispered, "and I'm alright."

He kissed her forehead as she filled his waterskin. The submerged vessel filled quickly. Neeve corked it and filled hers.

"I had a nightmare when I was young," Neeve said, the cold water freezing her hand. Bubbles undulated to the surface. "My parents came back from one of their trips, but it really wasn't them. Someone had taken their shapes and came home to steal their lives." She corked her waterskin, water dripping from her fingers. "It's been years, but I still remember that dream as if it just happened."

"Have you heard from your parents?" he asked. "Being apart this long can't be easy."

Neeve thought of the woman with the long raven hair, walking away from Erick when he was a boy.

She thought of the barrier in her mind that Erick had broken through, setting her chaos magic free.

"It isn't." She submerged Cassander's, the last to fill. "But they enjoy their work, and it's always fun to hear their stories when they return."

Neeve's hands shifted from young to old, the strength of her hold waning as wrinkles and liver spots emerged.

"Oh?" She glanced skyward, her voice changing in age and disappointment, her heart heavy. "Sunrise already?"

But the world didn't brighten with the dawn. It had not yet come.

"Seems a bit early." Erick studied her. "Something to do with the curse?"

"Gods above, please." Neeve sighed. "Will I be older longer?" Afraid, she met his gaze. "Will there come a time when I won't change back?"

He rested a hand on her shoulder. "We'll find your cure. No matter what it takes."

"A lofty promise."

The foreign voice came up from behind them both. Neeve whirled, knocking the bucket off the edge of the well, Cassander's waterskin going with it. The man was grinning, predatory malice in his eyes.

"I knew there was something suspicious about you lot," he said, looking from Neeve to Erick. "What kind of witchcraft are you using?"

"I didn't do this." Neeve stared, adrenaline coursing through her. "I was cursed." She hated how vulnerable she sounded, hated that she had to defend herself against this cretin. She owed him nothing but contempt.

The man chuckled, the sound rough in his throat.

"Walk away," Erick said slowly. "Cultist."

Neeve's eyes dropped to the man's boots, finding the telltale silver thread. Her hand went to her side, feeling only her clothes. The belt was upstairs on the table, the knife snug in its sheath.

"Not when there's a curse that needs breaking."

He drew the long knife hidden behind his back and looked for Erick to meet the challenge. But Erick was already moving in offensively, his own knife equipped and ready. In the dawn's light, Neeve glimpsed shadows limning Erick's body, his chaos emerging in defensive anger.

She looked around frantically, the back of the tavern rich with potential weapons, and the nearest was a spade. She choked the handle with both hands, arms weak as she lifted its metal end like a spear.

"You can't have her," Erick said. His voice, his stance, his eyes—

every inch of him was dangerous. The shadows feathered like smoke. "Leave if you value your life."

"I value the mission," he said with a severe look, his lips curling. "I give my life to the mission."

He moved forward slightly, body poised for any sign that Erick or Neeve would strike.

"Your life, your choice," Erick said, deftly flipping the blade to reposition it in his fingers. "I won't hold back."

The man offered one quiet, mirthless laugh. "I'd be offended if you did."

"It's two against one," Neeve said. "This won't end well for you."

The cultist pulled a blade hidden inside his trousers at his belt, the small knife made entirely of iron. "Don't underestimate the Order's training."

Iron made Neeve uneasy, but its reach fell short against what human blood flowed in her veins. She remained steady where Erick recoiled, the gesture subtle and instinctual before he countered with an aggressive step forward.

The cultist moved toward Erick first. She moved to strike as Erick made a defensive stance, but the spade altered her balance and her aged legs buckled. Her knees hit the ground hard, lightning shooting up her legs to her chest and arms.

"In league with a godborn," the cultist said, his chuckle revealing more of his discolored teeth. "Must be my lucky day."

"Your luck's run out."

From the inn came Darrow, his tall form dressed in the all black clothing common with Moonblade. With his fist, he struck the cultist as his other hand forced a dagger into the cultist's side. With frustration burning beneath her skin, Neeve abandoned the spade as she reached for the cultist's arm, hands glowing with light. He howled in pain as her touch burned.

Erick swept in, kicking the iron weapon out of the enemy's hand before his knife found his throat. The savage business was over quickly, the cultist choking on his own blood as he died.

Darrow kicked the iron knife farther, the toxic blade skidding to the tall grass, out of sight.

"He gave his life for the mission," Erick said bitterly, sweat gathering at his hairline. Going to Neeve, touching her shoulders and arms, his eyes traveled over her. "Tell me what hurts."

She touched her knees and back, pain flaring. "Curse this body." She searched him, hands and eyes passing over what she could see. "Are you hurt? Did he cut you?"

"He didn't get the chance." Erick helped her sit up. "Can you stand?"

Rage burned through her blood as her bones rattled against her anger. But she turned her focus to Darrow, who waited by the inn door.

"What are you doing here?" she asked. "How did you know?"

"You—" Erick looked from Darrow to Neeve. "You know each other?"

"A death reading," Darrow said. "I'm with Moonblade, and we're tracking Fallon. I was with you on the boat, keeping a low profile." He regarded Neeve with curiosity. "Are you on Fallon's trail, too?"

"No, but one he seems to be after." Neeve briefly explained the curse and the woman who cast it.

"It was after my reading?" Darrow considered, shaking his head slowly. "I didn't see anyone else when I left. Unless—" A thought pulled his brows together.

"What are you thinking, friend?" Erick asked, his hand resting on Neeve's shoulder.

"I'm not sure, but something—" He winced. "I'll see what I can learn."

"Thank you, Darrow," Neeve said. "For helping us."

"I'm glad about the timing." He lifted his waterskin. "Are you both alright?"

They were, though Neeve's bones still rattled within her.

Darrow filled his waterskin and helped them to gather their supplies. "I have to meet a friend, tell them what's happened."

"We're likely to meet again," Erick said, extending his hand. "Stay safe."

Darrow shook it with a nod. "You do the same."

Darrow didn't reenter the inn as he left. Neeve and Erick stood together in palpable silence, her hands shaking as her godborn power diminished, leaving her cold and weak. She smoothed stray pieces of hair from her face, shivering.

Erick didn't hesitate as he embraced her, his hold firm as he stroked her thin hair. She pressed her face against his chest, desperate for his warmth as tears threatened to fall.

"It's going to keep happening," she said, her voice muffled as he held her. "Why am I so *powerless*?"

"We didn't know," he said. "We've been so careful. There was no way of knowing someone suspected us."

She took a step back, wiping her face with unforgiving hands. "This damned curse, and this damned body."

They turned at the sound of someone rushing out. The owner of the tavern stared, hands holding his head, his skin several shades paler. "What the bloody hell happened?"

"Wandering Order," Erick said. "He accused my mother of being a witch."

"Is she?" He shook his head. "We don't want any trouble."

"Your concern for her wellbeing is touching, you bloody coward." Erick pivoted, still holding Neeve as he aimed his wrath at a new target. "You let Wandering Order scum stay here?"

"I can't discriminate against anyone with coin."

"Your guests are at risk." Erick admonished him as one would a child. "Is this really how you do business?"

"You lot brought trouble here!"

"You allowed trouble in," Neeve said, the cadence in her voice soft. *Specific*. She didn't break eye contact with the tavern owner as she said, "The Wandering Order shouldn't stay here anymore."

The man's mouth opened and closed. "They shouldn't..."

"They put everyone at risk. Murdering people in their beds." Neeve felt Erick's stare but didn't turn away. "Everyone's already afraid. Word will spread that they're in danger if they stay here."

"No, please—"

"We're leaving," Neeve said, her voice normal. The tavern keeper stared as though awaiting her judgment. "I know you'll do your best to keep everyone else safe."

"Yes, ma'am."

Erick retrieved their waterskins, making sure Cassander's was full before leading Neeve back inside.

"Well done." His smirked flattered him, even with fatigue showing around his eyes. "Surface thoughts?"

She nodded. "He didn't need much convincing. Planting the seeds may yield fruit."

"You gorgeous, clever woman."

Going upstairs wasn't difficult with Erick's help, but she sat on her bed as soon as they entered. Erick filled Cassander in as he helped Neeve to pack.

"Just now?" Cassander stared in shock. "This early in the morning?"

"It's as though he was waiting," Neeve said with a shudder as she put her knife belt back on. "How many of them are actually here?" Then, with a cold realization, she asked, "Are they keeping watch, just like we are?"

"I wouldn't put it past them," Cassander said. "Did you learn anything from him?"

"There wasn't time, and he wouldn't have been much help." Erick mimicked the man's words, "*I would give my life for the mission.*"

"Coward," Cassander said, the word like a curse. "I'm glad you're both alright."

"Physically, yes," Neeve said. "My mind and heart could use a break, though."

"I won't let anything happen to you," Erick said. "I promised your sister I would keep you safe."

I promised your sister.

And the way he dispatched that man without hesitating.

"Erick." His words sank in. "You promised, as in—"

His look answered her.

Their voices echoed in memory:

If anything happens to her, Mal'Erick, I'm holding you personally responsible.

I will keep her safe, Gretchen of Brightmere. I swear it.

"Gods, Erick. A sacred oath?" Neeve stared in disbelief. "Your life is hers, if you fail."

"I won't fail," he said, his confidence full. "And I would owe her my life anyway, even without the oath."

"Sacred oaths are serious." Cassander looked from Neeve to Erick, something glowing in his eyes when he met Erick's gaze. But whatever his thoughts were, he didn't give them sound.

Erick's response was simple. "So is staying alive."

"You can't give yourself away like that," Neeve said, shrugging stiffly into the straps of her pack. "Erick—"

"I've given myself to you, Neeve." He rested his hands on her bowing shoulders. "Giving myself over to Gretchen's will if something happens to you is the price I will pay for failure."

"She seems kind," Cassander said. "Not the sort to exact cruelty with such a promise."

"*Exact cruelty*?" Neeve looked from one godborn to the other.

"Some can take an extreme response to a sacred oath," Cassander said. "If a godborn gets caught in one, it can be catastrophic. But Gretchen didn't strike me as the sort to handle it with malice or irresponsibility."

Neeve remembered Gretchen's flushed cheeks upon meeting Cassander. Hearing him speak of her fondly almost overshadowed the concern Neeve bore for Erick's divine promise.

Almost.

"I'm not in any danger of losing myself, Neeve," Erick reassured. "It's as Cassander said. Gretchen is kind, and I will happily give my life to her if I fail in keeping you safe."

Her simmering anger kindled anew, but this time, the flames found her as their target.

Powerless. Afraid.

No. Not on my life, and not on theirs.

"We'll keep one another safe," Neeve said, resolve in her voice. "I burned the seven hells out of that man's arm, so that has to count for something."

"It does," Cassander said with a nod of approval. "Have you practiced much with your battle magic?"

She blinked. "*Battle magic?*"

"Not so much that," Erick said, pointing to himself. "Chaosborn teacher with a lightborn student. We've gone over the basics of godblood and its power."

Cassander regarded them both before turning to Neeve. "I will gladly teach you what I can if you are amenable."

She considered, not seeing a downside. "Lightborn battle magic?"

"Lightborn battle magic."

"Then, count me in." She stood, her bones creaking. "Unless this old woman's body has anything to say about it."

The trio made sure they had everything that belonged to them before leaving the room and the tavern for good, using the light of the dawn to guide their path ahead toward the ferry. They'd survived their first night in Ileden and their first confrontation with the Wandering Order, one that ended in bloodshed.

Turning back would be easy, with the promise of home on the horizon. The promise of her home, her bed, her family...

But disappointment would haunt her if she abandoned what remained.

I will return home as the woman I was, she thought, promising herself. *In my own body, with my own time, returned.*

CHAPTER 22

Sven had failed to tell them how far the coast was from Sun Glade. Hours. *Hours.* But the constant, soothing sound of water encouraged her, even more when the ferry and its passengers were in sight.

Her legs, however, were near to staging a revolt, so learning magic from Cassander was a welcome distraction.

"Channel through your core," he said, touching his stomach as they walked. "Fighting comes from instinct. Practice helps tell your body when and where to go."

"My instinct already tells me when and where," Neeve quipped. "*Now,* and *far away.*"

Erick chuckled. "That cultist would have a different perspective on your *instinct.*"

Neeve continued to carry frustration over that encounter, when her body had failed. But her spirit had succeeded, in a sense, pushing her through the pain to fight back.

"You can manipulate any light," Cassander went on. "Or you can conjure from within, though that may leave you fatigued. Using your energy to cast siphons your strength faster."

"Energy made light." Neeve nodded slowly. "I like where this is going."

"Manipulating the existing light works similarly to manipulating shadows," Erick added. "Same concept, different medium."

"And the two serve opposing, complementary purposes," Cassander said. "The hollow cold of shadow, versus the burning purification of light."

"And one is augmented by the other," Neeve said.

Erick smirked. "Philosophical *and* useful."

"Have you tried using your magic to ease your aches and pains?" Cassander nodded toward Neeve's legs and feet. "This has been a long walk."

"It hadn't occurred to me."

Neeve suffered her foolishness for only a moment before allowing herself the satisfaction of learning. They stopped as Neeve studied her aged hands, reflexively conjuring light to make her fingers and palms glow.

"Like this." Cassander pressed his palms to his hips, then his knees. "Send the warmth directly into the areas that ache. Channel it through, and your magic will take care of the rest."

Neeve obeyed, starting with her lower back and hips, pushing warm light into her skin and muscles. Relief was almost instant, and when she gripped her knees, the tightness eased, leaving sweet relief in its wake.

"That feels wonderful," she said, standing up straighter. "Why didn't I think of that?"

"You mean before being cursed or after being attacked by a cultist?" Cassander quirked an eyebrow, his half-smile endearing. "Battle magic and healing. Your heritage is remarkable."

Remarkable. Even as she had yet to learn the fullness of her divine gifts, what she held within reassured her.

This curse will be broken, and I will embrace my strength and power.

She yawned before she could control herself, pressing a hand to her gaping mouth.

"Here." Erick produced a linen sachet and held it out to her. "Some dawn's light. It's terrible to chew, but it'll help keep you awake."

"Thank you." She accepted the pouch and removed one petal. "You thought to bring some?"

"I wasn't sure what our days would look like with sleep and rest." He shrugged a shoulder, packing the pouch after she passed it back to him. "An unexpected boon in there being three of us is that we can take turns."

Neeve grimaced as she chewed, turning the petal to dust and coating her tongue in bitterness. She took a deep breath, wincing slightly at the acrid smell of sun-drying seaweed and salt. Gulls cried overhead as a few children laughed, playing near the water as their parents walked near them, their footprints deep in the wet sand.

Neeve practiced pulling light, thrilled as the beaming sunlight came to her hands. Its heat was tolerable, though a mortal's hands would burn. "Is it the same with firelight? Or would that be harder to use?"

"Light is light," Cassander said. "And your magic can control it."

"And shadows, too," she said, "though this feels more natural."

Cassander cupped his hands, walking so that he could face Neeve, and the light coalesced into a burning ball of glowing yellow fire. He pulled his hands apart, fingers tense as they held the magic, and pulled the light this way and that, reshaping it to his will. Then, carefully, he dispelled the ball of sun-made flame.

"Practice," he encouraged. "Learn how that feels and teach your body its muscle memory."

"Class dismissed," Neeve teased, her hands already mimicking Cassander's as he walked on.

Erick tugged at Neeve's sleeve, Cassander moving ahead. He glanced back briefly before continuing forward, likely reading Erick's face and determining that a private moment was in order.

Neeve squinted as she turned her face up to him. "Is something wrong?"

"I didn't want to ask," Erick prefaced, keeping his voice down. Their steps slowed as Erick struggled and Neeve waited. "About Darrow."

"Darrow?" Confusion lasted for a few seconds before realization hit. "Erick—"

"He isn't a fool," he said, looking down at his feet as he kicked at a small stone. "And he stepped in without hesitating."

"Likely from his training with Moonblade."

"It isn't his skill as an assassin." Erick bit his bottom lip. "Gods, I don't know how to say this. I probably shouldn't have—"

He hesitated, scratching above his ear.

"What is it?" Neeve slipped her hand into his. "Tell me."

"When you read him, did he strike you as a good man?"

"Yes." She squeezed his fingers. "His father was the one I tried to save. The one who died in the tavern fight."

He blinked, not hiding his shock. "Gods, really?"

"He thanked me for trying to save his life." She paused. "He's full of a lot of regret."

"He seemed like a good man to me," Erick said. "Before, when I shook his hand, I saw what I could from him. Gleaning surface thoughts and feelings. He—" He chuckled, though the mirth didn't find his eyes, an attempt at keeping his tone light despite the weight on his heart. "He sees you the way I do."

Neeve's words caught in her throat.

"He can keep you safe."

No. *No.* "Erick—"

"I would understand," he said, interrupting her, his tone kind. "I would understand if you developed feelings for him. He would be safer than a chaosborn in a cultist's crosshairs."

Neeve tugged at his hand, forcing him to stop. He glanced at her before looking down at their feet, dragging the toe of his boot through the dirt and grass.

"Look at me," she said, reaching for his face. She hesitated, seeing her cursed age next to his youth, but he needed her confidence then. "It's my turn to reassure you, isn't it?"

He leaned into her touch, closing his eyes. "From that night at the crossroads, Neeve of Brightmere, I knew."

"Me too." She tried to smile, anticipation and worry weighing it down. "From the moment I saw you."

The muscles in his jaw feathered. "This wouldn't have happened if I—"

She pressed her fingers to his lips. "Neither of us should bear her guilt and shame. Remember?"

Please don't say goodbye. Gods, please don't say goodbye.

The word teased her, as though it remained unspoken on the breath of the wind, waiting to be brought to life.

When he opened his eyes, his gaze didn't waver as he kissed her fingertips and pressed her hand against his pounding heart.

"I don't want you to leave," she whispered, her heart fluttering. Fear had cut her open. She'd never been more exposed. "But if you—"

"I won't," he said. "Even if you care for another—"

"I don't." Her lips threatened to quiver, her heart and mind discerning the feelings swirling within, fear coursing cold through her blood at the thought of another loved one leaving.

The way her parents had left her.

The way she had left Gretchen.

He lifted her face, earnestness in his eyes. "I'm not going anywhere, Neeve of Brightmere. Do you trust me?"

"I do." Her eyes itched, but the tears didn't fall. "I can't be myself with anyone else. Before, when the fight was over, the way you held me—"

He kissed her forehead, her breath catching at the pressure of his lips against her skin.

"I couldn't let my guard down while he was there. But you—" Her earnestness reached him, warmth coursing through her. "It's you, Mal'-Erick. It's *you.*"

He embraced her, heaving a sigh against her throat and shoulder as she wrapped her arms around his neck.

"You honor me, Neeve of Brightmere." His cool breath was steady against her skin. "Thank you. I—" He chuckled, the sound making her heart flutter. "I didn't expect this."

She held him tighter. "No one does."

For a moment, she heard her own voice say the words, her youth coming through as she laid her heart bare. But when the pair parted to continue, it was Godmother Neeve who walked beside Erick.

"I meant what I said." He took her hand, his grip firm. "I'm not going anywhere."

Her racing heart eased toward calm. "I'm worried about Gretchen, about leaving her alone, our parents gods-know-where..."

She stopped, hearing the bitterness in her voice. "I left her, just like they did."

"This is different," he said. "Are your parents trying to break a curse that ages them?" After a pause, he continued. "She's safe. She and Samson have each other. And we'll return home soon. I swear it."

Home. And he'd included himself. Home *with her.*

Now, more than ever, Neeve would see this curse broken. No one would rob her of the future she wished to see, one with a chaosborn with wine colored eyes and a mischievous grin.

***

THE FERRY WAS FURTHER down the beach, bobbing in the water with the steady movement of the sea. It was peaceful, a stark contrast to the boisterous activity of the tavern the day before.

"I used to want to live by the sea," Neeve said, weaving a band of light around her aged fingers. Its thickness rivaled a gold chain necklace, but the spell carried as Neeve twisted it this way and that. "I went with my parents when I was a little girl, and it was such a magical place."

"Too much sunlight for me," Erick said, shielding his eyes with a hand as he looked ahead. "But the sound of the water is soothing."

It was. Neeve imagined standing in the sand, the cold water sweeping over her feet and ankles as she slowly sank. Serenity and peace, and the act of letting go.

"I find peace in the mountains," Cassander said. "The quiet wind bringing the cold from the peaks, the crunch of snow beneath your boots." He nodded slowly. "That's my idea of heaven."

"It sounds nice," Neeve said. "But lonely."

Cassander didn't add to that, though his expression was jovial and upbeat. But *lonely* was all about perspective.

Neeve twisted her band of light to resemble the symbol of infinity before folding the band in on itself again and again. Soon, a ball of sunlight floated above her palm.

"Quick study," Erick said, impressed. "Now, imagine hurling that into Fallon's face."

"Better to hurl a string of them." Which gave Neeve the idea to separate the glowing orb into smaller ones. "Flaming missiles of sunlight."

Erick chuckled. "I love how your beautiful mind works."

They moved down the sand, booted feet sinking into the soft, wet ground. A family with two children walked further up the shore. One child squealed as she ran from the coming water. Neeve exhaled through a pang of homesickness, her heart reaching for the family she loved. Their touch had deeply rooted in her heart, and that knowledge fortified the areas where her strength waned.

That was love. Love accepted the weakest parts and strengthened them. Love treasured every peak and valley, filling the holes within so that nothing remained empty.

Neeve held onto the warmth as long as she could before guilt could sneak its way in, reminding her of Gretchen's solitude, her memories reliving the last time her parents had left.

But I'm not them, she reminded herself. *I'm going to save what remains of my life and return to my sister.*

"Looks full," Cassander said, his voice breaking through Neeve's reverie. "I hope there's room for us."

The ferry was a wide, almost flat vessel with enough seats for eight or ten. There were a pair of oars and no sign of a sail.

Slow-moving. *Leisurely.* They had time for neither.

Neeve took a fortifying breath, praying for patience as she counted those she could see. "Let's hurry, then."

Erick squinted as he shielded his eyes. "How long before the next one?"

"Hours?" Cassander shrugged with his guess. "Especially if he has them fishing."

They walked with more determined steps.

"I hope that family hasn't already paid fare," Neeve said.

"You share my thoughts." Erick was pleased. "How very determined of you."

"Hello!" The man holding a coiled rope waved to them. Turning to a passenger, he said, "What a busy morning it turned out to be."

"Is there room for three?" Cassander asked. "We're going to the Midlands."

"There's plenty of room," the man said, surveying the group until his eyes stopped on Neeve. "And we have a seat for you, young lady."

She politely accepted his compliment of *young lady*. "Thank you."

He extended his hand to each of them, introducing himself, "I'm Edgar, and this is River Spirit." He patted the prow with pride. "River will take us wherever we want to go."

They passed greetings and introductions, and Edgar turned to Erick and Cassander. "Have either of you fished before?"

"Yes," they both said. Cassander added, "Though, not a lot."

"Well, at the very least, you can help me sort the catches."

Neeve realized, then, what he'd meant about her having a seat. "I can fish too," she blurted. "Quite well."

"Very good. I didn't want you to feel obligated, especially with your sons here to help."

Edgar's quick assumption into their relationship made the facade easier to maintain. Neeve settled in to her role and amended, "Thank you. They're my grandsons. And I'll be happy to fish from my seat."

Edgar beamed, amused. "That's my girl. Right this way."

Erick moved beside her, shaking his head with a grin. "Milk it while you can, *Gran*."

She grinned, green eyes alight with mischief. "People are a lot nicer when you're old."

Neeve climbed aboard with help, the ten-passenger boat at capacity. One family sat their child between them, and Erick and Cassander assumed the same arrangement with her.

"It'll be hard to fish from here," Neeve said.

"Your line will reach just fine," Erick said, bumping her with his shoulder. "We wouldn't you want you to go flying off the edge, would we, Gran?"

"Setting off!" Edgar untied River Spirit from the dock and pushed off, two passengers manning the oars to move the boat forward.

A working ferry. Cheap fare, which Neeve paid, and the obligation to work for the rest. It wasn't a poor arrangement at all. Rather, Neeve remembered her girlhood a bit more clearly as she lined the bait on a hook and tossed it into the water.

Edgar began singing a common folk song, which a few passengers took up. The ferry was large enough for the eight passengers, plus the captain. But Neeve wasn't sure *captain* was the right word. He was more friendly and down to earth than Shea had been on their way to Ileden. But ship captains had to be stern. There was very little room for error when dozens of lives depended on strong leadership, especially out on the open water. Perhaps being a ferry driver afforded a bit more laxity, more room for enjoyment.

He certainly seemed happy enough, taking people back and forth while they fished for their fare. It wasn't a bad life at all, as Neeve watched him speak kindly with the passengers and laugh in good humor.

"To not have a care in the world," Neeve whispered aloud to herself. "What is that like?"

"We all have cares," Erick whispered. "It's the spirit that helps the person carry them."

"He just seems so happy," Neeve said. "And you shouldn't eavesdrop."

"I didn't mean to eavesdrop, but you don't mumble as quietly as you think."

"It was a *whisper*," she said, her glare playful, "not a *mumble*."

"Your whispers *are* mumbles, Gran," he teased. After a moment, he added, "Edgar's happiness is something he's given to himself. We all have that kind of power within us, too."

Each passenger received a rod and bait. Cassander's grip betrayed his inexperience, though he was brave enough to try. Neeve offered a few small suggestions to get him started.

"Thanks," he said. "I admit I'm embarrassed."

"Don't be." Neeve corrected his grip and patted his hand. "We all start somewhere."

"What brings you all to the Midlands?" Edgar asked, using the steering stick to help guide the rowers. He steadied a large bucket by his legs where their catches would go.

A few passengers answered first—some traveling west to see family, some looking for work further north. There was a moment's pause as the trio tried to collectively build a lie. When Neeve spoke up, Erick did, too, but he stopped, gesturing for her to proceed. *Of course.*

"We're looking for something." With no silver laces in sight, Neeve took a chance, reshaping the truth to avoid suspicious confrontation against a deathseer. "I had a dream about it."

This was a region rich with goddess worship. Would Neeve, acting on a dream, raise alarms among them?

"Oh." A man nodded to her, interested. "Dreams can be very significant."

Neeve perked up, casting her line and waiting for a bite. "Are any of you familiar with Brockdon Fields?"

"I am," another passenger said, a young woman maybe in her mid- to late-twenties. "I grew up there, though it's been a few years since I've been back."

"In the dream," Neeve said, speaking carefully. She could feel Erick and Cassander's eyes on her despite their work. "There was a statue of a woman surrounded by trees."

"Erys?" another passenger asked. "Her statues are everywhere in Ileden."

"But one in a forest?" The woman pursed her lips, thinking. "And you're thinking Brockdon Fields?"

"We're very sure," Erick said.

"Then it would have to be the twin statutes," the young woman said, looking from Neeve to Erick and lingering on Cassander. "Erys and Rhiann, together."

"You've seen it?" Excited, Neeve passed Erick her rod and rifled through her pack until she found the map. "Could you mark it for me?"

"I'll try."

The woman took the rolled parchment and readied her own pencil from the pack at her feet. She traced her finger over the terrain markings, going up from the coast into the lower central area of Brockdon Fields. "About here, I think?" She drew a light dot on the map before passing the artifact back to Neeve. "Erys faces the mountains while Rhiann faces the fields where farmers grow their crops."

"Symbolic," Cassander said. "Are all Erys statues joined with Rhiann?"

"No," she said. "Actually, this is the only one I know of. There aren't many sites with two goddesses together, even the sisters."

"The bond between sisters is strong," another passenger said. "Their worshippers will pay homage to both."

Neeve returned the map to her pack, encouraged, her hope clinging to a solid, tangible lead. She retrieved her fishing rod from Erick and allowed the anticipation to settle in, eager for their next step.

"That symbol on the map," Erick said, his voice low in her ear. "What do you know about it?"

"The claw and feather?" At this, Neeve smiled. "My mother is the wolf, my father the raven. They sign all of their maps that way."

"All of their maps?"

"They make a new map everywhere they travel and update this one. They love to track history and chart its paths."

Neeve caressed the edge of the map, wondering where her parents were in that moment, as Neeve traveled so far from home to save her life.

A curse has taken me, but you don't know. She breathed against the bitterness that stung her heart. *Why do you always leave?*

"Those statues will be a sight to behold," the woman said, her expression nostalgic. "Beautiful craftsmanship. Whoever sculpted them worshipped with every stroke of his hammer."

"Have you been before?" Neeve asked. "Is there anything I should look out for?"

"I was there when I was small," she said. "My parents brought me after the sun had set. The fireflies were out, and I knew that the world was made with magic." She hooked a finger beneath her collar, showing the leather cord bearing a wooden disc with carved spirals in the token. "I've been with Rhiann ever since."

Neeve had claimed Aishlin before learning of her lightborn blood. Erick's reassurance had been a comfort. Light and chaos working together meant she didn't have to abandon one for the other.

"I'm sure the magic is still there," Neeve said, readying her line. "I'm looking forward to finding it."

The journey remained pleasant as they fished, but Cassander fumbled, the rod nearly sailing from his hands with his first catch.

Edgar gently took the rod away. "Sorting the catch." He pat Cassander on the back. "That's much safer."

Neeve bumped Erick's shoulder, the calm joy of the moment

helping her to relax. "You seem quite comfortable out on the water like this."

"It's not uncomfortable. The day is nice, as is the company."

She raised an eyebrow, saying nothing, throwing her hook farther into the water as the ferry slowly moved down the coast. They worked like this for hours, the passage slow as the fish came fast.

"Good bait," the ferry master said, nodding sagely. "You're wasting your time, otherwise."

But Neeve could feel the tide turning, and it wasn't merely the bait's doing. There were good people in the world, *honest* people, who were eager to help and find joy in the very air they breathed. It reminded her of her family. Of Erick. Of Cassander and this new friendship. Comfort ran deep as she cast her line, but her mind disrupted what peace was there as she remembered Cassander's reading.

Had any choice diverted that path? Did killing the cultist at the tavern shift any weight on death's scales? Or were they following the line down to where Cassander would meet his end?

Neeve turned her face away, hiding the concern that pulled at the corners of her eyes and mouth.

Please, she prayed. *Make me strong enough. He can be saved. I know it.*

Please.

CHAPTER 23

The ferry docked when it was near to sundown, the collected fish secured and ready for trading. Neeve draped her shawl over her hair to prepare for the change, hiding as much of herself as she could. Her ferry companions had been amiable and helpful, but how far would that kindness go if they learned of her curse?

Erick stayed close, tracking the minutes as she did.

"You have kept my family fed," Edgar said, "and I am grateful to you all. Please, take one of your catches with you as my gift of thanks. There's more than enough."

They did. Edgar gifted Cassander a fish outright for his sorting work and said, "May you all travel well. There's a village nearby with a small tavern. I pray they have rooms for you."

"Thank you for your kindness," Neeve said, inching away. "All of you."

The change took her. She brought her hands up to her shawl to mask her face, but it was done.

"Gracious day," one of them said. "You're—"

"Cursed," Erick said for them, his body angling to shield her from them. "We're on a journey to break it."

"Not a grandmother then," Edgar said.

"A friend." Cassander eyed their faces. "A good and trusted friend."

The woman from before, a worshiper of Rhiann, approached Neeve with sympathy, resting her hands on her arms. "May you find what you're looking for. And may you be safe."

"There are Wandering Order idiots everywhere," someone else said, a man nearly as old as the ferry master. "Be on your guard."

Neeve bowed her head in gratitude, dropping her hands so that her face was visible.

"We'll be as careful as we can," Cassander said. "Thank you all for everything."

Carrying their fish, the trio followed the path toward glowing fires in the distance. No one was outside, save for two men outside of a large house with lanterns hanging by the front door, watching the passengers disembark and enter their village.

"Is that the inn?" Erick stared. "It's so—*small*."

"Let's hope there's room," Cassander said. "We may have to share with the horses."

"I'd rather sleep under the stars." Erick brushed his hand against hers, whispering, "Much more romantic, wouldn't you say?"

"Too exposed," Cassander said, oblivious. "A barn or a stall is better than nothing."

"Manure notwithstanding."

Neeve stifled a laugh, following Cassander as he lead them inside.

It was, in fact, the inn Edgar had mentioned, and when the innkeeper spotted them and their fish, she knew where they'd come from.

"We'll happily cook that up for you," she said. "Ale? Roasted potatoes?"

"Sounds like a dream come true," Cassander said.

After passing Cassander some coin, Erick led Neeve to a table while Cassander once again finagled room and board.

"How are you feeling?" Erick studied her as she removed the shawl from her head and returned it to her shoulders. Her striking hair cascaded over her shoulders.

"All right, I suppose." She narrowed her eyes, reading his expression as a curious one. "Why?"

He hesitated before he answered, gesturing at his hair as he stared at hers. "Um—"

She pressed her hand to her crown, matching the spot where he'd shown her. "What's wrong? What is it?"

"It's white," he said. "Like a stroke of paint in your hair."

Neeve's hair was already pale, but it had never been truly *white*. She turned, frantically looking for any reflective surface until she focused on her reflection in a nearby window. She struggled to see the true color difference in the dark, clear glass until Erick's hand came from behind, his fingers combing through the lock of white.

"How could you even see that?" She traced where his fingers had been, the texture unchanged.

"It's more noticeable than the window's reflection," he said, his voice low. "And, at the risk of sounding unsettling, your hair is enchanting. I admire it every time I'm with you."

Within minutes of their meeting at the crossroads, Erick had been drawn to her hair. She remembered his fingers, gentle with her curls.

An eyebrow rose, levity and flattery soothing some of her anger. "You stare at my hair?"

"*Admire.*" But her amusement didn't reach him. Concern furrowed his brow. "The curse is stronger, dear one."

Neeve watched Cassander approach from behind, thanks to the reflection. "What's wrong—*oh*."

Neeve turned, looking from Erick to Cassander before going back to their table. The server dropped off three tankards of ale, and Neeve immediately dove into hers, taking three deep gulps.

THEY FOLLOWED the same routine as before, taking turns to keep watch as they bunked in a single room. Luckily, though the inn was small, they secured a room with two beds.

"I'll take first watch," Neeve said. "I'm too angry to sleep."

"Spend this time wisely," Erick said, stretching out the bed nearest Neeve as she sat in the cushioned chair with their books in her hands.

"Plot her demise in the best possible way. A beautiful blend of light and chaos. Turn it into poetry."

"Gracious day," Cassander said, moving to the other bed. "I would suggest reading more than plotting your revenge."

"I can do both," was Neeve's answer.

Erick chuckled as he closed his eyes.

Neeve knew that reading couldn't be distraction enough. The curse had taken hold of her, doing more than changing her body. It stole from her, taking her life with no way for her to fight back.

If only the woman had used straightforward dark magic rather than this underhanded cruelty set on a delay.

I'm not powerless. Neeve mouthed the words to herself like a mantra, letting the light glow around her fingers. She missed her shadows, but the light burned in a way that satisfied her.

Mindlessly, her power manifesting, she conjured Titus, his form created in radiance instead of darkness. She stared, awestruck, as he stared back, silent, his burning eyes bearing into hers.

She dispelled him, the room falling to near darkness in his absence, and she stared at her hands, the lines of golden line dim but still visible.

A beautiful blend of light and chaos.

She pulled at the shadows, using the candlelight to fuel a test of power as her light magic entwined with chaos. Titus took shape, his raven's feathers made of shadows lined with gold.

"Amazing," she whispered, stroking a finger along his illuminated, smoky body, touching a stimulating blend of cool mist and dry warmth. "If only you could haunt that woman's nightmares. Or, better still, frighten her while she's awake."

The idea took shape as she studied the bird, its blended form patient, its smoke-filled eyes focusing with a golden iris as it watched.

"Go to her," she whispered. "Show me what you see."

She sent her magic through Titus, who flew from the room through the thin crack in the windowpane. He flew strong over the village, over trees and a field of grass and wildflowers glittering in the moonlight.

Yes. Show her. Neeve ignored the pooling fatigue weighing on her limbs. *Show her the power I possess.*

Titus flew hard and fast, the scenery passing quickly until he descended, eyes spotting a dilapidated shack densely surrounded by trees and brush.

A loud snore frightened her, jolting her body to consciousness, her scrying spell fizzling.

She opened her mouth but shut it quickly, the string of foul words remaining behind the white line of her lips. But Titus had shown her the shack. She was closer.

She leaned back in her seat, the use of magic spreading tiredness through her bones, but the rush of success left her satisfied. At the very least, it was something.

In *Spells and Curses of Order and Chaos,* she stared at the same incantation for a long time, her eyes unfocused and her thoughts racing. How much longer did she have before she wouldn't change back? Days? Weeks?

How much longer did she have to live?

Would she make it to the statue? To the dilapidated hovel in the woods? Would she last long enough to find her and have the curse broken?

Neeve stroked the hair made pale by the curse, stewing in her rage. What could she do in retribution? What fate could she give that carried poetry in its justice?

"Make her live her youth again?" She pondered the idea, remembering what Cassander had said. "Have her age younger and younger..."

It would be a blessing at first, feeling the strength and beauty of youth, until it didn't stop. Until *she* was helpless...

Neeve blindly turned the page. No wonder Fallon had pursued this woman. Silver laces and cold eyes, with hands like claws.

All because of one who'd let fear consume her.

"What makes you think you should have that kind of power?" Neeve whispered to the dark.

But the words rebounded back to Neeve, as though her own consciousness demanded the answer from her.

Why should you have this power when you let your fear drive your will?

She shut her eyes and clenched her hands, forcing the blooming anxiety to shrink. *I've saved lives. I've helped people. And I will break this curse.*

Abandoning her spell book for Erick's novel, it took Neeve hours to finish the chapter, the words slow to reach her very full, very chaotic mind. She woke Cassander first, remembering Erick's trouble the previous night. She was glad to see him finally resting, his sleep calm and superficially uneventful.

She stretched out on the bed and closed her eyes.

The curse.

The woman from the ferry, her eyes kind.

Book pages.

Sun-dried seaweed.

Burning frustration turned her insides to embers.

CHAPTER 24

Breakfast came later than they would have liked, but Erick was slow to call Neeve from her sleep.

"You looked like you were fighting someone," he said as she sat up. "Or some*thing*. Then, everything went calm. I didn't want to wake you when you finally seemed to rest."

Neeve didn't recall a dream, the lack of memory likely a blessing. She was grateful for the renewed energy, but time was irreplaceable.

"Thank you," she said, standing up with a groan as her back and hips resisted motion. "Is it just me, or am I getting older?"

She'd said it as a bit of a joke, something in passing, but there was weight to the question, as evidenced by the awkward silence in the room.

"This curse won't be the end of me," she said to them both, her determination either shadowed or emphasized by her aged voice and arthritic finger as it pointed at them. She couldn't tell which.

"It's good you rested up," Cassander said. "It's a couple of hours north of here. We'll have our work cut out for us. Unless we want to rent a pair of horses?"

"We've spent enough money." Neeve waved a hand, finalizing the thought. "We walk."

Erick snickered. "You haven't sounded more like a grandmother until this moment."

"You should respect your elders, young man," she said, grinning.

But their mirth wasn't enough to counter the weight of wondering. What if all this yielded nothing? It wasn't only her life that hung in an invisible balance. It was Erick and Cassander's lives. Gretchen's and Samson's. Her parents'.

What if Neeve made the wrong choice, and their world came crashing down?

"You're up to something," Erick murmured, leaning close to her ear. "What are thinking about?"

"The future, funnily enough." She took his arm to steady her, and he rested his hand on hers.

"It's this way," Cassander said as they stepped out of the inn, gesturing to the right. "There should be a footpath or a road most of the way. The last bit will be through the woods, though."

"I didn't sign up for a hike," Erick said, looking at Neeve. "Are you alright to make it?"

"I'd better be," she said, determined. "Because I'm going."

Neeve moved forward with her uneven gait, using the forward momentum as the distraction she needed from the doubt swimming around inside her mind. The morning breeze was cool, matching the internal frost from her fear, and she shivered, pulling her shawl tighter.

The humble beauty of the Midlands brightened with golden sunlight across the petals and leaves of wildflowers, complimenting the shimmer of tall wheat ready for harvest. Several farmers were already midst their workday, tending their crops with practiced rhythm.

The world is such a beautiful place.

She strove to fill her worried mind with beauty instead of fear, studying the shape of the clouds and the vibrant colors of the wild-flowers at her feet. Life was everywhere, and she was a part of this wild and glorious thing.

"What the world must look like to the bee that sits on the flower," Neeve said, "or the bird that flies above it."

"I'd always wanted to be a bird," Cassander said. "Ever since I was a boy." He looked up, squinting. "The freedom of flying, of seeing the world and traveling wherever you wished. That sounds like heaven to me."

"It was wolves for me," Erick said, walking with his hands in his pockets. "I'd always envied the devoted earthwitches blessed with shifting to wolfkind."

"Why wolves?" Neeve asked.

"Loyalty and unity," he said. "Compassion and ferocity."

Neeve knew so little of Erick's personal life, save for the brief memory of the woman walking away. She'd never asked him, but he knew so much about her—her family, her desires, her fears.

She looked up at him, apology in her eyes, understanding a bit more about the young man who walked beside her and why he was there. Loyalty. Unity. Compassion. Ferocity. He was all of those things, evidenced by this journey and by all the small things he'd done before.

She cast her eyes to the ground as they misted, blinking away the emotion that itched to be free.

"What about you, Neeve?" Erick asked. "What animal would you be?"

"I'm not sure," she said. "You both have strong arguments for birds and wolves."

"There are snakes," Erick teased with a grin. "Frogs, *newts*."

She pushed his arm before shuddering. "No."

"*Spiders*," Cassander added.

"That's enough." Neeve closed her eyes, scrunching her nose as her wince turned to laughter.

CHAPTER 25

The Midlands was a stretch of hills undulating like waves at sea, and each incline worked Neeve's muscles to their limits. Her legs burned, the downhill descent a thrilling relief, only to repeat the process over again.

But when they crested one large hill, Neeve holding Erick's arm for support, she gasped at the dazzling scene of sunlight glistening off of tall grass and wildflowers. In the expansive horizon, the dark blue silhouettes of mountains reached beyond the line of land ahead.

Brockdon Fields.

Every inch of Neeve's body endured every inch that she'd walked, but this moment of triumph made every step worth it. If only it would linger, reminding her how she'd overcame her body to see this through.

You thought this curse would defeat me, she thought, picturing the woman who'd left her to the consequences of fear. She still had steps to go, but she was proud of what she'd done. *I'm stronger than this. I'm stronger than* you.

"If we're on track," Cassander said, pointing toward their left at a copse of trees. "It should be there."

Neeve took out her map, trying to imagine the terrain from above to match the illustrations of the land they were on. She pointed a finger and tracing it up to the mark on her map. "It shouldn't be much longer now."

"Let's keep going," Erick said. "We can rest once we're in the trees."

Neeve agreed, though her body didn't. She pushed forward, listening to the birds calling from the small forest ahead, flying above the boughs before fluttering down to the branches below. Then a group of them fluttered up and away, chirping as they went.

Bright green grass augmented the rainbow of wildflowers at their feet. Neeve held her skirts, trying to step high and carefully to avoid any hidden holes or critters underfoot. Erick took her arm to steady her.

"Thank you," she said. "I'm alright."

"I know."

He didn't let go.

Rather than resist, she shifted to take hold of his arm, hand resting on his bicep, walking close to him.

He leaned to her, lowering his voice, the deep timbre pleasing to her ear. "Do you know what comes next?"

"No clue. I'm hoping something shows itself there. A path, a token, *something.*"

His expression remained neutral, but she could guess at his pessimistic thoughts. There wouldn't be anything to lead them to the next step. They would have to rely on a complete guess, much as they have been all along. Only, with their feet taking them through the unfamiliar, with their trip so close to a destination they'd carved for themselves, a wrong guess would be perhaps more devastating now than before.

"The history of the statue?" she asked, holding a thin thread of hope. "Maybe our magic can see something?"

"It's worth trying."

He brought his other hand to hers, holding her fingers against the curve of his arm. When they moved into the trees, she relied on him more as the uneven ground met her feet. Cassander moved ahead several paces before stopping to point.

"I think I see it," he said, glancing back at Erick and Neeve.

Carefully, Neeve navigated the trees with Erick until she finally glimpsed the blue-gray stone through the green branches of the pines. She stepped faster, eagerness rekindling her spirit, and saw her at last.

The face was just as she'd seen it in the vision, the calm and focused expression of Erys, goddess of the storm. Maybe it was the craftsmanship of the stonework or the reputation of the goddess herself, but Neeve would swear there was power in her stony gaze as it looked to the sky.

"Seeing it in person," Cassander said, eyes cast upward. "No wonder this site is revered as holy."

Revered by the woman, too, as Neeve remembered flashes of her death reading. Interesting for a chaoswitch to have shared devotion to the goddess of storms.

Releasing Erick's arm, Neeve moved to the side dedicated to Rhiann. The stone carver had elected to give them two forms in the same structure, as though the backs of their clothes were touching, with Erys's leather studded armor against Rhiann's long hooded cloak. The goddess of earth stood with her hood up while still showing her hair and face. And where Erys's gaze was heavenward, Rhiann's was down to watch life sprout from the earth at her feet.

"Such a waste of art," came a sneering voice from behind her. "Yet another skilled artist, squandered on foolishness."

Fallon, his blue-steel gaze locked onto her, with two other men at his side.

"Using obvious talent for such a useless endeavor." He looked at the statues in disgust. "No gods exist, and none will hear your prayers."

"You speak with ignorance," Cassander said, already drawing his sword. "Watch your tongue when you stand on holy ground."

Neeve, pulling her mother's knife, was overwhelmingly underprepared in a bladed melee. But she had her light and shadow, her magic tingling in her palms and fingers.

"We'll see how holy it is when your blood is shed upon it," said one man behind Fallon, moving with another to face Cassander and Erick. Their formation showed training...and planning.

This left Neeve with Fallon. He and the others drew their weapons,

Fallon's a pair of long daggers, while the others had short swords. A long, black holster hung from Fallon's belt, untouched, the silver clip glistening as it waited to be undone.

"Hello, little witch," he crooned, his eyes locked onto hers.

She swiped as a warning, feeling foolish as he jumped back with a chuckle.

"That's some curse on you," he said. "Do you feel it? The weight of years upon you?"

She sneered, hands trembling, palms itching with burning magic waiting to erupt.

"This can be done easily," he said. "No pain. No bloodshed. Just let me take what I want, and your friends will be unharmed."

Her palm burned, light erupting from her fingers. One hand strangled the knife handle as the other held minuscule suns aloft. Fallon stared, wonder smoothing the smugness from his face.

She sent each of them sailing, two searing Fallon's arm and thigh as he moved to dodge the others. The fabric of his clothes burned away, showing the angry red lines of burned skin.

"Fire magic?" he guessed, his grimace shifting to vicious loathing. "And here I pegged you for chaos."

It was Neeve's turn to appear smug, not bothering to correct him. *Let him rest in ignorance.*

Cassander's attacker rushed him as Fallon rushed Neeve, but Erick met his attack, gripping the cultist's wrist. Fallon cried out, his fingers loosening their hold on the dagger until it fell from his grip. Neeve moved to strike, aiming her knife for his side, but he pivoted on the balls of his feet, pulling away from Erick, who picked up Fallon's dropped blade to use against him.

"Get out of here, Neeve," Erick said, burgundy eyes alight with rage as he glowered at the cultists.

"No!"

A woman's voice, one Neeve would know even in sleep. Her blood ran cold.

"No! Stop this!"

The world slowed. When Neeve saw the shapes of her parents

running, bloodied with their hands bound, they were both familiar and foreign. She knew them by their faces, but this place, the danger around them...how were they here? *Why?*

Robert and Kaeli of Brightmere, tortured and beaten, held captive in Ileden, miles away from home.

Fallon and his men. Silver laces. Hands like claws.

A cultist rushed toward her, hands ready to grab her. She reacted without thought, the knife going into the man's gut. Shadows danced around her skin as she pushed harder, hearing him groan as blood oozed slowly. The wound might not prove fatal, but it hurt like each of the seven hells, and as Neeve yanked her weapon free, she kicked him to the ground to yelp in agony. He held his middle with one hand as the other tried to push himself back up.

But the use of magic cost her. What fatigue she had fought had increased tenfold. She found it difficult to catch her breath. Cassander's opponent managed a block that sent him staggering back. The man used the momentum of his first strike to lead into a second, but this time, he aimed for Neeve, swiping his sword toward her upper arm and cutting through fabric and flesh. The pain seared white-hot before simmering.

"Get back!" Erick shouted, facing two opponents as Cassander returned to his. "Run, Neeve!"

But she wouldn't. Living with leaving them behind was a fate worse than death.

"Neeve?" Her father's questioning look filled with horror.

As Erick struck their unnamed foe, their blades scraping as they tried to push and dominate, Neeve brought her bloody knife to the rope around her father's wrists.

"There's no time to explain," Neeve said quickly, sawing through the rope for her father, then her mother.

"Is that mine?" Kaeli narrowed her eyes at the knife in Neeve's hands.

"Had a feeling I'd need it." Neeve pulled the rope free from her mother's wrists.

More shouts came from the trees, thundering footsteps joining the entrance of half a dozen men and women dressed in black clothes with dark leather armor. Among them was Darrow, gray eyes narrowed at a cultist in murderous ferocity.

"That would be the bastards who caused all this," her mother swore. "Moonblade."

"What?"

"Let's get you somewhere safe," her father said, taking her by the shoulders. "When there's time, you're going to tell us everything."

Moonblade assassins faced the cultists with Erick and Cassander. Darrow spotted Erick, then Neeve.

Fallon prowled toward Neeve and her parents, stalking his prey. He readied his knife as his thumb went to the holster on his leg.

"When will there be time?" Fallon chuckled, piercing blue eyes moving from Robert to Kaeli to Neeve. "Oh, my. I think I can see the resemblance." There was cruelty in his laugh. "A little family reunion?"

Neeve rushed him, swiping with the knife as her other hand reached for his arm. They fell together, the shift in gravity jarring them both.

"Neeve!" her father cried.

Neeve held Fallon as hard as her old hands could manage, pulsing light magic through his skin, keeping him away from Cassander. He howled in agony, and she didn't relent, fueled by his screaming.

Sink deep, Anya, she prayed, channeling her fury. *Burn away his darkness.*

With eye contact came the gateway to his mind, reaching to the far corners to strike whatever vulnerability lay exposed.

"What are you most afraid of?" she whispered, pushing magic in to her voice. Surface thoughts, his mind betraying him.

He grunted through clenched teeth, fighting in vain as her magic met his body and his mind. His surface thoughts rendered the agonies given to others, fueled by hate and cruel victory, making it easy for Neeve to reverse the very same onto him. Fallon's screams echoed off of the boughs of every tree, vocalizing both pain and fear. Fueled by rage and encouraged by his suffering, Neeve pushed harder. Until—

"Cassander!" Erick, his voice full of panic.

Neeve shoved away from Fallon and scrambled to her feet, eyes locking onto Cassander's body on the forest floor. Blood pooled around him, staining the blades of grass and petals of wildflowers.

It had been here all along, not by Fallon's hand but by some name-less cultist. Stone and grass and tree, the vision came together as though a puzzle piece long-lost had finally been found. Only, the wildflowers...

His death flashed behind her eyes as she crawled toward him, recon-ciling what her eyes could see from what her mind remembered. This wasn't right. His body hadn't been among wildflowers, beauty framing the horror of his injury.

Fallon's hand grip her legs and skirts as she crawled, pulling her back as deadly rage distorted his hawk-like features. But a blade arched down, cutting into the flesh of Fallon's arm to the bone. Darrow's lethal gaze bore into the cultist with all the power of the seven hells.

"Curse you, assassin! Mercenary!"

Fallon tried to retaliate with his dagger as Robert kicked him in the chin, sending him arching back. Kaeli pulled at Neeve's arm to help get her beyond Fallon's reach.

Erick's cry pulsed chaos toward the foes that remained, not discrimi-nating the Order from Moonblade. Cassander's enemy, still on his feet, soared backward, landing hard against the trunk of a tree. Broken cracked as he crumbled to the ground, motionless.

Neeve crawled for Cassander, her hips and knees aching, her hands burning as she turned him over.

Voices cried out as the skirmish intensified, more cultists appearing seemingly out of nowhere. Darrow growled through the pain of a sword slicing his arm, but he didn't relent as he faced his attacker. Four Moon-blade remained, weapons poised and eyes wide as they watched the three standing cultists. The three gathered with Darrow, standing back-to-back in case more enemies surface.

"My, my." Fallon spat blood as one injured cultist helped him to his feet. His piercing eyes locked onto Erick. "A *godborn*."

Erick panted, arms out and fists strangling the handles of his bloody knifes. His body had changed, eyes black and skin shimmering a blue-gray. A swath of shadows hovered around his form like a distortion of light limning him in darkness instead.

"Chaos?" Fallon asked with a chuckle, he and his ilk slowly moving backward toward the trees. "This must be my lucky day."

"I will take joy in killing you," Erick said, his voice deeper, the rumble from the depths of the hells. "I will take my time to relish every second."

"Your friends will be dead long before then," one cultist said, his fear far stronger than his attempt at bravado.

"Friends?" Fallon looked at Neeve and Cassander with a mocking laugh. "Chaosborn don't have friends. They have *opportunities*."

"Shut your filthy mouth, hypocrite," Neeve snapped. "You are a waste of human flesh."

"Calling him human is generous," Darrow remarked, gray eyes keen.

"I don't spend my time worshipping someone's imagination," he said, sneering at her and Erick. "But magic is a plague upon this earth. It is undeniable, and denying it will ruin humanity as we know it."

"The only ruin in humanity is you," Kaeli said, her voice as rage-filled as Neeve's. "Soulless cretin."

"We are it's saving grace," Fallon said. "We will put things right."

Erick, growling, swiped his knife hand toward Fallon as though to strike him, but a wave of magic cut through the air, shadows like blades, colliding with Fallon's chest and sending him back, knocking him off his feet.

The other cultists ran, disappearing in the trees.

Moonblade pursued the fleeing enemies as Erick stalked toward his prostrate prey, but Fallon scrambled back, clamoring to his feet before breaking into a run, following the others. Erick didn't relent, his body moving with unholy speed.

Cassander shuddered a breath. Neeve was careful as she held him, wiping grass and blood from his face. The cut across his chest was deep.

"Village—" He tried to point left, wincing. "Healer—"

"We'll go," Neeve said quickly. "We'll get help." Though Neeve didn't know how they would get him there.

"Gods above," Kaeli said, kneeling at his other side. "This will take more than what a village healer can do. Unless they're godborn."

"Wait." He pressed a hand to his bloody chest. "Need magic—"

"Take it." Neeve didn't hesitate to take his hand, blood making her grip slippery. "Tell me what to do."

"Erick—"

"He's after Fallon," she said. "Tell me what to do."

"Too strong." He gasped, coughing, more blood wicking through his clothes.

"I can do it."

"No, Neeve." Robert rested a hand on her shoulder. "He's right. The magic's too strong. We're not full godborn."

We. But she couldn't look at her father, not with Cassander's shallow breathing. Tears stung as she watched him fade.

Death had prevailed. Inevitable. Unavoidable. No measure had prevented it, coming upon her without warning.

No, there was a warning. Fallon had been their warning. The cultist at the inn had been a warning. Neeve should have known better, her guard stronger, her attention keener.

Cassander would die in her arms, and it would be her fault.

Erick and the Moonblade members returned, panting.

"He's gone," Erick said. "Slithery bastard."

"Erick!" Neeve looked up at him, panicked, her aged voice high and piercing. "He needs magic but won't take mine. I don't know what to do."

Erick didn't waste a second, falling to his knees beside Neeve and pressing his hand to the wound over Cassander's heart. "Take it." His darkness slowly faded, the shadows disappearing as he returned to the man Neeve knew. "As much as you need."

Cassander pressed his bloody palm against Erick's hand, trying to keep his breathing steady.

"What—"

But Neeve didn't finish as Erick pressed harder. "Take more. I have it to give."

Cassander nodded, his chest slowly rising and falling. "Just enough," he said, still weak. "Thank you."

"He mentioned a village healer nearby," Kaeli said. "We have to get him there."

Cassander moved to stand, and Erick and Robert ducked under his arms, holding him up.

"Let's go," Erick said.

Neeve led the way with her mother close beside her, though she was only sure of the direction, holding branches at bay as Erick and Robert carried him.

"We are its saving grace," Fallon had said. "We will put things right."

He ought to be ripped from the world. Neeve set her jaw as she moved forward, allowing the dark thoughts to shadow her mind. *Let him meet Aishlin for himself. Let him see his folly too late.*

CHAPTER 26

The amber lights from the village were far, each step laborious as time derided them with fleeting minutes. Neeve glanced back to her friends and her father, ensuring all were still upright and following.

Cassander stumbled as he stepped, grimacing and groaning through clenched teeth. Erick and Robert adjusted to keep him upright.

With body and magic too weak to help, she could only walk ahead beside her mother, ensuring a solid path while making sure no other cultists waited for them. She pushed herself, walking through the aches in her hips and back, walking despite the ache in her right ankle.

Never had she felt more useless.

"Neeve," her mother said, her voice cautious. "What happened?"

"We were ambushed by the Wandering Order."

"No, I mean—"

"I know," Neeve interrupted. Then, apologetically, she added, "I don't have the energy to tell you."

Guilt stung, especially as she studied the marks and bruises on her mother's face and hands.

"You both have been through the hells," Neeve said. "I had no idea. Gretchen has no idea."

Her words came out with bitterness, even as she meant them with concern. The ache in her heart ran deep, glutting all optimism and leaving anger in its place.

"I could say the same for you," Kaeli said.

At last, the sun rested, and with it came Neeve's transition. In her younger form, her energy surged, and she raced ahead.

"Neeve!" her parents called, breathless.

But she ran, feet pounding against the ground as the wind stung her eyes.

"Help!" she cried. "Help us, please!"

She ran hard until she reached the edge of a modest town, skidding to a halt by a man leading a donkey toward a stable. Startled, the man stared before his eyes caught those following her, all of them bloody and bruised.

"By the gods," he said. "What—"

"Please," Neeve said, afraid that the mention of witch hunters would urge everyone into their homes behind locked doors.

"What's the matter, child?" one woman asked, stepping into the street. Others did the same, looking at the frantic young woman leading four bloody people into their village.

"I'm here," one woman said, running to her. Middle age graced her with gray hair around her temples and light crow's feet by her blue eyes. "Your friend. What happened?"

Neeve watched the woman place her hands on Cassander's face before inspecting the wound that crossed his chest. She had magic, though Neeve couldn't tell much beyond that.

She explained as much as she could remember—swords and knives, and Cassander bleeding everywhere. One villager, large and muscular, took Cassander from Erick and Robert, leading the way to a house down the street. Erick tottered on his feet.

"Not you, too." Neeve took his arm across her shoulders and held him tightly around the waist. "Stay with me. It's not much farther."

"At last, to hear you say those words...*stay with me...*"

He was exhausted, near fainting, but still wore that smirk she'd come to love. Neeve caught her parents sharing a look as she heard Erick's faint chuckle.

The home they entered was small and clean, modestly decorated with the comforting smells of flowers and brewed tea.

"By the fire, please," the woman instructed, and the man carrying Cassander laid him in front of the fireplace. She looked at Neeve and Erick. "There's clean water in that bucket there. I'll need some for him, then you're welcome to the rest."

The woman was quick to take up a bucket of water from the fire and pour the liquid into a bowl. Erick had already taken the liberty of sitting in a nearby dining chair at the table, shoulders slumped and head lolling forward.

"I'm Kenna," the woman said.

"Neeve." She introduced Erick and her parents on their behalf.

"Is he alright?"

Neeve rested a hand on Erick's shoulder. "I hope so."

"There are cups there." Kenna pointed to a shelf by a window. "The well is out back to the left."

"I'll fetch the water," Kaeli looked at her husband, who nodded once, staying close to Erick.

"You both need tending," Kenna said, her voice gentle. "Your wounds need care."

"In time," Kaeli said as she stepped through the rear door.

Neeve and Kenna worked quickly, removing Cassander's vest and tunic. He groaned, his grimace deep from pain.

"Sorry, love." Kenna shifted him to pull all the fabric free. "We're nearly there."

Cassander's brow furrowed, sweat gathering at his hairline. Even with Neeve's limited experience in healing, Cassander's rich brown skin was far too pale.

He's lost so much blood. She stared in horror, fringes of despair chilling her core.

The cut reached from his left clavicle across to the ribs on the other side, one heinous swipe of a blade that left a deep, angry line. Neeve had to look away. She'd never seen so much blood, so much wounded flesh before.

Was this what the vision showed? No matter how she focused on the fringes of her memory, the moment she recalled didn't match what she'd witnessed.

Even so, this could be Cassander's end. Their choices and steps may have led them to Death, after all.

Not today, Neeve thought, as though Death could hear. *Stay away from him. He is not yours to claim. None of us are.*

Kaeli returned with water, and Robert helped to pass cups around. But Erick didn't respond, his head dipped forward and shoulders bowed. Neeve clamored to her feet and touched his face, smoothing strands of hair behind his ear. He wasn't feverish, but his skin was clammy.

"Erick," she whispered, holding the cup for him as she continued to comb his hair back. "Water."

Rather than take it, he cupped his hand over hers, bringing the vessel to his mouth. He sipped carefully, eyes closed, his bottom lip touching her thumb.

"Thank you," he said. "I'm alright."

But he looked too weak for that to be true.

"What happened before?" Neeve asked, her voice a whisper. "What did he take?"

"Magic." He took another sip, his hand warm and gentle against hers. "Sons and daughters of Anya and Aishlin can heal one another and borrow magic to strengthen spells."

The sisters live for one another. Erick's words bore more weight as he swayed in his seat, as Cassander held on for his life.

"He could have borrowed mine," Neeve said. "He didn't have to take so much from you."

"It looks worse than it is."

But Neeve didn't believe him. "I'm godborn, Mal'Erick, not some withering daisy."

"And you'll need your magic to help keep him alive."

Erick reached for her, his fingers weakly gripping her wrist. Neeve sat beside him, fatigue filtering through her blood like cold water. She leaned against his shoulder, comforted when his head rested against hers.

Her parents had moved to help Kenna at her instruction, gathering dried herbs and a mortar and pestle.

"This is poison," Kenna said, delicately touching the feathering red lines around the wound. "Do you know what kind?"

Neeve stared as though Kenna had spoken a different language. "P—poison?"

"Whoever attacked him used poison." Kenna looked at each of them. "What happened?"

Neeve hesitated.

"I can't help him if I don't know what hurt him," Kenna said simply. "He's dying."

Neeve flinched, her hand tight around her cup.

"Witch hunters," Kaeli said. "We were attacked in the woods outside of town."

"The Wandering Order?"

Her parents nodded as they sat by Cassander. Neeve swallowed, the saliva passing down like shards of glass.

"Those monsters." Kenna stood, moving to a shelf of more herbs by her front door. "They use widow's veil on their blades in case they come across a godborn."

Erick met Neeve's eyes with dark panic. "Widow's veil is one of the few poisons powerful enough to take down someone with godblood."

Neeve studied the cut on her arm, appearing normal for a wound caused by a sword. They must not have coated every blade. "Is there a remedy?"

"There is." Kenna placed a series of jars and bundles of dried herbs on the dining table in front of Neeve. "I'm going to need your help. You both—" Kenna addressed Kaeli and Robert. "—grind those enough to make a paste. And you," she said to Neeve, "I need a fine powder. We're going to add this to what they're making."

Neeve studied the gathered ingredients as Kenna put a second mortar and pestle in front of her. She pulled two orange flowers from one jar and a purple flower from another, then two long, dried leafy stems from a bundle.

"I'll fetch more water." Kenna poured what remained of the bucket into a large bowl. "Grind these to a fine powder. We'll add this to the mixture they're making."

Neeve didn't want Kenna to leave with Cassander so close to danger. "I can get—"

"You four are on the edge of collapse, yourselves," she said, glancing at each of them. "Stay where you're safe and grind those herbs. I won't be long."

She left through the back door, and Neeve worked the petals and leaves in the cold stone bowl, grinding and tapping until everything blended to a fine dust. The job gave her hands and mind something to do, helping her to push the swelling emotion down so she could focus and be helpful.

Erick sipped his water, bringing a hand to Neeve's shoulder. "Not so hard." His voice was soothing. "You'll break the bowl."

But Neeve couldn't do this gently and keep her wits about her. Her eyes itched, but she didn't dare release her vise grip on the tools. Doing so would bring collapse.

"Neeve," her mother said. "What happened?"

All emotion drained from her voice as Neeve explained things quickly. From Eira to a deal at the crossroads to being cursed by a stranger, all the way to the present moment.

"A crossroads deal?" Disbelief ignited the fire in Kaeli's eyes. "You can't be serious."

"I suppose that's where you come in?" Robert regarded Erick with a knowing look.

Erick didn't hesitate. "It is."

But Neeve blinked at her father, incredulous. "How did you know?"

"A lucky guess," was all he said, his eyes lingering on Erick before he glanced at Kaeli, then the hearth fire.

Three loud knocks came to Kenna's door. Alarm moved through the room like a stone falling through water, the ripple effect stirring everyone's already anxious nerves. Kenna moved to answer, but Robert held up his hand.

"Allow me."

She nodded, staying by Cassander, and Neeve's father slowly opened the door. It was Darrow, his black clothes a silhouette against the night outside, stood there, panting. Hair had fallen from the tie at his neck, strands clinging to his clammy face.

"We chased them far into the woods," he said. "Couldn't get sight of a camp or anything, so they're likely somewhere licking their wounds." He glimpsed what he could see inside Kenna's home before nodding once. "Folks said you'd be here, and I wanted to apologize again for the misunderstanding."

"*Misunderstanding?*" Kaeli snapped, stalking to the door. "You accuse us of being cultists just so you can overtake the crystal mine, you—"

Darrow held up his hands in surrender. "I swear, I didn't know what they'd done." His eyes went from Kaeli to Neeve. "It happened after I left you. I swear, I didn't know."

Robert held his wife back from causing the man any physical harm.

Neeve moved to the door, standing beside her parents. "What happened?"

"There were others who accused them of being new recruits for the Order," he said.

"A load of horseshit," Kaeli spat.

"I agree," Darrow said. "It was done when I returned to them after the reading."

"Reading?" Robert looked down at his daughter.

But Neeve didn't pause to explain. "Moonblade did this to them?"

"It was the Order," Darrow said.

Kaeli's words came quick, each of them sharp and pointed. "But having us tied up certainly didn't help."

"It didn't," Darrow agreed, ashamed. "They were captured when they realized your father made the map they're so eager to get their hands on."

Father's maps. The Wandering Order.

There was so much Neeve didn't know.

"But I swear on everything holy." Darrow didn't relent, his earnestness genuine. "I didn't know until it was done."

"To be fair," Kaeli said, her anger cooling, "he tried to help us even before the Order came. And he came after us when we were captured."

Relief. Anger. Confusion. Bitterness. Hope.

Gods, how could so much happen all at once?

"Thank you for the news," Neeve said, magic tingling within her palms despite her fatigue. "And curse your damned guild for endangering my parents."

He chuckled, soft amusement lining his gray eyes. "I cursed them too."

Robert latched and locked the door as Darrow turned to go, giving him no further room to speak.

"The *nerve*," Kaeli said, stewing. "As though that is apology enough for what they did to us."

"They're after arcana crystal?" Neeve asked.

"For mist arcana," Robert said.

"The magic drug?" Erick scoffed, rubbing the bridge of his nose. "Of course Moonblade is involved."

"Heavily," Robert said. "Sales have filled a lot of purses, and the map shows almost every place you can mine it."

"Along with safe houses." Kaeli exhaled deeply, as though she'd deflate and sink to the floor. "The Order thinks Moonblade is hiding a chaoswitch they're after. Capturing us was a surprise."

Erick and Neeve shared a look as Kenna returned, remaining silent as she sensed the tension in the room. She brought the bucket of water to Cassander as she knelt beside him. "The powders, please."

Kaeli and Neeve both accommodated her, watching in forced silence as she mixed it all into a thick green paste.

"*Death readings*," Kaeli hissed, moving back to their conversation as though they'd never left it. "That's what Darrow meant, wasn't it?" When Neeve didn't answer, Kaeli went on. "Why in the hells would you—"

"It's hard to eat with no money," Neeve snapped, her temper flaring. "It put food on our table while you were gone."

Her mother's brow furrowed, anger behind her eyes. But Robert reached for his wife, his concern dousing whatever flames had kindled.

"You never received the money we sent?" he asked, his voice soft and calm.

"What money?" Sarcasm lingered in her biting tone. "We never saw a single coin."

"We sent money every week," Kaeli said. "Whatever we could manage. Gold and silver."

Neeve stared, rectifying the idea that her parents hadn't forgotten them.

Fury flared in Kaeli's eyes. "That *bitch*."

Every eye stared at Neeve's mother as she said, "She stole from them, Robert. Every last coin."

"Breathe, love." Robert rubbed soothing lines up and down Kaeli's back. "She isn't here. Save your anger."

Kaeli breathed carefully through her nose, her pupils still pinpricks.

"I see where you get your temper from," Erick muttered with a slight smirk.

"And *you*." Kaeli aimed her anger at Erick. "How could you—"

But Neeve, rightly predicting how her mother would react, moved in front of him, physically cutting her off. "He did exactly as I asked. I knew what I was getting myself into, and I said yes. Don't lay this on him."

"You knew what you were getting into?" Kaeli's sharp look showed disbelief. "What was that, Neeve?"

"I almost killed Eira," Neeve said. "I wanted my magic gone. But I'm *godborn*." She seethed, watching them share a glance. "Something you'd think my parents would have mentioned before I went, broken-hearted, to the crossroads."

Several seconds passed with Neeve's heartbeat thrumming in her ears before Kenna's soft voice broke through.

"Wash your hands and help spread this all along the wound," she said. "Once we've done one pass, we'll do it again."

Neeve obeyed as Kaeli paced the length of the room, her fingers flexing in and out of fists. The fresh water Kenna fetched was for their hands, which Neeve was grateful to finally have clean. They each took turns to scrub away the dirt and blood, the water horribly soiled when they finished.

Neeve knelt beside Cassander and applied the prepared medicine, starting at the opposite end of the wound from Kenna.

"When you saw Cassander's death..." Erick's words were slow, his exhaustion severe. "Was this it?"

"I don't know," she said, her throat tight. "It may have been. But it didn't feel right."

"What do you remember?"

"Grass and trees." She blinked furiously to see where her fingers applied the medicine. "And Cassander, bloody. But I don't remember the flowers or this kind of wound on him. There was so much blood."

"Do you think you stopped it?"

She shook her head. "I'm not sure. I'm afraid to say yes." She sat back on her heels, hands shaking. "I don't know."

"Were you trying to stop it?" her father asked.

"Yes," Neeve said, "but I didn't try hard enough."

Distracted. Hyper-focused. Selfish.

But she admonished herself for taking on the actions of others as a trigger for her guilt.

You didn't do this. And you're working to save his life.

Guilt and grief and fear threatened to choke the life out of her. She forced air in, unconscious of her wavering focus and resolve, unprepared when Cassander's death flooded her mind once more.

The same flashes of his death flooded behind her eyes with more images, more lights, more colors.

Iron. Fire.

And Fallon's eyes.

Neeve gasped, hiccuping through a sob. Erick's hand touched her back, his broad palm warm between her shoulders.

"Let me, Neeve," he whispered, gently urging her back.

But she shook her head, wanting to mend his broken body with her own hands.

"What happened?" Kaeli asked, her tone calmer, but her words still clipped.

Neither Erick nor Neeve answered. Robert whispered something to his wife, prompting her to nod quietly and step back.

"Magic," Kenna said to Neeve. "It's all over you and your friends."

"We don't want any trouble," Erick said.

"You're safe here," Kenna said. "We have worshippers and magic folk in our village. The Wandering Order has been closing in for some time, using the smaller magical communities to bolster their resolve."

Kenna's work was gentle and steady, evidence of experience. "They're too scared to go West, though. Or to the islands near the Sound. Bloody cowards."

"We'll leave as soon as our friend is well enough to travel," Erick said. "We didn't mean to bring this to your doorstep."

"It was here before you," Kenna said. "I swear on my life, you're safe in my home."

The silence that followed amplified the crackling fire in the hearth and Cassander's agonized breathing. Neeve's fingers worked with the last bit of medicine before Kenna took the bowl to make more.

"How did a cult like this find its beginning?" Neeve asked.

Fallon and the two other men, their ill intent toward complete strangers simply because of what they thought they knew about them. How did something like that happen?

"How does hatred of anything start?" Kenna asked. "Fear makes people do unthinkable things. Things that may not have been in their nature to do."

"It's in their nature," Erick said, looking down into his empty water cup. "Make no doubt about it."

Softly, Neeve's father added, "Hatred like that doesn't come from nothing."

Neeve remained silent, wishing she could disagree. She took the water bucket and stepped out the back, finding the well close by. She used what remained to wash her hands before working the well rope to bring fresh water. Her hands moved with mindless automation until the task was done.

Cassander, on the brink of death. Her parents, beaten but alive. Erick, his consciousness dangling by a thread.

Tears fell as she leaned against the side of the well, palms pressed against the coarse stone, the edge cutting into her palms. Her lungs struggled to accept the breath she tried to swallow down, her muscles far too tight. A hand touched her shoulder, and Neeve started, choking a gasp as she turned into her mother's arms. Kaeli enveloped her without a word, holding Neeve against her, stroking her hair.

The dam within broke at last, and Neeve's arresting sobs would have had her on her knees had Kaeli not braced her against her chest.

A second pair of arms held them both. Neeve's father, his cheek resting on top of Neeve's head.

"We didn't know," her father said. "We thought you and Gretchen were cared for."

"We trusted the wrong person," her mother said. "We're so sorry, Neeve."

"You—" Neeve's throat spasmed, her breathing unsteady. "You didn't forget us."

"Gods, no." Kaeli held her tighter. "We thought of you every second."

"Why did you leave?" Neeve pulled back, meeting her parents' eyes, darting from one to the other. "Why in the seven hells did you leave?"

Her ragged voice ripped the words out at last, confronting the hollow fear that left her haunted and cold.

"We have something to tell you," her father said. "About the work we do."

Her mother nodded. "And who we do it with."

Neeve's stomach dropped. Moonblade. Wandering Order. Assassins and cultists fighting at Erys's statue, and her parents bound and bloodied.

She stood straight to look each of them in the eye, to watch them tell her the truth at last.

"There's an organization," her mother said, "that works against the Wandering Order."

"It was started by a woman in Thurin, and it reached us in Shaylon Plains."

"Only because your father is the best mapmaker in Sheraton."

Neeve narrowed her eyes as a piece fell into place at last. Erick, noticing the symbol on the map. Her father, making updates and copies.

"It is called Feather and Claw," her father said, his voice low. "And we are Sentinels."

Her mother explained further. "We're guardians of safe houses and areas with resources, places where members and those we're protecting can recover."

"The maps," Neeve muttered.

"One of our maps was stolen," her father said. "A ship captain in Runa lost his copy, and we've been in turmoil trying to get it back."

"One thing led to another," her mother said. "And Moonblade crossed our path."

"That's how you got captured? But—" Confused, Neeve tried to make sense of it.

"They wanted the arcana crystal," her father said. "We were scouting a prospective mine north of here."

"They used the Wandering Order as an excuse to capture us," Kaeli said. "So they could get the crystal all to themselves."

"All the way in Ileden?" Even as Neeve's emotional wounds filled and the pain eased, the familiar ache returned. "You traveled to another continent. What if—" The words caught in her throat. "What if you—"

Her mother embraced her tightly again before she could finish her question.

"We're safe now," she said. "We're all safe now."

But relief didn't reach Neeve's heart, which waged a war of anger within her. Working with a group determined to counter the Wandering Order, to save the magical people harmed by their principles and actions —all of that was noble and good and even righteous.

But Neeve's frustration simmered, selfishly wanting her parents to choose *her*. To choose Gretchen. To choose their daughters over some mission that carried him so far away.

She said nothing, letting her parents comfort her before they each went back inside to face the next stage of what was to come.

CHAPTER 27

An hour later, Neeve and Kenna made more medicine and applied it to Cassander's wound.

"It looks better," Kenna said, "but he still has a long road ahead. The poison is pulling away from his blood." She pointed to the blush around the wound, lighter than before. "He's strong. He'll heal in time."

"How much time?" Neeve felt callous for asking, trying not to imagine Fallon's ice-blue eyes.

"Soon." Kenna regarded her first, then Erick. "Are you running from the Order? Or did your paths cross by other means?"

"We're looking for someone," Neeve said. "A woman cursed me."

And Neeve explained everything, from the failed reading to the attack by the statues that reunited her with her parents and almost killed their companion.

"Gods above, Neeve," her mother said. "Hearing you say it again…" She clasped her hands together. "I can't promise I won't wring her neck when we meet her."

"You and me both," Erick said.

"The woman and the curse," Kenna said slowly. "And her path put you alongside the Wandering Order."

"That's what it looks like," Neeve said. "They were after her, and now we've garnered their attention."

"It's going to take some time," Kenna said, looking at Cassander. "The medicine is working, but he'll need continual care until the poison is gone. I'll stay up with him." To Neeve's parents, she said, "I have a room for you both." She held a hand toward the dark hallway leading to unseen rooms before speaking to Neeve and Erick. "I have bedding for you to stay close to him, in case something happens."

Before anyone could agree, Kenna left the room briefly, returning with an armload of blankets and thin but serviceable pillows. "Get as much rest as you can. The process will be long."

"Thank you." Neeve didn't argue, her body desperate for rest. If she was near collapse, it was a marvel that Erick remained conscious. "Wake for me for anything."

"You have my word." She nodded to Neeve's parents. "I'll show you to your room."

They left together as Neeve laid out bedding for her and Erick both.

"You're not keeping us separate?" He raised an eyebrow, staring at the way Neeve had arranged their respective beds together.

"What's the point?" she asked. "We're already taking up so much of Kenna's home. And—" She hesitated, looking at her hands. "Is it strange that I would feel alone otherwise?"

"No," he said, groaning as he descended to the floor. "Not strange."

"I don't think we'll have any trouble sleeping." Neeve smoothed her pillow.

Kenna returned without a word, going to the fire with a book. "Rest well."

"You too."

Erick leaned close, his breath warm, and whispered, "It took a near-death experience to get you close to me. Feel free to use my arm as your pillow."

She pushed his shoulder. "Behave yourself, Mal'Erick."

"*Oh*." If possible, he leaned in closer, his mouth almost touching her ear. "Say it again."

Despite the shiver down her spine, she elbowed him in the side. From across the room, Kenna chuckled.

"You have my word." He raised his hands in obeisance. "Perfect gentleman."

"I've no doubt of that," Neeve said, the levity doing much to soothe what tension remained. "You know what I'm capable of."

He laid back, grinning, and sleep took him quickly. Neeve laid on her side, watching him breathe. The soothing rhythm of his chest rising and falling with the quiet ambience of Kenna's home wrapped Neeve in a calm embrace, and when she awoke, her body was old again, the sun well past its rising.

In sleep, she and Erick had found one another, his arm draped over her side as the other supported his head. Up close, Neeve fought the overwhelming temptation to sweep across his long lashes with her fingertips, to feel their feather-light touch. She reached to brush an errant lock of dark hair from his eyes, but she recoiled, seeing her aged hand.

No dreams. No restlessness. Just the quick passage of time, her youth spent in sleep.

She sat up, grunting through the ache of her back and shoulders. Erick's arm slid from her, leaving a trail of warmth that cooled far too quickly. She craned her neck to see Kenna still awake, whispering to Neeve's parents. They were all seated close to Cassander, sipping steaming liquid from their cups. Their eyes found Neeve as she struggled to her feet and hobbled toward them.

"I didn't mean to sleep this long." She rubbed her eyes and face. "How is he?"

Erick groaned from the floor beside her, stretching. But he didn't move to rise, sleep still enveloping him.

"He's alright," she said. "The poison is gone, and his body is slowly healing itself."

The feathering poison had gone, the cut no longer a deep, foreboding red.

Tears misted in Neeve's eyes. Bracing her mind, she touched Cassander's hand, glad to feel its warmth. "You saved his life. Thank you."

"I'm glad to do it," she said. "I'm only sorry that this is how we met." She gestured to the chair opposite hers and poured a fourth cup of tea.

"Thank you." Neeve sat, accepting the cup and breathing in its aroma. "This smells lovely. What blend is it?"

"Lady's ivy and skydrop," she said. "Very good for muscles and joints."

Neeve said nothing, knowing the blend was for her, another sign of Kenna's kindness.

"If this isn't too personal a question," Kenna said, regarding Neeve. "How do you feel when you're young again?"

She looked at her parents, hoping her words would be reassuring. "I feel like myself, as though nothing's wrong."

"No residual aches or pains?" her father asked. "No fatigue?"

"No. I feel the energy of my real age."

But Neeve spoke nothing of the growing effects of the curse.

Kenna leaned back, studying her. And, to Neeve's surprise, she didn't feel under scrutiny when Kenna stared. "Why not simply keep you aged? Why dawn and dusk?" At Neeve's curious look, Kenna added, "I watched you change while you slept. I'm sorry if that sounds intrusive."

"I think we all did," Kaeli admitted. "Sorry, love."

But Neeve was relieved, not offended. "Have you ever heard of anything like this before?" She glanced at her parents. "Have you?"

But they each shook their heads, and Neeve accepted the bitter tinge that replaced the sliver of hope she'd allowed in.

"Nothing like this." Kenna sipped her tea. "How difficult it must be to have your youth for mere hours in a day."

"What's difficult is finding the woman who did this." Neeve struggled to keep the hardness out of her voice. "If she would break this curse, I could get what's left of my life back."

"What if you can't break the curse?" Kenna's expression was kind, though straightforward. She was someone who cared enough to ask and tell her the truth.

"I'd be lying if I said I hadn't considered it," Neeve said.

"So have we," her father admitted. "What happens if the curse isn't broken?"

Neeve stared at the amber liquid in her cup. "I haven't let myself think that far."

"That's understandable." Kenna moved to a pot that simmered over the fire. "It may do you more good, though, to think about what could come next."

Neeve closed her eyes, reluctant to accept it. The moment she considered the outcome of the curse remaining was the moment the quest would be lost. She would see this path through to its end, no matter what her body went through.

Kenna returned to the table with a steaming bowl of oats and fruit for Neeve. "Picked those wildberries this morning."

"Thank you. But aren't you tired? You've been up all night."

"I keep odd hours."

"Go rest," Neeve said firmly, looking at Cassander. "Is there anything I need to know? Or do?"

"He'll need more medicine by the time you're finished eating." She brought a closed jar to the table, the contents a thick, dark green. "It's all here."

"Did you make this last night?"

"I did."

Impressed, Neeve watched as Kenna disappeared down the short hallway she'd gone to before. Only, this time, she didn't return.

Erick rose then, touching Neeve's shoulder as he passed her for the pot of food. "Oh, she made a *lot*." Kenna had left out a bowl and spoon, and Erick helped himself. "Did you all sleep alright?"

"Yes," Kaeli said. "You?"

Neeve took a bite, the oatmeal fresh and delicious. It reminded her so strongly of Gretchen that her chest ached.

"Well enough. Have you noticed that Kenna doesn't keep iron in her house?" He gestured vaguely with his spoon. "I wonder if she's magicborn." He took Kenna's seat, taking a delicate bite of the hot food. "Mm. That's good."

The guests ate together in comfortable silence. In some strange alternate reality, this could have been any other morning with Erick coming for a meal and company and Neeve's family welcoming him. But more and more, her eyes studied the age in her hands, the smell of

Cassander's medicine finding its way in her nose despite the fragrant breakfast.

"We'll wash up," Kaeli said, standing and taking their bowls.

"And Kenna will need more firewood," Robert added. "I need to keep busy."

They stepped outside, Kaeli glancing back only once, her eyes darting from Erick to Neeve.

They were purposefully letting them have time alone.

"Your parents are very perceptive," Erick said.

"Why?" She narrowed her eyes. "What are they thinking? What are *you* thinking?"

"That we need to talk." He leaned forward, his expression soft, his mahogany eyes a rich well of knowledge. "Something happened, Neeve."

"What happened?"

"I watched you last night, when you put medicine on him."

Neeve froze, the secret bearing the weight of shame.

"What did you see?"

She exhaled, too defeated to fight. *Fight against what? What good is keeping this to myself?*

"How much of me do you see, Mal'Erick?" Neeve's laugh was quiet, its mirth a mask for the emotion that trembled beneath it.

"You wear your heart out for everyone, so long as they have eyes to see." He touched her hand, his voice quiet and sweet. "Tell me."

She struggled not to gulp for air as the weight pressed harder. "Iron. Fire." Her lips tightened as she fought the urge to cry. "And Fallon's eyes."

"Gods above," he whispered. "We didn't stop it."

"Or it hasn't happened yet." She steadied herself, lips trembling. "Or we've changed everything without realizing."

"We keep our eyes open," he said, squeezing her fingers. "We won't let that bastard win."

She nodded, fear's grip loosening with Erick's resolve.

"I'll take up our bedding," he said, standing. "You take care of Cass."

Neeve raised her eyebrows, the weight on her chest breaking. "*Cass*?"

He shrugged a shoulder. "He almost died trying to stop evil cultists from murdering us. I can cut him some slack. *Some*."

Neeve took up the jar, inhaling its earthy scent as she unscrewed the lid, and Erick folded the blankets and stacked them neatly out of the way.

She struggled to crouch at Cassander's side, using a chair to sit as she awkwardly leaned over him, the salve on her fingers. The wound had sealed but still carried a slight fever.

"I hope you can rest, too," she whispered to him, her touch gentle as she finished. "Thank you, Cassander."

She studied him, the steady rise and fall of his chest, the almost serene look on his face. Death had almost taken him, and the threat of it loomed even still. "We'll do what we can to keep you safe."

"His healing is slow but steady," Erick said, taking Cassander's hand. He was quiet for several seconds, concentrating, before letting go. "That should help."

"Don't give too much of yourself."

"I've already given myself to someone, dear one." He kissed her forehead. "But, on a more serious note, are you alright with waiting?" He took her hand in both of his. "This was a complication we didn't see coming."

She stared at their hands together, barely processing his question. "I won't leave without him."

"Your devotion is endearing. How's the curse?"

She wanted to say something sarcastic, something to keep the mood light and make him smile, but his touch was gentle, as a man caring for his beloved. His beautiful hands stroked her aged ones. It wasn't *her* hand he held. This body belonged to someone else.

She slipped free of his hold, her shame overshadowing any confidence she'd had. "Erick—"

"What?" His eyes grazed over her. "Are you in pain?"

She shook her head, dejected by her own doubt. Weakly trying to keep the mood light, she teased, "You shouldn't flirt so shamelessly with an old woman."

"You're not an old woman." He rested a hand on her shoulder. "I see you, Neeve. *You*. Not the curse you bear."

She met his gaze, marveling at how unflinchingly he stared, as though to shove the truth into her mind with the power of his eyes.

"I don't see the curse," he repeated, taking both her shoulders. "I'm not being poetic or kind. I see through the magic." His earnestness made his touch both firm and tender. "I only see *you*."

The hope she'd let in before now tried to bloom again, the stem and leaves pushing hard against her crushing fear, petals desperate to open despite claustrophobic doubt.

Hope had pushed through, the pressure building in her chest as tears welled in her eyes. Erick pulled her close, his arms tight as she cried into his chest. He stroked her hair and kissed her crown as she grasped him like a lifeline, lest she be swept by the waves of a wide, expansive, lonely sea.

With Erick, she could be herself, wholly and completely. All of her wanted by all of him.

She hugged around his neck, burying her face as her tears fell freely. She wanted nothing more than to surround herself with his warmth, in his strength.

"Can you hold me tighter?" For a moment, her voice sounded young. Even within a delusion, longing continued to root through her. She would be herself again.

He answered by obeying, pressing her firmly against him. His hold was a welcome vise, not easily broken. Their bodies were nearly one, even as the dam broke further. She breathed in his comfort and strength as everything collapsed within. Days of existing with more questions than answers, the unknown remaining an oppressive force as she tried to keep her eyes forward. But she always glanced back, seeing very little progress in the path behind.

"Neeve—"

Erick pulled back, a hand in her hair, her moon-white curls wrapping around his fingers.

She stared, awestruck, and looked at her hands.

Her youthful, smooth hands.

"What did we do?" She held her own hands, rubbing her palms and knuckles before her fingers went to her hair. "What did we do?"

But the age spots slowly returned. Her hair shortened and thinned. Neeve's chest tightened further, anger burning like a wildfire with every heartbeat.

She struggled to keep her voice down as she cursed the witch who did this. "Would that I could see her judgment." Her whisper was knife-edged, slicing the air as Neeve forced herself to breathe slowly through her nose, but the tears returned as her own body became her cage.

Erick surrounded her, arms tight, one hand cupping her head as the other spread across her back. He wouldn't relent, even as Neeve trembled in his embrace.

"Tell me what to do," he whispered. "Gods, Neeve. I'll do anything."

"Don't let me go." Her breath caught in her throat, her chest tight. "Don't let me go."

Magic hummed through his skin as she focused on his breathing, tension in her body leaving as the flow of emotion finally loosened its hold while Erick tightened his.

"I'll never let go." He kissed her shoulder, her hair, her cheek. "Worlds will end, but I will never let go."

CHAPTER 28

It was nearly dusk when Cassander finally awoke, swearing like Captain Shea. He took several deep breaths, pressing a hand to his forehead.

"*Seven hells.*" When he tried to sit up, he swore again.

From their place by the fire, helping Kenna prepare supper, Neeve and Erick shared a grin.

"Welcome back, Cass," Erick said.

Kenna met him quickly, hands going to his chest and shoulders. "Easy." She helped him to recline back. "You're out of the woods, but the wound is still serious."

Cassander looked down at himself, touching the red line down his chest and stomach. "I thought it was a dream."

"If only," Neeve said, helping Erick cut vegetables. Neeve's parents stepped in from outside, arms laden with more herbs and firewood.

"Meet my parents, Robert and Kaeli," Neeve said. "They were captured by the Order."

"But only after Moonblade accused us of being cultists," Kaeli said. "It's nice to see you awake, Cassander."

"Thank you for helping our daughter," Robert said.

Cassander stared, the shock slow to recede. "It's nice to meet you both, though I'd much prefer the Order not have been involved."

Kenna gave Cassander the finer points of his injury, including the poison and current state of recovery. She helped him with supper, a simple meal of seasoned vegetables and broth.

"Meat is expensive," Kenna said. "I'm sorry I can't offer more."

"This is more than enough," Cassander said, eagerly drinking the savory liquid. "I owe you my life."

"You don't."

"I do," Cassander insisted. "This was beyond kindness or duty. I am alive because of my friends and because of you."

Her appreciation shined through. "I'm glad to have helped."

Neeve regained her youth halfway through the meal, flushing as the others watched.

"Hello, everyone," she said shyly. She swept her hair out of the way and took another bite.

The food was satisfying, and Erick was the one to take the dishes for washing again, this time with Neeve's help. They used the cooking pot as a makeshift basin, and Kenna gave them two washing cloths before they stepped out.

"Though I won't say no to your company," Erick said, "it's all right if you want to stay and help Kenna."

Being near Erick grounded her in a way that she'd never imagined. Gretchen and Samson were close in the way they kept Neeve centered and content, but Erick had added a layer of peace she didn't want to live without.

"My parents can help." Neeve closed the back door behind them and followed his lead to where he'd washed the dishes last time. "I need some air."

Once at the well, Erick drew water from the bucket and set it between them.

"What you said before," Neeve said, carefully working the food away from the bowl with her wet cloth. "About seeing the curse."

"About *not* seeing the curse."

She looked up at him, glad to see his burgundy eyes fighting her vulnerability to ask him outright.

But it wasn't vulnerability with Erick. It was honesty. *Trust*. Gods, how her heart warmed and calmed as she allowed herself to feel his safety, as though a thick layer of ice that had surrounded her heart had finally melted.

"You really don't see it?"

"The glimmer of magic is there, but my eyes are godborn."

"But you can see the age." The statement was almost another question.

"I can see the tethers of a curse upon you." Her eyes flickered to his mouth as he spoke, watching his lips form the words. "It almost looks like faint wisps of smoke or shadow. If I look at you a certain way, I can see the older version of you. But I only see you." He paused for effect, his resolve unwavering. "I see Neeve."

She opened her mouth to speak but stopped, holding her breath as he leaned closer, his face level with hers, their noses almost touching.

"I see the same woman I've always seen. The same woman I love to see." He paused, pleased. "I'd like to think it's because I'm *special* to you."

She prodded him with her elbow. "You *are* special to me."

The burn of his stare warmed her skin as she focused intently on one particular spoon that was already clean.

Without another word, he continued washing the dishes, and Neeve didn't look up as she gathered hers to take back to Kenna. But as she turned, he was close to her, his mouth almost touching her ear.

"I would break the world for you, Neeve. By your command."

She blinked, words failing as her breath caught in her chest. He chuckled, walking ahead of her into the house.

"By the gods, Mal'Erick."

He looked at her over his shoulder, giving her a wink.

THE NEXT DAY had Cassander sitting upright, eating and talking and laughing, even as he winced and held his stomach.

"It's good to see color return to your face," Kenna said. "I'll go see about supper. Keep yourselves busy while I'm gone."

"Gone?" Neeve asked.

"I'm off for the market, but I shouldn't be long."

"May we join you?" Kaeli asked Robert. "We lost most of our supplies after we were captured."

Kenna's face lit up. "I'd love your company."

Neeve almost offered to go with her, though her bartering skills left something to be desired. Instead, she dug into her purse and pulled three silver pieces.

"It isn't much, I'm afraid." Neeve held out the coins out to her.

Kenna shook her head, but Neeve took her hand and held the coins against her palm. "You've given us your home for a time and saved our friend's life. Now, you're out of food." Neeve curled Kenna's fingers over the money. "You've done so much for us. The least I can do is make sure we can eat."

"I thank you." Kenna bowed her head to them before stepping out.

"I'm sorry," Cassander said, looking from Neeve to Erick. "We've lost so much time."

"Only because you lost so much blood." Erick teased, one eyebrow slightly upraised. "Don't bleed so much, Cass. It slows us down."

He chuckled, groaning as he clutched his chest. "I'll keep that in mind."

"Gretchen said something similar to me once," Neeve said. "We were just girls then. Our parents had returned from Sudor with trinkets and stories, and they'd found relics near a mine that showed Sudor was once devout."

"Sudor?" Cassander furrowed his brow, astonished. "That must have been long before Jesper."

"My father thought the same thing," Neeve said. "Which added to the romantic notion of relic hunting and mapmaking. So I was playing pretend one afternoon and cut my hand on one of my mother's mining tools." Neeve showed her aged palm and drew a line where the faint line of a scar remained. "I bled a *lot*, and Gretchen was furious. She said if I couldn't handle the job, our parents would never take us to Alvar."

"Oh?" Erick perked up. "What part of Alvar did you visit?"

"We didn't end up going," she said. "There was another job in the Ghostlands that reached them first. But we would have visited the northwestern coast. There's a port town said to have evidence of the battle between Shanna, Erys, and Aishlin."

"Greystone Port," Erick said. "Stories of that battle circulate heavily there."

"I'm from a village near there," Cassander said. "Thornvale."

"You're from Thornvale?" Erick blinked. Neeve didn't remember seeing him this surprised before. "Were you there long?"

"Most of my life," Cassander said. "Until the last few years in Ileden. Why?"

"I grew up in Greystone," he said. "I returned there after my brief time in Falkirk."

"We were so close to one another," Cassander mused. "Hours apart."

Neeve said nothing as she witnessed something between them strengthen. A bond initially forged out of necessity had grown to friendship.

An hour passed with Erick and Cassander sharing their experiences in Alvar while Neeve listened, tidying Kenna's home and brewing more tea. Erick settled at the dining table with his book, a candle close by for light. Neeve hadn't realized that Cassander had dozed.

"How long have they been gone?" Neeve asked. "Do you think they're alright?"

Erick left his book open, face down, on the table. "Not sure. You want to look for them?"

"I do."

"Excellent," he said. "You lead."

You lead. Excitement laced through Neeve's blood as she helped Erick unfold their bedding and sit, facing once another.

But Neeve's frustration mounted as she looked to the window, the fringes of daylight lingering at dusk.

"Is the curse late?" Neeve asked, looking at her hands and arms. "Or am I impatient?"

He didn't answer at first, concern knitting his brows. Something was wrong, and the truth of it stabbed Neeve in the center of her chest.

"It's getting worse."

"We're going to break it." He took her hands, his grip firm. "Believe in it. Trust in it. We're going to break it."

She nearly said the words back to him, but she couldn't bring herself to lie. Not to him.

"This despair won't win," she muttered. "This fear won't win."

"You have the strength and magic to do whatever your heart desires," he said. "Trust yourself and what you can do."

"Are you sure?" She scoffed a laugh. "Your motivational speech is inspiring."

"We've been in each other's minds, Neeve." He kissed her palm, pressing the length of her fingers against his cheek. "You are capable of wonder. Shadow and light. Order and chaos."

Shadow and light.

Titus would be perfect.

She cleared her throat, tightening her fingers around his. "Let's find Kenna and my parents."

Neeve closed her eyes, her magic tingling in her palms as the shadows coalesced, their chilling touch reassuring. Determination pushed her to dig deep, proving that she was capable, proving that this curse wouldn't stop her. She conjured Titus and sent him searching.

Her vision soared. Her raven cawed, its voice ethereal, its wings flapping as she saw through its eyes. Titus flew beyond Kenna's home to the market, watching the thin crowd of villagers pass along the thoroughfare.

"They're not in the market," she whispered. "Can you see what I see?"

"Yes, you clever woman. Titus is seeing for us both." His thumbs grazed her knuckles, stroking back and forth. "Go easy. You'll find them."

His voice was quiet, its tone and gentleness reserved for her. She listened, easing her magic as her scrying eye searched.

You are capable of wonder.

Neeve hadn't expected his confidence to take root within her, steeling her resolve to see this spell succeed. There was nothing she could do about the curse, but she could control and maintain her own magic.

She searched, passing over faces she didn't recognize until she found them walking toward the butcher. Her parents, arm in arm, talked animatedly as Kenna looked heavenward, taking in the night's first shimmer of twinkling stars as the sky darkened.

"Kenna looks at peace," Neeve said, glad to have Erick's hands to hold.

"Just like Edgar," he said. "They want what they already have."

Kenna used one of Neeve's silver pieces to buy meat. As the butcher wrapped it, Neeve pulled the spell back and opened her eyes, finding Erick watching her.

"Wanting what you have is difficult," he said.

She looked down at their hands, glad to see that she'd changed. The curse hadn't taken her completely.

I'll always be Neeve. She willed the words to sink in. *I will always be Neeve.*

Erick's hand broke from hers, cupping her cheek. "Where did you go, love? You're a million miles away."

Her eyes traced the curves of his face, from his cheekbones to his jawline, to his mouth and the perfectly shaped cupid's bow. She met his gaze when his hooked finger touched beneath her chin.

"Your eyes are like wine," Neeve whispered, the words passing from her lips without thought.

His gravity pulled her closer, the power in his eyes unyielding.

"Drink deep, love."

Her lips parted as his grazed hers with the barest whisper of touch. Lightning surged across her skin.

Kenna's front door opened.

Erick and Neeve parted, a gust of wind sweeping around them as they whirled to see their host and Neeve's parents return.

"If you both are amenable," she said, looking down at her feet as she kicked off her dusty boots by the door. Kaeli and Robert glanced over at Erick and Neeve with a questioning look but said nothing, going to the hearth to settle by Cassander.

"I would love for you both to help me make supper," Kenna said. "Vegetables and meat."

Neeve rose too quickly, her knees popping as she stood. Erick's arm steadied her.

"We'd love to," he said, swallowing.

Neeve almost avoided looking up at him, only to be relieved to see his face as flushed as hers.

"So." Erick leaned to whisper. "Do you like wine?"

Her face burned, but she didn't back down. "I've only had a sip. I'll need more to know for sure."

Firelight shimmered in his eyes. "Good answer."

CHAPTER 29

"Are you asleep?"

Neeve's whisper was barely audible, but Erick answered by shifting, turning from his back to his side as he opened his eyes.

Kenna's home was quiet but for the low crackle of the fire in the hearth. The amber light competed with the cool glow of the moon shining through the window glass, both tones blending across the features of Erick's face.

She held the blanket to her chin, though she wasn't cold. "I wondered about the scope of my power. What I could do."

"Because you've done touchmagic in the past?"

She nodded, and he edged closer. "I still rely on my hands in a fight."

"Touchwitches can accomplish many things," he said. "From healing to pain, from seeing to learning. Objects and people all have histories and futures. Touchwitches can tap into that thread and see where it's been and where it leads. Even with your godborn blood, your practice with touchmagic makes gives you control."

"Godborn touchmagic and control—" She held her breath before letting it slowly release through her pursed lips. "It wouldn't be diminishing greater power but channeling it."

He said nothing at first, reading her expression in the dim light.

"What are you thinking?" she asked.

"That you don't hate your power anymore."

"It wasn't hatred for the power," she said. "Only the weight that comes with it. But knowing you has made it worth it."

Neeve had nearly missed the tension in Erick's jaw, watching it dissolve as his expression softened.

"While we're both struggling to sleep, shall we try to reach Gretchen?" he asked. "Scry for her first, then try to speak with her?"

They sat up, knees touching, fingers interlaced. She gripped his other hand, her thumb stroking the curve of his palm. The corners of his mouth twitched upward.

"This magic is yours to control," he said. "It's farther to reach, but I'm here. Use me."

She closed her eyes, momentarily distracted by the way his hands held hers, fingers flexing.

"Let the magic take you," he whispered. "You know how to find home. The magic will take care of the rest, but it will need you to push."

She obeyed, allowed the arcane pull to take enough control to allow her consciousness to soar. Using Titus, she eased her will to guide him toward Gretchen, connecting her magic to the ring on her finger. Her sight passed over land and sea. The rush of speed was breathtaking as she remained grounded beside Erick on the floor.

"This feels right," she whispered, remembering what he'd done before.

"You're doing well," he said. "Remember to breathe."

She inhaled deeply as she pushed her magic toward Shaylon Plains, soaring past the mountains and hills from Alvar and Thurin all the way to the rolling plains, flowing southeast until she reached the small village of her upbringing.

She breathed faster, the strength of the spell growing, the need for energy increasing. The vision darkened without losing its momentum, as though Titus traveled through a space utterly devoid of light.

"Use me," Erick whispered, tightening his hold. "I'm here."

But she didn't. The spelled carried her, the sensation euphoric.

Swirling. Traveling through the dark. She could almost feel the wind in her hair as she soared.

But it was so dark. Thunder growled overhead, a storm close by.

"She didn't light the fire," Neeve said, heart aching. "I always remember before sleep. Did she forget? In this storm?"

There would be no moonlight or starlight. Gretchen should have prepared a fire for warmth.

"Gretchen?" Neeve whispered. "Are you cold?"

If Gretchen heard her, she didn't answer.

"She must be asleep," Neeve said.

"You can't see anything?"

"No. The storm is close." Wood creaked as the wind howled. "She'll wake up cold. Maybe Samson is with her."

But the ache in Neeve's chest didn't diminish. Gretchen, alone, forgetting about the fire. Did something happen?

"I shouldn't have left." Worry and regret mingled like long-lost friends.

"Did you feel the spell connect?" Erick asked. "You're pulling away, Neeve. Focus."

She pushed harder, the darkness pervasive within the storm's shroud. The rain pelted the roof outside.

"Yes," she said. "It connected."

"Can you see anything?" he asked. "Are you in total darkness?"

"Nearly. There's no moonlight or anything."

"She's alright," he said. "She's likely sound asleep with Samson."

"Yes," she said, concern unraveling within her. "She's alright."

Neeve released the spell, her consciousness reeling back as the magic gracefully fell away.

"Well done," he said. "How do you feel?"

"Worried," she admitted. "I can't shake this feeling that something's off."

She hadn't felt the tears fall until Erick gently wiped them away. His hand lingered against her cheek, his fingers in her hair. "It's only a storm. She'll be alright."

She closed her eyes, trying to remember anything else. But there was only darkness and the sounds of thunder and rain.

"She's alright, Neeve."

She leaned into his touch, opening her eyes slowly to allow herself to let go of the worry gnawing at her core. She pressed her hand to his, turning her face slightly to kiss the heel of his palm. Gratitude filled her heart at his unwavering, steady strength.

Her eyes lingered on his face. The prominence of his brow, the shape of his eyes, the peaks of his cheekbones, the cupid's bow crowning his mouth. She couldn't help but stare, the moonlight pouring in from the window gracing every curve. His lips parted as an invisible cord tugged at Neeve's core.

Closing the space between them was easy. Her fingertips traced the peak of his cheekbone before curving around his ear. Pleased at his shock and wonder, she relished the moment before pressing her lips to his, her touch gentle, curious, lasting seconds before she pulled back.

She searched his face, lingering on his eyes, almost shivering as his hands moved from her hips to her back, molding to the curve of her waist. He kissed her with delicate urgency, his rhythm slow as his tongue sought permission before deepening the kiss.

Wildberries and vanilla.

She'd never known a closeness of this kind before, made more intense by her certainty in him.

Mal'Erick. Charming and loyal and fierce. Chaos and shadow and deep, unwavering trust.

When their lips parted, he pulled her closer. "Gods, holding you like this." He nuzzled her throat and shoulder. "My arms have ached for this, Neeve. They have ached for *you*."

With her arms around his neck, words failed. But never had her heart been more full.

"Neeve." He exhaled, his breath cool. "You bring me so much peace."

"Even with all this?" She combed her fingers through his hair. "With everything that's happened?"

"There is so much light in you. Just being near you..." He finished the thought by holding her tighter.

"You have light in you too, Erick."

"Not with all this chaos. There's a lot of darkness here. So much of it."

The pressure of his arms filled pieces of her that had emptied, the warmth reaching areas long cold. "There is light and dark in us both."

He brought a hand to her hair and stroked her curls gently, reverently, sending shivers down her spine.

He stilled. "Are you cold?"

"Don't stop," she whispered, flushed by her boldness. "That feels nice."

He obeyed, his fingers gentle as they combed through. "I've dreamed of this."

"You've dreamed of my hair?"

She could feel his smirk. "Is it strange if I say yes?"

Mischief glimmered in her eyes. "I was attached to it, right?"

His laugh nearly erupted before Neeve pressed her hand to his mouth.

"Hm?"

Neeve and Erick froze as Cassander shifted, a quiet groan escaping before deep breathing continued. As she lowered her hand, he kissed her. She stared, mouth agape.

"I get immeasurable joy in surprising you."

"You're certainly good at it."

His mischief faded to something softer as he touched her face, his thumb tracing the curve of her bottom lip. "I hope I am not too much shadow for you, Neeve."

She'd never seen him so vulnerable. Something flared within her, be it protectiveness or something more. She was determined to have him remain at her side.

"I've always been comfortable in the dark."

THE HOUSE WAS dark when Neeve awoke in Erick's arms, one as her pillow and the other draped over her side. The ties of his shirt collar were loose, her eyes lingering on the shadow at his clavicle and throat before Neeve's fingers traced where the light touched. He inhaled as though awake, curling his arms to bring her closer. She wanted to hear him speak, to feel his kiss, but sleep kept him.

What remained of her youth ticked away with every passing second, leaving Neeve to relish the remaining time, dozing beside him. And when the shift came, the magic tugged her into consciousness, as though an internal alarm sounded to wake her ahead of Erick.

She made it to her feet in a quiet struggle and shuffled to the hearth where Cassander still slept. The wound was nearly gone, last she saw. Their stay with Kenna would conclude soon, the knowledge bittersweet.

Would that they could rest and linger in peace. But the Wandering Order wouldn't stop. Fallon wouldn't stop. And Neeve needed this curse broken before it consumed her remaining days.

Healing comes in rest, Gretchen had said, likely repeating those words from their mother.

If only rest was enough. The curse remained, even as Neeve's magic grew. The moment with Erick had given her hope, when their embrace had returned her youth, but it wasn't enough. Nothing they had done had rendered anything permanent. The curse lingered. Neeve's fear lingered.

Her mind and spirit were at odds with the limitations forced upon her, and all she could do was wait.

She put water over the fire to boil, giving herself a task to banish the thoughts that would breed bitterness and anger.

Keep going forward. Keep moving ahead.

The moment you look behind is the moment you move backward.

But she wanted to glimpse the progress she'd made, to reassure herself that all of this hadn't been for nothing.

She kept her internal eyes fixed forward, too afraid to turn.

CHAPTER 30

"You rose early," Erick said, speaking low into Neeve's ear. He moved to sit beside her at the dining table, placing himself across from her father's scrutinizing look. Kenna and Kaeli brought steaming bowls of porridge to the table. "Is something wrong?"

"No." It wasn't untrue, so why did it sour within her? Speaking up to include the others, Neeve asked, "When will we be set to travel?"

Kenna glanced at Cassander before answering, "Barring any severe discomfort, I would say that you could continue today or tomorrow. But you're welcome to stay as long as you need."

"I feel well enough," Cassander said. "Your kindness and generosity have meant a lot."

"I will be in the orchard today," Kenna said. "Apples are ready for picking. I want to send you with some before you go."

"We can help," Cassander said, leaning forward at the idea. He eagerly looked from Erick to Neeve. "It would be nice to pitch in."

"You're sure you feel up for it?" Neeve asked. "You won't start bleeding?"

"Apples are easy enough," he said. "Very little physical strain involved."

Erick poised his cup for a sip. "Except the part about climbing ladders and reaching through branches."

"With all of us helping," Robert added, "it shouldn't take long."

"If you would like to help," Kenna said, "we divide the harvest among the helpers. You could sort them without having to climb into a tree."

"Done." Satisfied, Cassander relaxed. "Thank you."

Erick leaned to Neeve, his mouth close to her ear as he whispered, "Are you up for it?"

She nodded. "It will feel good to do something."

"I'll fetch my baskets, then." Kenna stood. "Finish your breakfast, and we'll head over to the orchard."

She disappeared down the small hallway as Robert leaned forward to Erick. "May I speak with you?" He nodded his head toward the rear exit. "There's something I should tell you."

"Rob—" But Kaeli stopped as Robert shook his head.

"He should know, Kae."

Erick stood slowly, eyeing Neeve as he followed her father out.

"What was that about?" Neeve asked.

Kaeli sighed, resting her head in her hands and closing her eyes. "Your father didn't just know Erick was chaosborn. We—" Her lips pressed together in a white line. "We know his mother."

Neeve stared. "You what?"

"She's with Feather and Claw," Kaeli said.

Erick and Robert returned minutes later. Erick, his expression devoid of emotion, held eye contact with Neeve before returning to his seat beside her.

"Let's go outside," Neeve whispered, taking his hand.

"Ready?" Kenna returned, holding two baskets stacked together. "Harvest should be good this year."

"Later." He kissed her temple as he stood, helping her to her feet. "Later, I promise."

They set out for the orchard, Kenna and Neeve watching Cassander. He winced as he took those first steps before moving more comfortably.

"What hurts?" Kenna asked.

"Your medicines work wonders," he said. "There was a slight ache, but it's passing."

"Your muscles and skin are still stitching themselves together," Neeve said, "even with your natural healing."

"Fallon's attack was specific," Erick said, bitter hatred in his voice. "Hurting those with magic gives him sick pleasure."

"Their comeuppance will be severe," Kaeli said.

Erick smirked at Neeve. "Couldn't have said it better myself."

"The Order's hatred brings only more hatred," Kenna said, her voice pained. "It hurts to see what fear can do."

"I won't compromise what you've done for me," Cassander said. "And I appreciate you all helping me do something other than lay and heal." He chuckled. "That was the hardest part of all of this. Doing nothing."

"The sun's touch must feel good." Kenna's expression was kind. "A contrasting warmth to the cold of the poison."

Fleetingly, Neeve imagined the touch of the sun magically healing the sons and daughters of Anya. And there was Erick, basking in moonlight, strengthened by the blue-white touch of Aishlin.

Neeve opened her mouth to ask as several townspeople joined them toward the orchard. They all greeted Kenna, casting glances at Erick and Cassander. Very few of them noticed Neeve.

Rich red and deep green expanded before them as Neeve stared at the trees, awestruck by their simple beauty. Several already carried buckets and ladders with others opting for fabric slings.

"Here," Kenna said, leading the group to a pair of wooden tables ready for sorting. She pointed to the tub on the ground to the right. "The good apples go here, and the bad—" She pointed to the tub on the left. "—go there."

"Seems easy enough," Robert said.

"We'll divide the harvest once it's ready. There's a chair in the shed," Kenna said, moving toward it.

"I've got it," Erick said. "I'll get buckets, too."

"I'll help," Kaeli said, going with him.

Kenna stayed with Cassander, Neeve, and Robert as Erick and Kaeli left and returned. To Neeve, he said, "There's a second chair in there. Should I?"

"Maybe soon," she said, taking a bucket. "I'd rather work on my feet for a bit."

The work began, villagers moving through the rows of apple trees with practiced hands filling their buckets. Neeve took a deep, luxurious breath of sweet earth and apples with a trace of the coming rain.

"If I may," Kenna asked Neeve, her voice low as they worked beside one another. "How are you faring? You seem well today, despite the curse."

"I think the effects are lingering," Neeve said. "I'm more old than I am young."

"Curse? Old and young?" one person asked, overhearing.

"I've heard of those," another said. "Wears the body out. I've heard of a curse like that from a deathwitch."

Neeve flinched at the unforgiving term.

"That's hearsay," a third said. "People don't know half of what they're talking about when Aishlin's concerned. Any witch can draw up a curse like that."

"Sure, but it's the ones who dabble in chaos who lean toward that kind of creation."

"And I suppose you've never met a man made of twig and bone?"

It wasn't often people spoke of Aishlin in any kind of positive light. Only a few were brave enough to face Chaos. Erick listened too, his eyes darting to each speaker as he quietly worked.

An older woman near Neeve edged closer. "Do you know the person who cursed you?"

"No. Not even her name." Neeve focused on her aged hands handling the apples. "Taller than me. Long, dark brown hair, dark brown eyes. Agitated and furious."

"You or her?" someone quipped, laughing at their own joke.

A man chuckled from his perch on a ladder, stepping down to offload his bucket. "Sounds like my sister. But she's useless at magic. Claims she can communicate with the souls of the dead." He chuckled. "She was tangled up with one group, I think. Trying to get her hands on arcana crystal."

"Moonblade?" Robert asked, glancing at Neeve.

"No, not them. Something else. *Claws.*" The man curled his fingers and swiped down.

"Feather and Claw?" Kaeli muttered, stepping closer. "Is your sister about my height?"

"Close to, yeah." He looked at each pair of eyes now studying him. "What's she done this time?"

Not holding out any hope, Neeve asked, "Did she recently leave for Sheraton? And maybe returned to Ileden?"

He narrowed his eyes, looking at them over the plants. "Said she was meeting someone for a job. Didn't say what, though. My sister has a penchant for getting herself into just the right amount of trouble after trying to get something for nothing. Using grief and spirits is not surprising. But she's harmless, otherwise."

"Ethically sound, your sister," Erick said.

Hope slipped from Neeve's fingers, the lead too thin to grasp. "She's never tried to curse someone before?"

"The curse?" Kaeli studied her daughter, realization sinking in. "That woman cursed you."

"I didn't mean—" He shook his head, physically retreating with a half-step back. "No, she's never cursed anyone. She's a swindler who pretends to be good at magic."

Neeve, emboldened, asked, "If she were to return to Ileden—"

"I can't." The man took a full step back this time, leaving tree and bucket. He would flee any second. "Jackie's a crook, but she's family. I'll pay hell if I betray her."

"Jackie?" Neeve asked, the thread longer, her hold stronger.

"Jacqueline," Kaeli said. "She's the one we sent to you and Gretchen with our money."

"Gods." Galla grimaced. "You gave her money?"

"I promise no harm will come to her," Cassander said, stepping in. "We need her alive and well so she can break the curse."

"No. I can't. I won't." He was shaking his head so fast, his jowls wobbled. "I probably shouldn't have said this much." He backed up further. "I'll have to live with this for the rest of my life if something happens to her."

"Something already has happened to her," Erick said coldly, sharing little sympathy for the man's plight. "She's tangled up with the Wandering Order."

A chilling silence fell over the orchard.

"They're after *her*," Erick went on, relentless. "We think that's why she sought Neeve out, to see her future. But she was too impatient."

The man paled, horror in his eyes. "The Order?" His lips moved without sound until, "They won't stop until she's dead."

"We will do our best to make sure that doesn't happen," Cassander said. "All life is precious and worth defending."

Neeve shared a look with Erick, her thin eyebrow raised, but said nothing.

"If she came back to Ileden," the man drawled, the syllables coming slowly as though to stall time. "And if she were in trouble, she'd to go a small shack in the woods, north of here."

A hovel, dilapidated. Neeve had seen it before while scrying.

They were on the right track at last.

"Can you show us?" Cassander moved to Neeve. "We have a map."

The man hesitated, wincing as Neeve pulled the worn parchment from her bag. But he pointed, a spot past a cluster of trees north of the town.

"It's quite a walk," he said. "A couple of hours on foot."

"I assure you," Neeve said, rolling the map and returning it to her bag. "I only want the curse broken. That's it." He still looked worried and scared. "Please, believe me. I want my life back before it's over."

He flinched, nodding. "I'm sorry she did this to you. I'm—I'm ashamed."

"Her sins are not yours to bear," Erick said, "but that doesn't make this any easier."

"What's your name?" Neeve asked, extending her hand to him. "I'm Neeve."

"Galla." He shook her hand. "I hope you're free from this curse soon."

"So do I."

CHAPTER 31

Kaeli rhythmically hit her thigh with a fist, her expression tight with anger. "This is all my fault."

Gathering their share of the harvest, Kenna led them back to her home, arms leaden and hearts heavy.

"How is her curse your fault?" Neeve asked, even with the bitterness swelling in her core. Her parents had chosen to leave. They'd chosen to trust someone. And somewhere between those two points, that trust led to Neeve, cursed.

"She played it off as though everything went smoothly," Robert said. "Gods, she even—" He stopped, the first glimmer of anger shimmering in his eyes. "She said you and Gretchen loved us, and that she fell in love with Samson."

"She used everything we'd told her about you against us," Kaeli added. "Stories we'd shared, confessing to how much we'd missed you."

You wouldn't have missed us if you'd never left. Neeve clamped her teeth together, keeping her words to herself. *None of this would have happened.* The curse, leaving Gretchen...

The corners of her mouth tugged down, but her lips did not quiver.

Townspeople traveled with them down the worn path toward

homes and businesses. The sky darkened prematurely as a storm steadily swept in.

Cassander extended his arms to Neeve. "I can carry—"

"No." Her tone was resolute. "If you so much as wince in pain, Cassander, I swear to the gods you'll never hear the end of it."

Mischief brightened his dark eyes. "As you wish, *Gran*."

She chuckled despite herself. "*Cassander*."

"Worth it to see you smile," he said, the sunlight working wonders on his skin and eyes. A true son of Anya.

But the levity didn't last as Kenna chimed in on the subject of Jacqueline once they were inside. "I understand your wish to go to the shack Galla spoke of." She set her bucket on the dining table, Neeve and Erick doing the same. "I only ask that you be careful."

Cassander agreed. "The Order will find it, eventually, if she's hiding out there." He sighed. "We've lost so much time."

"Do you know where it is?" Neeve asked, hope still flickering despite everything. "Is there a faster route we could take?"

Robert was already unfurling his map, tracing a finger along a northern path.

But Kenna looked to Cassander. "The medicine heals quickly, and your godborn body is strong, but I would recommend you wait one more night with the coming storm."

As if the sky and Erys herself had heard her, thunder rumbled overhead. Disappointment tingled in Neeve's heart, but she knew Kenna was right. Cassander was on the mend, but it would be foolish for anyone to travel into the unknown during a storm.

"One more night," Robert said. "We can do that."

"We have another lead," Erick said to Neeve. "This is far from over."

She braved a look in his eyes as he touched her shoulder. Time was not on their side. With every hour, the hold of the curse grew stronger, and the one woman who could break it kept moving farther and farther away.

"Let the storm come," Kaeli said, confidence in her voice. "We leave in the morning when we have the sun."

They each did their part to help Kenna prepare their meal as the rain fell and thunder rolled. They lit candles and added wood to the fire, the interior of her home a haven from the darkness outside.

"I've only just learned her name," Neeve said, almost laughing to herself. "We've been on her trail for almost a fortnight. I've just met her *brother.*"

"I didn't know she's the one you're after," Kenna said. "I have little to tell you, I'm afraid, though Galla was being honest about her—" She paused, searching for the word. "Opportunistic tendencies."

"That was the most diplomatic thing I've ever heard," Robert said, impressed.

"Jacqueline is misguided," Kenna went on. "I hate that she's in the cult's crosshairs, but she isn't exactly discrete."

Erick glanced from Kenna to Cassander before settling his eyes on Neeve's. "What if they've already found her?"

"She's eluded them this long," Neeve said, trying to hold on to the thread of hope the afternoon had given her.

But no one can run forever.

She didn't voice her fear, instead taking a seat by the fire with Cassander, who'd elected to lie down and rest. Somehow, within minutes, Cassander had dozed into sleep, his breathing deep and even, his body relaxed.

Iron. Fire. Fallon's eyes.

No one can run forever.

"Oh, to have such a talent," Neeve said, using her voice to break the cycle of thoughts in her mind. "He can sleep absolutely anywhere."

Erick agreed. "Infuriating, isn't it?"

Kaeli and Robert said goodnight as they quietly passed to their room, Kenna not far behind. Neeve stared at the dark portal, curious about Kenna's life outside of healing strangers and helping neighbors harvest apples. If Kenna had the day to herself, what would she do? Garden? Read? Sleep?

Neeve unfolded the bedding for her and Erick. "What you and my father talked about. Do you have the energy to tell me?"

He helped smooth the bedding and ready the blanket before lying back, Neeve parallel to him. He stared at the ceiling as he formed his answer. "Your parents and my mother. It's been Feather and Claw. All this time."

Neeve turned to her side, watching his face in profile. "The man that she was with. The one I saw when our minds linked."

"I never learned his name," he said. "I've seen him twice, and both times, he took my mother with him."

He opened his arms for her, and she slid closer, resting against his shoulder with her arm draped over his chest. He smelled like the orchard. She drew a long, deep breath.

"I still think about the last time she left," he whispered. "It was so long ago, but I—" He turned his head slightly, emotion trying to cage his voice. "It's like what you've said to your parents. About choosing."

"That damned group." Neeve watched the gentle rise and fall of his chest, matching the rhythm of his breath with hers.

"It's a strange fate, Neeve, having the same grief shared between us."

"By fate or grace," Neeve said, "so that we don't have to bear it alone."

"She left me in Falkirk," he said, "all those years ago. But I still feel it." He pressed her palm against his chest, his heartbeat strong. "I wish she'd stayed."

"Do they know where she is?"

"Yes." He paused, the silence rich with meaning.

The distant rumble of thunder overhead only added to her stream of consciousness. Slowly, Neeve's body changed, the only signal that the sun had set with the darkness already enveloping the world in the storm.

"You and I are always searching for something," he said. "Parents. Jacqueline."

"Youth." She chuckled. "They could have found her by now. The shack that Galla mentioned, I think I saw it days ago when I scried."

"And you're afraid she's moved on."

"Or was captured."

"We won't know until we look. And we'll keep looking." He rubbed her back with perfect pressure. "I swear it."

Neeve wanted to imagine a life after the curse, returning to her youthful self and living as she had before. But that was a world away. Everything had changed, and it had only been days.

This life wasn't hers anymore. It was Godmother Neeve's, for all that meant.

"Tell me a dream," he said, massaging her arm. "What is something you've always wanted to do?"

"Travel." She stared ahead, wistful, anticipating the promise of adventure. "All of this life to live, and I want to see it all."

"Where will you go first?"

The whole of the world lay in front of her. How could she choose? "Anywhere. Everywhere. What would you recommend?"

"Alvar, if you're starting in the continent," he said. "Then, Hymoor. Specifically Falkirk."

"Start with Alvar. Describe it to me."

He hummed as he thought, and she heard memory in the sound. "Everywhere is green. The air itself is pure magic. The woods are alive with lights and singing, and the grass is the softest you've ever touched."

He paused, the pattering rain a soothing accompaniment to the crackling fire in the hearth.

"That would be where I'd want to spend my last days," he said, "if I were given the choice. Something so beautiful, *so peaceful*..." His words were melancholic, tinged with longing. "As for Falkirk," he went on. "That's where I was when my mother left. I met an old woman named Dania who was kindness itself, in human form. I didn't think any one person could be so compassionate. She was one of the most genuine people I'd ever known."

He paused, remembering her, his attachment significant. Even though Neeve only knew the woman's name, Dania's touch had reached her through Erick. What power, to share compassion through others.

"Falkirk is a place for people to start over," he went on, "from a mercenary raising her daughter alone to a stable hand who was a general from Kema and had seen unspeakable atrocities in war. Their kindness meant so much because it came from darkness. They were welcoming and gracious and giving with their food and their stories and their time, all of them bearing scars and still living each day with love."

"Whatever you've lived through," she whispered. "I am grateful to Falkirk and to Dania." Without thinking, she brought his hand to her lips, kissing his knuckles. The gesture was as natural as breathing. "Have you been back since?"

"No, but I'd like to. Someday."

Someday. What would someday look like when it reached them?

But it is all mine to make. She steeled herself against the despair of aging before her time. *Why wait to travel when the curse is over? Why wait to do anything when the curse is over?*

"I look forward to showing you the world, Neeve."

The thrill of his words thrummed in her heart, but reality remained ever present. "I've been too afraid to think about the possibility that this won't pan out in my favor."

"Are you thinking about it now?"

After a second's pause, she nodded.

"What are your thoughts telling you?"

"The fear of inevitability, coupled with the disbelief that it's actually happening, alongside the will to fight with my last breath."

"That's a lot for one mind to process all by itself."

"What if I'm never young again?"

"You changed back before," he reminded her, his voice gentle. "Something happened to you then. I wish I knew what we could do to recreate it, to channel it and make it permanent."

Her sigh was heavy. "That almost makes it worse. Something that I can do without Jacqueline, something within me. But—" She winced. "What if it never breaks?"

He kissed her head, holding her closer. "It will break, Neeve, because we will break it."

She sighed, allowing her body to melt against his.

This body is the truth and the lie.

What if it never breaks?

But withering fear dissolved to anger as she loathed the hand that forced her.

Whatever Jacqueline made, Neeve would see it unmade.

CHAPTER 32

Neeve sat up, her body still young. The light of morning hadn't come, prompting the question of how long she'd slept.

"You're up early."

Her mother sat at the dining table in front of a steaming cup. Neeve rose, a light headache thrumming behind her eyes.

"Seems to be a recurring thing these days," Neeve said, sitting down.

"Did you sleep well?" Kaeli poured a second cup and set it in front of the closest seat.

Neeve sat, wrapping her chilly hands around the warm cup. "I did."

"You two have gotten close." Kaeli glanced at Erick before studying Neeve. "He's been with you since the deal at the crossroads?"

Neeve nodded, not trusting where this was going. "I don't want to argue about the deal."

"I don't either," Kaeli said. "I'm grateful he's been with you, helping you." She sipped her tea, eyes staring into the liquid as though to read the stray leaves at the bottom. "After finding out about Jacqueline stealing from us, going back on her word, it's good you've had someone looking out for you."

"Gretchen and I looked out for ourselves." Neeve held tighter to the cup, her frustration coming to the surface. "Can I ask you something?"

"Always."

Neeve took a slow breath through her nose before speaking. "Why did you have my mind blocked?"

The time had come for an answer, and Kaeli met her daughter's eyes with shame and pleading.

"You were so young," she said. "You'd come to us with tears in your eyes, heartbroken over something you'd seen."

Neeve waited, staying silent, Kenna's house completely still.

"You would describe your *nightmares*, as you called them. They came to you when you touched someone." She smiled at her with lips pressed together. "You saw their deaths, and you were so scared. And we couldn't help you."

"But we're godborn," Neeve said.

"Your father is," she clarified. "Half godborn, half human."

"And me and Gretchen?"

"Gretchen hasn't manifested any innate magic, though her knife throwing is beyond human." Kaeli's steady gaze didn't waver, earnestness in her voice. "But you—you could death-read with touch. Your father and I had no idea such a power could come from a lightborn."

A beautiful blend of light and chaos. "They share blood."

Kaeli nodded. "We realized that, but you were already suffering with your power."

"And blocking my magic?" It was hard for Neeve to keep the sarcasm from her voice. "You really felt that was the best solution?"

"An outcome we didn't foresee," she admitted. "We thought the healer could block only the deathsight, but it took over all of your magic."

They were silent for several minutes, sipping hot tea and processing together. Kaeli reached for Neeve's arm, her hand resting gently as her thumb stroked up and down. "I'm sorry. For so many things."

"Me too."

Kenna emerged from the hallway, hair slightly tangled and eyes still filled with sleep. She offered a tired smile, brightening when she saw the tea.

"Thank you." She sat with Neeve and Kaeli, holding her cup steady as Kaeli poured. "You both look rested." She looked at Neeve, her cup poised for her first sip. "And resting has done you well."

Neeve accepted the compliment, though she didn't agree. The curse would still come, its hold stronger and longer.

"And the blessing of family and friends," Kenna went on, looking at Kaeli. "It's a relief that you all found one another."

"A relief and a blessing," Kaeli said.

Neeve, feeling obligated to add to the conversation, said, "We are very lucky."

"I don't believe it's luck." Kenna winked before she sipped. "There are some who believe in fate and the will of the goddesses. And I don't discredit that, but I also think that what we do shapes our outcome, no matter if there's actually fate at play."

"I like that," Neeve said. "I never liked the idea of seceding control to something unseen and arbitrary. Not that the deities are, themselves, arbitrary, but faith certainly is."

"That's very true," Kenna said. "No two people believe the same thing. Not really. Everyone's path is different."

Neeve sipped her tea. "And our path leads us onward, it seems."

"What will you do if nothing changes?" Kaeli asked. "How will you move forward?"

"This life is still mine," Neeve said. Her conversation with Erick had given her the idea of what she would seek after all this was over. "I'd like to live *more*."

Adventure. Love. Discovery. All of it, open to me. All of it ready for me to take my first step.

"I can appreciate that." Kenna looked past Neeve at the sound of someone stirring. "Especially with loved ones to live a bit more alongside you."

Contentment warmed Neeve's heart, and even as her body transformed with the dawn, she held onto that feeling of completeness, as though to prove to her old body and to the curse and powers that be that she is and will be all right.

Erick stretched and yawned, running a hand over his hair. Cassander wasn't far behind. Kaeli helped Kenna brew more tea and prepare breakfast.

"I can't thank you enough for your hospitality," Cassander said to Kenna. "Your kindness has truly meant a lot."

"You are all most welcome. If things—" She hesitated before continuing, her tone a bit more delicate and careful. "If things don't go well at the place Galla mentioned, you are welcome to return here. My home will always be safe for you."

"Your generosity is appreciated," Cassander said.

"It's more than kind," Erick agreed. "We come to you out of nowhere, and you've been so gracious."

"You are endeavoring something important, and that isn't without its dangers." Kenna stood, moving to the fire to prepare her cookware for breakfast. "A lot of places aren't safe for those with magic, whether it's the acting government or a delusional cult."

"Or a woman who likes to sling around curses." Neeve made herself chuckle.

"Gods above, be safe. And thank you for sharing my table with me." There was a hit of sadness in Kenna's smile. "The days have been nice with your company."

"Waiting was the right choice," Cassander said, pulling the collar of his tunic down to show the top of his wound. The scar had almost faded completely, the line barely visible. "When we run into trouble, I'm much more capable now than I would have been."

"Emphasis on *when*." Erick quirked an eyebrow. "I appreciate your realism, Cass."

"Fallon, Charis." Kaeli rubbed her forehead. "A warden and preceptor for an anti-magic cult, and we're likely headed straight for them."

"Charis?" Erick sat up straighter. "She's here?"

"She's the one who captured us." Kaeli studied his face. "You've met?"

"Briefly," he said, his expression remaining neutral but for the flash of red in his mahogany eyes. "It wasn't pleasant."

"She's especially heinous," Cassander said. "Charis was there not long after Fallon—" A muscle in Cassander's jaw feathered, the words still difficult to say. "She made sure there were no survivors."

"She knows we're in Feather and Claw," Kaeli said, touching the healing bruise on her jaw. "She tried to learn what she could from us."

The blood and bruises when they'd escaped Fallon and the others. Those had been Charis's doing.

Power crackled beneath Neeve's skin like stored lightning, waiting to strike.

"You said warden and perceptor?" Neeve asked.

"*Pre*ceptor," Kaeli clarified. "She trains new recruits and determines if they're ready for promotion."

"*Promotion*," Erick said with a scoff, his voice rich with sarcasm. "A reward for a job well done."

"Fallon's a warden with aspirations for more," Cassander said. "From what I've seen, there is animosity between him and Charis, which likely holds him back."

Neeve liked the sound of that. "Let the two of them fight amongst themselves and see who comes out on top."

"It will be Charis," Kaeli said. "Of that, I have no doubt."

The dangers on the horizon had multiplied. Even with Cassander's healing and the reunion with her parents, Neeve saw the road ahead congested with violent opposition.

Only Neeve's stubbornness could have overshadowed the unease in her core. If she were any less resolved, her apprehension would have stopped this journey from the very beginning. But she saw no other choice than to pursue this to the end. There was no way in the seven hells she would turn back now.

Robert emerged, the most disheveled of them all. "Gods, I slept like the dead." He rubbed his face before combing his tangled hair back with his fingers. "What did I miss?"

Kaeli smirked. "Existential inevitability and the gravity of our mortality."

"Is that all?" He eyed the steaming food on the table. "Oh, breakfast."

He thanked Kenna for the meal before digging in.

CHAPTER 33

The rain had done wonders to the world. Yesterday's storm enlivened the earth, and with Erys's embrace, Rhiann could thrive.

Just like Cassander and Erick, Neeve thought. *Sons of Anya and Aishlin, capable of keeping one another alive.*

Neeve's steps were steady, though her aching body wanted vengeance for the work it did the day before. She hobbled, stubbornly pushing through the stiffness in her legs and back.

"Are you all right?" Cassander asked.

"I have sympathy for my grandmother," she said with a chuckle. "Simple things are more difficult as you age. I've taken a lot for granted."

"Remember what we practiced," he said. "I can offer my magic if you need it."

Self-healing. Light magic.

"Practice?" Robert looked from Neeve to Cassander.

"Light magic," Cassander said. "I've shown her a few things."

"Light *and* chaos?" Robert's eyebrows rose in surprise, looking at Neeve. "Gods be praised, daughter. You've been in strong company."

"You could tell Erick was chaosborn, but not that Cassander was lightborn?" Neeve held her own arms, sending light to her aching joints and limbs. Tension eased. "How is that?"

Robert hesitated, eyes meeting Erick's. At Erick's nod, Robert answered. "He and his mother bear a strong resemblance."

"Oh, gods, that's right."

Cassander blinked at Erick. "Your mother is in Feather and Claw?"

"It would seem so," he answered. "And they have crossed paths."

"I last heard she was headed to Alvar," Kaeli said, looking between Erick and her husband. "We received word that a bloodborn was eager to help us against the Order."

"A bloodborn?" Cassander and Erick both raised the question simultaneously, both locking eyes with one another. "How long was I asleep?"

But Cassander's levity didn't reach them. Neeve looked up at Erick, a slight furrow in his brow, a touch of tension at his mouth. She slipped her hand into his, glad to feel her grip returned.

"I haven't heard from her in a long time," Erick said.

Robert nodded, his expression wary. "She's alive, despite the Order's best efforts."

"She spoke of you often," Kaeli said, speaking up. "And how she left you with good people in Falkirk."

"She did," he said. "They were good people."

Neeve stayed silent by his side as they continued on. They moved north, stepping carefully through grassy terrain and the hills of the Midlands. The overcast provided some relief from the bright afternoon sun as the day waned, and for a brief, blissful moment, she nearly forgot about her cursed body and the age it bore. Erick, who'd kept the world at arm's length, had let her in, and she could read the anguish on his face as they walked together. But an hour into their trek, the familiar aches resurfaced, starting at her knees and hips.

"An hour is impressive," she said. "Staving off the effects of a curse isn't easy."

Cassander offered his hands, but Neeve refused. "Save your magic. I'll be alright. I'm coming to terms with what may actually be."

"And what is that?" he asked.

"That I will have to live as my older self for the rest of my days."

Erick squeezed her hand. "Neeve—"

"I will do my best to accept whatever comes."

"Don't act like we're already defeated."

She stared, the frustration in his voice controlled by the soft way he always spoke to her. But she could hear it, still.

"There is a chance we fail," Cassander said. "But there's hope."

"All magic can be undone," Robert said, and Kaeli repeated the words like a mantra of hope that called for other voices to give it life.

"All magic can be undone," Neeve said, a hint of sarcasm in her words. "Whether through more magic, through destruction, or through death or divinity." She glanced at each of them. "Right?"

Cassander winced slightly, nodding. "Those are the strongest ways, though divinity is rare."

"Death certainly isn't."

"It won't come to that," Robert said, his eyes full of love and concern. "We haven't lost yet."

But rather than suffering the sourness in her core, Neeve stood as tall as her bowed shoulders allowed. "But this life thread is far from its end. And I certainly won't let the likes of her be the reason it's cut short."

"Fight it," Erick said, stealing a kiss as he pressed his lips to her temple. "She will rue the day she knocked on your door."

They stopped for food and drink once they reached a line of trees, the forest stretching before them. They rested on a fallen tree and large stones as they ate what Kenna had given them. The trees whispered amongst themselves as the birds fluttered through their branches. The ground was soft beneath Neeve's feet, and the breeze was cool. At least here, with everything spinning around her, life was beautiful.

Cassander finished his food and dusted off his hands. "Where did Galla say it was?"

Neeve pulled out the map and looked, the mark among trees much like the ones that surrounded them. "Oh, we shouldn't be far. How big is this forest?"

Erick eyed the surrounding trees and brush. "Let's hope not very."

They'd walked for hours going north, and the air that touched them brought a chill from the mountains, nostalgic of the border between

Shaylon Plains and Thurin. Neeve breathed in as though to smell snow, its scent often on the air as the wind swept down to the fields.

All the more reason to see the world, Neeve thought. *How much more of it is like home? How much of it is so different that it will take my breath away?*

Moving on, their steps carried them through the trees to a clearing, one often tread with a footpath well worn.

"It has to be close," Robert said, pointing at the path and tracing down. "Someone passed through here a day or two ago. Maybe three."

Neeve maintained her momentum, spite fueling her resolve. She would confront Jacqueline at last and see to the end of this wretched affliction.

There! A wooden roof peeked through the boughs of the trees until she reached the clearing. But her relief was short-lived as she took in the derelict state of it. The roof had caved in on one side, and on the other was a devastating hole in the wall, as though something large had broken through. A sapling, likely from a buried acorn, was growing up from within the shack, along with large patches of long grass and wild flowers. The front door was off its hinges, hanging pathetically in its portal with a delicate sway in the breeze.

Neeve remembered its shape, the peaks of the roof, the shadow of the house against the sunlit land. But it was far beyond any hope of repair, let alone safety.

"What on earth—" Cassander stopped, staring at the broken structure before them. "There's no way anyone could hold out here, hiding from the Order."

The footsteps on the path had shown someone's recent passage, but there was nothing that Neeve could see of Jacqueline being close.

But Neeve had seen this place. When she scried, seeking Jacqueline, her sight and shown her.

"Did he lie?" Kaeli asked. "One last attempt to save her skin?"

"Maybe not," Cassander said. "Maybe he didn't know."

Neeve pulled the front door it to see more inside, but there was nothing. As her hand held the damp, mildewed wood, a tingling danced up her arm to her shoulder, to her chest and back, turning into a thousand needles piercing through her skin and muscles. She gasped, the pain fleeting, like a limb that had lost circulation. But her entire body froze.

"I can't move." Panic trembled through her voice as she tried to breathe, her chest far too tight. "I can't move!"

An invisible net had ensnared her, thin threads made of the strongest fibers, holding her in place. Her parents were quick to her side, only to be caught with her.

"It spreads," Kaeli said to Erick and Cassander, the two stopping in their tracks to reach them. "Don't touch it."

And then the spider emerged.

Jacqueline looked at each of their faces in wonder. "Oh, look at all of my visitors. Apologies for the trouble."

Her eyes met Kaeli and Robert, a bit of the color leaving her face.

"Good to see you both again." Then, seeing aged Neeve, likely put all the pieces together. "Oh, you found one another. How sweet."

"Break the curse," Neeve said. "That's all we want."

"As return the money you stole," Kaeli spat. "You greedy—"

"I can't." Jacqueline blinked at Neeve, her expression unreadable, before she said, "There are a lot of steps to break it."

"Then take them," Neeve said. She heard Erick whispering quietly behind her, unfamiliar words coming fast to finish his cast. "I want my life back. The life you *stole*."

"You betrayed us, Jackie," Robert said.

"Don't call me that!"

"You stole from our daughters." If Kaeli's gaze could kill, Jacqueline's last moments would be in agony.

"Nothing has gone the way I'd like," Jacqueline said, as though that was her defense. "Gods, even Moonblade wants what they think is theirs." With a hint of remorse, she said to Neeve, "If I said I didn't expect the spell to turn out this way, would you believe me?"

"What did you expect?" Neeve spat. "My death?"

"Gods, no! I had to get out! Which, by the way—" Jacqueline tugged her pant leg up, showing the shadow of a bruise on her ankle. "Your little touchmagic stunt took *days* to heal. I was limping my way to the port."

"No less than you deserve," Neeve hissed.

"Why stop for a reading?" Cassander asked. "You've harmed someone, and for what?"

"I didn't mean for this to happen!"

Neeve felt her bonds break with Erick's final word, and the three of them swarmed Jacqueline, the woman screaming as she tried to flee. But Erick pulled from her pile of tricks and ensnared her, his magical net stronger.

"Let me go!" Jacqueline wiggled and screamed. "They'll find me!"

"They sure will, with you giving away where you are," Erick said, a look of disgust on his face. "Keep screaming, you careless, pathetic witch. Make them find you."

Kaeli moved closer to her, her gaze burning with anger. "Know that we don't trust you and automatically assume you're lying."

"Even if I said I can't break the curse?" Jacqueline raised her eyebrows in a challenging look, as though she dared them to call her bluff. Her eyes, unblinking, darted to each of them. But, rather than her bravado giving her a look of confidence, the fear of a caged animal was in her eyes. "I can't break it."

"Then you're taking us to someone who can." Erick shrugged. "Either way, you're coming with us."

"They'll kill me," she said, her loud whisper raspy as it grated against Neeve's hearing. "Please."

"You shouldn't worry about *them*." Kaeli's voice was dangerous. Robert gripped her shoulder, genuine concern in his eyes.

"You made a mistake, Jacqueline," Robert said. "One you will have to fix."

"You didn't have to curse me." Neeve's voice was like acid. "I tried to help you."

"I didn't mean to." Tears welled in her eyes, but neither Neeve nor the others bore any sympathy. "There was a seer who said to beware the one who sees death."

"You just made that up," Kaeli said.

"Do you believe the lies you tell, or do you still have a grasp on reality?" Neeve shook her head. "*Beware the one who sees death* doesn't mean *go to her home and ask for a reading.*"

Erick snorted a laugh as Jacqueline sneered, trying to counter the chaosborn's magic.

"If you know how to break these bonds," he said, "then you're quite the powerful witch."

Challenge flared in his eyes as he watched her cast spell after spell, all of them yielding nothing.

"Can those bonds go with her?" Neeve asked, her patience thin and anger burning. "We should keep moving."

Erick moved his fingers and whispered the spell, keeping Jacqueline's arms bound but her legs free. She tried to flee, but her invisible cocoon limited her mobility. She fell, nearly face-first, and thrashed like a fish out of water.

"How can I trust you?" Jacqueline hissed, strands of hair sticking to her face. "After what I've done, you want my head on a stick."

"If you don't trust us," Neeve said, "trust that we need you alive."

Cassander helped her to stand. "Take us to someone who can break the curse, and we'll part ways."

"So long as you stay the hells away from Sheraton," Kaeli said.

They waited, Jacqueline eyeing them uneasily. "Keep me alive and make sure nothing happens to my brother. He only wanted to keep me safe."

"Well, he did a great job, didn't he?" Erick's voice was knife-edged. "Such a loving brother."

"This would move a lot faster if you'd tell us where to go," Cassander said.

Erick crossed his arms, satisfied. "Still can't break the bonds?"

Kaeli nodded in approval. "Nice work, Erick."

Her glare was deadly as she struggled, arms immobile. "Head west. There's a camp of deathwitches near the coast. Just a boat ride away from Hymoor."

"At least we don't have to go all the way to another continent," Neeve said. "*Again.*"

"The children of Aishlin are everywhere," Jacqueline said, looking at Neeve as though she were an idiot. "No one country or continent can hold a group as powerful. These are in the Midlands. One of them sold me the curse."

But Erick shook his head. "I've heard enough." And, with a flick of his fingers, he pulled Jacqueline to her feet and pushed her west, setting her to lead them.

"Sons and daughters of darkness," Jacqueline said to bait him, though there was reverence in her voice. "Sons and daughters of chaos."

His burgundy eyes flashed with frustration, his mouth hard-set as he tightened his hold on her. Jacqueline cried out.

"Erick—"

But Cassander's warning went unheeded as Erick persisted, his anger dominating his senses.

"What do you know of chaos?" His voice deepened, shadows feathering around his feet. "You petulant, immature witchling. You are a mockery of her power."

Jacqueline's eyes traced his form, understanding making her expression go slack. She stared, awestruck. "I'm sorry. I didn't realize." Hers was a gaze of admiration. "May I—May I know your name?"

"No." With his magic, he turned her around and pushed her forward. "Take us to the camp and see that this curse is removed. Then I hope to never see or hear of you again."

"I didn't know." Jacqueline shook her head, panicked. She fought against the movement, wanting to stop and explain. "I didn't know she was yours."

"She belongs to no one." Erick's voice dangerously trailed a knife's edge. "Now *lead*."

Jacqueline fumbled in her steps to keep up with Erick's magic, and Neeve and Cassander exchanged curious and alarmed looks.

"A self-proclaimed acolyte of Aishlin has pissed off a chaosborn," Cassander said. "An interesting turn of events."

Robert chuckled. "I appreciate the irony."

Neeve hurried to Erick's side, enduring the aching pull in her back and legs. He moved too quickly for her to read him, to know how best to comfort him, so she resigned to stay in his presence with space enough for his thoughts and feelings to run their full course, unimpeded and uninterrupted.

Jacqueline was the sort of chaos worshipper who drew Erick's disdain, and she had no inkling of how dangerous that was. Someone as loving as Erick enduring such darkness kindled a fire within Neeve that burned in the palms of her hands.

Hurting Neeve with a curse was one thing. But hurting Erick? Bringing him to anger because of her ignorance and selfishness in the name of Aishlin?

How tempted she was to see how far her connection to light and chaos could go...

CHAPTER 34

Jacqueline moved painstakingly slow, as though to punish the group for keeping her.

"You only delay the inevitable," Cassander said at last. "The sooner you help us, the sooner you're free."

"You're right," she said, her tone mocking. "I should comply and make this easy for myself, despite this forced journey to a place I don't want to go."

"I wonder what that's like," Neeve said, her tone knife-edged. "To have your hand forced because of someone else's actions."

"Why don't you want to go?" Erick asked, pleased with her predicament. "Are you in trouble with them, too?"

Jacqueline only tilted her head in a near shrug, one that answered *yes*.

"Is there *anyone* who would be happy to see you?" Neeve asked, awestruck by the woman trudging on in front of her. "Or does everyone have a reason to seek retribution from you?"

"Careful, *Elder*," Jacqueline said with a sneer. "You wouldn't want to slip and break a hip."

Erick's hand landed on Jacqueline's shoulder. "Speak to her that way again, and you won't be able to speak at all. Whatever happens to her happens to you."

"Ooh." She winked at him. "Promise?"

"I warned you." Exasperated, Erick wove his fingers in the air, muttering.

Jacqueline laughed in silence. Horror-struck, her gaze turned inward as her hands went to her throat. She mouthed *what did you do* over and over until she screamed. The group watched in relief and blissful silence as the villainess cried out with no voice.

"I like him," Kaeli muttered to Robert, but Neeve overheard.

"I have to say I do, too," he said.

Neeve smiled despite her annoyance at Jacqueline, one corner of her mouth tugging upward.

"It's terrible when someone curses you, isn't it?" Erick's vocal inflection was full of mocking, though his expression was stoic. "Take us to the witch who created the spell, and I might give you your voice back. If any harm comes to my people, harm comes to you."

Jacqueline screamed again, this time reaching for Erick with her fingers like claws. But Neeve intercepted, grabbing Jacqueline's wrist in her aged grip. Neeve sent a trace of light through her skin, enough to shock the tantrum out of her.

"You're the reason you're here, you petulant child," Neeve said. "Your choices have led you here." She let her go. "And your choices can help you now, if you let them."

Jacqueline's eyes were deadly as they bore into Neeve's.

"Careful," Neeve warned, not backing down. "I just might finish that death reading."

Neeve wiggled her fingers over Jacqueline's arm, and she recoiled. Neeve didn't contain the cackle that emanated from her throat, instead relishing the freedom it gave.

"Being old has its benefits," Neeve said. "An old crone with biting sarcasm suits me just fine."

"Gods," Kaeli said, smiling, "you sound like my mother."

Hours passed while walking before they rested for food and drink. Jacqueline held her stomach with both hands, mouthing *hungry* over and over again.

"We would've rested much sooner if you hadn't slowed us down,"

Erick said to Jacqueline. "Remember what Neeve said about choices having consequences?"

She threw a string of curses at him, all of them inaudible.

Kaeli chuckled. "I can't express how satisfying that is."

Erick, with a smiling side-glance, agreed.

They sat where they could and rifled through their packs for what food they could share with Jacqueline. Neeve dug deep, reaching for whatever food was the oldest, when thundering footsteps caught her attention—footsteps that were fading.

Cassander was fast. Neeve would have sworn wings of light came from his back as he intercepted Jacqueline's hasty attempt at escape. Jacqueline's mouth opened in a silent cry, stomping her feet.

"I like him, too," Robert said to Kaeli, who nodded. "Our daughter keeps good company."

Cassander's gaze was steel, though it hadn't lost its kindness. "You will have no peace until it is done."

"*I will have no peace,*" she mouthed slowly, with Cassander repeating the words out loud. "*I will have no peace, no matter what happens.*"

Unlike Cassander, Neeve bore no sympathy. "And that is the life that you created."

Jacqueline spoke too quickly for Neeve to read her lips. Something about *say that again* and *my choices.*

"We will share our food with you, and you will make sure we arrive safely." Kaeli counted her terms on her fingers as she verbalized the ultimatum. "You will also make sure the curse is completely broken and my daughter is returned to her original state. I don't know how we can make it any clearer, thief."

More curses escaped Jacqueline's mouth, and Erick grinned at Neeve. "That might be my favorite spell."

The cool breeze swept over them as they ate, bodies glad to rest.

"How much farther?" Erick asked Jacqueline. "Another hour?"

She waved her hand in a see-saw motion.

"When the witches helped you," Cassander said, "did you pay them?"

She nodded.

"Was this curse your idea?"

She shook her head vigorously and mouthed, *"I didn't know."* Then, slowly, she mouthed, *"Wanted to slow him down."*

"You didn't know what the spell would do," Robert said, his tone rich with disbelief, "yet you cast it at my daughter instead of the man it was meant for?" He shook his head. "Save your lies and save your breath."

Jacqueline glowered at him.

"Slow him down," Cassander repeated. "Fallon?"

She nodded and mouthed the witch hunter's name with another's: *Charis.*

"Gods above, you can't be serious." Kaeli shared a look with her husband. "If she's telling the truth, Charis is after her, too."

Jacqueline glared at them. *"It's true."*

"Which part?"

"All of it!"

Kaeli chuckled as Erick muttered to Neeve, "I love seeing her so frustrated in forced silence."

"Serves her right," Neeve said. "Poetic justice."

"I suppose I can let her speak for a little while," he said. "Just to remind her of what's in store when she completes the job as directed."

"No rush on that," Kaeli said.

But Erick cast to diminish his hold on her voice, granting her the freedom to speak.

"You bastard," she said immediately. "How long will this reprieve last?"

"As long as you behave yourself."

Neeve looked past Jacqueline, dark gray clouds rolling in the distance. "That storm is moving fast."

"Will we reach their camp before the storm?" Cassander asked.

"We'd better," Kaeli said. "We are *not* setting up camp with her."

Jacqueline glanced skyward, thinking. "We still have awhile to go."

Would that I could cast a truth spell. But something else occurred to Neeve, remembering her training with Erick.

She met Jacqueline's eye, guiding her will to Jacqueline's consciousness.

"Are you telling the truth?" Neeve's power brushing over her surface thoughts, but the attempt yielded nothing. Casting through Jacqueline's mental wards would take more time and focus than Neeve could afford.

"Mostly," Jacqueline said. Neeve's magic confirmed with a warm touch against her skin that her word was honest. "We're close, but I can't remember exactly where it is."

Neeve raised an eyebrow, glancing at the others. "Keep our eyes open, I guess."

"Let's go," Erick said, dusting his hands off before offering one to Neeve to help her stand. "We won't have any shelter until then."

He moved close to Neeve, a slight smirk flattering his mouth. "Well done, by the way."

She bumped his shoulder with hers. "Glad you noticed."

Jacqueline had to eat while walking as clouds continue to sweep overhead, sunlight coming and going like waves on the sea.

"It's almost as though Erys is urging us on," Cassander said, looking wistfully heavenward. "She wants us to succeed."

"Even so," Erick said, "I like our self-reliance. I've never been one to wait around for a divine touch or intervention."

"That's likely why the goddesses are keen to help," Cassander said. "Because we're helping ourselves."

"Your faith must be unwavering," Jacqueline said in bitter disbelief. "How can you stay so devoted?"

"Faith requires *all* of you," Cassander said. "Only giving parts of yourself won't help you reach full and satisfying power. Your selfishness won't give you the connection you seek."

"Don't preach at me, lightborn."

"Then don't open the door and walk through it," he bit back, his tone severe, "if you don't want to see the room where one lives."

"Be careful about insulting the children of Aishlin's sister," Erick muttered. "It would do you well to remember that he and I bear the same blood."

Neeve chuckled. "You have a remarkable habit of burning the bridges you need to cross."

"It's true we don't like you," Robert said, "but we have no interest in taking your life. The same can't be said for the Wandering Order."

"We could be the only thing keeping you safe," Kaeli added. "The irony isn't lost on me. Believe me."

Jacqueline was silent as the group walked on beneath the sky, shifting in light and shadow. In the far distance, thunder rolled.

CHAPTER 35

Static grew in the atmosphere as the dark stretched overhead, the storm clouds inching closer. Neeve drew a long breath, smelling incense and sage mingling with wood smoke. The perfume of magic.

"Not much further," Jacqueline said. Neeve watched her gulp as she stared ahead, eyes unblinking.

What is she walking into? Neeve watched ahead, ready for any sign of the camp. *What are* we *walking into?*

As though to answer, voices whispered through the air, questioning the strange travelers venturing too close.

Strangers.

Visitors.

Why are they here?

Why do they come?

"They already know we're here?" Neeve asked Erick and Cassander.

But it was Jacqueline who answered. "They did the same to me when I came before. They have wards all around this place."

"The wards themselves aren't dangerous," Erick said. "I can feel them. They're more of an awareness spell, letting them know when someone's close."

"Are the wards whispering to us?" Robert asked. "Or are the witches?"

"That would be the witches," Jacqueline said. "Unsettling, isn't it?"

"It caught me off guard," Cassander admitted. "But they have to protect themselves."

There was a deep inhale, as though the earth readied a deep breath, before a voice carried a single word. "*You.*"

The voice, a smooth alto, caught their attention in its abrupt address as the woman appeared, her black robes worn but cared for. Her dark hair was bound and woven into the knot at the back of her neck, and her violet eyes were bright beneath the stormy sky as they bore into Jacqueline, who trembled, eyes wide and mouth weakly shaping around words she couldn't speak.

Two others joined the first, walking effortlessly on the uneven ground, though their feet made no sound. Their robes matched, emphasizing the differences in hair and height. Their eyes locked onto Jacqueline with dark delight.

"You've returned after we forbade you to come," the first woman said to Jacqueline. But her eyes darted to Erick, realization softening the hard lines around her mouth. The other witches did the same, their eyes locking onto him in such synchronicity that Neeve's nerves trembled beneath her skin. Reverence replaced the disdain the woman held for Jacqueline as she stared at the chaosborn before her. "We are blessed, my sisters. A son of Aishlin has come."

"A son of Aishlin," the second witch whispered, her chestnut hair full as it fell past her shoulders. Her rich blue eyes regarded him with unabashed wonder.

"A son of chaos." The third showed her palms in supplication, the copper rings around her fingers nearly matching the color of her eyes. The length of her braided blonde hair reached far over her shoulder.

And they each bowed to him, humming their words of praise.

"Please," Erick said, retreating a half-step back, grimacing in discomfort. "It's not as though I am Aishlin, herself."

"No, but you are of her line," the first said. "We are honored to have you among us."

She introduced each of them, starting with herself, her palm over her heart. "Isa." She gestured to the brunette. "This is Genova. And Moira." The blonde bowed her head as Isa introduced her.

Then their eyes flashed to Neeve, Robert, and Cassander.

"Three lightborn," Isa said.

"That sounds like the beginning of a prophecy," Moira said before laughing quietly to herself. "Or a bad joke."

Isa reeled on Jacqueline, who, during this interlude, had tried to tiptoe her way out. She bumped into Cassander, who sneakily blocked her path, and had to face the chaoswitch who cleared the distance between them.

"You dare curse a godborn?" The storm in Isa's eyes darkened. "You dare use my magic against a vessel for Anya's power?"

"I didn't know!" Her voice was shrill with panic. "The spell went wrong!"

Neeve rolled her eyes at Jacqueline. "Stop acting like you're the victim when you've caused the trouble you're in. The spell went exactly as it was meant to."

"Of course it did," Isa said. "My magic is precise."

Jacqueline's eyes shot daggers at Neeve, but Isa continued. "I don't take kindly to those who use my magic like this."

"How would you like it used?" Erick looked as uncomfortable as Neeve felt.

"It was intended for the cultist," Genova spoke up with hatred in her voice. "The one with ice for eyes."

"We're looking to end the curse," Erick said. "We've traveled a long way to see it done."

Sympathy mingled with Isa's analytical gaze as she regarded Neeve. "Interesting."

That was the last thing Neeve expected to hear. "What do you mean?"

She glanced at her parents, who held the same confused expression. *Interesting?* Her mother mouthed with a shrug.

"We are just about to dine," Isa said, breezing past Neeve's question. "We would be honored to break bread with you."

Neeve opened her mouth but stopped herself. *Move with them. The timing will come. Let the flow lead you.*

Their camp was simple with necessities, and it looked much more transient than it actually was. They'd been there for days, maybe even weeks, without moving from this spot.

Genova and Moira took their time looking over Neeve, Erick, and Cassander, upon whom her eyes lingered.

"Mortals, chaosborn, and lightborn," Genova said, toying with her chestnut hair. "An interesting traveling group."

"We're friends," Erick said, a hint of authority in his voice as he edged toward Cassander. It didn't escape Neeve's notice as Erick tried to protect them from any misgivings or intentions the witches may have toward their lightborn companions. "We only seek to end her curse."

"The cursed typically have the power to end the curse themselves," Moira said. "Have you tried fighting the magic?"

Neeve raised an eyebrow. "Have I tried *not* being old?"

"Let us eat first," Isa said, passing a bowl of stew to Erick first, then Neeve, then Cassander. "Magic is best done after hunger is sated."

Patience. They'll help you. Of that, she was certain.

"Are you from Ileden?" Neeve asked, making conversation.

"I am," Moira said. "Genova and Isa are from Willow Hill."

Genova didn't hide her watchful gaze, waiting for any reaction at the mention of such the infamous region in Hymoor known for its dark magic. Isa took her first bite of food, seemingly unaffected.

"My parents and I are from Shaylon Plains," Neeve said, feeling it only polite to share.

"It must be beautiful this time of year," Moira said. "Everything in full bloom."

"Willow Hill has such moments," Genova said. "But I've found it more similar to Melia than Shaylon Plains."

"Trees, mushrooms, *bogs*." Isa giggled. "Melia doesn't have bogs, Gen."

"I said it was *more* similar," Genova defended, "not identical."

Moira leaned closer to the trio and muttered, "You'd think they were sisters."

The mention of *sisters* brought Neeve's thoughts to her own. She pressed her lips together, wishing that the phantom touch of Gretchen's embrace was tighter.

The rest of the meal continued with Moira and Genova going back and forth, the rest of them remaining mostly silence as they ate and listened.

"Jacqueline," Isa said, still eating. "Tell me why."

Jacqueline stayed quiet for several seconds before she nearly coughed out, "I panicked."

"You were to use this curse on that spawn of slime," Isa said, her tone dangerously calm. The eye of a storm. "How could you be so careless?"

"I could feel him on my trail," she said, her words coming fast. "He would have been at her doorstep any second. I had to get out of there."

Isa set her spoon down into her bowl, looking at Jacqueline with a clear, level expression. "I don't understand your level of panic pushing you to curse an innocent woman performing a task you asked her to do."

Neeve marveled at the quiet anger in the chaoswitch before her. Every inch of her held *control*, even with something so wild as chaos magic.

Jacqueline choked out a sob. "Please, forgive me."

"While I am not pleased to see my magic wasted in such a way," Isa said, "it is not I who can forgive."

All eyes fell to Neeve. The embarrassment was an extra layer of pressure she didn't need.

"Don't hold your breath," Neeve said. "I have no intention of letting this go."

"But—"

"It's as Isa said," Neeve interrupted. "You were careless. You *are* careless." Her voice came out ragged, even as she worked to control her anger. "You've changed my life in a drastic way that has forced me and my friends to step into a dangerous situation to reverse your stupidity."

Jacqueline's repentant look flickered to anger for the briefest moment, her eyes and mouth hardening as she moved to speak.

"Don't." Steel supported Neeve's words, sharp and unyielding. "When it comes to me letting this go, keep your expectations low."

"That last bit rhymed," Moira mused.

"She's her mother's daughter," Robert said, shaking his head at

Jacqueline. "They're practically god-touched when it comes to holding grudges."

Isa waited until everyone had finished eating before having Moira and Genova clear the dishes. Then, with four sets of eyes upon her, she began.

"There isn't a way to break this curse," Isa said.

Neeve stared, disbelief freezing all thought in her mind.

"Which she knew." Isa's eyes flickered to Jacqueline before returning to Neeve. "This is something you have to do."

"What?" Neeve's reaction was barely a whisper. No emotion, no breath, no heartbeat. There were too many things passing through her mind that her body detached completely.

There isn't a way to break this curse.

This is something you have to do.

The moment with Erick, where her body had returned, only to shift back to Godmother Neeve.

She hadn't expected the folklore adage of *the power was within her all along* to be the linchpin for her own success. It was a cheap way out.

No, not cheap. Clever. Because Fallon wouldn't have figured it out, either. The curse would have consumed him with either age or madness, whichever took him first.

But disappointment soured Neeve's stomach again.

"I thought you were joking," Jacqueline said, breaking the resulting silence. "Something to threaten Fallon with. Make him sweat." Genuine panic laced in her words. "Every curse can be broken."

"Yes, and this one can be remedied, but it isn't something that anyone can do." Isa's eyes meet Neeve's. "Anyone except you, Neeve Deathseer."

Jacqueline swore, eyes flashing to Erick and Kaeli. She quivered beneath the burn of their respective gazes.

"If she dies," Erick said, his voice dangerously low, "you die."

"How could I—" Neeve struggled, glancing from Isa to Jacqueline to Erick. She caught Cassander's sympathetic eye. "Everything I've tried has failed."

Neeve set her jaw, hating her words, hating her despair. *Don't let fear win.*

"It's not that type of curse." Isa's kindness remained, even with the bluntness of the truth. "And it's not that type of cure."

She held her hand out for Neeve to take. At their contact, magic flowing beneath Neeve's skin. Isa, though not godborn, was very strong in magic.

"The cure rests within you," she said. "Love and appreciate yourself as you are, not as you feel you should be."

"But I do!" Neeve gripped Isa's hands tighter, as if to prove it to her. "I have a wonderful life!"

Isa raised her eyebrows. "Then the curse should have no hold over you."

But the curse had consumed her like a flash flood beneath a relentless rain. Its flow was impossible to tread, the surface rising higher as every drop fell.

"I've had the power to break the curse." Neeve said the words out loud, though she still didn't believe them. "All this time?"

Isa nodded, her expression solemn. "All this time."

Erick rested a hand on her shoulder, but Neeve stood up. "I—" Her throat was too tight. "I need some air."

"We're already outside," Jacqueline said, only to receive a withering look from everyone.

"This close to getting silenced again." Erick pinched his index finger and thumb together, squinting at Jacqueline. "*This close.*"

Moira giggled.

Neeve walked a few paces, still keeping the group in her sights. It was the closeness of them, each of them breathing and watching and thinking, when her mind overflowed.

She took a deep breath through her nose, smelling herbs and wood and salt water and damp earth. In the quiet, she thought of home.

I don't love myself? Is that what all this means?

But that didn't feel right. She had wonderful parents, a beautiful sister.

A wonderful life. A wonderful family.

Her eyes found Erick as he watched her, a flutter in her stomach souring beneath a tinge of guilt. She wanted to kiss him again, to explore the extent of what she felt.

Those feelings haven't carried me, either.

She looked down at her weathered hands.

Because I won't let them.

A chill coursed through her, one deep and not easily quelled. Her next breath shuddered, her body buckling beneath the swell of emotion that would overwhelm her any second.

This is what Isa meant. The power that I hold to stop this stupid curse—

Her stomach churned, foolishness and guilt mingling in her core.

She shivered, frost spreading through her. Erick, Cassander, Gretchen, all that they've done *with* her and *for* her, the significance of everything bearing down all at once.

"I could have stopped this long ago," she whispered to the listening trees. "If I hadn't been so afraid."

The wind whispered back, the rustling boughs and falling leaves a quiet chorus.

She closed her eyes, understanding the longing in her heart more than ever before. Adventure, *love*—those things can't be done in fear.

"Oh, good." A voice behind her. "You're all here."

Neeve spun, wide-eyes finding Fallon's smug face.

"That will make this much easier."

CHAPTER 36

"How—" Backing away from Fallon, eyes darting to each cultist, Neeve nearly lost her footing, the soft, uneven earth ill-equipped for her anxious steps. "How did you—"

Her legs quivered beneath her. *Gods damn this body.*

Fallon sauntered toward them, the two other cultists at his flank. He glanced over his shoulder. "You did well."

A man stepped forward from the trees, fear alight in his eyes.

Galla.

He swallowed, wincing in shame. "T—Told you."

"You and your sister have held up your end of the deal so far," Fallon said. "That won't be forgotten."

"You *and* your sister." Light tingled her palms, begging for use. "You *coward.*"

"Jackie started all this." Trembling, Galla gulped, recoiling back. "It's been months. *Months.* Gods, I haven't slept since."

Months. From the very beginning. Jacqueline in Feather and Claw, a Wandering Order plant. Going to Neeve's home and cursing her.

All this time.

"Oh." Fallon's sinister grin widened. "Speaking of sisters."

Behind him, more cultists emerged from the brush, one of them gripping the arm of a beautiful brunette, her curls haphazard around her shoulders.

Gretchen, her lip bloodied, her cheek bruised. The man holding her collar had a dagger to her back.

Fire licked through Neeve's veins. The world stopped as she traced every bruise, every bloody mark on her sister's face, neck, and arms.

Light gathered around Neeve's hands, the heat in her palms almost aching beneath her skin. "You will all die screaming."

"I'm alright," Gretchen said right away, grimacing as the man shook her. "Two of their friends aren't, though."

The world dimmed as Neeve siphoned the glow from the surrounding rays of sunlight. Her green eyes flashed from Gretchen's captor to Fallon. "I will make you beg for death."

Fallon's satisfied smile sharpened the angles of his hawk-like face, making him even more predatory. "Now, now, little witch. Play nice. We've had our eye on her for a while now."

Footsteps thundered from behind as Erick and the others reached her.

"Gods," Cassander said. "*Gretchen*."

"Gretchen!"

Kaeli and Robert stormed forward before skidding to a halt. Gretchen winced, the man behind her tightening his hold against the dagger.

Kaeli's hazel eyes flashed murderous rage. "I will skin you alive, you useless waste of flesh."

Fallon chuckled, eyes traveling from Kaeli to Neeve. "I see the rage is hereditary."

Jacqueline moved around them all, her bound hands extended toward Fallon. With a disgusted sneer, he shook his head toward one of the other cultists.

"Cut her bonds. She delivered as promised."

The others watched in stunned silence as the cultist did as he was told. Jacqueline rubbed her freed wrists, the burning red marks angry where the rope had been.

"Inept at magic," Erick taunted, "but accomplished at lying."

"You were with them?" Neeve shuddered, memories of the death reading and the curse coming back in flashes. "The death reading. It was so you could—"

"I knew you'd see," Jacqueline said. "I had orders. But they never said you'd have to *read me*."

"*Orders.*" Erick's grin was manic, laced with rage. "You had orders to go into her home and curse her?"

"That bit of flavor was extra," Fallon said with a smirk. "The curse has been an unexpected little perk."

"Explain what you said before," Neeve demanded, glaring at him. "You've had your eye on my sister."

"The sister to a deathseer," Fallon said, as though the concept were simple. "Leverage to use against one who struck a deal with a chaosborn."

Fallon's eyes brightened as Erick stepped beside Neeve, shadows swirling around his form. He strangled the handles of his knives.

"Our time in Brightmere was enlightening, to say the least," Fallon went on. "A deathseer was a fortuitous discovery. And as soon as we got wind of a chaosborn granting deals, our Preceptor made it a priority to gain his capture." Fallon's eyes fell on Erick. "Something about unfinished business."

"Deathseer." Neeve's eyes flashed from Fallon to Jacqueline. "They weren't after you?"

"After her?" Fallon laughed, the sound echoing off the trees. "Silly girl. We've been trailing *you*."

"Gods," Cassander said, disbelief heavy in his voice. "It wasn't Jacqueline. It was—"

"A ruse," Fallon said. "Well acted and well executed."

"Enough," Erick said, burgundy eyes aflame. "This ends here."

"Ends?" Fallon grinned. "This is only the beginning, chaosborn."

"Your Preceptor has delusions of grandeur, much like yourself." Erick's voice deepened, his chaos power surfacing. "Her obsession with me would be flattering if it weren't for her murderous intentions."

"And she sent you to do her dirty work," Neeve taunted, "like a good little errand boy."

Fallon's face reddened, nostrils flaring, lips twitching.

"There was darkness when you brought her to Ileden," Neeve said, her thoughts racing. Pieces fell together as the grim truth revealed itself. "I couldn't see her."

"I heard you speak," Gretchen said, grimacing at knife point, "but I was gagged and couldn't answer."

"Ah." Fallon, composing himself, straightened his shoulders. "A bit of stealth was required as they sailed near the Sound. Stormwitches made their lives hell as they navigated the waters near Storm Key. The ship nearly capsized."

Neeve stared at the cultist's grip on Gretchen's arm, the beds of his fingernails white. Gretchen at sea alone, surrounded by monsters. She could have been lost, and Neeve would never have known.

Shadows laced through the threads of light swirling around her hands and feet, their cold touch desperate for human warmth.

"Snatching loved ones from their beds?" Isa said, hands already poised for a fight. "You cultist dogs have no honor."

"Speak to me of honor, witch, when you are purged of your darkness."

Moira and Genova whispered together. Isa joined them. Neeve pulled on her shadows as they swirled and spread around her, the distraction exactly what she needed.

"This doesn't have to be difficult," Fallon said to those gathered. "We leave with the godborn and the deathseer, and all is well."

But the witches didn't stop, their magical voices growing louder, a quiet cacophony of whispers designed to disorient and obscure. Several cultists blinked against it, the reach of the magic already deep in their minds.

"Your loved ones will never see you again," Neeve said, her voice low, eyes locked onto the man holding Gretchen. The power beneath her skin bloomed, the sensation new and vitalizing. Shadow and light formed a line of small orbs that revolved around her hands. "There will be no bodies to bury, no rites to perform. You will fall to nothing."

"Now, now, little witch," Fallon crooned. "Careful."

Gretchen cried out as her captor jabbed the dagger against her back. Neeve's world turned red, the orbs swirling faster, every remaining touch of fatigue fading. Her magic grew, her mind broadened to the arcane energy in the air.

"It's a shame none of you pray," Erick said. "You've no idea what you've done, and what mercy will be denied you."

One cultist snickered. "We know exactly what we've done, godborn. Nothing you can do can sway us."

"Oh, I'm not talking about me." His burgundy eyes fell to Neeve. "I'm talking about *her*."

Connecting to his mind was easy. No guards or fortifications stood in her way as her magic slipped in. Neeve's pulse thundered in her ears as she watched his gaze turn inward, his pupils shrinking to pinpricks. He groaned, trying to resist her assault on his mind. But his mental strength was weak, his mind prime for the taking.

Live the nightmare, you wretch.

Blood oozed from his nose, his face flushed a deep red. Then he screamed.

Gretchen turned and struck, her hit landing hard against his throat. She took the dagger from his hand and plunged it into his gut. He crumpled to the soft earth, screaming. Gretchen pulled the sword from his belt and moved like a freed predator, claws out and ready to strike.

Neeve threw her magic at the gathering of cultists threatening Erick, Cassander, and her parents, nearly a dozen coin-sized orbs of light and shadow hurling at their enemies. Several found purchase against their foes, but the others, including Fallon, dodged.

One cultist ran forward, blade aloft, until Kaeli raced forward and slammed a tree branch into his gut. Robert was not far behind, bringing another branch down onto his head.

Fallon's lip curled. "You seem to think this is a fight you can win."

Gretchen poised the knife to throw, aiming it at Fallon, until a whistle pierced the air, preceding a bellow of agony. The hidden bowman sank an arrow into Robert's shoulder. Kaeli held him as he bent in pain, the wooden shaft between his bloody fingers.

"Dad!" Neeve and Gretchen screamed.

How many bowmen were there? One? Ten? The forest was closing in, unseen villains lurking in its hiding places. Could Neeve's magic reach them all?

The three witches continued their dissonant whispers, the hisses growing louder and more discordant.

Cassander rushed to him but skidded to a halt as an arrow whizzed past, missing him by inches.

"Cowards." Erick sneered, lifting his shadow-laced arms, his form becoming more abyssal as he reached his darkness toward the trees.

Another arrow found purchase, this time in Moira's leg, before unseen cultists screamed from the boughs above them. Erick's whispering grew louder seconds before archers fell from branches with thuds, the sickening cracks of bones nearly drowned out by their panicked cries.

The whispers faltered as Moira collapsed, her injured leg sticking out as Isa and Genova surrounded her. Neeve moved with Gretchen, hastening out of their line of fire.

Genova lashed out, aiming her hands at those who came from behind. The bowmen and Jacqueline cried out, Genova's magic potent, and the three of them collapsed to their knees.

"Jackie!" Galla rushed forward but crumbled beneath his own gut-wrenching pain from Moira, one bloody hand at her shoulder and the other aimed at Galla, fingers curled like claws.

Fallon and the other cultists faltered in their advance, his bright eyes fixed on Moira.

"Now!" Fallon called out. "Take them!"

Isa joined her friends as Erick and Cassander fought beside Kaeli and Robert, weapons and godborn magic coalescing in a stunning display of light and shadow.

"I would much rather bring you both in than fight you," Fallon said to Cassander and Erick. "Our complicated past notwithstanding, the Order would love to meet you."

"*Complicated past.*" Cassander sneered. "You absolute wretch."

"Darrow was right," Neeve said, more magic swirling. She pulled the knife from her belt, light magic coating the weapon with radiance. "Calling him human is generous. What does one call the scum on the bottom of their shoe?"

Erick stood with Cassander, edging around so they would defend one another's flank. "Hopefully *dead*."

Fallon laughed. "It is fascinating how our perspectives of one another are so similar."

"It's true," Neeve said, tightening her hold on her knife handle. "We both believe we're fighting evil, don't we? But one side is right, and the other is a bloody cult."

The satisfaction at seeing his rage also prepared her for his retaliation as he moved in, the cultists with him following his lead.

"Careful, Gran," one cultist laughed. "Wouldn't want to break a hip."

Neeve's retaliation was quick, using her knife as a distraction while her free hand reached for his gut. The pulse of light magic was potent, sending him back against one villain facing Isa and the others. His tunic burned, his hands pathetically patting the smoking fabric and burned skin as the other cultists fumbled. Isa and Genova finished them quickly.

Another cultist pulled a short sword. Gretchen responded with her bloody knife, aiming true as it landed at the bend of his arm above the elbow. He howled, recoiling, the sword loose in his grip. Neeve didn't relent as she touched him, pulsing flames through his body as her magic surged. His cry echoed against the trees as he fell.

Another arrow, this one through Gretchen's shoulder. Her scream tore through Neeve like a fiery blade, searing skin and muscle. Gretchen fell to one knee, reaching for the bloody weapon with trembling fingers.

There. In the tree. Neeve shot a bolt of light, careful of the branches as it found its mark, striking his leg. He screamed as he fell, his voice muffled by the skirmish surrounding her.

A shadowy form moved through the trees as the man fell. More cultists. More eyes and arrows and hands waiting.

Something hard slammed against her back. Winded, she fell, her old body immediately weakened with blinding pain and the need for breath.

"Neeve!" Gretchen, screaming, bleeding and bruised.

A rough hand pulled at Neeve's arm, nearly popping it out of joint. Her hand slammed against his throat, touching what the V of his collar bared.

"You will die for what you've done," she whispered, pulsing every inch of her burning nightmare into him. "You will never touch my sister ever again."

Fear filled his gaze as he shook his head, jowls quivering. "I—I didn't—"

"You did." She pushed harder. "*You all did.*"

She stabbed his mind before stabbing his body, her magic inflicting damage as her knife pierced below his ribs. As he fell, Neeve turned to see Fallon facing Cassander and Erick, the holster at his leg open and a long iron poker in his hand. Back-to-back, the godborn faced the gathering of men as Fallon watched with predatory glee. Isa, Genova, and Moira cursed and struck, the men facing them hearty and still fighting.

But Neeve's magic no longer had its tether. Nothing reined in the reach of what she could do.

Her power touched each enemy's mind, the magic begging to reach farther, to dive deeper, to push until every mind was at her whim. Tendrils and shadows and wisps of light whispered as each cultist fell, her victory a chorus of dark, jubilant voices.

"Gods above." Beside her, jumping from the low bough of a tree, was Darrow, sweaty and bloody but otherwise alright. "You're incredible."

He sees you the way I do. But what would Darrow do if he glimpsed all of her shadow as well as her light?

Erick sees it all. Neeve pulled harder at her shadows, watching him fight with Cassander. *He sees it all with love in his eyes.*

"The bowmen in the trees are from the Preceptor," Darrow said quickly. "She's here somewhere. We're surrounded."

A scream pierced the air, pulling Neeve's gaze to Moira as she watched Genova fall, the cultist in her grip falling with her. Both were dead, Genova with a sword in her gut and the cultist with black veins stretching throughout his body.

Moira screamed again, her injured leg at an awkward angle beneath her as her claw-like hands struck cultists within her reach. Darkness spread from her eyes through her skin like ink, her blonde hair darkening to a rich black. She channeled her magic with every ounce of anger she possessed. Power hummed over the air as even the clouds overhead pooled their shadows to hide the sun and darken the earth.

Her darkness was Neeve's. Unbridled chaos in response to anger. And grief.

Neeve had never taken a life before this, but Fallon and his band of hatred had brought out a darkness she never wanted to reach.

Humans are capable of extraordinary things. Darkness and light. Order and chaos.

Moira's power grew. Fallon and the cultists groaned, hands reaching for their foreheads or stomachs. Neeve rushed Fallon, gripping his arm and shooting more pain into his body. Her deathsight also captured glimpses of his last moments alive with no sense of place or time. He was in agony as he died, his final breath passing in solitude. No aid, no resource. Only death. And that was enough.

But it was not today. He still had time upon this earth.

The hum of power stopped. Moira gasped in surprise as a blade protruded from her core, one held by Galla, panting and wide-eyed with fear.

"No!" But Darrow grabbed Neeve's arm as a cultist raced for her, using his foot to slam the man down. Neeve sliced her arm through the air toward him, a blade of light sinking into his skin, leaving him screaming.

Moira sneered as she reached a hand for his face before he yanked the blade free, causing her to fall. Her breathing was shallow, creating small clouds of dirt in front of her, before her breathing stopped altogether.

Two more cultists slipped through the trees, their deadly gazes locked on Darrow and Neeve.

Kaeli's keening wail reverberated off of the forest ceiling as she charged, a foreign sword in her hands, likely from one of the fallen. Her father remained with Gretchen, each of them standing close to Moira's fallen body, protecting it from cultist hands and blades.

Darrow and Kaeli's blades clanged with the cultists, and Neeve's light danced around their ankles and wrists. She tugged, as though controlling puppets on burning strings, but dissonant whispers slipped into her ears, into her mind.

It was Isa, channeling her chaotic magic with unbridled rage, her murderous eyes piercing into Galla.

But knuckles collided with Neeve's cheekbone, the distraction costing her. Her aged body twisted as she fell, feeling pain in her left knee before her body met the earth. Her face thrummed with a throbbing pulse, her palms and fingers burning as they broke her fall on the forest floor.

Erick and Cassander were quick, the other cultist dead at their feet as they rounded on Fallon. But both godborn were pallid and bloody, sweat gleaming on their faces.

Iron sickness, and it would settle in soon. The remedy was beyond Neeve's skill.

Gretchen screamed, a cultist grabbing her by the hair and holding a knife to her throat while another faced Robert, their swords clanging. Neeve tried to reach one might, her sister's attacker briefly making eye contact, but pain thrummed throughout her body as her breath came short. Gretchen landed a blow in his gut before slamming her forehead against his nose.

But another cultist was ready. Neeve screamed for Gretchen, but it was too late as the other attacker rammed the pommel of his sword against the back of her head. She crumpled to the forest floor, consciousness fleeting.

With a piercing scream, Neeve struck, light stabbing the man's back and chest. Robert felled his enemy before slamming his body into the cultist who harmed his daughter. Kaeli raced for them, screaming in anger before she rammed her sword into his gut. Robert crawled to Gretchen as Kaeli raced for Neeve, hands ready to help her stand. Neeve rose, her hips and knees weak.

"We came prepared." Fallon said to Erick and Cassander both.

"Prepared for war." Isa's voice was like the wind of the frozen north. "A war that will be your end."

"Personally, I'm glad you chose to fight." Fallon laughed, the sound manic and cruel. "This was much more fun."

Fallon struck Cassander first, the lightborn growling against the burn of iron on his skin. Flashes of his death invaded Neeve's mind, pulsing like a heartbeat in her skull.

Erick and Cassander, fighting for their lives.

Cassander, falling.

Light and chaos, both nearly at Fallon's feet.

More cultists appeared, blades and nets among them, ready to capture them like animals. Moonblade assassins moved in and around them, striking where they could in a whirlwind of human violence. But they were outnumbered. The Wandering Order had mustered an army.

"My, my." A woman's voice came through the din, the calmness in opposition with her surroundings. "All this for a prisoner transport?"

Neeve watched the blonde woman approach with a dozen of cultists with bows, arrows nocked and ready. Her sword gleamed at her side, her keen eyes appraising their success in the fight.

She'd seemed kind before, asking where she could repair her boots, trusting Neeve to help her. But to see her now, face hardened and eyes murderous, was to see her true face. The mask had lifted.

"You." Neeve narrowed her eyes. Her light answered the summons, but they were thin. Neeve had little energy left to give.

"Found a cobbler." Charis smirked as she tapped her boots with the end of her sword. "I see you've run into a spot of trouble, deathwitch."

Neeve sneered at the remark. *Deathwitch* on Charis's tongue was an insult, a curse uttered with disgust.

"Galla!"

Jacqueline's scream ripped through the air as Isa gripped his throat with one hand as the other pressed against the center of his chest. Galla groaned, eyes and mouth wide open as Isa pulled him close, her mouth inches from his. As he exhaled, the sound unnatural and unsettling, Isa breathed in. Shadows emanated from her touch, her face displaying a blend of anger and euphoria before Galla collapsed, pale, to the ground. His eyes were open, unblinking, staring into nothing.

Jacqueline raced toward her, a battle cry ripping through her throat, but Isa shoved invisible force magic toward her, knocking her back. She landed hard, winded, staring, dazed, at the sky. Isa pushed more magic toward Fallon.

Charis lifted her hands, and her archers raised their readied arrows.

"No!"

Neeve pulled at whatever magic remained within her. Her headache pounded like a war drum as light burst forth. A few bowmen missed their marks, but it wasn't enough to stop them. Neeve's breath came quick, her knees buckling as she crashed to the earth.

"Oh, my." Neeve didn't have to look up at Charis to see the smirk on her face. "Your magic is spent, Elder."

"Neeve!" Erick cried, fighting alongside Cassander, both of them surrounded. A hit landed somewhere against his side, forcing him to double over. Neeve couldn't see if there was blood.

Darrow tried to run to her as a cultist swept his legs with remarkable dexterity. The thud was loud when his body landed.

Neeve's fingers dug into the soft earth, her anger burning without the energy for flame.

"Glad you could make it," Fallon said to Charis as he approached. "What kept you?"

Charis laughed quietly, her mouth closed and eyes deadly. "The Moonblade pests have been infuriating, as you know."

Fallon pulled Neeve's hair, forcing her to look up at them both. But her hands found his bare arm. Even with the meager allowance her magic could give, Fallon cried out, shoving her to the earth and kicking her hard in the shoulder. Fallon had something sharp embedded in the toe of his boot, and the secret blade scraped against her clavicle. Pain coursing through her body like lightning.

"Leave her alone!" Erick's dark magic flared, several cultists moving back. Even iron sick, he was formidable. "It's me you want!"

Erick. Her heart ached more than the agony in her shoulder. *Stay alive. Erick, please. Stay alive.*

Through bleary, tear-filled eyes, Neeve watched Erick run, his form wreathed in shadow, his eyes crazed with chaos. But the nets found him first. Nets with black laced through the hemp, and Erick screamed as the iron burned against his skin.

"Erick!" Neeve pushed herself up, only to collapse back to the earth. This body was old and weak, far too fragile to sustain the young spirit that fought within it. "Erick!"

"You monsters!" Cassander's eyes brightened, their glow like sunlight.

But when he lashed out, Fallon struck, a short blade peeking from between his fingers as he punched the lightborn hard beneath the ribs. Light peeked out from the wound, thin rays of white shining against the river of red that flowed.

"Iron weapons," Fallon said, his voice low in Cassander's ear. "Iron rope." He yanked the blade free. "I told you we came prepared."

Fallon kicked Cassander to the ground as Erick thrashed in agony within the iron net. Neeve blinked through the pain misting her eyes, watching Cassander fall slowly as they dragged Erick away. One cultist took up one of the burning sticks from Isa's campfire and set their tents ablaze.

Iron. Flame. And Fallon's eyes.

But she hadn't seen Charis. Her vision had only given her enough information to fill her with dread and the false hope of success against a single enemy. But Charis was the unseen predator, lurking, waiting to strike.

I've been so blind. Anya, forgive me. What have I done?

Hands found her and pulled her upright. Charis's bowmen. Unlike Fallon, they wore leather gloves that reached their elbows, protecting them from bowstrings and touchmagic.

"Join your wretched family, godborn." Fallon sneered at Cassander before he turned to go. "We were interested in forcing you to do our bidding. Mist arcana is a remarkable boon in this war against magic." Mania turned his otherwise smug into something infernal. Hells-touched. "Another lightborn hasn't been as elusive as you, and she's taken well to our...*treatments*." Fallon snickered. "It brings me unutterable joy to see your end, knowing your final moments will be soaked in failure."

Isa collapsed to her knees, all of her energy spent. The bowmen's hands gripped Neeve's shoulders hard, holding her in place. But they didn't strike her with a weapon or tie her in chains. They forced her to watch as they dragged Erick, screaming, wrapping in iron-laced hemp.

"You were on our list," Charis said, looming over her, "but this chaosborn has saved your life. He's far more valuable." She smirked. "I'm dying to know how mist arcana affects him."

"I'll kill you if you touch him."

Charis laughed. "You're adorable when you're angry."

She turned from Neeve and barked a command to her subordinates. "Prisoner transport will be a challenge. But he is to remain alive."

"Yes, Preceptor." The cultists left with Fallon and Erick, the bowmen last to leave until Charis nodded. They released Neeve with a shove that forced her down, her shoulder landing hard on the unforgiving earth.

Jacqueline left with them, grieving eyes staring at her brother before her wrath turned to Isa. "This isn't over."

"Save your breath, cultist," Isa hissed. "While you still have it."

Every ounce of Neeve's strength went into crawling toward Cassander. If he were soaked in failure, as Fallon had said, she was right beside him, devastation leaving her hollow and cold.

"Iron weapons," Cassander said. Light still shimmered from the wound, though not as brightly as moments before. "We should have expected—"

He gasped, struggling to breathe. Isa reached for him, panting and weak.

"Iron and widow's veil," she said. "Those bastards."

"No," Neeve said, shaking her head, forcing her arms and legs to work. She sat up, growling through the limitations of this cursed body. "We can help him. We can save him. *Cassander.*" She touched his face with bloody hands. "Cassander, you have to fight."

Darrow reached them, as did Neeve's family, their hands holding wounds as their eyes watched, helpless.

His eyes opened and closed with alarming slowness. Nightmare drenched her reality with Erick at the hands of the Wandering Order while Cassander lay dying in front of her.

There's nothing I could do. Death will always find who it seeks.

Cassander. Erick. Their deaths—

No. She would reshape the world, bend it to breaking. Her loved ones would survive even if the earth shattered beneath their feet.

Her parents. Gretchen.

Cassander.

Erick.

Her heart fluttered like a small bird in a cage, panic blinding it as it sought a way out.

"I'll need your magic to try," Isa said, taking Neeve's aged hand. "But it may already be too late."

It may already be too late.

"No. No. It's not too late." Neeve steeled herself against the familiar doubt creeping in. "Tell me what to do."

CHAPTER 37

Iron. Fire. And Fallon's eyes.

But Neeve hadn't accounted for so much blood.

Jacqueline had sentenced her to an unknown region of the hells when she struck her with this curse. Her magic faltered, her body far too weak to sustain what Cassander needed from her.

Swelling bitterness threatened to consume her.

"Focus," Isa coached. "You can do this."

Neeve took a deep breath and forced her body and mind to comply. *Cassander doesn't have time for your despair.* His light dimmed with each passing second. *I have light enough to give.*

Isa's words and hands were quick. "Press harder on the wound. Pull as much of the iron and widow's veil as you can."

How had Kenna accomplished such a feat with mundane medicine? Was that why it had taken Cassander days to recover?

Your magic will help him heal faster. He'll live, Neeve. Do whatever it takes. He doesn't have time. Erick doesn't have time.

"It's alright." Cassander's voice was meek, a sign of his frailty. "We fought as—"

"It's not over," Neeve interrupted. "I need your help to save Erick. I need your help to put Fallon in the ground."

He managed a weak smile. "Pity the earth that bears that wretch's remains."

Isa exhaled a quiet laugh. "You have life in you yet, lightborn. Let's do our goddesses proud and use every last breath to give those bastards all seven hells."

Cassander winced, grunting through the pain. "One layer at a time."

Darrow whispered something to Neeve's parents and Gretchen, but his words were too quick and quiet for her to hear. Too much blood flowed loudly through her body, pulsing in her ears. Kaeli still tended to Robert's wounded shoulder as Darrow helped Gretchen, wrapping makeshift bandaging around their wounds. The three each said something to Darrow as he finished Gretchen's bandaging. He turned to look at Neeve, sadness in his storm-gray eyes, before he nodded once and walked to the trees.

A tiny pinprick in her heart acknowledged that she would likely never see him again.

The poison that had spread through Cassander's blood, calling for Neeve to reach deep in blood and sinew. "By the gods," she whispered. "It's everywhere."

"Breathe." Isa placed both of her hands on Neeve's. "We're doing this together."

Neeve obeyed, pushing her magic further, touching the parts in Cassander's body that felt wrong. He groaned but remained still.

"It's like sucking venom from a snakebite," Isa said. "Let your magic absorb it, then pull it out. Cycle through until it's gone."

Save him, Neeve. Save him.

But her body shuddered as more magic coursed through her. Light reached in, collecting poison from his blood. Is this what healing was like? What could she be capable of at full power?

Her hands remembered the phantom burning of her light magic as she conjured and fought Fallon and his team of monsters. Natural, instinctual, *powerful.*

"It's working," Isa said. "Keep going."

Isa's magic moved with hers, even as Cassander's innate healing moved through the parts no longer afflicted by iron and widow's veil. She'd only ever known the dangerous side of her magic, the pain-sending, death-seeing. *Mindwalking.* What healing she'd done had been minimal, helping her body to walk with stronger steps as fatigue and age set in. But life?

The world was made in chaos. The world thrives in the order that chaos demands.

That was something Erick would say, philosophizing about life and existence. Gods, she wanted to wrap her arms around him and never let go.

I could have done this long ago, had I not been so afraid.

"Almost there," Isa said. "It's almost gone."

And then, at last, the final trace. Neeve sat back on her heels, staying upright by sheer will. Cassander's fatigued muscles fell slack as his body surrendered to rest. The wound slowly sealed itself with threads of flesh, blood oozing until the red line closed.

Isa smoothed the hair from Cassander's face. "Rest, son of Anya. We still have quite a fight ahead."

Cassander nodded, not opening his eyes, weariness sweeping over him. "Thank you."

"You rest, too," Isa said to Neeve, her own exhaustion coming through. "We are useless to Erick if we go to now. He needs us at full strength, or we're all as good as dead."

Neeve looked to her family, noting Darrow's absence. The questioning in her eyes was enough for her mother to explain.

"He said a nearby Moonblade outpost was ravaged by Charis. He has to see what's left and report in."

"*Report in.*" Isa chuckled. "Such organization for a league of assassins."

"He has to tell them what Jacqueline did," Gretchen said. "She blinded them, too."

"Gods," Gretchen said, exhaling. "Who hasn't she hurt?"

"Humans are capable of incredible things, both in bravery and in fear," Isa said. "Jacqueline's fear has cost her."

Robert knelt with a groan beside Neeve and Cassander. He rested a hand on her back. "You look like hell, love."

"I feel like it." She leaned against her father's shoulder.

One saved, but one still in danger.

What do I do?
How do I save him?
How will my body cope?
Is this where I die?

Neeve closed her eyes against the onslaught of questions that she lacked the energy to ask. Warmth filled her, energy returning in a slow, steady stream. She peered up at her father's concerned face, though he offered a soft smile.

"I'm sorry, Neeve," he whispered. "We wanted to protect you from seeing death, not block your magic."

"I know." Hearing him acknowledge it, hearing him apologize as he sent healing magic into her, softened the bitter ache in her chest. "I understand why you did it."

"I never imagined you would have deathsight," he said. "It's not a common power for lightborn. We're healers and fighters. Not *seers*." He rubbed her shoulder as he tightened his hold. "But the threads of life are the sisters' specialty."

"Healing, fighting, seeing." Neeve held up her aged hands, turning them over, remembering the shadows and light that swirled around them. "There's still so much I don't know."

"So much that you can learn."

"And Erick—" Her throat tightened around the words she wanted to say, the reassurance she needed to hear.

"He'll be alright," Robert said. "He is the son of chaos."

"In the hands of monsters who know how to hurt him."

"That was their mistake," he said. "Hurting him hurt you, too, and they have underestimated the gravity of what they've done."

Robert's green eyes matched hers, and the love and admiration deep within them gave her the strength to let go, tension easing from her muscles as her tiredness swelled, finding room at last.

But there were the dead to look after, the aftermath of hate and fear. "We can't leave them here."

Isa agreed. "But it's going to be hard without a shovel."

"It's already hard."

Isa and Kaeli used Genova and Moira's bedding to wrap them, taking great care as she brought the fabric around their cold bodies.

Gretchen helped where she could, one arm cradled against her chest. But her wound had mostly healed, likely thanks to their father.

Neeve looked down at Galla in pity, wondering what choices in his life lead him to such a fate. A wasted life was its own specific tragedy.

With each of them wounded and tired, it took them hours to bury Genova and Moira, their hands rubbed raw from stone and dirt as they returned the women to the earth.

"There's a river close by," Robert said. "It comes in from the southern coast."

Neeve hesitated, seeing Galla, remembering him harvesting apples with the rest of his village. But his body would return to the earth, regardless if his grave was cool water or soft loam.

So, the river became the resting place for Galla and the cultists left there to rot, abandoned by their depraved leaders. They dragged the bodies to the river bank and pushed them in, watching them bob and float as the flow of the water swept them away.

They washed their hands, soothing the abrasions, wiping away the marks of the earth they'd just moved.

"Your body has been through an ordeal," Isa said to Neeve.

"This isn't my body." Neeve spoke without thought, the words pouring out of her as though Isa had turned a spigot.

"It is, Neeve." Isa's voice was gentle. "This body has come too soon, but it is yours. It deserves your love."

Neeve winced, frustration mounting. But Isa hadn't spoken an untruth. Nothing she'd said was *wrong*. But it also wasn't *right*.

"Rest," Isa said. "You look like you're near collapse."

"What about you?"

"I'll prepare us something to eat." She gestured to the ground near where Cassander lay. "We'll take turns watching over him."

"But they burned the tents," Neeve said. "How is there anything left?"

"We keep our valuables underground." Isa raised one eyebrow, smug. "This isn't my first encounter with the Order, and it certainly won't be the last."

"I'll help you," Gretchen said. "Everyone else should rest first."

Cassander, near death, and Neeve, nearly depleted, as though nothing had progressed from Kenna's home to the camp with Isa. The only change was Erick, given over to the hands of malice as he tried to go to her, to help her.

Those wine-colored eyes, soft and loving as they gazed upon her. So full of wrath and ruin as his shadows gathered in vengeance.

Her guardian, her love, wrapped in iron and hate.

Her fingernails nearly broke the skin in her palms, memories of his screams echoing in the chambers of her mind.

Curse this body and the woman who tried to break me. Curse the cultists who only know hate.

Neeve sat on the soft, cool ground, groaning through the pain in her knee as she extended it.

Her left arm still throbbed, the cut and the stab wound working together to keep her from fully relaxing. But her body was too tired to let the pain win.

This body is yours.

It deserves your love.

Erick regarding her with reverence, his hands gentle, his lips eager. Her body remembered the phantom touch of his embrace, warmth and strength surrounding her for mere seconds before reality reached her.

It deserves your love.

Neeve pressed her hands to her mouth to muffle the sob that climbed from her throat, making it hard to breathe.

CHAPTER 38

Get some rest.

But no rest came. Even in dreamless sleep, Neeve awoke bearing the remnants of exhaustion. She blinked in dull confusion, looking for the face and hands that weren't there, her memory flooding back in excruciating detail.

Erick was gone, taken by Fallon and the others, suffering iron-laced hatred.

The sun had set with Isa and Gretchen by a fire, delicious steam feathering steadily from the pot as Isa stirred. Neeve's parents slept close by, her mother resting on her father's uninjured shoulder.

"Good," Isa said. "You're awake." She turned the spoon around in the pot to aim the handle at Neeve. "This is ready. I've already had some." She yawned, stretching her arms.

"Sorry," Neeve said. "I didn't mean to sleep."

"Don't apologize for what your body needs."

She watched Cassander breathe, relieved to see life commanding his body to survive. Color returned to his skin, the rich hues as they should be.

This was one victory. Another loomed in the distance, time and healing separating her from pulling Erick out of an iron-filled hell.

Without a word or thought, Neeve took Erick's pack and pulled out his book, hands pressing firmly to its cover with intent. The book still carried his touch, her magic connecting with it quickly.

Show me where he is. There was no light left except within, but the shadows answered, Titus coming to life and spreading his ethereal, smoky wings. *Show me where he is.*

But the world was pitch dark, the night so dense that she had no sense of direction. The path remained indiscernible even as her eyes tried to adjust. Titus soared, the spell connecting without issue, but her raven of smoke could see nothing in the dark.

Is he alright? But the power didn't have an answer, the vision in her mind limited until Neeve let go.

"Anything?" Isa asked.

Neeve shook her head. "There was too much darkness."

She winced, the meaning of her words deeper and sharper than she'd intended.

"They could be in something," Gretchen said. "A cave, a structure without fire. We'll know more after daybreak."

"He's not—" Neeve shook her head, unable to say it. "Is he alive?"

"Did you feel the spell reach him?" Isa asked.

"I think so."

"It wouldn't have connected if he was dead."

Neeve blinked through stinging eyes.

"He's alive," Isa said. "Trust that. And trust your magic."

Trust your magic. Neeve didn't feel such confidence and assurance in herself. The longer she remained, the longer Erick remained at Fallon and Charis's mercy. "That feels impossible."

Neeve shivered, the fringes of her mind coming up with answers she didn't want to face.

"Neeve." Isa leaned closer, firelight dancing in her eyes.

"Cassander looks much better," Neeve said, stopping whatever Isa had prepared to say. There was a glimmer in her storm-colored eyes that Neeve wasn't ready for. She turned to her sister. "Your turn. Time to sleep."

Gretchen yawned, nodding vaguely, before lying down where Neeve had been.

Several quiet moments passed, Isa and Neeve listening to the sounds of the night and of their companions' deep breathing.

"What about you?" Isa asked, that gleam still in her eyes. "How's *your* healing?"

With a playful attempt at avoidance, Neeve asked, "Rest. I'll keep watch."

"There's something about your magic that stops you from using it."

She said nothing, an internal argument flaring. But it was only a sizzling flash before it dissolved beneath Isa's knowing gaze.

"Something happened," Isa said.

"A friend," Neeve said. "My magic hurt her in a way I'd never expected. I didn't mean to, but it happened. And I can never take it back."

Isa listened, her attention unwavering and her expression devoid of judgment.

"Her name is Eira." Neeve sat with the steaming bowl in her lap, breathing in the savory, herbal aroma and stirring the vegetables in the thick broth. "We toyed with chaos magic. Me, in my inexperience with a barrier in my mind."

"Wait," Isa said, lifting a hand. "A barrier?"

Neeve explained meeting Erick at the crossroads to pull her magic from her, only to learn that she was godborn.

"My parents try to help me with my deathsight," she said. "But it blocked almost everything. I struggled to use magic, even though it was all I wanted. Power, connection. And Eira helped me. She—" Neeve winced, jaw clenching. "She wanted to connect our minds."

"Deathsight is a rare godborn gift," Isa said. "Mindwalking is powerful magic that you accomplished, even with thin instruction and a barrier blocking your progress."

"Gift?" Neeve didn't look up, ashamed. "Her parents had to take her to Alvar for healing. I don't—" Neeve struggled, lips quivering. "I don't think I'll ever see her again."

Isa waited, the calm night surrounding them. "What happened, Neeve?"

She clenched her jaw. "We wanted to see where my parents were. They left for some job in Sudor and Melia, and they said they would be gone for months." Neeve stared at the bowl in her hands, seeing nothing except the day her best friend nearly died. "They're gone so often, but Eira and I thought that, with magic, we could find them."

"You attempted to scry," Isa summated. "Knowing it was possible."

"But not *how*." Neeve hesitated. "It almost worked, and Eira—she connected me with her mind, to build a world together. But I didn't—"

Emotion gripped her throat in a vise. She choked out a sob before pressing a fist against her mouth.

"But she survived," Isa said. "She's alive now, in Alvar?"

"As far as I know." Neeve shook her head. "What if she's dead? What if I—"

Ida rested a hand on Neeve's arm. "There is nothing wrong with what you can do."

Neeve closed her eyes, unable to erase the memory of Eira, blood coming from her nose and ears, her eyes vacant as they stared into the limitless distance.

"Gods, I miss her." Neeve sobbed, pressing a hand to her mouth as the other steadied the steaming bowl.

"Connecting with another person's mind is a remarkable power. You did it without training or formal practice."

Neeve opened her mouth to argue, but Isa stopped her, resting a hand on her arm.

"But remarkable power is a burden, Neeve." Isa paused, letting that sink in. "The godblood that flows in your veins has gifted you an incredible resource for magic, but your soul bears the weight of everything that comes with it."

"My recklessness cost me someone I love." Tears fell down her warm cheeks. "I don't want to risk that kind of failure ever again."

"You must forgive yourself."

Forgive yourself. Erick's voice, soothing in memory.

"No." It was the first time Neeve had rejected the notion out loud, the first time her voice slapped down the idea like a housewife swatting a fly. "Forgiveness is impossible."

"You said the same thing to Jacqueline," Isa said. "But the grudge you carry doesn't discriminate against yourself."

Neeve's brow furrowed, sarcasm building behind her trembling lips, but her heart throbbed with the truth. Forgiveness isn't a gift that flows in a single direction. It returns to the giver, bringing them peace.

Forgive yourself.

"Your heart is good, Neeve, and it deserves your love."

"It's not worth the risk," she blurted. "I tried leaving that door open. I tried accepting it and controlling it. But bad things keep happening."

"Because bad things happen," Isa said. "Not because you make them." She held her hand out for Neeve to take. "Let me show you how forgiveness is possible."

Neeve hesitated, knowing what she would see. But Isa insisted, bringing her hand closer.

"Take my hand, Neeve. Please."

Neeve slipped her fingers into Isa's palm, startled by the force of the witch's grip.

When the flashes of Isa's life came, Neeve closed her eyes, watching a serene, beautiful childhood surrounded by thick trees and countless wildflowers pass by. A woman's voice, a man's laugh, and their dances beneath the moonlight.

Years progressed in love. She explored magic, worshipped Aishlin, and touched the depths of chaos with eager hands.

Then there was fire. Voices screaming.

And the power in Isa's hands swept over the villains who burned her home and her loved ones. Lightborn. Cultists. Villagers who let superstition champion their ability to reason. Human beings filled with terrifying hate.

Isa gasped, her breath shuddering. "So many dead, several by my hand."

The burning of Willow Hill. Isa's last memory of the fight showed her hands around a man's throat, shadows pulling light from within him. *His soul.* She was a soulwitch, and a powerful one.

"You lost so much." Grief held Neeve's breath hostage. "Gods, that's my worst fear, and you lived it. How did—" Her lips trembled. "How did you make it through?"

"I almost didn't," Isa said. "If it weren't for love, I wouldn't have lived beyond my grief." She held tighter to Neeve's hands, studying her before answering. "Tell me what you're afraid of."

"Losing everyone I love."

"But it's more than that," she said. "It's how all of this started." Her smile was kind, even as sadness lingered in her eyes. "You feel abandoned."

Magic tingled from Isa's touch, likely confirming the truth as Neeve internally collapsed.

Abandoned.

"If I can forgive myself for what I did willfully and in anger," Isa said quietly, "so can you, for something done in innocence."

Neeve's heart sank, reliving Isa's darkest moment and following the path to her present, watching her friends fall to cultists.

And then—

Neeve gasped, seeing her death. *Very soon.*

"I already suspected I wouldn't survive this," Isa said. "The Wandering Order bears no soul and no conscience. No value for life. I am at peace with what is to come."

Neeve eased her grip but didn't pull away first. Isa squeezed her fingers before letting go.

"We're powerless against death and loss," Neeve whispered, her grief arriving before the time had come.

"Death and loss isn't what you fight *against*," Isa said, her voice as soothing and gentle as ever. "It is *life* that you fight *for*."

Neeve blinked, her mind quickly trying to discern meaning when everything she'd survived spoke to the contrary.

"It is *life* that exists. Aishlin is the patron of chaos and our guide to what comes after. Death is simply a term mortals use to understand what happens when we leave this mortal plane." She paused before adding, "I believe there is no death. We would not exist were it not for chaos bringing us into being, and chaos carries us on after these bodies turn to dust."

Chaos carries us on. Eternity and fullness. Light and shadow, both.

"Nothing ever stops," Isa went on. "We grow and we change."

"How boring would it be if we didn't grow?" Gretchen had said. "If we didn't shed this skin to accept something new?"

The wisdom of her loved ones, coming back to her through a stranger. All because Neeve refused to see.

"You will not be the same woman tomorrow," Isa said. "Or the day after that. You can't punish yourself for something *you* didn't do. That was a Neeve of the past who has learned and grown because of her actions and choices. You've walked this path to become who you are. *Keep walking.* There is so much more to see."

When Neeve took a breath, it was a gasp for air as the emotional tide rose within her. She let the tears fall freely, feeling the burden of a weight she'd carried for so long finally roll away.

"You deserve all the love in the world," Isa said, "especially love from yourself."

She could almost hear Erick's voice speaking Isa's words.

Forgive yourself, Neeve.

"When the past stifles our present," Isa said, "it's difficult to overcome because we can't take it back. Forgiving ourselves is the hardest thing of all."

"It isn't the past."

"Because you won't let it be over. You bring it into the present where it doesn't belong."

Neeve pressed her lips together, her stomach tight, more tears falling.

"What happened is done. Eira has help, and I believe she's alright. What comes next is what *you* decide."

"How can I trust myself?"

"Because we must, Neeve. We must trust and forgive ourselves. We know our hearts more than anyone else can, and your heart is good."

"How do you know?" She took a shaking breath, speaking through the tears. "How do you *know*?"

"Because there is light in you."

They were Isa's words, but Neeve heard Erick's voice.

There is so much light in you. And the way he'd held her, breathing her in, the moment between them sacred.

"There is hope and kindness," Isa went on. "There is love."

Silence passed between them, Neeve staring at her hands as they touched the smoothed edges of the wooden bowl. The steam from the stew feathered up to her tear-streaked face.

"How do I let go?" Neeve whispered, speaking more into her bowl of food than to Isa. "How do I let this go?"

"It won't happen quickly," she said. "Nor should it. Believe in the good you can do." Isa slipped down from her seat to the blanket prepared on the ground, laying her body on its side facing the fire. "Trust yourself, Neeve."

Neeve slowly spooned stew into her mouth, grateful for the warm meal to combat the chill in her core.

Trust. Forgiveness. When the world made it so hard to do both.

No, not the world. She pressed a hand to her chest, against her pounding heart. *You.*

CHAPTER 39

Neeve let her eyes lose focus as she stared at the fire. Isa, Gretchen, and Cassander all rested soundly, the ambience of the night surrounding her in a peace that rivaled the storm within. She allowed her mind to empty, to let it blissfully wander into nothing, devoid of sound and thought until peripheral movement pulled her gaze.

Kaeli sat up, eyes alert, though Robert continued to sleep soundly beside her. She rose delicately, moving to sit beside Neeve.

"Hello, love." Kaeli kissed her temple. "Did you manage any rest?"

"Some," Neeve lied. "You?"

"Too much, maybe." Kaeli didn't break her gaze from Neeve. "I overheard your conversation with Isa."

Ice cold water flowed through Neeve's veins as she tried to recall every word she'd said. How much of it broke her mother's heart? How much of it hurt her feelings?

I said nothing that was untrue. But that reassurance was useless. The truth was barbed and unrelenting.

"Mom—"

Kaeli raised a hand. "Don't apologize." She took her daughter's hands, her touch filling an aching void within Neeve that had long been numb. "Your father and I never meant for you to feel abandoned."

Neeve clenched her teeth, making her jaw ache. But the well of emotion surged forth despite the weak barrier Neeve tried in vain to raise.

"I left Gretchen," Neeve choked out, the words coming out on her breath to stay quiet. "How she must have felt, alone, And to be taken by the Order—"

Kaeli embraced her, rocking her steadily back and forth. Neeve's walls had broken. She pressed her hands to her mouth to keep her cries from waking the others.

"What other choice did you have?" Kaeli's hand massaged circles between Neeve's shoulders, the pressure maternal and soothing. "An aging curse only has one outcome, love. Staying would have killed you."

"But I'm the one to break it. I could have stayed."

"Did you know how to break it?"

Neeve shook her head.

"There's your answer. You needed this journey, Neeve." Kaeli stared at their hands as she stroked Neeve's fingers. "But the work we've done has taken its toll.

The work. Feather and Claw. It would be easy for Neeve to curse the name and all it stood for, but it helped others like her. Still, she allowed herself room to hate it.

"You didn't abandon your sister," Kaeli said. "And it would be easy for me to say *we didn't abandon you, either*, but that does little when you *feel* that way."

"I know you didn't leave *me*," Neeve said. "I know it, in the depths of my heart, but gods, Mama, I am *so angry*."

Kaeli embraced her tighter, stroking her curls, her breath shuddering as she inhaled through the emotion that gripped her.

With arms tight around one another, they cried quietly, the hole within Neeve's heart sealing itself.

Another set of arms embraced them.

And another.

Neeve hiccuped a gasp, seeing Gretchen and their father, the family embracing as tears fell.

"The loves of my life," Robert whispered. "It is by the grace of the goddesses that we're still here."

"The Order won't stop," Gretchen said. "The work you do is important."

"But it's not worth the two of you," Kaeli said. "Your father and I—"

"No." Neeve sat up, knowing what her mother would say. "Gretchen's right. She and I can—"

"No." It was Robert, not Kaeli, who interrupted. "It's too dangerous."

"It's too dangerous without your daughters," Neeve said with a laugh. "Knife-throwing and light magic."

"We've decided," Gretchen said with a chuckle. "And without even talking about it first."

"We'll rid this earth of their pestilence," Neeve said. "And we'll stay together."

Kaeli and Robert shared a look, one that mingled pride with fear.

"The right thing is never easy," Kaeli said. "We'll send word to Cynthia as soon as we can."

Robert kissed each of them on their foreheads. "I love you all more than anything."

They responded in kind, holding one another until Kaeli pointed to something shimmering by the fire. "What's that?"

On the ground near them was a small clay bowl filled with water, firelight dancing across its still surface. Neeve didn't remember seeing it there before.

"What's that floating in it?" Gretchen asked. "Is that rosemary?"

Fill a small bowl with fresh rainwater. Add a pinch of salt and a sprig of rosemary.

Beside it was a candle, unlit, with rosemary embedded in the wax. A small leather pouch sat at the candle's base, likely holding amethyst and quartz crystal.

Neeve pictured the spell, its words scripted across the parchment. All that was needed was a circle of Anya, and the spell would be ready.

Neeve stared at Isa, expecting the chaoswitch to be watching her realize what she'd prepared. But she slept soundly, at ease even as Neeve and her family discovered the components laid out for her.

"What's it for?" Robert asked, and Neeve explained, showing them the book.

Gretchen touched the cover. "Didn't Erick give you this?"

"He did."

The path is set. I have to be the one to move forward. I have to be the one to see it done.

Dawn peeked over the horizon, the golden rays shifting the deep blue of night to shades of burning. Neeve watched her hands and arms change, but instead of looking upon the wrinkles and age spots with hate, she touched her hands with the same love she showed the book.

Love.

She took up the candle and pouch first, lighting the wick and arranging the crystals until they made a circle and a cross, the symbols overlaid to represent the power of four, the strength of seasons, the eternity of life as a cycle ongoing. The candle looked beautiful, surrounded by the crystals.

Neeve was careful with the bowl, the water undulating until it came to rest after she set it in front of her. Slowly, quietly, she recited the words.

"Balance within, balance without, steady the soul, dispel all doubt."

The touch of magic didn't come, but the words were soothing as she whispered them to herself.

"Believe that you can. Believe that you will. Knowledge of self. Trust, instilled."

Gretchen joined her, then her parents, their whispers harmonious as they carried on the early morning breeze.

"Balance within, balance without, steady the soul, dispel all doubt."

Old Neeve would be powerless to save Erick, to help Cassander, to stop Fallon.

Stop thinking of yourself as powerless. Old and young, you still have life in your body, pulsing and coursing through your veins.

"Believe that you can. Believe that you will. Knowledge of self. Trust, instilled."

Blood that ignites in anger at injustice.

Blood that warms in love when you look into Erick's eyes.
Blood that flows when Gretchen hugs you so tight you can't breathe.

"Balance within, balance without, steady the soul, dispel all doubt."

Hands that love with their touch.
Hands that fight with their power.
Hands that create with every motion.

"Believe that you can. Believe that you will. Knowledge of self. Trust, instilled."

Her heart raced as the circular motion of her hands took her body, the whispered words coming on their own as she let the sound surround her.

I am Neeve. Lightborn. Wielder of light and shadow.
And I am loved.
This curse may take me before my time.
But I am loved.
If the afterlife claims me, light and chaos will surround me.
And I will be loved.

An unspeakable peace swelled within her, even as she opened her eyes to find the dawn. Tears had fallen in hope and joy, and she wiped her face as she smiled at her family. Even with this body that slowly became more like home, she would pull Erick from the edge of hell crafted by human hands.

She held his book against her heart, eyes shut and mind focused.

Show me where he is, Titus. Show me.

There was more radiance from sun and fire as Titus soared, his body blended with light and shadow. There were peaks of tents erected in haste, four or five of them surrounded by trees and brush. The campfire burned with healthy flames as dawn brightened.

A large camp meant a lot of cultists, with Erick bound in iron chains.

Hold on. She wished her thoughts could reach him.

Her mind lingered there, picturing his smirk that appeared each time he'd gotten under her skin. His deep, genuine laugh, his voice whispering her name. The light shimmering in his eyes, the shadows coalescing around his chaosborn image.

She would hold him again. She would kiss him until they both ran out of breath.

She sent Titus in, a wisp of scrying shadow slipping into the tent. Charis stood before him, wiping her fingers on a bloody cloth. Erick was weak but alive, defiance in his wine-colored eyes.

"You wear your nightmares on your sleeve, Preceptor," Erick taunted. "You'd never carry this guilt if you—"

She struck him, his head whipping to the side. "Enough. Sit and stew with all this iron, godborn."

Charis left him in the dark tent alone. Neeve fingers tingled, wishing for a burning wrath to consume her whole. But even with the rage, pride swelled within her heart at Erick's victory over her.

She sent Titus to perch on Erick's knee, its golden eyes staring.

"Hello, dear one," Erick whispered. He smiled, his mouth weak and swollen eyelids drooping. Her fingers ached to comb his hair back from his face. "Stay alive for me, won't you? I'll see to these cretins."

He wanted her to stay away, but Neeve wouldn't dream of leaving him there at the whim of madness and hate.

I choose you, Mal'Erick Chaosborn, and I will come for you with all that I have left.

Titus rubbed his head against his bound arm before disappearing, lest Charis or another cultist walk in.

"Neeve?" Cassander blinked, hand going to his bloody shirt where the wound had been. "Everything all right?"

She opened her eyes, the vision breaking. Cassander stretched from his spot on the ground, wincing and pressing a hand to his stomach.

"Take it easy," Kaeli said. "You're godborn, but a stab wound is no trifle."

He chuckled. "*Trifle.*"

"At least you're in good spirits."

He eyed the book, sobering. "Did you see anything?"

Neeve described the camp as best as she could, though there wasn't much to discern where Erick was.

Worried, Gretchen asked, "How many tents did you say?"

"Maybe five. But there could be more."

Cassander sat up, rubbing his stomach and lifting his shirt to see the wound. It was a still a red line, though the healing had done a lot to seal it. "We need to go. Too much time has passed already." With some trepidation, he added, "I heard some of what you spoke about." He looked from her to her family, embarrassment tinting his cheeks. "I didn't mean to eavesdrop."

Neeve's confession about Eira and the fear she harbored. The healing of wounds with her family.

"I wanted to let you know that you're not alone. Our experiences are different," he admitted, "but the result is still *loss*. The result is still *grief*."

Neeve took a breath at the ache in the dead-center of her chest, as though his words had physically struck her. *Grief*.

"That's why I went to the crossroads," she said. "To remove my magic and any risk of hurting anyone ever again."

"That guilt is a lot for one person to bear."

"With your father and I always leaving," Kaeli said, "you wanted reassurance. Stability."

Tears willed her eyes as she closed them, the wetness seeping through and falling down her warm cheeks. Her parents embraced her as Gretchen helped Cassander get to his feet.

Forgive me, Eira.

Her lips trembled. There was no use stopping the emotional tide that flowed higher.

Forgive me, Neeve.

"I'll scry again when we get closer," Neeve said. "I won't stop trying until we find him."

"That's the spirit." Isa, waking up, yawned and sat upright. "Leaving already?"

"We should eat something." Kaeli looked at the pot, which Neeve had removed from the fire during her watch. "We don't know how long we'll be walking."

They ate quickly, Neeve helping Isa to clean up their camp while Cassander and Kaeli prepared their weapons for travel, cleaning and sharpening. Gretchen and Robert saw to food and other supplies while trying to pack light.

Neeve scried once more before they began their search, though nothing much had changed. "The fire's out with two men sitting by it. I can't see their faces."

"Can you describe the trees?" Isa asked. "Flowers?"

Cassander asked, "Is there a water source in sight?"

"Not that I can make out," she said, studying the scene. "The trees are tall and full alongside brush that's a light green, almost white. The ground doesn't have much, but there are some small white flowers in the shade."

"Small white flowers in the shade," Cassander said slowly. "Where have I seen those before?"

"They're a common weed," Robert said, "but they grow well where the shade is thickest. That gives us somewhere to start." He pointed ahead. "The trees get denser the farther we go. That's something."

And they set off, with Neeve glancing behind at the makeshift graves of the dead they'd buried.

Rest well.

CHAPTER 40

With one hand, Neeve clutched Erick's book close to her chest, the edges of the cover and spine pressing into her as though to make an impression through fabric and skin. With the other, she rubbed the ring from Gretchen, forcing the metal to spin back and forth on her finger.

"Oh, I forgot to mention," Gretchen said, "Samson is with Carissa and Zayn."

"Thank the gods," Kaeli said. "Though I have to ask how this arrangement happened."

"That was my question," Neeve asked. "If you were kidnapped, how did they know to help?"

"I was preparing to leave." Gretchen glanced at her family as they walked through the tall grass, which masked the stone-laden terrain. "The Wandering Order actually saved me the price of passage to Ileden."

"You can't be serious," Robert said. "What if we'd never found each other? What if you died at sea?"

"All those *what ifs* will ruin your life," she said. "And I had every faith that I would find you."

Brush and twigs grabbed at Neeve's skirts with every step, as though to warn her to stay back.

If this is your caution, Rhiann, you're wasting your time. Neeve acknowledged the boughs of the trees as though to pay reverence to the goddess that made them. *Nothing short of death will stop me.*

No one has ever chosen him. But I do. With all my heart.

The terrain didn't relent, but neither did she.

Neeve stopped, holding the book between her hands to scry again. This vision was much the same as before. Only one man sat by the remains of their campfire, rather than the two from before. Neeve studied what she could of the terrain.

"Small white flowers beneath the trees," she said. "A few trees have lighter leaves, more yellow than green."

"Those grow more west than north," Robert said. "Those leaves angle their undersides away from the sun. That's good. We can use that."

"Wait." She watched a second man emerge from the trees, carrying waterskins. "There's water nearby. A stream or river." Neeve used the direction of the morning sunlight, mumbling to herself. "That's east, so he came from...the south..." She drew imaginary lines in the air, trying to orient herself. "Water to the south."

"Excellent," Isa said. "We're on their trail."

"That's my girl," Robert said with pride. "The cartographer's pen is yours when you want it."

Neeve froze as Fallon stepped out of the large tent, wiping his hands with a handkerchief and looking up at the midmorning light. Concern lined his face and weighed on his brow as he slipped the handkerchief back into his pocket before turning for the tent again.

There, she urged. *Follow him.*

The vision obeyed her, the thrill of movement surging her own body forward as her steps pulled after the spell, following Fallon into the tent. Behind him, Charis, bruised with a bleeding lip, glared, her expression murderous.

Erick was still bound to the old wooden chair, face bloody and bruised. He grinned at Fallon, eyes swollen, revealing reddened teeth. "The hawk's come to do what the fox could not."

Erick laughed, but Fallon remained silent, reaching for the holster at his side and flicking the latch open. Slowly, he pulled out an iron poker, oxidized in places. Erick's humor faltered as unseen pain replaced it.

"He's alive." The swell of anger in Neeve's chest was cataclysmic. If given the chance, she could level mountains with the force of her touch. "Fallon has iron."

The vision stopped. Neeve growled, trying to push her magic to see more, hands clutching the book.

"That was good, Neeve," Gretchen said, resting a hand on her shoulder. "Are you alright?"

She didn't answer right away, hugging the book tighter. "I'll be alright when their blood stains the ground." She exhaled through her nose. "We have to get him out of there alive, or the world will burn."

Neeve pulled the map from her pack and unrolled it, holding it out for everyone as they stepped closer.

"There." Both Robert and Isa pointed, their fingers finding the river that was likely used by Fallon and the others.

Robert added, "Water to the south, and here—" He drew an invisible circle around the drawn trees to the north of the river. "This must be where they are. We should find those trees you saw."

Determination touched hope as Neeve stowed the map. "We have something to work with."

Hold on, Erick.

She studied the terrain as they walked, haste in their steps and even in her old bones. *Water to the south. Yellow-green leaves.* But Erick's horror-stricken face haunted her. Fallon wielding iron while Erick faced him, bound and alone.

Neeve rubbed her chest, urging her heart to calm and her lungs to fill with air. *We're going to make it. We're going to find him.*

This is all my fault.

She grimaced, the truth stinging in a deep place.

I have to let this go. Neeve nearly spoke the words aloud.

There is light in you, Isa had said, speaking of both *light* and *forgiveness.*

There is so much light in you. Erick, his voice soft in her ear. *You bring me so much peace.*

Her lips trembled, hearing his voice.

How boring would it be if we didn't grow? Gretchen's words returned. *If we didn't shed this skin to accept something new?*

We must forgive ourselves. We know our hearts more than anyone else can, and your heart is good.

Shed this skin and accept something new.

Balance within, balance without,

Steady the soul, dispel all doubt.

Neeve had to break out of this chrysalis if she had any hope of surviving. She'd broken free from the tower of her mind only to cage herself in another.

There is nothing wrong with me.

This suffocating fear was a shell surrounding her. She willed her body to accept the truth, to harden and strengthen and fight against the cage of her own making.

Steady the soul. Dispel all doubt.

Come on, heart. Keep beating.

She collected memories of her childhood with Gretchen and her parents, hearing their voices and their laughter.

Your heart is good.

She forced herself to remember Eira, the look of mischief in her dark eyes as they would play and keep innocent secrets and explore the world with eager, curious eyes and hands. Eira was a loyal, loving friend, one that Neeve would see again.

You're alive, aren't you? The healers of Alvar have helped you?

Warmth spread from her heart, reaching through her chest and stomach, down her arms and legs, until it felt as though warmth rooted down to the earth from the soles of her feet. The peace from the spell the night before seeped into her body once again.

I am flawed.

I am light, and I am chaos.

I will face the day knowing that I am Neeve, the same as always, but stronger.

"Neeve," Gretchen said.

She opened her eyes to find them all staring. Isa regarded her as one victorious.

"It isn't dusk yet," Cassander said.

Gretchen blinked, tears falling. Kaeli and Robert held one another, watching their daughter with reverence and hope.

Neeve looked down at her hands, still holding the book, and watched as her skin wavered between old and young.

"Believe it," Isa said, delicate urgency in her voice. "Deep in your heart. No doubts. You know exactly who are you, and you are magnificent."

Neeve let those words sink, swallowing them down.

"You are fierce and loyal," Isa said. "You love with your entire being."

Fierce. Loyal.

Light. Chaos.

I'm stronger than I was before.

Isa's words were no different from Erick's. But Neeve hadn't given herself permission to believe them. Not until now.

I'm sorry I'm so late to your love. She willed Erick to hear her voice, silently praying to the goddesses that he would know. *Thank you for waiting for me.*

The snap wasn't audible, the breaking more a sensation in her core than of something that bound her. The relief that came washed over her like a soothing wind on the hottest day, encouraging her body to relax so that she could breathe in the glorious air of freedom.

She looked down at her youthful hands and touched her face.

"You did it," Gretchen said, grinning. "You did it!"

"Of course she did," Isa said, looking at her proudly.

Neeve pressed a hand to her chest, feeling her heartbeat strong beneath her touch. She thanked her body for staying strong. She thanked her mind for breaking free. And she thanked her heart for never giving up.

I'm sorry it took me so long. She rubbed circles of comfort against her chest, speaking to her heart. To Erick's. *I'm here now.*

Neeve's family surrounded with arms and voices, Gretchen's coming through elated tears.

If she'd have been kinder to herself, this would have gone so much faster.

No, don't think that way, she self-chastised. *It had to happen this way. How else would you have learned?*

Light thunder rumbled in the distance, though the sky above them was still bright. They moved on, Neeve's body handling the terrain with much more finesse now that the curse had broken. But the sky darkened sooner than they'd hoped, the thunder rolling closer as rain pattered in the near distance. A few drops fell on Neeve's shoulders, chilling her with the change in the wind.

"This will be good cover," Cassander said. "We should try to hurry and take advantage of it while we can."

"We still have to cross that river," Isa said. "The storm could make that harder."

"We'll make it." Neeve, her hope rekindled, found her optimism. "Nothing has stopped us so far."

"And nothing will." A light of pride flickered in Kaeli's eyes. "With the magic and might among us, we are formidable."

"They crossed the wrong soulwitch," Isa said, a dark tone of eagerness in her voice. "They will not live much longer to regret the choices they've made."

A witch of soul and chaos alongside children of light.

Trust your instincts, she thought. *You'll do this or die trying.*

The weight of it pressed upon her shoulders, the reality a hefty burden.

You'll do this or die trying.

CHAPTER 41

They kept their steps light as they traversed the wet ground through the storm. Lightning flashed in the distance, the rumble of thunder rolling toward them.

"We're getting close," Cassander said. "I think I hear the river."

"How?" Gretchen asked, hearing only the pattering of rain and the rustling of branches. "I can't hear past the storm."

He pointed ahead, drawing a line for the river Neeve still couldn't see. "It's not far. If you focus, you can hear it."

But discerning *water* from *water* wasn't Neeve's talent. Her feet swam in her boots as she tried not to squelch with each shivering step.

"There." Cassander, satisfied, pointed ahead and then touched his ear. "Hear it?"

Neeve and the others stood still, focusing, and, with a grin, Isa said, "Nicely done, Cassander. You must be a dazzler in taverns. *And for my next trick...*"

They reached the river soon thereafter, the banks narrow enough to cross.

"We're already soaked," Neeve said, lifting her skirt up to her calves. "Let's swim through."

Kaeli had already waded in. "Like minds."

Neeve's arms burned as she held up her pack, safeguarding what valuables remained, and her arched back threatened to riot if she didn't correct her form soon. The opposite bank was several yards away, and when she reached it, her muscles ached with tiredness and the weight of water-soaked clothes. Neeve squeezed buckets of river water from her skirt, Gretchen doing the same.

"We're wearing trousers next time we go gallivanting across landscapes," Gretchen remarked. "Skirts are highly impractical."

The group shivered as they continued, their steps miraculously silent as they watched and listened.

"We're close," Neeve whispered, not daring to blink as she stared through the trees toward the camp. She smelled the faint scent of wood smoke not suffocated by the rain.

She took Erick's book in her hands, lamenting its wetness as the raindrops fell. *Show me the camp.*

The vision was the same, with the campfire lit and two men sitting by it beneath a fabric canopy. The larger tent had lights burning from within, and Neeve could make out faint shadows moving.

"Two outside," she said, returning the book to her pack. "More in a larger tent where they have Erick."

Isa wove her hands in the air, eyes half-closed and muttering words to a spell, but before she finished, she held one hand tight as though gripping a small ball, eyes alight as they moved forward. Cassander pulled his sword, reciting words akin to a prayer as he unsheathed his sword. Neeve pulled her knife, having no prayers, but she called to the rage in her heart.

Firelight flickered through the trees and brush, the two men huddled close to the healthy, warm flames. Their canopy bowed with the weight of rainwater, their setup hasty and likely to fall if left as it was.

With neither word nor warning, Isa finished her spell and pushed her hand toward the men. Neeve watched and waited, the world silent but for the rain and crackling fire, until the distant sound of a woman reached her. She was crying, whoever she was, further into the trees.

Isa's eyes gleamed like lightning in a storm. "I thought a distraction may be a good idea."

Robert shuddered. "Gods, above, that's haunting."

One man stood, glancing toward the sound before turning back to the other. He carefully made his way to the trees, his hand resting on his sword handle.

Shadows fluttered around her form, her eyes murderous. "I'll have him all to myself."

And she left them, skulking around the camp, to meet her target alone in the woods.

"What about the archers?" Gretchen asked. "They were in the trees before."

But Neeve couldn't call for Isa to come back. Quickly, she reached for the shadows and conjured Titus, surveying the boughs with haste. "I don't see anything."

"Your eyes," Kaeli said. "They're white."

Neeve blinked, breaking the spell, seeing her family's shock with wide eyes and open mouths.

Robert beamed with pride in his eyes. "You've accomplished so much."

"Accolades later," Gretchen said, studying the cultists visible at the camp. Other tents were still, the calmness of the camp unsettling.

Neeve jabbed Gretchen with her elbow. "Thanks, sis."

"*Later*," she said with a smirk. "We'll sing your lightborn praises over a hot meal when this is over."

"We'll go around," Kaeli said to Robert and Gretchen. There were more tents further on, other cultists likely resting during the storm. "One by one. Don't let yourselves get surrounded."

They were slow and steady as they maneuvered around the camp to its other side, Neeve watching until they disappeared among the trees.

With Cassander, she crept toward the other unsuspecting cultist, approaching him from behind as thunder rumbled overhead. Their movements were precise, Neeve with her hands poised to cover his mouth as Cassander readied his blade. She struck fast, stifling his cry as her touchmagic did its work. She pulsed pain until he fell unconscious. He hit the ground with a merciless thud.

Isa cackled, her voice echoing through the trees.

"Let's hope they don't hear that," Cassander whispered, looking at the tent. Two shadows moved within. "We'll have to act fast."

Blunt force struck the back of Neeve's head, sending her to the ground. Cassander, too, fell beside her.

"Not fast enough."

Neeve stared, bleary-eyed, at the smug face of Fallon, one of his cultists sneering beside him. Fallon's hands were empty, his sword at his side and his holster clasped shut. But the man beside him griped his sword handle, eyes locked on Cassander.

"Welcome," Fallon said. "So glad you could join us. Though I expected you sooner." The infuriating gleam in Fallon's eyes set Neeve's nerves on edge. "It was difficult to keep your friend alive and well this long. It was tempting to finish him more than once."

Neeve bared her teeth in a silent snarl, her palms tingling. "You're a monster."

"I know my calling," Fallon said, unshaken. "I know my mission. And I love it when I succeed."

"You haven't succeeded in anything," Cassander said. "Your hands are stained with innocent blood that will never be washed clean."

"*Innocent*," Fallon said with a laugh, stalking around them with a showman's bravado. "As though those with magic and divine blood are impervious to blame simply by possessing power that no mortal should hold."

"Who are you to make that judgment?" Neeve asked. "You are as flawed and broken as anyone else. You're no better."

"Yes," Fallon hissed, the light of anger flashing in his eyes. "I *am* better."

"Better off dead, I would say." Isa emerged from the woods, black smoke feathering into her hands as though she siphoned life from the air itself. Her eyes were bright, an ethereal quality carrying from them as they bore into Fallon.

Fallon raised a brow. "Did you leave him alive?"

"I'm no fool, cultist."

He grit his teeth and glanced at the man at his feet, stirring to consciousness from Neeve's magic. He held his head as he rose with Fallon's help. Seizing their chance, Neeve and Cassander scrambled to their feet, crawling away toward Isa to regain their bearings. But at their movement, the man with Fallon reacted quickly, lunging for Neeve and scratching at her arms to grab her. She kicked at him once, twice, and the third time, the heel of her boot landing hard against his knee. The unsettling pop preceded his howl of pain as he reached for the injured joint.

"You'd better act quickly," Isa said, extending her hand to the man clutching his knee. "I'm still hungry."

Isa siphoned his soul, his living breath shuddered in his chest as he tried to scream. Fallon watched, awestruck.

"You are no deathwitch," he whispered, staring at her in horrified disgust. "Abomination."

Her eyes burned with the soul she'd consumed, light limning the violet dark of her irises.

"Save Erick," she said to Neeve, locking her predatory gaze on Fallon. "Leave this wretch's soul to me."

"What's this?" Charis's light blue-green eyes bore into Fallon's with pointed, lethal rage. She walked with determined steps from the large tent, a bare sword in her hand. "You didn't think to tell me when our guests arrived?"

"You were busy." Fallon didn't pull his gaze from Isa. "The chaos-born has kept our hands full. I thought it prudent to divide and conquer."

Voices sounded from the distance, but nothing lingered in the air. Quick bursts of a shout that was quickly quieted, coupled with the rustling of leaves and branches, caused everyone to stare at the line of trees bordering the rear of the camp.

Neeve's family, evening the odds.

"Gods," Charis said, glaring at Fallon. "What about the rest of them?"

"We have the power to handle them." Fallon's furrowed brow crowned his angry eyes, his mouth opening and closing through a retort he couldn't verbalize. "Don't be afraid to use them."

"How dare you put our people at risk?" Charis's hands flexed at her sides, likely itching to do Fallon severe physical harm. "Do their lives mean nothing to you?"

"They mean everything," Fallon retorted, "and they understand the needs of the mission."

Charis sounded a sharp whistle and aimed two fingers toward the sound of the fight. Rustling in the trees shook branches overhead as someone jumped through them toward the fight.

"Archers!" Neeve screamed, praying her family would hear. "In the trees!"

Charis closed the distance to Neeve in two strides, striking her across the face with the palm of her empty hand. But Neeve reacted, gripping Charis's arm with her burning touch. The Preceptor cried out, jerking her body away, as the standing cultist with Fallon moved to subdue Neeve. Cassander intercepted with his sword, deflecting the adversary's blade and shoving him back.

Charis staggered back as more cultists emerged from their tents, drawing weapons. A dozen of them, bladed and eager.

"There's more behind the camp!" Charis shouted, waving cultists to go toward Neeve's family. "I'll see to the chaosborn, since he means so damn much to them."

"No!"

But an approaching cultist thwarted Neeve's pursuit, moving around her like a predator toying with its prey.

"You won't get your hands on me, witch," he said, running his tongue over his teeth. "Though I wouldn't mind it, in other circumstances."

Her eyes locked onto his. "I don't have to touch you to get what I want."

Her mindwalking probed his mind, leaving nothing to grace or mercy as she rent his consciousness to shreds. He fell to the ground screaming, his sword hitting the ground as his hands pressed against the mounting pressure in his skull.

Glass shattered behind her, and she spun on the balls of her feet. Green smoke billowed around Isa and Cassander's feet. Feathers of it reached Neeve, and it took her breath, lungs seizing. Something metallic graced Neeve's tongue.

Iron.

"A special blend," Fallon said, a cloth tied to cover his nose and mouth. "Iron, toxic herbs, enough for mortals and godborn alike."

Iron and widow's veil? Or something weaker to keep us alive?

Neeve's vision blurred, trying to focus on the surrounding threat. Cassander and Isa were the first to fall to their knees, the smoke choking them, their veins protruding from their necks. Three cultists swarmed them, cloths around their faces.

"Neeve!"

Her family, running, arrows whizzing from the trees. But they were alright, their blades bloodied and eyes alight as they ran for her before more cultists swarmed them.

"Gods damn you!" Gretchen cried, swinging a stolen short sword as her parents met her shoulders, a bladed trinity.

Neeve coughed, tasting blood, torn between staying with Cassander and Isa and running for Erick.

There were too many of them.

Let go, Neeve. The voice in her mind resonated with peace, the decision already made. *Let go.*

Neeve aimed her magic at Charis, pooling light-laced shadows around her feet and wrists before pulling hard. Even if she didn't cause the woman to stumble or fall, it would stall her, change her focus, bring her wrath to Neeve instead of Erick.

Charis cried out, surprise smoothing the expression around her eyes and mouth before she narrowed her steely gaze at Neeve. Even at a distance, Charis's eyes were clearly visible.

"Kill her!" Charis commanded before screaming in agony.

Neeve clawed her way through the cultist's mind before an arrow pierced through her shoulder, breaking her concentration with white-hot pain.

"Neeve!" But Cassander couldn't rise, the iron-laced smoke slowly killing him. He sputtered a cough, droplets of blood spraying from his mouth.

Charis, in a fury, disappeared into the tent.

"You never learn," Fallon said. He had the nerve to click his tongue against his teeth, as though chastising a child. "Serves you right, death-witch. You should have known better."

"I am no deathwitch." She wanted to smirk, but the smoke wracked her lungs. She coughed up a spray of blood, struggling to her feet. "You ignorant fool."

He chuckled, satisfied, as his ice-blue eyes bore into Cassander. "My face was the last thing your beloved saw before she died."

Cassander met his wretched gaze with hatred in his reddened eyes, tears welling from the smoke.

Fallon gripped the lightborn's throat. "Please allow me to reunite you both."

CHAPTER 42

Neeve rushed Fallon, screaming through clenched teeth, bringing godborn and cultist to the ground with her. Cassander scrambled to his feet despite the poison in his lungs. Blood sprayed from his mouth as he coughed.

Neeve's shoulder raged, the flames fueling her fight against Fallon as she strangled his wrist. Light passed through her, burning him as he growled through clenched teeth. He reached for the arrow still lodged in her shoulder and pulled, straining the shaft against the tender wound. Her cry of agony erupted light magic all around them, but another wail in the distance stirred fear, rattling bones as Neeve's blood ran cold.

Erick.

Gods—

But her diverted attention cost her as Fallon bested her, using the arrow's leverage to maneuver behind her and pin her to the ground. He grabbed her wrists, barking orders for a nearby cultist to bind them.

Voices shouted, bodies scuffled, but Neeve couldn't turn her head to see. Hands gripped her hard, knees leaning on her back.

"Make sure her bonds are good and tight," Fallon instructed, getting to his feet as a stranger held Neeve to the ground.

Her captor said nothing, tightening their grip as rope passed over Neeve's wrists.

"Damn you!" Fallon called. Neeve glimpsed a body falling, the man level with her with his eyes and mouth agape.

Isa cackled, victory gleaming in her eyes. But the cultist wasn't dead. He moved quickly, pulling a knife from his belt and lunging for her.

"Isa!" Neeve choked on dust and the remnants of Fallon's toxic smoke, but her warning came too late.

"Die," the cultist growled. "Death*bitch*."

Neeve struggled until the cultist on top of her pressed into her wound, her arm going cold from pain and diminished circulation.

"Wait." Jacqueline. "Trust me. *Wait*."

"Gods above, where did you come from?"

"Hold still."

"Why in the hells should I trust you?"

Jacqueline worked quickly, tightening the ropes around Neeve's wrists before closing Neeve's fingers around something small, made of metal.

Neeve hissed, cutting herself on the sharp end of a knife.

"Careful," she whispered. "Get on your feet."

Jacqueline made a show of pulling Neeve up roughly, helping her upright and guiding her toward the others.

Cassander fought alongside Gretchen and her family, all of them bleeding but upright. Nearly a dozen cultists littered the ground in various states of consciousness and life, but they remained everywhere.

Among them lay Isa, facedown, in a growing pool of blood. Just like the vision.

How much longer before all of this was over?

"You and your loved ones have remarkable spirits," Fallon said, looking down his nose at Neeve. "It's admirable. And it makes our victory that much sweeter."

Neeve spat at him. "Suffer in the hells, cultist."

"If the hells even exist," he said with snark, "You'll come to learn their many layers before I step foot anywhere near them."

He unclasped the holster at his leg and removed the iron poker. It only took seconds for Cassander to suffer a misstep, leaving an opening for his opponent to strike.

He'd endured Fallon's toxins only to falter against iron once more.

"You bastard!" Neeve gripped the knife, desperate to cut the rope. "You will suffer for everything you've done."

"I *have* suffered." He bent to her, his sharp eyes unyielding as they stared into hers.

She moved quickly, seizing the opportunity to scramble his mind. He winced against the unseen foe of her magic, recoiling with his empty hand going to his head.

But he struck her, his fist landing hard on her cheek. Her concentration broke as the blinding pain disrupted all thought. She spun and hit the ground, landing almost parallel to Isa's still form.

"You've done well," Fallon said to Jacqueline. "I'm sure Elias will be pleased."

Elias?

Jacqueline didn't respond, eyes avoiding Neeve and the fight beside them.

"Perhaps he will want to experiment on the deathseer now." Fallon glanced toward the tent. "Watch her. Maim her if she moves."

Sheathing the iron poker and clasping its holster closed, Fallon strode to the tent, shoulders straight and chin elevated in self-claimed importance. As soon as he disappeared, Neeve worked fast against the ropes.

Jacqueline crouched to help. "Quickly. While he's distracted."

"Whose side are you on?" Neeve asked. "My head is spinning, trying to keep up."

"I'm on no one's side now." Jacqueline worked on the ties at her wrists. "Cynthia's gone too far this time."

"Cynthia?"

"Feather and Claw." Jacqueline pulled hard on the rope. Neeve groaned as her injured shoulder and wrists throbbed. "She's asked far too much from me."

"What are you talking about?"

"*Infiltrate the Wandering Order*," Jacqueline recited, "*by any means necessary*. Well, I did. I used Feather and Claw. I used Moonblade. And, finally, I convinced them to let me in if I promised them someone valuable."

"Was it Erick?" Neeve sneered. "Or did it start with me?"

"You. Elias is very interested in what a deathseer can do. They weren't expecting a chaosborn in the bargain." She paused. "Neither did I."

Neeve stared, stunned, her anger burying any coherent thought or word.

"Your parents don't know about Cynthia's orders," Jacqueline said. "It's probably better they never do."

Her parents, sending Jacqueline with money and news, trusting her to help her daughters survive.

"You sacrificed me to them," Neeve uttered, hearing her loved ones fight. "You sacrificed my family."

Light prickled its burning ache in her palms, eager for a target.

"It wasn't meant to go this far, but they used my brother as leverage," she said. "Just like they used your sister."

The truth did little to dull the sharp edge of Neeve's anger.

"That's why I asked for a death reading," she went on. "They were there, waiting to see if your magic was true."

Fallon in the tavern.

Charis, asking for a cobbler.

"He and Charis have saved a modest stockpile of mist arcana to test on those with magic. Some of them have worked, which is bad for the rest of us."

"Mist arcana. *Experiments*." Neeve stared without seeing. "Gods. That would kill me."

"Taking enough of it certainly would. But they'd likely have what they need from you before then."

"To use me," Neeve uttered, looking down at her dirty hands. "How many others have they used?"

"Too many." Jacqueline stared into Neeve's eyes, self-assured and angry. "Did you bury my brother?"

An ache bloomed in Neeve's chest. Galla. Human leverage. His final moments had been in anguish. "We sent him downriver."

Jacqueline nodded, nose and mouth twitching as she fought back the emotional tide that likely welled within. "He didn't deserve this. He didn't deserve any of it."

"Neither did I."

"The aging curse was a feeble attempt to knock them off your scent." Jacqueline's eyes held apology, though her lips never uttered the words. "I expected that you'd break it, not pursue me to another continent."

"Why didn't you tell me this before?" Frustration sparked within her, but Neeve stayed silent. "When we found you at the shack—"

"And the Wandering Order was on your heels?" Jacqueline's gaze was steel. "How can you still be this naïve? They've watched your every step. They watched *me*." Jacqueline extended an open hand. "May I get that arrow out of your shoulder now, or would you like to interrogate me some more?"

Neeve pursed her lips, bracing herself for the agony to come. Jacqueline snapped the arrow shaft and yanked the weapon free without hesitation or caution. Neeve screamed through closed lips, pressing her hands to her mouth.

"Here." Jacqueline pressed a small lump of blue-green arcana crystal into Neeve's hand. "Can you heal with this?"

Neeve nodded, the power of the crystal already soaking into her skin.

"Him too." Jacqueline nodded toward Cassander, fighting hard. "He's going to need it."

"You have another one." It was a guess, but Neeve said it with authority and held out her hand for it. "Erick will die without it."

Jacqueline hesitated before revealing a larger piece. "Only because I almost killed you with that curse. Don't show this to Darrow."

"Darrow? Why?"

"Moonblade gets angry if you steal from them." She winked, placing the crystal in Neeve's palm. "This makes us even."

"As long as Erick and Cassander survive." But Neeve wasn't eager to relinquish her grudge.

Neeve pulled a sword from a downed cultist and ran, drawing from the power of the crystal to fuel the light gathering around her hands. One cultist charged forward, blade ready, ire aimed at Neeve as she blocked the strike of his blade, her arm and injured shoulder shuddering against the weight and strength of him. Cassander blocked his own opponent as he kicked toward Neeve's. The cultist faltered, giving Neeve room to end him quickly. She tried not to focus her eyes on the way her sword cut through him, turning her gaze from his body as he fell.

"Here." Neeve passed Cassander the crystal, slipping it into the pocket of his trousers. "Stay alive."

"You too."

Neeve fired two orbs of light at the cultists fighting her parents, the miniature suns sailing to their backs. The cultists arched in searing pain, their cries echoing off the boughs overhead. Neeve's parents and Gretchen finished them before moving in defense against others.

Nearly there. Neeve hurried to the tent. *Just a bit longer.*

The front flaps of the largest tent moved, shadows surrounding the arm that separated them. Erick emerged, eyes burning red, skin shadowed with Chaos. Shadows stretched from his back like massive wings.

Neeve froze, terror gripping her heart.

Charis and Fallon followed, haughty and challenging, as they regarded Neeve from behind Erick's chaotic form.

Charis admired Erick like a proud parent, as though she'd made him in his magnificence. "What a marvel he is."

"Erick—" His name was barely a whisper as Neeve took a step forward, halted by Fallon as he unclasped the holster, reaching once more for the iron.

"Not so fast, deathseer." He grinned. "He's ours now."

CHAPTER 43

"A curious thing, arcana crystal," Fallon said. "The dust from it drives magic folk into madness."

He made a show of unsheathing the iron poker, his wild gaze challenging Neeve to react. But she didn't have to, as Erick slammed his fist against Fallon's chest. He crashed into the tent, nearly collapsing it on top of himself.

"Remarkable," Charis said, awestruck.

"What did you do?" Neeve glared at Charis before taking in the red depths of Erick's eyes. "What did she do, Erick?"

"Mist arcana," Charis answered, producing a vial from a pocket. The powder was iridescent green and blue and shimmered in the sunlight. "Remarkable what even a small amount can do."

She moved toward him as a hand grabbed her wrist to pull her back. She whirled, ready to retaliate, but Erick's chaos magic struck the cultist hard in the chest, sending her breathless to the ground.

At this, Neeve ran, reaching Erick even as Charis moved to strike her. But Neeve's magic reached her with Erick's, the Preceptor subject to cold affliction and burning rage as the chaosborn and his lightborn deathseer unleashed their complementary magic through her body.

She crumpled to the ground, quivering, and Neeve crushed the vial of mist arcana with Charis's hand, glass and bone cracking beneath the heel of Neeve's boot. The Preceptor screamed, unable to rise from the magic she'd endured, consumed in pain.

"Neeve—" Erick's voice, deeper in his chaos form, was soft as he said her name. "Neeve, I—"

His breath shuddered, waves of chaos creating tremors of shadows around his body.

"How can I help you?" Her free hand cupped his face as the other brought the arcana crystal to his chest. "Will this help? What can I do?"

"Run."

She shook her head. "Not on your life, Mal'Erick."

The crystal seemed to have no effect, his power still thrumming with remarkable strength. Neeve waited, seeing no change.

"This power," he said. "All of this chaos, I can't—"

A pulse came from his form as though it had built up too much pressure. As though it couldn't be caged. It swept over Charis and Fallon, each of them crying out as chaos amplified their suffering.

"Tell me what to do." She hugged his neck, the crystal gripped in her fingers, desperation making it hard to think or breathe. "Tell me what to do."

"You can't." His hands found her waist, and Neeve feared he would push her away. "This poison is crawling through my veins."

She took his hand in hers as another pulse of chaos shot around them. Erick growled through clenched teeth.

"Neeve—"

Fallon and Charis cried out in pain, shadows giving them anguish and nightmare. But Neeve remained.

"You can't hurt me," she said, kissing his hand. "I love you, and I'm not afraid."

Tears fell from his red-lined eyes before he squinted them shut, his bared teeth clenched as his lips trembled.

"I love you," she said again, "and I'm not afraid."

He quivered, the shadows gathering darker around him. He was colder, as though the dark siphoned away all of his warmth.

"Look at me." She touched his face, her heart a hammer against her ribcage. "Look at me, love."

He pressed her hand to his face, fear and shame weighing heavily around his eyes as he obeyed.

Even with mist arcana coursing through his blood, he'd removed his guards for her, and she slipped into his mind. Neeve tread carefully, mindful of her presence and her touch as she saw the day's memories.

THE IRON TORTURE from Charis and Fallon.

Blood. Bruises.

Exhaustion weighing on weakened shoulders.

But Erick had enough spite within him to give Charis a blood-laced smirk.

Charis gripped his face in one hand, forcing his sneering lips to pucker. She opened her mouth to speak but stopped at the sound of agonized screaming from outside. It was the man Neeve had attacked, ripping through his mind.

Charis straightened, looking over her shoulder toward the tent's opening. "What in the hells..."

Erick grinned, shaking his face free of her grip. "That would be the love of my life, coming to reclaim what's hers." He watched Charis's expression with triumph. "Isn't she magnificent?"

"Your little deathseer pet?"

He glared at her through his lashes. "Diminish her power at your own folly."

"I have to admire your tenacity, chaosborn," she said in the memory. "And the way you love her."

"You will lose your hands if you touch her."

"Is that a promise?" She bent to his level, her smirk infuriating. "Your feelings for her will be useful."

"You wish for death," Erick said, thrashing against the ties that bound him. "I would consider it an honor to give it to you."

Neeve screamed, terror and rage filling Erick as he lashed out, chaotic magic pulsing from him as he screamed his rage in Charis's face. The Preceptor fell, landing in a heap at Erick's feet.

"We won't kill her if you comply," she said, holding a vial between her thumb and index finger as she stood. "We only need to test a small amount to see what it will do."

"You really want to test that on a chaosborn?" Erick laughed, mirth not reaching his eyes. "It's your funeral, Preceptor."

Charis uncorked the vial and waited, eyeing Erick's mouth. For the briefest moment, his courage faltered before he controlled himself again.

"I will force you to watch while we kill her." Charis poured a small amount of powder on the tip of her index finger. "But if you take this, I'll see that she remains unharmed."

Fallon stepped in, eyeing the two of them with a curious lift of his brow. "Am I interrupting?"

"Aren't you always?" But Erick didn't take his eyes off of Charis. "If you go back on this arrangement..." Erick's voice, dangerously low, sent shivers down Neeve's spine. "If she so much as gains a scratch, your neck will break for it."

"My neck, my hands. Make up your mind." Charis offered her finger, and Neeve watched as Erick opened his mouth. Anger burned through her bones as Charis touched his tongue, drawing a short line with mist arcana.

The change took effect almost immediately, shadows and chaos coalescing around his body. Neeve's body suffered a phantom sensation of euphoria and terror, her heart fluttering, her blood flowing. Chaos burned beneath her skin, her body no longer strong enough to house its power and strength. It wanted *out*. It needed *freedom*.

This is what Erick has suffered.

Neeve's bones would have shattered, but Erick's body endured.

"Darktouched," Charis whispered, a smile gracing her face, making her appear years younger. "Remarkable."

Fallon kept his distance. "How much did you give him?"

"Enough."

Erick stood, breaking the bonds and the chair. Fallon staggered back, hand reaching for the iron holster, but Charis stopped him.

"We need to see what he's capable of." She stared in reverent awe, as though in the presence of divine greatness. "No iron until it's absolutely necessary."

But Fallon kept his hand on the clasp, eyes wary.

"How do you feel?" Charis asked Erick. "Is there pain? Elation?"

His eyes flashed infernal anger, lips sneering. Shadows swirled fast around his hands.

"Tell me, chaosborn, before I shove you so full of iron—"

"Show her to him," Fallon said. "The deathseer."

Erick's gaze snapped to Fallon, his sneer sharpening. His fists unfurled, fingers taut like claws. Shadows limned his form in darkness, as though all seven hells haloed around him.

"She's the leverage to make him comply," he went on. "And he's leverage for her."

"Finally showing your usefulness." Charis opened one of the tent flaps for him. "After you, chaosborn."

⁂

Neeve slowly let go, easing her way out of Erick's mind.

"You're stronger than them," Neeve whispered, hooking her arm around his neck. "You're stronger than what they've done."

She clutched the arcana crystal, its power fueling the light magic that warmed her skin. He took her empty hand and pressed it against his chest, his heart pounding against her palm. He leaned into the curve of her neck and shoulder.

"This will not break you, Mal'Erick, my love." Waves of light passed from her, filling him with love and warmth. "Because nothing can."

"Say it again," he whispered, his chaotic voice low in her ear, his breath warm against her throat. "Gods, Neeve, say it again."

"Mal'Erick." She kissed his temple, tasting dirt and sweat. "My love."

He shuddered, the effects of mist arcana still holding him hostage, but she felt him lift his head as he targeted the remaining cultists around Cassander and her family. She turned, staying in the safety of his arm, watching his extended hand aim darkness and strike.

One cultist fell.

Then another.

Neeve aimed her light alongside his shadows, their bolts felling two foes at once.

Charis screamed as Fallon scrambled, hurrying to flee.

"You monster!" Charis's hand reached up, clawing at Erick's arm. He cast her aside, forcing her to land hard against the earth.

The next swipe of his hand seized Fallon, unseen magic gripping him by his throat. Erick's fingers curved as though holding the cultist by the throat, lifting him from the ground.

"You struck her," Erick said, his voice laced with the seven hells. "My promise to the Preceptor applies to you, too, Warden."

"Pr—prom—" Fallon struggled, his face and neck purple with veins protruding.

"You don't deserve his death on your conscience," Neeve said. "Though the temptation to wipe his stain from the earth is strong."

"Very strong," Erick said through clenched teeth. "When our minds connected, I saw through your eyes. How he hit you..."

Erick's grip tightened. Fallon's eyes rolled back.

"I know your heart, Mal'Erick," she whispered. "This will follow you."

His hold on Fallon released, the cultist crashing on the earth with an audible snap. He wailed, hands reaching for the knee Neeve had kicked before.

Erick tightened his hold on Neeve's waist as he moved with her toward the remaining fight, one cultist somehow still standing with the others, battle weary.

"Our friends need us." His burning eyes scanned the trees. "More are coming."

"More? Gods above, they're like vermin."

"Charis sent for the other Preceptor. He wants *you*. He'll bring whatever rodents are in his camp, but their resolve is breaking." Erick smiled down at her, his shadow form magnificent. "Let's see it done."

But Erick faltered, something hard striking him from behind. It was Charis, her injured hand cradled against her chest as the other gripped Fallon's iron poker. She ripped the hook from Erick's back, tearing his skin and bringing him to his knees.

Behind her was Fallon's body, motionless in the bloodstained grass. His throat had been slashed, his leg holster crudely ripped open and empty.

"See you in the hells, chaosborn."

CHAPTER 44

Neeve's movements were quick, but the passing seconds were as minutes, her mind stock still as her body reacted. One hand clutched the arcana crystal as the other struck Charis's chest hard, radiance and anger colliding in her bones, making her breath catch and step stagger. Neeve dropped the crystal and seized Charis's face with both hands, screaming her rage as she pushed Charis back, the pair nearly tripping over the fallen cultist near Isa's body.

As their eyes met, Charis paled with whatever nightmare Neeve burned into her mind, pupils shrinking to pinpricks. When Neeve released her, she struck Charis once more, her knuckles colliding with her nose. Lightning shot up Neeve's arm on impact, but the satisfying crack of cartilage reverberated, bringing joy to Neeve's fury.

"Preceptor!"

Neeve turned as Charis scrambled back, trembling, tripping over her own feet and stumbling away, dropping Fallon's iron poker in her panicked attempt at escape.

"Preceptor!" A male voice from the trees. "Preceptor! We're here!"

Thunderous feet running. But Neeve couldn't tell how many. She rushed to Erick, Gretchen slinging the poker away from the two godborn as Cassander inspected the wound, inflamed from iron.

"Take them!" Charis commanded, her scream high-pitched and panicked. "Kill them all!"

One man among the cultists stood out, with silver hair and eyes the color of night. He found Neeve among the crowd and broke into a run, hands unsheathing the daggers from his belt.

The other Preceptor.

"Here!" A voice from the trees, followed by rallying cries from men and women clad in black.

Moonblade. The cavalry had arrived.

"I'm no fighter," Neeve said to Cassander, taking up a discarded sword from the nearest cultist body. "But I can buy you time."

"Neeve—"

"Heal him," she said, "and stay alive. In every death I've seen, you've survived."

"Neeve." It was Erick, his breath shuddering. "Don't. Please."

She knelt in front of him, the surrounding fight raging as cultists and assassins swarmed closer to her loved ones. "Let Cassander heal you, Mal'Erick, and give them hell."

She kissed him before conjuring her light, stepping to the nearest cultist in the fray. He turned to her, dagger in hand, mistaking her for easy prey until the bolt of yellow-white light slammed into his chest. Others cried out as beams sailed toward them, hopping on the balls of their feet to avoid them.

"Gah!" one cried out. An orb slammed against his arm. "It burns!"

Neeve pulled harder, commanding her light to bind them, to wrap in them in her searing wrath, but one cultist carried a black-bladed knife.

"*Witches hide and witches flee,*" he sang, his voice rumbling like shifting stone. "*None escape the Order's decree.*"

"Oh, hells. You've got a *song*?"

"*Hunt them high and hunt them low.*" He grinned. "*Where witches hide, the Order goes.*"

"You must be the favorite at the campfire."

He edged closer, twirling his iron knife, dark eyes gleaming. But cries and shouts disrupted whatever intimidation he'd attempted as one runners clad in black stormed the fray.

Darrow.

Bless him, Anya. Keep him safe.

Her hands moved quickly before she brought her hands together, fingers tight around the hilt of the sword. A deep *boom* sent a wave of force that shoved the cultist back. With a twist of her hands and a flick of her fingers, the light coalesced, rising like a round wall around her and her enemy. Others cried out, caught off their guard until, one by one, they stepped into the radiant wall to surround her. But the barrier muffled their screams, the light filling their mouths and throats, choking them.

Neeve held on, magic flowing through her as it had always wanted. The iron-wielding cultist's playful taunt had shifted, eyes widening in violent rage.

"Your corruption will yield nothing but sorrow," he said, hand strangling his weapon. "I look forward to seeing your end."

"Your eyes will fail you before you get the chance."

The light swirled faster before funneling into every orifice of the cultist's face. His cries of fear and anger surrendered to the light Neeve poured into him.

"Greet your fellow monsters in shame," Neeve taunted. "In the gutter of the Chaos Realm."

He died choking, his body collapsing to the earth as her radiance took him.

When the light dissipated, the other cultists had fallen in a half-circle around him. The dust settled, but the fight was far from over.

"Well done, Neeve." Erick stood behind her, his chaos form returned. He labored to breathe, but whatever damage the iron had done, Cassander had it healed.

"Yes," one cultist said with a sneer. Sweat poured from his brow, one arm cradled against his side. "Well done, witch. You've proven us right."

"Then take that truth with you to hell."

But as Neeve readied her magic, Gretchen screamed, throwing a knife from a yard away to land in the man's shoulder. Erick struck, his shadows quick as they surrounded the man before flowing into his mouth. He fell to the ground, body seizing, hands clawing at his throat.

The next raced to Neeve. The world brightened as she met his challenge, light surrounding the sword as she stepped toward him.

"Gods—" He took a half step back. "Your eyes—"

He fell, his ankle rolling as he stepped on a rock, but his cry came from fear, not pain. He scrambled backward, leaving his sword behind.

"Please—"

"You beg when you raised your blade against my loved ones?" Her vocal pitch resonated with a layer of depth, a second voice that was god-touched. Power surged through her blood, coating her muscles with energy. "If they'd begged, would you let them go?"

His hesitation was her answer. But another cultist rushed forward, screaming, daggers raised. Neeve moved in defense, giving her opponent the opportunity he needed to stumble to his feet and run.

Their blades clanged when Neeve blocked the first dagger with her sword, bouncing on the balls of her feet to avoid the strike from the second.

"Pretty little dancer," the cultist said. "Watch your step."

Neeve winced. "Does that line actually work for you?"

He rose to her challenge, pride bright in his eyes, but as he squared his shoulders, staring into Neeve's eyes, the severity of his sneer weakened.

"You should have known better," she said, her voice echoing in his mind.

Her movements were quick, making no ceremony about triggering his fear as she mindwalked. He flinched at unseen foes before crouching, hands pressed against his head, body trembling.

Darrow was several feet ahead, his bleeding arm cradled against his chest as he defended with only a sword, each successive blow from his opponent coming harder and faster. Light came to Neeve's call, sailing fast and colliding with the swordsman, sending him back several feet where he landed hard against the ground. A nearby assassin saw to his end swiftly before moving on to the next.

Neeve jogged to Darrow, the wound on his arm severe. "You're losing too much blood."

Darrow offered a half-smile, his face sweaty and pale. "But this isn't where I die."

"That doesn't mean you become a fool with your life." She rested her hand over the wound, warm light working through the deep cut across his bicep. With a gentle touch, Neeve's light repaired the damage, leaving a dark red line in its wake. Cassander and Isa would be proud.

"Gods above." Though still weak, Darrow tested his arm, bending and flexing. "You're magnificent, Neeve of Brightmere."

"Guard your life, Darrow." She picked up a fallen dagger and passed it to him. "No future is certain."

Dual wielding blades, he nodded with a wink. "We'll see where the road leads."

"Yes," came a deep, smooth voice. Neeve turned. Elias, the second Preceptor, approached. Tall, with a commanding gaze and a longsword coated in blood. "Your road, Deathseer, leads to me."

"I decide where I go." Neeve strangled the sword handle as her other hand pulled more light, glowing threads swirling around her hands. "No one commands me."

"We'll see when this is over." He drew a knife from his belt, edging closer as he circled her. "This doesn't have to end in blood. None of your loved ones have to die."

Neeve fired a streak of light, which he dodged without tearing his eyes from her face. But he knew better than to meet her eyes, keeping his locked onto her mouth and chin. Without the direct connection, Neeve's mindwalking wouldn't go through.

"I've been so eager to meet you since I heard about the deathseer in Brightmere." The softness in his voice made her skin crawl, the notes of danger melodic beneath the veneer of sweetness. "My spies had some interesting stories to tell. Forecasting the end of a life thread, trying to save poor wretches who still got themselves killed..." He glanced at Erick. "...A romantic interest in a chaosborn." He chuckled. "I can't wait to learn what makes you *tick*."

She aimed more light, this time at his feet. He avoided each one with a dancer's grace.

"If you touch anyone I love," she said, "I will keep you alive through every agony you suffer."

"Promise?" He grinned. "Our spirits align, Neeve of Brightmere. I can't wait."

With a flourish of his weapon, he rushed her, eyes fearless, body swift and sure.

A bolt of shadow slammed against his chest. The man staggered but his not fall, his malicious, eager eyes bright as they stared at the healed chaosborn who returned to Neeve's side.

Erick bore a bloodied sword in each hand. His chaotic form wreathed him in shadow, complementing Neeve's radiance with darkness.

"Cassander and the others are alright," Erick said, flicking his wrist to swing his sword in an impressive arc. "A lot of cultists have fled with Moonblade at their heels."

"How precious," the man crooned, his voice full of mocking. "Lovers joined in divine blood."

"Your numbers are wearing thin, Preceptor," Erick said, shadows deep in his voice.

"And your time is running out."

"Be careful," Neeve said to Erick. "He has more than meets the eye."

"And I have you." He winked at her. "Let's show him what darkness and light can do."

CHAPTER 45

The three came together in a rush of blades and anger. The Preceptor blocked their attacks swiftly, as though divinity coursed through his blood to grant him exceptional dexterity.

"My." He grinned at Erick. "You look like someone I've met before. A woman. Long hair, black as night."

The shadows darkened around Erick's body, his eyes burning red.

The man's grin broadened. "I've had my eye on her, too."

Erick growled as he unleashed several strikes, each of them blocked or dodged. Neeve tried to aim her orbs of light at their foe, staying back while Erick's bladed fury sought purchase.

But their enemy seized an opening, shoving against Erick's attack and kicking him hard in the stomach. Erick staggered back, nearly falling.

Neeve flew in, desperate to make eye contact, to touch the man's skin and make him burn, but he swung the longsword. Neeve dodged to miss the brunt of the strike, but the blade cut through Neeve's sleeve and skin. The cut burned as it bled.

"Careful, little witch."

He met her gaze without fear, but as she sought to touch his mind, she met a barrier.

"You're warded," she said. "*By magic.*"

He tapped his temple. "Don't think we don't have what we need to fight the pestilence on this earth. You wield fire, so will we."

Mist arcana. Experiments on those with magic.

To use me, Neeve had said before, when Jacqueline unveiled the Order's true intent.

Elias straightened his shoulders, his chest broad as he watched her. "You see now, don't you?"

"Your hypocrisy, Preceptor." she said.

"Hypocrisy over abomination." He sneered as he grinned. "Your filthy incestuous blood."

"Incest?" Erick cocked his head. "You think we are..."

Elias's gaze sharpened. "Goddesses mating—"

But Neeve's laugh cut him off. "That is not how godborn are made, you ignorant wretch."

"Goddesses touch the chosen," Erick said slowly, as though explaining this to a child. "Their offspring are godborn from blessed blood."

"*Blessed blood.*" Elias, undeterred, laughed so fully that it further stoked the flames in Neeve's core. "We'll see how blessed."

"Aw, how cute," she said to Erick. "He thinks I care."

Erick smirked, pride beaming in his eyes.

"Oh, little witch," Elias said. "Soon, you'll see."

"Should I warn him about underestimating you?" Erick asked, his playful tone bolstering. "I'd much rather let him find out the hard way."

"The hard way works for me."

And Elias rushed at them both, sword and knife drawn. Neeve moved to flank the cultist as Erick defended against each attack. Elias was skilled at fighting two opponents, where Neeve was hardly skilled at physically fighting one, but she didn't relent as she tried to balance melee force with light magic. As Elias swung, Neeve kicked at his knee, giving Erick the window to strike. His sword pierced Elias's side.

But Erick's look wasn't triumphant. He grimaced, brow furrowing, eyes finding Neeve.

Elias had stabbed him, too, the knife blade between his ribs.

Neeve gripped Elias's damp hair and pulled him back, sending the cultist bleeding to the ground, as Erick faltered to his knees. Light swayed at her whim, coalescing into a dome that surrounded the Preceptor even as he screamed to escape it. He beat his fists against the wall of light as she closed her hand, sealing him inside.

"That's my girl." Erick smiled, revealing bloody teeth. "My radiant Neeve. It's not—" Erick grimaced, bracing his hand next to the wound. "It's not that bad."

"Don't talk." Neeve pressed her hands on either side of the knife, feeling with her magic to see what the damage had done. "Don't you dare talk. Don't you dare die."

Erick chuckled, bringing a bloody hand to her face. "You're cute when you're angry."

"Gods, Erick." She channeled her magic in the way Cassander had showed her, helping his body to reject the knife and sew itself back together. "Will you please stop getting stabbed?"

"I can't have Cassander besting me in the number of wounds and scars we earn." He laughed feebly before wincing in pain.

Her magic was working, and, gods be praised, the wound wasn't deep. "Haven't you been through enough?"

He swept a lock of hair from her eyes. "I told you I would break the world for you."

She pulled the knife, making him groan. His godborn healing sealed the wound as her light magic hurried the process. "Then stay alive and do it, Mal'Erick." She kissed his cheek and met his gaze. "Stay alive and break it with me."

"Preceptor!"

A cultist raced for the dome, trying to break free with his sword. The blade sliced through, and the Preceptor cried out in agony. Horror shrank the cultist's pupils to pinpricks before his eyes fell to Neeve, where anger replaced fear.

"You want him?" Neeve opened her fingers, muscles and tendons tight as she held the spell. "Join him."

Closing her hand once more, the dome swallowed them both, the light swirling. But something hard collided with her between the shoulders, stealing her breath as she blinked through stars. Erick struck fast, his sword stabbing whoever was behind her, but the spell dissipated as her hold diminished.

Glancing behind, there was no one else, the newest body a heap at her feet. What cultists remained were dead or scattered through the trees. And Neeve's loved ones were still standing, weak and breathless, bloody and bruised. But they were alive.

She kept a hand on Erick's chest, their magic coalescing. Shadows and light, entwined as one. Order and chaos.

Elias was on his knees, holding his arm with the opposite hand, blood trailing down his fingers. He glowered at Neeve, a dangerous blend of emotions burning behind his eyes. The cultist with him screamed in agony, holding his forehead with one hand as the other feebly held his sword.

"You will never know mercy," Elias said, rising to his feet. "The next time I see you, I kill you."

Elias dragged the screaming cultist with him, trying to hurry with weak, faltering steps. Neeve had nothing left to stop him from running. Erick's lips pulled back from his teeth, sharing her frustration. But as the dust settled and the afternoon grew quiet, Neeve closed her eyes, focusing on the sound of Erick's breathing and the rise and fall of his chest.

Their remaining enemies fled. The world returned to calm, though the ground ran red with their violence.

"Who's alive?" Gretchen called, panting. "Everyone yell their name."

Neeve's family was battered but alive, as were Cassander and Darrow. Erick, taking her hand, pulled her close and kissed her crown.

Gretchen's impromptu census confirmed a bittersweet outcome: Neeve, Gretchen, her parents, Erick, Cassander, Darrow, and a few other Moonblade assassins.

But the field was littered with cultists, assassins, and—

"Where's Isa?"

Neeve went to where the soulwitch had lain in death, the spot of bloody grass empty. Isa was nowhere to be found.

"Fallon's gone, too," Erick said, pointing to a large swatch of red in the grass.

"She feigned death?" Kaeli asked, surveying the dead. "Or did she..."

Kaeli regarded Robert with a knowing look.

"There was arcana crystal," Cassander said.

"What do you mean?" Neeve asked, remembering the shard she'd dropped while fighting. "What would the crystal do?"

"She's a soulwitch," Erick said. "And a powerful one."

"You mean—"

"A soulwitch with arcana crystal," Robert said. "And she'd absorbed souls during the fight."

"Explain it to the mundane human in the group," Gretchen said, panting. "What would that do?"

"Give her incredible power," Erick said. "Soul magic is connected to chaos and light magic. She would have power over the life threads of every living thing with the ability to manipulate them, to *use* them."

"Necromancy," Neeve whispered, putting the pieces together. "Fallon."

Neeve didn't have to elaborate. Everyone nodded solemnly as Erick said, "It certainly looks that way." But he chuckled, despite the gravity of it. "The tenacity of a soulwitch."

Silence swept over them. They took their time tending to the wounded and the dead, their already exhausted bodies pushed to the brink.

But when the task was done and dusk teased the sky, the group walked to find a place to camp. Darrow and the other assassins bade farewell as they diverted for their nearest safe house.

"It was an honor to fight alongside you all," Darrow said. Then, eyes locking onto Neeve, he nodded. "Thank you. For everything."

She offered a smile as he departed, feeling Erick's curious gaze.

"Care to elaborate?"

"I will," she said, looping her arm around his and walking close beside him. "There's that tone in your voice."

"Which tone, love?"

"The one you use when you want something."

He laughed, the sound fresh, as though Neeve hadn't heard it in ages. "If I said I wanted to kiss you..."

The statement remained unfinished, but Neeve stopped, looked up at him with more love than she'd ever thought was possible.

"Here's your chance, Mal'Erick. You'd better take it while—"

His lips pressed against hers with gentle longing, hands cupping her face. The cool touch of shadows mingled with threads of light, hearts beating as one.

THE DAYS that followed held rest, the group imposing on Kenna's hospitality once more, grateful for her sanctuary and hot food. News of Fallon's death and the cultist massacre of the Midlands had reached nearly every ear, and none of them spoke a word to correct it. None knew who was behind the bloodshed, and many voices rose with rumors.

"The deathwtiches killed them all, and good riddance."

"They captured a godborn. As though they could handle that kind of magic."

"The goddesses themselves culled their plague from Ileden."

Neeve and the others remained silent, listening with closed mouths as the stories grew grander and wilder with each retelling.

"But the Wandering Order is still out there," one person said, lifting his tankard of ale to sip. "Have they cut the head of the snake? Or is this just the beginning?"

"Something that big doesn't go away overnight," another replied. "Their network is vast, from what I hear. Even into Sheraton."

"They wouldn't dare touch Kema or the Ashlands," Erick said quietly with a chuckle. "Magic and holy devotion run deep there. They'd have their asses handed to them."

Cassander laughed, tapping Erick's tankard with his own before taking a sip.

Some said that fear spread like wildfire, but Neeve reckoned it had spread like disease. The contagion of fear was hard to quell, even with preparation and precaution. Eventually, it will find another victim, whose body and mind would have to be strong enough to fight back.

Where Fallon had been strong and formidable, his fear made him weak. And it made him dangerous. What of the remaining members of the Order? What of those like Elias, where their hatred and dogma made them fearless? They were widespread, and their numbers were only growing.

She glanced at Gretchen, her expression similar, and they sipped their ales.

"You still in?" Neeve asked.

"Joining Feather and Claw? Fighting the Wandering Order?"

"Yeah."

Gretchen nodded. "It's the right thing to do."

"The Wandering Order keeps growing," Neeve said, looking at her friends and family. "We're doing to do everything we can to stop them."

Erick took her hand, giving her a reassuring squeeze. "We've dealt them a serious blow."

Cassander nodded. "It may not take them long to recover, if their networks are as vast as people say."

"And you're not doing it alone." Erick winked at her. Then, turning to Cassander, "You in?"

Cassander answered by lifting his tankard. "I wouldn't dream of missing it."

Kaeli and Robert shared a look before drinking deep from their tankards of ale.

CHAPTER 46

Light and chaos mingled within Neeve as she stood with Erick at the doorstep of a mansion in Alvar.

Alvar was far greener than Neeve could have ever imagined. Lush hills, rich forests, shimmering fields—it was the stuff of dreams. Even the massive mansion they stood before reflected the perfect serenity of the country, with rich ivy growing up the gray stone facade. Though, in the dimming light of the setting sun, the mansion's silhouette bore a foreboding image.

Erick gripped her hand tightly, eyes darting everywhere.

"You can still turn and run," Neeve said. "We don't have to be here."

"No, I—" He cleared his throat, smoothing his hair. "I want to do this."

"How long has it been?" she asked.

"Gods. Twelve years?" He cleared his throat. "I was so young then."

Neeve slipped her hand into his. "Remember to breathe."

He inhaled, inflating his chest, and knocked three times, holding the air in his lungs for several seconds until, at the sound of the latch turning, he exhaled.

The woman who answered was striking as her expression shifted from surprise to confusion to, finally, joy. Her long black hair was modestly bound behind her neck, cascading down her back like a shining, inky waterfall.

"Erick?"

He shifted his feet. "Hello, Mother."

"What—you—" A hand went to her mouth as tears welled in her burgundy eyes. "You're *here*."

"It's been a long time," he said, hesitating. But he wanted to reach for her, his hand holding Neeve's tighter instead.

When his mother opened her arms to him, relief spread throughout Neeve's body as Erick released Neeve to step into his mother's arms. She turned, giving mother and son privacy despite her proximity, the moment tender between them.

"Erick," his mother said, emotion heavy in her voice. "I can't tell you how sorry I am. There aren't enough words."

"Feather and Claw," he said. "I know."

"I didn't know it would be like this." She pulled back, tears streaking down her flushed cheeks. "It wasn't supposed to be—"

"I know."

"I went back to Falkirk, but you weren't there." She wiped her face. "I've looked for you, but there was nothing. No trail, no leads. And when I tried to scry—"

"I had wards," he said. "I was looking for you, too, but the Wandering Order showed their interest. I had to hide."

At the mention of the cult, his mother sneered. "Those animals."

They were quiet a moment, his mother touching his face and hair, before she turned to Neeve, kindness and love rich in her wine-colored eyes.

"This is Neeve," Erick introduced. "She helped me find you. And Neeve, this is Mirelyn, my mother."

Neeve extended her hand, which Mirelyn took. "It's lovely to meet you."

"Thank you." Her smile was sweet as more tears welled in her eyes. "Thank you for helping my son. For—" She looked at their joined hands, then back to Neeve's face. "Oh, my dear girl. You have been through a lot, haven't you?"

"Her magic lets her see what's past," Erick explained. "And your life thread has come through quite an ordeal."

"It certainly has." But Neeve didn't connect her magic to Mirelyn, electing to have her future remain unknown.

"Gods above." Mirelyn stared at Neeve, recognition awakening behind her eyes. "*You're* Neeve."

"Yes." Neeve's reply was almost a question.

"There's someone here," she said, her brows flexing over her eyes, knitting together before releasing, then back again. "Gods, she has no idea."

"Who?" Erick asked. "Someone here knows Neeve?"

Mirelyn nodded. "She's upstairs."

Neeve's heart thrummed within her ribcage. *She's upstairs.* Someone in Alvar...

"Eira?" Neeve whispered her name, the quiet pushing it back to her.

Mirelyn guided them inside. The interior was cozier than the outside hinted, with warm wood furniture and earth-toned decor and colors. Wall sconces bloomed with light, and the hearth fire provided a lovely ambient glow. Mirelyn took a candlestick from a nearby shelf and brought it with them up to the second floor.

"It's quite dark, isn't it?" Erick asked.

"As requested," Mirelyn said. "Light hurts her eyes. But she'll get stronger."

Darkness, a quiet house.

"There are others who live here and nearby," Mirelyn said. "You've caught us at a quiet moment, which is fortunate."

The wood creaked beneath their steps as they climbed, the silence enhancing the rustling of their clothes.

"I ask that you brace yourself," Mirelyn said, one hand holding the skirt of her dress as the other held the candlestick aloft. "She is not as you knew her."

Guilt and anxiety mingled in her core, reunited like long-lost friends. But the familiar sensation was unwelcome, especially as each step forward felt shakier than the last.

Erick rested a hand on Neeve's back, between her shoulders.

"What have I done?" she whispered.

"You didn't," he said. "Remember that. *You didn't.*"

The very thing that weighed on her conscience would confront her at last. Here was her chance at redemption, but as she climbed higher, she wanted nothing more than to run.

At the top of the stairs, the long hallway stretched before her. There were four rooms, two on each side, and a fifth at the end of the long corridor.

"She's just here," Mirelyn said, walking to the first door on the left.

It was Erick's reassuring hand that helped Neeve to move forward, to walk into the opening doorway and see into the room where her absolution would come.

The room's fireplace held a modest flame, lighting the room enough to see and walk. Two chairs sat in front of the fire with a table between them, books stacked with marks showing progress in each. The area rug was large and richly dyed, its design an intricate pattern of swirls that guided the eye toward the four-poster bed.

And there, propped by pillows, lay Eira.

Neeve stared, her friend recognizable but for her eyes. White all but replaced their typical icy blue, the irises seeming to glow in the dim light.

She sat up, eyes wide, mouth agape. "Neeve?"

Her voice was smooth velvet, slightly deeper in tone than usual. She threw the blankets from her legs and stood, gripping the post of the bed to help her stand.

"Gods, Eira." Neeve rushed to her, only to stop as Mirelyn warned her.

"Be careful," Mirelyn said. "She's still getting her feet under her."

"What have I done?" Neeve approached her carefully, taking Eira's hands before embracing her. Her body was frail in Neeve's arms. "What have I done?"

"No." Eira tightened the embrace with more strength than Neeve expected. "It was me, Neeve. It was me."

Neeve leaned back, taking Eira's face in her hands. The pallor of her otherwise richly toned skin oddly complemented the depth of her inky hair and the startling white of her eyes. "Tell me what happened."

"My parents found a healer," she said. "But they couldn't see a way to pull me out of my mind."

"You were locked in your own mind?"

She stroked Neeve's hair, the silence passing between them before she answered. "I was a prisoner there until I died."

"Died." The word was a whisper caught by the crackling fire, barely audible. "You died?"

"And was resurrected," Erick said.

"But the spell didn't work as expected." Eira tried to smile, apprehension weakening whatever reassurance she tried to convey. "But I'm getting stronger."

"Bloodborn," Erick said. "How do you cope?"

"That's where I come in," Mirelyn said, her steps quiet as she moved closer. "Helping her to manage the craving for blood. The urge to hunt."

Neeve's heart fluttered in fear. "Eira, this is all my fault."

"No, Neeve." Eira embraced her again. "I wanted the magic as much as you did. I cast the spell that welcomed you into my mind. But I didn't expect being trapped there."

Eira's words did little to assuage the guilt and grief storming Neeve's insides. But her best friend held her. Her best friend spoke to her. Her best friend had a heartbeat.

Both alive and dead, brought from the afterlife and into a body that wasn't quite whole, a body that hungered.

"I am coping, and I am learning," she said. "And I am eager to bring my talents in the fight against those devils in the Order."

"Calling them devils gives them too much credit," Erick said with a chuckle. "Though a lower ranking term escapes me."

Neeve regarded Eira, looking upon a young woman with remarkable power, even as her mortal body adjusted to how it had changed. Neeve praised the goddesses for the privilege of holding her best friend's hand once more.

"But we're not alone." Neeve pulled Eira closer, kissing her temple before wrapping her in an embrace. "We'll face them all. Together."

EPILOGUE

The tenacity of a soulwitch.

The Storyteller had been especially proud of that line.

She closed the book, this latest volume one story closer to the life thread she sought. One page at a time, the full tale would be told.

The Storyteller hoped she would do it justice.

Shelved beside the earthborn who dreams, the book of light trembled, restless, eager for more.

"Rest now," the Storyteller whispered, touching the spine with loving fingers.

"She was there," the soulwitch whispered, lingering in the open doorway. "The Preceptor." Firelight flickered across her form, making the shadows dance around her. "Are you alright?"

"I will be," the Storyteller said. "Everything, in time."

The soulwitch turned, her undead thrall following her, his blue clouded eyes unblinking.

"Nice touch," the Storyteller said, nodding toward the thrall. "It's no less than he deserves."

Shadows feathered off of the soulwitch's fingers as she closed the door behind her, leaving the Storyteller to the next tale that awaited her, the soul's power ready.

With ink and parchment ready, the Storyteller began.

ACKNOWLEDGMENTS

Once again, this book would not have come to life without Jesus and coffee. Praise to Him, from whom all blessings flow, especially the excellent coffee that always finds its way into my cup. <3

To my family and friends who've shown consistent enthusiasm and support: I cannot express what your love means to me. I say this book wouldn't have happened without Jesus, and that's in large part to the people He's put in my path. You are living blessings that I cherish, and I am so grateful to have you, especially when I'm a writer goblin who hasn't seen the sun in three days.

And to you, dear reader: Thank you for picking up this book and giving the Dark Library Series your time and support. Whether this is your first time in the library, or if this is your third enthusiastic dive into this world, you mean the absolute world to me. Thank you for giving this indie author a chance.

About the Author

When Morgan's not writing, she's playing video games. Find her on social media @morganreallywrites (except X, which insists on being DIFFERENT — @morganrlywrites).

Find all of her stories on Kindle Unlimited:
    amazon.com/author/morganreilly

Stay up to date by signing up for her newsletter here.

Also by Morgan Reilly

Short Fiction

Secrets of Northanger Abbey

The Dark Library Series

Book One: The Book of Water

Book Two: The Book of Dreams

Find all of her stories on Kindle Unlimited:

amazon.com/author/morganreilly

Stay up to date by signing up for her newsletter here.

9 798889 473004 2